Sadie
and
Summer
Plan the Wedding of the Century

ELISSA MARKS

Copyright © 2024 Elissa Marks
Cover by Sunny Williams (@sunnibugs on Instagram)

This is a work of fiction. Names, characters, places, and incidents either are the product of the author's imagination or are used fictitiously. Any resemblance to actual persons, living or dead, events, or locales is entirely coincidental.

All rights reserved. No part of this book may be reproduced or used in any manner without written permission of the copyright owner except for the use of quotations in a book review.

All brand names and product names used in this book are trademarks, registered trademarks, or trade names of their respective holders. The author is not associated with any product or vendor in this book.

ISBN: 9798343924848

A letter from the author
to the rom com lover
on behalf of

SADIE AND SUMMER PLAN THE WEDDING OF THE CENTURY

This book is a love letter to the rom com and everything it is: The frivolity, the unrealism, the simplicity, the predictability.

What one person calls frivolous is really someone else's most important thing. Simplicity and predictability are comforts when real life is complex and unexplainable. And while some would say that the rom com kind of love is unrealistic, is fictitious, I can say with certainty and from experience that it is not. All that which the world uses to try and weaponize the thing you love is not its deficit. It is everything its critics think it is, and so much more.

Think of this book as a sappy love confession to love, to the unapologetic rom com, and most importantly to the people who love those things. Please never let a disapproving glare keep you from the things that make you happy.

And Red, please never forget that you, exactly as you are, have inspired and informed every piece of art I have made since I met you. You are deserving of all that you have, all I can give you, and so much more. I love you.

Warning:
Pages 397 to 400 contain explicit sexual content. Reader discretion advised. *(Mom: I am begging you, **skip these pages**.)*

Other notable content: adult language, off-page cheating by past partner, off-page body-shaming by past partner, recreational consumption of alcohol, very brief mention of child death in a car accident by a minor character, mild descriptions of grief/mourning by a main character, illness of a pet (no death), discussions of unaccepting family (homophobia, transphobic microaggression)

Sadie
and
Summer
Plan the Wedding of the Century

Chapter One
Sadie Keeps It Pretty

"I really think you'd love her," Felix says, dark eyes fixed on his reflection in the mirror before him as he packs a makeup brush with eyeshadow. The sun is just starting to set, a pinkish glow spilling through the window of the annoyingly picturesque little house my best friend shares with his annoyingly perfect life partner, Julian. It's the kind of life the average apartment-dwelling, single gay (read: yours truly) could just choke on with jealousy.

"Sit still," I reply, running product-covered hands through the puff of jet black hair atop his head. The motion comes to me like second nature; I've been Felix's personal hairdresser since we were preschoolers, six girls deep into a braiding chain.

"She's a great girl," he continues. "I mean, she's Julie's best friend, so you know she is. A *baker*. Actually- remind me and I'll send you her business Instagram. She's trying to launch her own bakery. I'm not saying I won't miss my homeowner tax on all those delicious baked goods, but, you know..." He scrunches his nose at the fresh swipe of colorful shadow on his eyelid. "It'd be awfully nice to get her out of our guest room and into your bedroom."

I can't help but roll my eyes a bit at Felix's repeated attempt to thrust his and Julian's reclusive houseguest onto me. Despite spending at least three nights a week here, I haven't seen even a trace of the mysterious baker best friend in the almost-month since she got into town. "Yeah, I'm definitely waiting with bated breath to fuck the unemployed cake maker crashing on your couch. Besides, I've conducted a post mortem on dating and decided that it's best for me *and* the rest of the single population if I take myself off the market."

"Baby, why?" Felix moans like a little kid seconds before a tantrum. "I know the last couple sort of blew, but... you're such a catch! Anyone would be lucky to fall in sweet, gay love with you! Or *make* sweet, gay love." He drops the brush, abruptly turning in his chair and making my hands slide right out of his gel-covered hair. "Honey, if you're swearing off romance, so be it, but at *least* stay getting laid! God, what's the point of life if you aren't?"

I laugh, knowing (or perhaps hoping) he isn't serious - if only for Julian's sake. "You've got me there, Felix."

"At least look at her picture," he says, already reaching into his pocket for his phone. "I'm telling you, she's gorgeous."

"Later," I reply, fully facetiously. I clap my hands together. "Now turn back around. Happy hour won't last forever."

"Happy hour?" Felix repeats, carefully applying more eyeshadow. "We're not in college anymore. I can afford full price drinks. Why are you in such a hurry?"

My stomach squirms as I try to remain nonchalant, pulling the final errant strands of hair into place. What Felix thinks is just a regular hangout for the two of us tonight has actually been orchestrated by Julian- after what seems like one billion years of blissful, unproblematic, home-owning love, he's finally popping the question. It's gotten increasingly difficult to keep the biggest day of his life so far a secret from my best friend in the world, but I only need to hold out for two more hours.

"If we miss sunset, our pictures are going to totally suck," I tell him, and he nods seriously.

"I'm *almost* done." He squints at his reflection, applying a thick wing to the corner of his eye with laser-precision. "There." He slides his circle glasses back onto his nose.

"Hold on," I say, turning around and pulling a dark pink rose from the vase I brought over from Inspiration Florals, the flower shop where I work. I gently push the stem over his ear and under the arm of his glasses. "It goes with your sweater."

He beams, admiring the bloom nestled against his dark hair. "I have to say, Sadie, you're pretty good at that."

I snort, grabbing my purse. "Maybe I should make it a living."

Felix stands grandly, his arms swinging outward. "Alright, gorgeous. Let's drink!"

I make a mental note to make sure his drinks top out at a glass and a half. Felix is energetic enough when he isn't hammered, and I doubt Julian's perfect proposal plan includes his new fiancé flashing his top surgery scars at oncoming traffic and whooping like a howler monkey.

"Right behind you, Felix."

"You know, I hear there's a new dessert shop on 5th," I tell Felix an hour later, ever-so-casually, without even looking up from my glass.

Just as expected, he gasps in a manner that denotes an impressive lung capacity. This kind of overreaction to sugar is present even when he's stone cold sober. "What do they have?"

"The works." I feel almost devilish rattling off the script Julian frantically texted me last week. "Gelato, cookies, muffins, cinnamon rolls, croissants, crepes, cakes..."

"We have *got* to go!" He shoots upright, the sudden motion scooting the table toward me with an unpleasant sound.

A smile cracks across my face. "Totally. Let me finish my wine."

The temperate Pennsylvania July air feels nice against my skin as we step out onto the sidewalk, and I'm grateful for a minute that Roseport can charitably be called a walkable community. Felix skips down the street like a wobbling puppy, all joy and little direction. If he's this happy about dessert, I can't wait to see his face when he sees the ring.

"You know, Sadie," he says, looking up into the street lamps, "I think Gabby was an asshole."

My shoulders tense. I don't want him to spend the day he's getting engaged worrying about my personal life, especially not about the most recent in a stream of bad relationships. "I'm over it."

"No, I mean it," he says, screwing his nose up in a show of disgust. "You don't just *do* that to people. Charlie and Reagan and Ben were bad, but Gabby…" He scowls, making an emphatic swatting motion with his hand. "I wanna hit her with my car."

My heart stings, but I have to stay focused. I hang a left, grabbing his wrist to make sure he's still following me. The cute pink awning of *So Sweet* comes into view, and my heartbeat starts to race. "Come on, babe."

A bell rings through the little space as I open the door, and I swear I hear a quick *shhh!* from the far corner. Felix swaggers up to the counter, a comfortable smile on his face as though he's already at home here among the baked goods. I pat his shoulder. "Go ahead and order, babe. I've gotta pee."

A childish giggle bubbles in my stomach as I race off, darting into the hallway. Julian peeks over the swinging kitchen door, his dark skin, curly mullet, septum piercing, and big brown eyes unmistakable. I shoot him an enthused smile and a thumbs up, then burrow into the corner as he nudges the door open with his shoulder, a tray in his hands carrying a round, pastel-frosted cake. I turn to watch him go, eagerly biting my lip, as another figure exits the kitchen.

I don't think much of it until the body settles next to mine, turning toward the mouth of the little hallway. I flick my eyes to the side, looking at the pale redheaded woman dressed in a bright pink *So Sweet* apron. I'm immediately uneasy, both for the proximity in this tight space, and for the extreme attractiveness of this girl.

My unfortunate tendency when coming into contact with beautiful people is similar to some people's reaction to a bug, and this woman is about as beautiful as they come. Her features are strong and striking - a sharp jaw, defined cheekbones, dramatic dark eyelashes, full lips - and the bright ginger hair tied neatly at the crown of her head only adds to the impact. Her skin is almost glowingly pale, and in our closeness I can even see faint brown freckles running up her cheeks. Her *So Sweet* apron hugs the curve of her waist, highlighting a gentle hourglass shape.

"I can't wait to see this," she whispers to me, leaning even closer. My stomach turns. I guess if a proposal is happening at her place of work, she's perfectly entitled to watch it go on. But I hate the pull in my chest that brings me closer to her, even more now that I've sworn off dating. Almost without my permission, my legs take a definitive step away from her, hoping in vain to break the magnetic spell.

There's another loud Felix gasp from around the corner, and we both rush forward to peek around.

"Jules!" Felix puts his hands to his face, looking up with adoration as Julian sets the cake down on the table before him. "I- What are you doing here?"

"I got you something special," he says with an almost shy smile, and Felix turns his attention to the cake, and gasps.

"Felix Nguyen," Julian says, getting to one knee. The girl next to me squeals, and I have to contain a similar reaction. "You're the love of my life. You've been with me and supported me through so much. I've loved every version of you, and I can't wait to love all the ones to come. I want to spend the rest of my life with you."

Felix says something, fully garbled by tears. Julian reaches for him, pulling him into his arms. "Will you marry me?"

"Yes!" Felix wails, hugging onto the other man. "Obviously, yes!"

The pair springs to their feet, Felix peppering Julian's face with kisses. Cheers echo through the shop, and Felix nestles his face onto his fiancé's shoulder, the pink rose in his hair perfectly matching the sleeve of floral tattoos on Julian's arm. I grin to myself, quickly snapping a picture of the embrace before rushing to greet them.

"Baby!"

"Baby!" Felix cries, turning and flinging himself into my arms. "You knew?"

"Of course I knew," I tell him, squeezing tight. "Who do you think kept you fully dressed, mostly sober, and out of the way of the planning?"

"You're the greatest," he says.

"Nope," I reply, letting go of him and stepping to the side. "You're an engaged man now. I can't always be your number one."

"Gross, I have to spend my life with him?" Felix says playfully, sticking his tongue out at Julian and then giving him another kiss.

"Congrats, you guys!" cries the redhead, who I've only just realized is here with us. Julian whoops and turns to hug her.

"Thank you so much for helping with the cake! It turned out perfect." Julian's dark clothes and tattoos stick out like a sore thumb against her pink apron.

Felix's eyes go wide. "You made this?" He scrambles for a fork, and Julian laughs. "I didn't even know you worked here!"

As his fiancé digs in, Julian turns to me. "Sadie, this is my best friend Summer." Her face lights up with a welcoming smile.

My head gets hot. It was probably a total delusion to begin with, but I'd managed to convince myself that it would be no problem turning down Felix's offer to date their serial-baking houseguest - and, just my luck, here she is drop-dead gorgeous.

"It's nice to meet you." The words feel brittle. I want to extend my hand, but it stays firmly at my side. Summer's brows raise ever so slightly.

"Oh my god, this is delicious," Felix muses, mouth audibly full of confection. "Sadie, you have *got* to come try this."

"I'm alright," I say, nausea stirring in my stomach.

He cocks his head to the side, dark eyes boring into me with their extreme concern. "Baby-"

"It's buttercream icing," says Summer almost abruptly, crossing to point out her handiwork. "And I know how much you loved that chocolate ganache I made, so it's actually in between the layers here-"

Felix practically dives into the cake. "No fucking way. Summer, I love you."

A blush fills her face and it feels, frustratingly, like sunshine filling a dark room.

We go our separate ways after a bit, the boys bidding Summer and I adieu as Felix explains, while lovingly draped over Julian's shoulders, they are off for celebratory drinks. The walk back to my car feels jarringly quiet - the rest of tonight, when I was focused on helping make Felix's proposal perfect, felt like a movie. Bright and energized and unreal, like it was all taking place on a painted nighttime backdrop in an old film studio. But now with only my thoughts, my walk down the street is disappointingly real. Which, quite appropriately, has become a much more familiar feeling lately.

The key, as always, fits jaggedly into the lock, and it's a full-on assault just to wrench the door open and step into my tiny apartment, the familiar tornado-style decor littering the floor and countertops. Ethel, my geriatric beagle, waddles toward me and I stoop to scratch her ears. She wags her arthritic tail.

"Just you and me tonight, old girl," I tell her, as if this is any sort of surprise. I think Ethel learned not to get too attached to any "new parent" back when I was in high school. I kick off my shoes and lift her up onto the couch next to me. She settles in quickly, snoring contently in what seems like seconds. At least one of us isn't feeling the pain in our sudden change of lifestyle.

It's all too easy to let myself fall asleep there on the couch without even changing out of my clothes, old sitcom reruns almost like white noise in the background. Despite all my best efforts, I've felt aimless in the past few weeks. Once I'm alone, with nothing to distract me and no one else to prioritize, I can't help but shut down.

Chapter Two

Summer Makes Things Sweet

"Table for seven, under Jefferson," Felix says, vibrating with excitement. The hostess nods and leads us back, and Felix turns to grin at me and Julian. "I can't believe that. Soon I'll be Felix Jefferson." He beams at the ring, then looks up, head cocked to the side. "Jefferson-Nguyen?"

"Nguyen-Jefferson," says Julian definitively, flashing an almost shy smile as he grabs his fiancé's hand. I can't help but to start beaming at them. Julian catches my eye and, as per usual when he's with Felix, he looks the happiest he's ever been. It makes my heart swell- I remember meeting him back in college, when I was the only other trans person he'd ever met, and he told me once in a drunken stupor that he felt like no one would ever really love him. It's safe to say now that fate itself helped prove him wrong.

When we sit down at our table, I pull a container from my purse and set it in front of us. "Happy engagement party, you two!"

Felix gasps, popping the lid and marveling at the simple white-frosted cake pops I made. "You had these in the car? How do you keep sneaking dessert past me?"

"It's white chocolate frosting and milk chocolate raspberry filling," I tell him, pushing the container toward him. Both men reach for a pop, and I watch with relish as they take their first bites. "Good?"

"Holy shit," says Julian.

"Summer, I adore you," adds Felix.

"How are things at So Sweet?" Julian asks, sliding off his leather jacket to reveal his heavily tattooed arms.

"It pays," I reply, my smile wavering. "It's better than doing something else, you know?" I don't like to dwell on the negative, but there isn't much else I can bring myself to say about it. "My boss is nice."

"And how is Sweet Summer Confectionaries?" Felix says, mouth already full of a second cake pop.

Even hearing the name of my personal bakery brand brightens me for a second, but I'm still struggling to keep from deflating on the subject of my current career. "I haven't had much time for it," I say with a frown, fidgeting with my hands in my lap. "I'm still baking all day, but… at So Sweet. Not my own recipes, which feels so… And it doesn't help that I'm making less of the money."

Both men nod sympathetically, and Julian leans across the table to lovingly pat my arm.

"Things will get better, love," says Felix, and though this is the exact kind of attitude I always try to maintain, something about his tone feels a little too certain.

"What does that mean?"

His eyes light up and he springs out of his seat. "Baby!"

I turn in my chair on reflex, and it's no shock to see Sadie striding toward us. There's a pang in my chest; she's lovely, her stylish brown pixie cut tousled with the same sort of effortless charm that seems characteristic to her entire being, soft features and sparkling green eyes giving her appearance a distinctly friendly quality, and a blindingly genuine happiness emanating from her as she embraces her best friend. Somehow my day feels brighter just from looking at her.

"You remember Summer," says Felix, motioning my way, and I remember the reality of her presence. It's like a switch flipping: her posture goes stiff; her beautiful, slightly crooked smile vanishes into a polite grimace that looks like it pains her; and she waves awkwardly.

"Nice to see you again." My mood dissipates as she slides into her seat, her gaze turned anywhere but to me.

A peppy young waitress walks up, a notepad open in her hands. "Hi there! Are y'all waiting on more people?"

"Yes," says Julian, right as Felix, bounding in his chair, tells her, "It's our engagement party." Julian blushes and covers a small smile with his hand.

"Congratulations!" Her customer service smile is thousand-watt. "Can I go ahead and get some drink orders?"

"Long Island iced tea," says Felix immediately.

"I'll just have whichever white wine is your favorite," Sadie says.

"Could I get a gin and tonic?"

Forever the hitch in the system, I have to glance at the drinks menu on the table in front of us. "Oh, I'll try the cherry martini."

She nods brightly, and it only seems like a couple of seconds before she's back with our drinks in tow.

Sadie stares into her wine glass like she's looking for something. "Do we have any updates on when Georgia, Khalil, and Rio get here?"

"We actually invited you two a little early," Felix says, straightening in his seat. "We wanted to talk to you."

Sadie shoots me a glance, then looks back to the couple. "To us?"

"The wedding's going to be really small," says Julian. "We don't want anything too flashy. It's actually gonna be in the backyard. It's really special to us that we've gotten to have a home together, so…"

I can't help but touch a hand to my heart and gasp a little bit. "That's so sweet."

"So we talked about what we'd be willing to actually spend a little money on," Felix adds, "and you know how Julie feels about flowers."

"And Felix has always wanted a massive dessert bar at our wedding," Julian finishes. "So we thought…"

"You want me to do the flowers for your wedding?" Sadie cries, her face lighting up like a lantern.

My lips turn up at the corners. "I could totally do a dessert bar," I say. "That's awesome."

"It would end up being most of the planning," Julian says hesitantly, "and we're both so busy, and you know us so well, so of course we'd trust you to do your jobs…"

"You'd basically be planning the whole wedding," Felix cuts in again. "Obviously we'd check in, and approve things, but neither of us has nearly enough time to do it on our own, and you're professionals."

Julian scratches his scalp, ruffling the long curls. "We know it's a lot to ask."

"And *obviously* you're also both the *only* candidates for maids of honor, so if you don't want to, we absolutely understand." Felix gesticulates emphatically, drink in hand.

"Are you kidding?" Sadie says, grabbing her friend's hands. "Felix, I've been dreaming of this since we were kids. I've worked a billion weddings. I'll be *glad* to do this one."

"I figure it's about time Sweet Summer Confectionaries got the chance to prove itself," says Julian, raising one brow.

"Thank you both so much," I say, shaking my hands to try and release some of the excitement coursing through me. "I promise, I won't let you down."

Julian grins at me, his nose scrunching and his big brown eyes sparkling. "Not possible, Summer."

"God, I'm so fucking excited," Felix says, his voice sounding a little froggy as he fans misty eyes. "You guys are gonna make this day so magical. Oh, come hug me!"

Sadie and I both spring from our seats, and soon Felix is wrapped in a tight group hug. Sadie and Julian both coo unintelligibly into his ear.

"Okay, okay, I'm good," he says after a second, and we all let go. Sadie looks sideways at me and tucks in her arms, and my stomach churns. We sit back down, and my hands return to fidgeting in my lap.

"When's the date?" Sadie asks, settling back into her chair. I notice now that her right canine tooth sticks out ever so slightly, sharp like a cat's.

"We're thinking about May," says Julian. "We need to get everything cleared with the HOA, so we'll make real save-the-dates later."

"Do you guys still want a cake?" I brush a strand of hair that escaped from my updo behind my ear. "Or just the dessert bar?"

"Maybe a little cake for us to cut," Felix says, taking a long sip. "I think it's so cute when couples feed each other."

I nod. "I can't wait to get started!"

"We really can't thank you guys enough," says Julian, looking sideways at Felix in that way he does, like he still gives him butterflies.

"Well, if it isn't the men of the hour!" A tall, smartly-dressed man walks up behind Felix and Julian, resting his hands on their shoulders.

"Hey!" Felix exclaims, turning in his chair with a big smile. "Look at you. Always on time."

"Always early," the man corrects good-naturedly. He's handsome, with thick dark brows, a well-trimmed beard, and a shaved head. His dark skin is clear and dewy, and his button-up shirt is crisp without a single wrinkle in sight. He carries an intense aura of confident, mature charm. "Good to see you, Sadie."

"Right back at you," she says, grinning behind her glass.

He turns to me, holding out his hand. "Khalil Brown. It's a pleasure to meet you."

I shake it. "Summer McConnell."

He settles into a chair at the end of the table, forcing Sadie to scoot her chair ever so slightly toward mine. The bright, springy scent of freshly cut flowers flies across my nose.

"I work with Felix," Khalil tells me, looking casually at the drink menu. "And I hear you're from Chicago."

"I wouldn't really say I'm *from* Chicago," I respond, taking a sip of my drink as my stomach squirms ever so slightly. "I lived there for about two years, but I grew up in Serenton, a few miles from here."

"Summer went to college with Georgia and me," says Julian.

"Then welcome back to Roseport," says Khalil with a smile. "How's the engaged life, you two?"

Felix starts giggling like a little kid into his drink, and Julian says, "It's been great." He clears his throat. "How are your partners?"

"Eleanor's dad is sick," he replies. "But Cecily, Axel, and Matthew are great."

"Oh, give Eleanor our best," says Julian with a sympathetic cluck of his tongue.

"Isn't Axel's birthday coming up?" asks Sadie.

"Yes," Khalil says. "They'll be the last of us over the 30 line."

"God, I always forget you're *old*," Felix prods playfully.

"You laugh, but you're getting there," says Khalil, rolling up his shirt sleeves. "Today you're a sweet little twenty-something fiancé, and tomorrow you're a wrinkled thirty-two-year-old *husband*."

"Husband," says Felix dreamily, looking into Julian's eyes.

"*Awwww*," I coo as they kiss.

Julian looks toward the door and smiles. "Speaking of college…"

I turn in my chair and grin. "Georgia!"

They look our way from the hostess stand, numerous facial piercings glinting in the overhead lighting. She runs to us and Julian and I jump to embrace them. When I pull away, I take in her appearance: the same blonde buzz cut, copious facial piercings, sharp pixie features, and edgy, masculine fashion I remember them for.

"It's so good to see you, Summer!" They shoot me a smile, snake bites flipping upwards. "I told you you never should've moved."

"I know," I reply with a grin, internally appreciating their discretion about *why* she'd advised me not to move. I cover a wince at the memory. "Next time, I'll listen."

"Hey, Sadie," she says as they sit down across from Khalil. "Felix. Congrats, you two."

It doesn't seem like Felix will ever get tired of being reminded that he and Julian are engaged. He's practically glowing.

"Oh!" I cry out. "I forgot- I made cake pops."

"You're the sweetest," Georgia exclaims as she and Khalil both reach for one. "Rio here yet?"

"Never," Felix says. "You know them. It'll be fifteen more minutes at least."

Georgia laughs, a mouthful of cake pop muffling the sound.

"Rio?" I ask.

"Right! You've never met Rio," says Julian. "I did a tattoo for them about a year ago and they hit it off with Felix."

A yell rings out through the restaurant. "My favorite boys!"

"I wonder why," Sadie deadpans, smiling into a sip of her wine.

"Rio, you're early!" Felix says, standing out of his chair to greet them. Rio is colorfully dressed, round and cheerful with brown skin, bold makeup, and shaggy hair dyed messily in shades of green and blue.

"This is an important event," they tell him, bright red lips parting to show gapped front teeth. "I wanted to be on my best behavior."

"Best behavior," Khalil repeats with a playful grin. "Does that mean you're topping out at five drinks instead of six?"

"Blow it out your ass, old man," they say, sticking their tongue out at him. "You just wish you could have more than half a glass of red without getting a headache."

"I concede the point," he says with a small nod.

They look at me as they take the seat between me and Georgia. "I'm Rosario Hernandez, pleased to make your acquaintance."

"Summer McConnell."

"You know, you are *gorgeous*," they say, snapping their fingers like a drag queen and showing off the little teddy bear tattoo on their inner forearm.

"*And* she made these cake pops," Georgia adds, shaking the container enticingly.

"Holy shit," says Rio, snatching one up and looking around the table. "I like her. Is she part of the group now?"

"Hello, Rio," says Julian with a faux weariness.

"Oh my god," they cry, whipping around. "I'm so excited for you two. Show me the ring or I'll die."

Felix makes a play at false reluctance, but it can't last more than two seconds, and suddenly everyone is leaned into the center of the table studying his finger.

"That setting is gorgeous," Khalil muses, his finger under his lip like the caricature of a college intellectual.

"I love the color," says Georgia, of the warm brownish orange stone which sits prettily in the silver setting.

"Absolutely," I agree. "So unique."

Rio is halfway onto the table, straining to see. "Is that citrine?"

"Topaz," Felix preens.

"It looks like it was made for you, babe," says Sadie with a smile.

"Must have been a pretty great fiancé who picked it," says Felix, and he turns to nuzzle into Julian.

"You know what we should do," Rio says, grabbing another cake pop and waving it as they speak like a toddler with a plastic 'magic wand'. "To celebrate."

Julian cocks his head to the side. "What?"

"We should go clubbing."

Khalil laughs lightly. "I think some of us might be a little past clubbing age, Rio."

"Nobody cares about your opinion," they reply. "Let the boys decide! It's *their* engagement party."

"Anything you want, honey," Julian says, tipping his head toward his fiancé.

"Let's do it!" Felix exclaims. "I miss partying. Plus, if you pretend to propose again, I bet we'll get a *bunch* of free drinks."

Everyone laughs, and Rio looks around. "Did you guys have a waitress or what? I need to try this signature cocktail."

"I'm starving," Georgia agrees.

The rest of the evening is full of laughter and celebration, and as Georgia, Rio, and Khalil leave (Khalil with the rest of my cake pops to share with his partners), I realize I haven't felt this happy in quite a while. I'm looking forward to settling back in here and spending more time with Julian, Felix, Georgia, and my new friends.

"I'd better be heading home," Sadie says, looking across the table to where Julian and Felix, the latter still slightly tipsy, snuggle like two teenagers on a first date.

"Wait a minute," Felix says, sitting up. "I have to pee. Don't leave 'til I get back." He starts to stand, then stumbles. Julian catches him at the elbow, helping him stay upright.

"Looks like I'm going, too," he says, slinging Felix's arm over his shoulder and leading him toward the bathroom.

Awkwardness settles like a blanket over Sadie and I the second our friends are out of sight. Despite her vibrant personality shining through all of dinner, for some reason she's still yet to warm up around me.

"So, you do a lot of weddings?" I ask after a second, some anxiety within me refusing to let me stay quiet.

"Yeah," she replies, twisting the ring on her index finger. "Have you ever baked for a wedding before?"

"Just a few parties," I say.

She pulls out her phone, laser-focused on the screen before she turns it toward me. "This is my phone number. So we can figure out planning stuff."

I nod, entering it into my phone. "What's your last name?"

She cocks her head to the side. "Why?"

I look up, oddly defensive under the intense cast of her gaze. "All my contacts have a first and a last name."

"What, like you're my sixty-year-old mother?" she says, and I realize with a pang that this weird affectation she's taking on is a playful one. But seemingly just as I notice this, so does she, and her eyes dart to one side. "Levine."

"Sadie Levine," I repeat slowly, slightly thrown by the interaction.

"Baby!" comes Felix's voice, and Sadie gets out of her chair and rushes to him, taking his embrace directly as he falls from Julian's grasp. "I fucking love you, Sadie."

"I love you too, dork," she says. "Congratulations again."

"I love you," Felix repeats emphatically.

"Bye, babe," she says like she's talking to a dog, then gently pushes him back into his fiancé's arms. "Bye, Julian."

"Bye," he says, kissing her on the cheek and hugging her with his free arm. "Drive safe."

She turns back to me, her face once again halfway into and out of a polite smile. "I'll see you later, Summer."

I nod, my heart thrumming dully in my chest. "See you later."

When we arrive back at the house, Julian leads Felix into their room and quickly bids me goodnight. I make the walk to the guest room, but my hand stops on the doorknob. My mind is racing and my fingers seem to itch, so my feet carry me back to the kitchen.

I try to be as quiet as possible as I rustle through the cupboards, gathering ingredients like second nature. The noise in my head begins to quiet down as I measure out sugar, flour, baking soda. It isn't long before I'm standing over the sink and eating chocolate chip cookies, finally settling now into a bit of relaxation.

I turn my head at a noise, and there's Julian shuffling into the kitchen with messy hair and sleepy eyes.

"What are you doing still up?" he asks, rubbing at his septum ring.

"I'm just so excited about the wedding, I couldn't get to sleep," I reply, leaning forward to rest my forearms on the counter.

He doesn't seem to buy it - he knows me too well - but he doesn't say anything, just joins me at the sink and nicks a cookie.

"Jesus Christ," he says through his first bite. "That's a *chocolate chip cookie*. How on earth did you make it *better*?"

I laugh a bit, but don't respond. I grab another cookie, if only to have something to do with my hands.

"Summer." He gently nudges my shoulder with his. "Everything's gonna be okay."

It's all I can do to stop a tear from falling down my cheek. I let my head fall onto his shoulder, and he rests his cheek on my hair.

I can't help but feel guilty about staying here, even though I know he and Felix would never view me as an inconvenience. I'm too old to be starting over and crashing in my friends' guest room, especially knowing where I came here from.

I just have to stay positive. It should only take a few more paychecks from So Sweet before I can get an apartment and get out and stop burdening Julian. He's been such a wonderful friend to me, and as much as I know I shouldn't be, I'm ashamed to have needed the help.

Chapter Three

Sadie Plays It Cool

"Oh, hi!"

My heart skips as Felix and Julian's front door swings open to reveal Summer, radiant even in grubby sweatpants and with a swipe of flour on her cheek.

"Hi," I reply, shifting the bouquet in my arms. "I just came to give this to the boys."

"Oh, totally, come on in!" she says, stepping out of the doorway. "They're at the grocery store. You can wait for them to get back."

I follow her, an overwhelmingly sweet scent slapping me across the face practically the moment I'm past the threshold.

"Hey, since you're here, do you wanna start some planning?" she says, rushing into the kitchen and picking up an oven mitt.

I swallow. "Sure."

The counter is littered with plates, each containing a veritable pile of some different sweet treat. "I've been trying out some recipes."

"I couldn't tell," I reply, probably a little too under my breath for her to hear.

"You can help yourself to anything," she says, halfway disappeared under the counter as she reaches into the oven. I instead busy myself with grabbing a vase out of the cabinet and arranging my bouquet.

She springs up from the oven like a Jack-In-The-Box, a tray of brownies in tow. She sets the pan down and crosses the island.

"This is gorgeous." She leans in, taking a big whiff. Her eyes literally roll back in her head. I feel my face grow warm. "And oh my god, the *smell!* God, your place must be like some kind of fragrant floral wonderland."

I squirm a bit under the sincerity of her gaze. "No, I, uh, don't keep flowers in my apartment."

"What?"

"I don't really like to bring work home," I say with an uncomfortable shrug.

"Gotcha," she says, going back around to tend to her brownies. "Well, it's great work."

"Thank you."

"Were you thinking of something like that for the wedding?"

"I don't think so," I reply, looking at the varying white and purple shades. "Since they're having it in the backyard, I think I'll try to blend with the colors they already have in the garden."

"Cool," she says, picking up a cupcake and biting into it with a pensive look, furrowing her brows. "I've been really struggling to decide what I should do. Weddings are *so* important. And those two, they're like… I mean, it's what we're all looking for, right?"

I avert my eyes. "I'm actually not dating right now."

"Oh. Any reason?"

The half-lie rolls off my tongue easily. I even manage to summon up the charisma to really sell it. "I've done enough awful weddings, I don't know if I really believe in all that 'love' stuff anymore. People are so insane about it. They want exactly this, or it'll ruin the whole day. 'Baby's breath will literally ruin my wedding.' 'If the peonies don't perfectly match the napkins, I don't even want to do this.' It's nuts."

She cocks her head to the side, thinking for a second before she says, "That sounds like you don't really believe in all that 'wedding' stuff. You didn't say anything about love."

I'm embarrassingly caught off guard by this callout. My stomach drops to my toes. "I-"

"I was standing right next to you when Julian proposed. I don't know... I think maybe you do still believe in love." She shrugs, taking another bite of the cupcake. "A few floral maniacs shouldn't be enough to make you stop believing. If it's something you want, I don't think you should give up hope that easily. What good would that do?"

I don't want that to hit me the way it does. It would do a lot of good for me to just give up on ever finding something like Felix and Julian have. Wouldn't it?

My stomach churns. I don't like the way it feels, this pretty girl standing here and telling me things I don't want to hear.

As nonchalantly as I can muster, I reply, "Just not what I'm looking for."

"That's okay, too." She tucks a piece of bright ginger hair back into her bun, then turns her attention to the brownies. She waves her hand over the steaming dessert, wafting it toward her face. "I wonder if brownies are a little too, I don't know… commonplace for a wedding? I mean, they're not very fancy."

"It's a *backyard wedding*," I say quickly, my tone so frank she looks like a kicked puppy for a second. "The point is to celebrate Felix and Julian. They don't care about 'fancy'. They just want to have a day with the people and things they love."

Her eyes gradually brighten as she seems to realize I'm being *nice* to her. I can't blame her, considering my abrasive delivery.

"And I guess you'd pretty much be the authority on things Felix loves," I continue, my voice softening a bit. "Dessert-wise." I clear my throat. "I don't think you have to work so hard."

"Thank you," she says with an air of slight surprise, looking at me with a meaningful expression that makes me feel like shrinking down to the size of an earthworm and wriggling out the door.

"Baby!" Felix's voice echoes through the foyer, following the sound of the front door.

"Hey, Felix," I call, his presence a breath of relief as I turn away from Summer and that earnest expression. He and Julian appear in the kitchen, grocery bags in their arms.

"These flowers are so pretty," Julian muses. "Thanks, Sadie."

"Are you ready to hit the club, babe?" Felix says, setting down his baggage on the single square foot of empty counter space and breaking into a goofy dance.

"Shit, that's tonight, isn't it?" I tuck my hair behind my ear and look down at the simple, very un-clubby jeans-and-shirt combo I'm sporting. "I totally forgot."

Felix gasps. "You should get ready here! It'll be like prom night."

"I don't have clothes here," I say, looking awkwardly over my shoulder, very aware that Summer is still in the room.

"You know I have clothes that fit you," Felix says dismissively. "Please? It's technically still my engagement party." Now he breaks out the puppy dog eyes, which he *knows* I can't resist.

"Fine," I reply. "But you're doing your own hair."

"Sadie Levine, you've got yourself a deal," he says with a grin. "Summer, pack up those treats and let's all get pretty."

Half an hour later - as I usually do - I regret having bent to Felix's will. It seemed innocuous at first when he passed me one of his pre-op party shirts, a flirty mesh number adorned with rhinestones which is cropped just below boob level. Even before his top surgery, it was a loose fit on skinny Felix - not so much on me. I've worn it a million times before and never had a problem. But, I realize upon catching my reflection in the mirror on the way to the foyer, that was months ago, and now I very much have a problem.

I half-consider turning right back around and stealing something less skimpy, but just then is when Summer emerges from the hallway with the guest room, and I don't think I could move if someone used a forklift.

Her short green dress holds tight to every curve of her body and a light layer of makeup only enhances the striking quality of her features, but what really grabs me is that I've never seen Summer's hair down before, and it is *curly*.

It's not a big deal. It's not even like I'm that crazy for curls, but somehow this revelation just serves as one more nail in the coffin for how gorgeous she is and how uncomfortable it is for me to be around her. It only heightens her overall beauty, framing her freckled face perfectly.

I feel like the world's biggest Disaster Bisexual being totally thrown for a loop by bouncy red curls, and as I reflexively tug at the bottom of what can charitably be called my shirt, this self-loathing stacks on top of the horrible knowledge of just how much of my body is showing.

"We look hot," Felix announces, linking his arm with Julian's. "Let's go, sluts."

"You're going to drink *so* much tonight, aren't you?" I ask, forcing a wobbly smile through the growing upset at the base of my stomach.

"And there's no way your shirt is staying on," Julian says affectionately, adjusting the collar of his 'formal' leather jacket.

"I paid good money for these titties," Felix says, slapping a hand to his collarbone in mock offense. "I'll be damned if I don't show them off every once in a while." He tugs at his shirt, a fun-patterned button-up that sits like a second skin against his flat chest. "Now come on. We're wasting moonlight."

The four of us are first at the club, a new gay bar called Spectrum where Rio supposedly knows people. Forever proving their priorities, they're the next one there, sporting a pair of floral neon pink-and-orange overall shorts.

"Are you alright?" Julian asks, looking up at the dramatic mascara stains running down Rio's cheeks.

"Oh, I'm great," they reply, plopping down next to him on the plush purple couch where we've been seated. It's, luckily, far enough from the dance floor that we can actually hear one another speak. "I was listening to the end of *Les Misérables* in my car."

This revelation settles over the group as many of Rio's contributions do: with a moment of bemused silence before anyone can formulate an appropriate response.

"The book or the musical?" Summer ventures, her head cocked to the side.

"The musical," they reply, nonchalantly wiping away the residue with a tissue from their purse. "It's what I always do before I go to the club. Like a pregame."

"That's fucking genius," says Felix. The rest of us laugh.

"Listen, you gotta try their signature drink," Rio says, leaning forward almost as if telling us a secret. "It's like fifteen bucks, but we'll all split one. It's *delicious*."

"And dangerous," Georgia chimes in, sitting down next to Summer, who hugs them. "You can't taste the alcohol at all."

"Which is why we're splitting one," replies Rio, scrunching their nose at her.

"Sadie, you look really cute," Georgia says.

My face burns, but I resist the urge to pull down on my shirt. "Thanks."

"You know, I've been meaning to ask," they continue, fiddling absently with the stud at one side of the bridge of her nose. "Are you still seeing that one girl?"

Felix tenses and immediately locks eyes with me. I feel sweat slide down my legs and onto the fabric of the seat below me.

"No," I reply casually as my heart pounds. My hand sneaks up to the shirt now, pulling it over the sliver of my stomach that was exposed. "That, uh, didn't work out."

My whole body tenses as I wait for somebody to ask a follow-up question, already scripting out the half-truths I'll tell. Felix knows more than anybody, but even he has only some of the details of what happened with Gabby, and he's already got murderous intent for her. If everybody knew the whole story - especially Georgia, who's known for being essentially a pierced, gay guard dog - they would freak out. And I don't need to dwell on it any more than I already am.

"Shame, shame," says Rio instead as Khalil flies onto the scene, joining us on the couch. "Right on time is shockingly close to late, Mr. Brown."

"I was *here* ten minutes ago," he says, straightening his tie, a deep purple piece with metallic stars. I breathe out, eternally grateful for this group distraction from my dating life. "I just had to circle the parking lot five times to find a spot."

"That's because this place is awesome," Rio says. "You're welcome."

"*And* because of that boat-sized minivan you drive," adds Felix, seemingly also appreciating the change of subject for my sake. "I don't understand why anyone without kids would ever volunteer to get behind the wheel of that behemoth."

"You just can't fit a saturated polycule into a sexy sports car," Khalil replies with an exaggerated shrug. "Sorry, Felix."

The group falls into a comfortable conversational rhythm like they always do, and to add to my discomfort, Summer slots right in as if she's been here all along. While she lights up and jokes with that signature sweetness, I freeze up and get in maybe a sentence or two between thinking about the loud club music and my exposed boobs and stomach and Summer's delicate curls perfectly framing her face.

"Holy shit," Summer says, taking a sip of the communal cocktail. It's bright pink in a tall glass with swirling glitter and a curly straw. I half expect heart-shaped bubbles to emerge from it like some kind of magic potion. "This tastes *amazing*."

She passes me the drink, a small smile appearing on her lips as we make eye contact. I wordlessly decline, unable to pull my focus from the tiny pink lipstick stain on the straw. Rio reaches out, taking it instead, and my face burns.

"I told you," Rio gloats, guiding the straw toward their mouth with two fingers like they're holding a cigarette. The second the sip hits their throat, they let out a whoop. "Hot damn! Who wants to dance?"

Khalil laughs, grabbing the glass from their hand. "I'll pass."

"You *know* I'm in," Felix declares, jumping to his feet and ceremoniously undoing the top button on his shirt. "Jules?"

"Sure, honey," says Julian, sliding off his jacket and lacing his fingers with his fiancé's.

Felix turns back to me, raising his brows. "Baby?"

My stomach is still sour, and the thought of my shirt moving while I try to dance makes me feel like I could throw up. "Eh, not right now."

"Georgia?"

"I'll dance when they play a song I like," she says, running their hand over their buzzed hair. "None of this EDM crap."

"Snob," Rio says playfully, and then pulls the boys toward the dance floor.

"Oh, Summer!" Khalil exclaims, leaning forward. "I just remembered. Axel fell in *love* with those cake pops I brought home."

"That's great!" Summer says, her face shining.

"They want a big party for their birthday next month. Could we hire you for it?" he asks. "Whatever your rate is, we're willing to pay it."

Her whole demeanor changes, her eyes going wide. "Really?"

"Of course," Khalil says. "We've got the flexibility, and we'd be supporting a friend, not just a great artist."

"Khalil, that-" She laughs breathlessly. "That's so sweet. What, um, what would you guys want me to make?"

"Enough cake pops for all our friends," Khalil replies, straightening his tie. "And considering there are five of us, I'd put it around forty attendees."

Summer's eyes dart like she's doing some quick math in her head, and then she locks onto Khalil, her smile huge. "Holy shit. That's, um." She reigns herself in, clearing her throat. "That's the last I'd need to put toward getting my own apartment."

"I'm glad," he replies, nodding. "You have a serious talent, Summer. You are deserving of every dollar."

Georgia grins. "Absolutely."

Summer stands up, half hovering over the couch. "I'm gonna- Can I-" Khalil nods and she throws her arms around him. "I seriously can't thank you guys enough. Tell Axel, too."

"They'll be happy to hear it," he says, patting her back. "After those cake pops, we're *all* enamored with you."

Against everything logical in my mind, this makes me feel even sicker. This is in no way a come-on. Khalil has been at maximum partner capacity for almost as long as I've known him, and he's complimenting Summer's *cake pops*. But even if he were hitting on her, I have less than no reason or right to be bothered by it. I can't stop Khalil or anybody from being interested in people *I* find attractive. Even still, my queasiness doesn't lessen until they break from the hug.

The music playing on the dance floor changes, and I hear Felix shriek from across the room. Before I can fully register it, he's back at the couch, pulling me up by my wrist with a smile reaching each of his ears.

"It's our *song*," he exclaims.

"What?"

"Sadie," he cries, feigning dramatic offense. "You're a horrible friend. *Our* song! We danced to it at junior prom!"

I can't help but laugh. "I'm sorry, I can't believe I would forget such a thing."

He tugs again. "Come on!"

"I love this song," Summer says, standing up too.

"Everybody!" Felix says like a kid on Christmas morning. "On the dance floor. I demand it!"

Khalil and Georgia exchange a glance, then join us as Summer makes a run for it and Felix drags me onto the floor.

I desperately want to be able to let loose as Felix dances and I even start to recognize the music. The whole group is there having a great time, and it hurts not to be part of it. But I can't make myself do much more than an awkward shuffle as I feel my shirt threatening to ride up at any moment, and Summer looking gorgeous in the corner of my eye makes it all the more terrifying. The rest of the night is a blur - my mind never relaxes, and I barely notice much outside of my own body. Georgia eventually leaves the dancefloor to flirt with a cute femme at the bar, Khalil checks out around midnight to "go home and sleep" (Summer is sure to thank him again before he goes), and about an hour later I start to really feel the emotional lag of my zombie evening.

"I'm gonna head home," I tell Felix over the music.

"Can we come see Ethel?" he yells back.

"Sure," I say by reflex, watching Julian and Summer appear over his shoulder. Rio has long since disappeared into the pulsating mass of dancing bodies, never to be seen again.

"What's happening?" Summer says, brushing the voluminous red curls behind her ear.

"We're gonna stop by Sadie's before we go home." Felix replies. I gulp against the lump in my throat - yet another wonderful facet of the neverending fun of this evening is the promise that Summer will see the disastrous state my apartment is in. *Great.*

"Welcome," I say dryly as the door swings open, and Felix pushes past me and darts into the apartment.

"Ethel!" he cries, racing around like a toddler.

A waddling, pudgy ball of fur instead trots toward Summer, who coos. "Hello!"

She and Julian squat to pet Ethel, whose tail is going about as fast as it can go. Felix joins them, running his hands across her fur.

"Ethel and I go way back," Felix tells Summer, grinning. "She's been around since we were in middle school."

"What a sweet old girl," Summer muses, cupping the dog's snout. Ethel, horrifyingly, lunges forward and covers practically the entire surface area of Summer's face with her tongue.

I step forward. "Sorry, she doesn't usually-"

Summer giggles, a bright sound like a bell that makes my knees weak. "Thank you, Ethel!" she says, scratching behind the dog's ears and planting a kiss on the end of her nose.

"She knows good people," says Felix, scratching at her hip.

"I missed you," Julian whispers almost intensely, staring straight at Ethel's face.

"Hey, that's a badass oven," says Summer rather suddenly, craning her neck back to look into the kitchen. Ethel strains to follow her. "They had one of them at an old job of mine. I swear, you can do a batch of cookies in like half the time with that thing."

"Okay," I say slowly, not exactly sure how to respond. She looks inherently out of place here, beautiful and put-together crouching on the dusty floor and petting my ancient dog. It's worlds colliding in the worst way: utter perfection gracing my ungodly pigsty.

"Thanks for coming out tonight," says Julian, climbing to his feet and hugging me.

"Wouldn't miss it," I reply, a little wooden.

"You can just give my shirt back whenever," Felix says, standing up and kissing my cheek. "I love you, babe."

"Love you too." I look at Julian. "Both of you."

"Have a good night," Summer says, joining the boys at the doorway. Ethel starts to follow her, and she laughs. "Silly puppy."

I gently push Ethel away from the door as I open it for them. "Goodnight, guys."

"Night," the boys chorus, and the three of them disappear.

As the door shuts, I cast a glance to Ethel at my side. "Traitor."

"Morning." It comes out robotically as I come through the back door of Inspiration Florals.

My coworker Macy turns at the sound, her dark ponytail flicking around with the movement. "What happened to you?"

I join her at the counter, pulling on my black embroidered apron. "I forgot I'm twenty-seven and work on Saturdays."

"Okay, didn't know you were a bad girl," she teases as she carefully slides a dahlia into the large vase in front of her. "Why don't you tell Rob you're on your period and call off? That's what I do when I'm hungover."

"I'm not hungover," I tell her, clocking in on the computer. "I was out late at my best friend's engagement party."

"I'd call off anyway," she shrugs, her eyes sparkling behind the thick winged eyeliner she always wears. "But whatever, you can be a goody-goody if you want."

"As opposed to the edgy, flower-shilling rebel *you've* always been," I reply with an eye roll.

She laughs. "God, come for my throat why don't you." The last dahlia leaves the table, but her vase is still mostly empty. "We just got some white lilies. Will you bring them over here?"

"Sure."

"Thanks, toots," she replies through a thick accent, slightly rearranging the flowers in the vase.

Work goes by on autopilot - Summer's probably right about me having fallen out of love with my job. It's easy as ever to do it well, but it's just as simple to let it all happen almost without me. I can do it asleep: joke with Macy, make arrangements, help customers. I've been doing it all for so long that it really has lost its shine. And it doesn't help that every time someone moony-eyed comes in looking for a romantic gift, it cuts a little bit. There's so much love in the world - so much in *my* world, with Felix and Julian and Khalil and his partners - that it makes everything I've gone through instead of love feel even worse.

Chapter Four

Summer Moves Out

"There, that's the last of it," says Julian, stepping out of the house and setting another box in the trunk of my car.

I look between him and Felix, my heart swelling. A car full of boxes is a bittersweet sight for me since moving here, but it's the happiness that overwhelms me looking at the two wonderful men who've let me into their home. I find myself holding back tears. "I don't know how I can ever thank you guys."

"Don't mention it," says Felix, looping an arm over my shoulder affectionately. "That's what friends are for, Summer."

"It's nothing," Julian agrees. "I'm always here to help you."

I know he means it, but I can't quite chase away the guilt at having inconvenienced them. "Just," I say finally, "thank you." They both hug me, and I hold on tight. As much as I'm glad to have my own space, I'm going to miss living with them too.

"Alright, let me just pee first and then we can get on the road," says Felix, and leaves Julian and I leaning against my car.

"Is it weird that I'm a little sad to be leaving?" I ask him, smiling wistfully. "Always having people in the house… it was like college."

"We'll still hang out, I promise," he says, nudging my shoulder with his. The ring on his left hand sparkles lightly - sometime over the last week, Felix must have given him the private, sentimental proposal he's always dreamed of.

"I know." I tighten the hair tie around my ponytail and twist the ends around my finger absentmindedly. "It's really nice making new friends. I haven't…" There's an ache in my chest, and I trail off. Julian nods knowingly.

"I'm really glad, Summer," he says. "It's been so great to have you back in town, you know. I missed you."

"I missed you too." The tears start to creep up again, and I gulp back against them. "Everyone's, uh, everyone's so nice."

"They are," he replies with a smile. "What do you think of Sadie?"

I tense a bit. I don't think telling him that his fiancé's best friend is weird and cold to me is exactly a good idea - especially since it's probably a little soon to pass too much judgment on her.

"I haven't had much time to get to know her," I reply carefully. "She hasn't come on quite as strong as the others."

He nods. "She can be that way sometimes. But she's really sweet."

"I guess we probably just don't have much in common."

Julian turns to look at me just as Felix emerges from the house. "Alright, let's move!"

The rest of the group meets us in the parking lot of my new building, everyone dressed in their best mover chic. Felix immediately starts giving everyone orders like the world's most femme construction foreman, sending the group on systematic trips upstairs. In no time, I'm overseeing box placement from the kitchen and Sadie and Julian are carrying in the last of the load.

"Where do you want these?" Sadie asks me.

"The bedroom," I reply, taking my hand out of the box full of kitchen utensils to gesture in the right direction. "That top one is books and CDs. You can go ahead and start putting them on the bookshelf, if you don't mind."

"Aye aye," she says, a twinge of dryness to her tone that irks me, then disappears down the hall. Julian sets his set of boxes, the top clearly marked **LIVING ROOM CLUTTER**, on the couch and starts going through them.

"It's beautiful, Summer," says Felix, admiring the place with his arms crossed in front of his chest. "So much sun."

"Hey, Boss Man," calls Georgia from where they and Rio are kneeling in the corner of the kitchen. "How about you help us unpack all this stuff?"

"Oh, right," he giggles and scrambles to their side. He pulls a hand mixer from a box, holding it up like James Bond with a gun. "Boss Man reporting for duty."

"Don't worry too much about where to put stuff as long as it's all like with like," I tell them, rooting through my own box. "I'll move things later if I really need to."

"Yes ma'am," Rio says cheerfully. "I swear, I've never seen this many different baking supplies in my entire life."

"Proud to be that for you, Rio," I reply with a smile, sliding open a drawer and placing several wooden spoons inside.

Khalil pops up from behind the TV stand, a clump of cords in his hands. "Summer?"

A group of plastic spoons joins the wooden ones. "Yes?"

"You only needed a couple of these for the TV," he says. "Where do you want the rest?"

"I have a basket in my room," I tell him, closing the drawer. "Here."

He hands them to me, and I start down the hallway. When I open the bedroom door, I see Sadie sitting on the floor in front of the bookshelf.

"Three copies of *Romancing the Drone*?" she says to herself, pulling a charcoal gray book from the box which perfectly matches the two books already sitting in front of her. She raises her voice upon hearing the door open. "What is this girl, George Lucas's manic pixie wet dream?"

"One copy is signed," I tell her through a grin.

She doesn't turn at the sound of my voice. "Are you George Lucas's manic pixie wet dream?"

"I'm a romantic," I shrug, pulling the cord basket out from under my already-made bed.

"You're a weirdo," she counters, turning over her shoulder to look at me with a cocked eyebrow and a playful grin. "I get 'romantic', but *this* is shameless robot smut."

"You think the girl with three copies doesn't know that?" I offer a similar smirk. Under usual circumstances, somebody making so many disparaging comments about my favorite misunderstood, actually very comedic smutty romance book wouldn't sit so well with me. But I've heard how she talks to the rest of the group, and this level of familiarity makes me think that finally, finally I might have cracked her.

But as if realizing that she's on the verge of making a good impression and needing to remedy that immediately, she suddenly drops the whole demeanor and turns away, silently slotting the books into an empty spot on the shelf. I deflate, a little wounded.

"We talked on the phone for hours," Georgia is saying as I come back into the kitchen. "I felt like such a teenager, giggling into the night."

"Who's we?" I ask, digging back into my box.

"That girl they were flirting with at Spectrum two weeks ago," says Rio, stacking two cupcake pans on top of each other and stowing them in a cabinet.

"She asked me to be her girlfriend two days ago," Georgia says, a blush spreading across their face. The whole room erupts in a chorus of "aw"s and exclamations.

"What's her name?" asks Khalil.

"Carrie," she says sheepishly, and we all cry out again.

With the combined power of all six of my little helpers, things are mostly unpacked in almost no time. I dismiss everyone before dinner, and my night quickly turns quiet.

I'm lying in my new bed, a rickety queen wrapped in light pink bedding I haven't used in a bit more than two years. It's well past when I usually try to be asleep, especially with work in the morning, but I've been here with my eyes closed for what feels like forever.

Well, I decide as I climb out of bed and shuffle to the kitchen, *might as well go ahead and get a handle on the new appliances.* It's lucky I moved in with a full stock of groceries.

The hours fly by in a cloud of flour, powdered sugar, and a carton and a half of eggs. The baking trance feels almost like dreaming, but I don't get a wink of sleep all night.

The next morning, balancing a sugary frappuccino (the only way I can drink my coffee) in my hand, I set down my array of sweets on the So Sweet break room table. There's a sizable *thump*, causing my coworker to look up from her phone with a bemused look.

"What is that?" she says, barely holding back a laugh.

"Treats," I say simply, grandly sweeping my arm and taking a sip of coffee. It does little to perk up my tired body.

She shrugs, reaching for a cupcake. "As long as *these* don't come out of my paycheck."

"There," I announce, closing the oven door. "That'll be about fifteen minutes in the oven, then cooling time."

Sadie gives a detached look from the other end of her kitchen counter, where she fiddles with a small bundle of flowers that could become a boutonnière. She's wearing a pair of thick-rimmed glasses I hadn't seen before today, which ever so slightly amplify her eyes. "Good."

I scratch the scalp beneath my bun, the practical hairstyle left over but fairly messied from my admittedly long So Sweet shift. "I think they'd both like the chocolate and caramel in the cake," I say aloud, fairly confident that Sadie isn't listening to me. "And the…" My brain seems to lag, struggling to recall the ingredients I *just* put together. "Uh…"

Her green eyes go wide. "Are you okay?"

My body takes this cue to suddenly take on the texture and consistency of a croissant, and my eyelids suddenly feel heavy. "I'm fine," I say quickly. "Just a little tuckered out from work. And I haven't been sleeping great the last few weeks…" I don't mention the extracurricular cake pop preparation for Khalil's partner's party that I've been squeezing in between shifts, as even I realize how extreme all these things sound when explained in quick succession.

"Why don't you take a nap?" Her response is so abrupt and her tone so sharp that it takes me a second to realize she's actually being kind. "On my couch. I can wake you in an hour or two."

My face feels hot. "I- I couldn't."

She straightens her posture and holds firm eye contact with me, the dark emerald hue somehow incredibly intimidating. "Fifteen minutes in the oven, right? Then onto the rack to cool? I think I can handle that."

I falter. "I don't know if-" But my body betrays me, forcing a huge yawn up from my throat, the kind where you have to close your eyes and stretch your arms out. When I emerge from the seconds-long affair, her gaze is unrelenting, and I can't argue.

It's more than a little alien settling onto her couch - *Sadie*, who hasn't warmed to me at all in a month of knowing one another, who seems to be uncomfortable any time I enter a room, who I would have previously assumed just didn't possess this kind of caring streak (at least not for me), inviting me to curl up and take a cat nap in her house. It feels almost absurd.

But the couch is surprisingly comfortable, and I discover as I pull it over my body that the blanket draped over the back has the kind of texture I'd attribute to an angel's embrace. What's more, Ethel walks up with her droopy face and her big brown eyes, slightly cloudy, and climbs up with me, cuddling into my side like a space heater with a heartbeat. Sleep finds me easier than I can remember in months, like a soft hug from an old friend enveloping me in peace and quiet.

I wake up on my own, the refreshed feeling so unfamiliar I almost dislike it. Ethel makes a groggy sound of protest as I move ever so slightly to look over the back of the couch into the kitchen. Sadie leans over the counter and a variety of flowers, laser-focused. She's a different kind of pretty than I've known from her before in her glasses and a slouchy pair of sweats; more casual, unexamined, domestic. I feel almost affectionate, waking up from a good sleep and looking into the distance at a beautiful woman, as though we're two different people with a totally different relationship. Even as it is, I feel different seeing her now. I'm pleasantly and utterly surprised by this unprecedented act of kindness. But if she's done this, I have hope that maybe she could really be my friend one day after all.

It takes me this long to look a little to the left and see my cake on the cooling rack. It's *perfect*. A silly bit of pride builds in my chest at having exactly estimated how long it needed in the oven.

"Thank you," I tell Sadie a bit later, breaking a long silence as I slice up the cake and put it into some containers to take home.

"Don't worry about it," she says shortly, not looking at me, and I get the sense that she really means that. It's a bit of a blow, but I suppose I shouldn't have expected her to change up entirely.

"Are you going to be at Axel's party next week?" I can't quite tell which answer I'm hoping for.

"No," she replies. "We don't know Axel that well, so we're sitting this one out. It'll probably be more of Khalil's boring adult friends."

I shrug. "Boring adults like desserts, too."

"And they have money," she adds.

I collapse onto my couch and mindlessly switch on the TV. I just dropped off the cake pops at Khalil's place after a long So Sweet shift, and now I feel like I can finally let go - until tomorrow, at least. I'm not even sure whether I get to sleep, just that the sound of some random real estate show dwindles to a dull hum and my mind drifts out like a boat to sea. I'm startled awake an indeterminate time later by my phone ringing.

"Hello?" I say groggily, not even bothering to look at the caller ID.

"Summer!" Khalil's voice is energetic, and I quickly switch him to speaker phone. "I've got great news."

"Let me hear it," I reply, stretching out my arms in an attempt to shake my sleepiness.

"You were a big hit at the party," he says. "Everybody spent practically the whole time raving about the cake pops."

"That's great!" Even as long as I've been baking, it never quite gets old to know that my stuff makes people happy.

"I gave your social media to a *lot* of our friends," he tells me. "And I think it's safe to say you'll be our go-to baker when we've got an event."

"Thank you, Khalil," I say, though there's a downward pull on my good mood. I want to be grateful for this probable push to my business, but suddenly the thought of squeezing in Sweet Summer Confectionaries with my day job like I've been this last week makes me feel like I've been hit by a train.

"It's no problem," he insists. "Thank *you*."

We exchange our parting pleasantries and I set my phone down in front of me, the fatigue like a weighted blanket on my shoulders.

It will all be okay, I tell myself, not a small amount unconvincing. *It will have to be.*

Chapter Five

Sadie Opens Up

I turn the key in the lock of Inspiration Florals' front door just as Macy appears behind me.

"Morning," she says cheerfully, a coffee in hand.

"Morning," I reply without any of her enthusiasm.

"You can at least pretend to be happy to see me," she prods.

I take in a deep breath before deadpanning, "Oh my god, Macy. I'm so excited to see the person I see almost every day at my full-time job." I hold eye contact as I pull the door open.

"Much better," she says, pushing past me and into the shop.

We both clock in and pull on our aprons, and she stays behind the counter while I go around turning on all the lights.

"So a few of us are going to a bar after work tonight," she calls as I flick on the bulb over a group of pre-arranged bouquets. "You in?"

"I'm busy tonight," I reply, skipping the perfunctory *I wish I could* as I don't quite feel the conviction to lie. "I'm helping plan my best friend's wedding." *And dreading it*, I neglect to mention. Going to Summer's place is sure to be weird, especially considering the last time I saw her I let her sleep on my couch. All my attempts not to like her are failing, and I'm sure she can tell. I comfort myself, at least, with the memory that tomorrow I get to see Felix for his birthday.

"Fun," Macy says. "But one of these days I'm gonna get you to come out with us. I *know* you're more fun than you look."

"I think you're *exactly* as fun as you look," I counter, flicking on the open sign.

She laughs. "You got me. What would I do if I had to work with boring people?"

"How do you know I'm not?" I ask, crossing back to the counter. "You've never gotten me out of the shop."

"Which is why I'm not giving up," she says. "But whatever, enjoy *planning your best friend's wedding*." She adds a goofy lilt to it, faux-mocking me. That's sort of Macy's M.O., irony wrapped in irony.

"I will," I reply flatly, and I honestly can't tell whether or not this is a lie.

"Alright, I've had a lot of ideas," says Summer in lieu of a greeting as she lets me into her apartment. She's got a bit of a jittery vibe which starts to make sense when I notice an empty coffee cup on the countertop.

"Let's hear," I reply, setting down the bouquet I brought from work on the kitchen island.

She holds up a plate of what looks like an array of whipped cream dollops. "Two signature desserts tailored to the tastes and personalities of the grooms." She shakes the plate. "I already made vanilla meringue cookies with blackberries and raspberries for Julian."

"Cool," I reply. That does sound like something Julian would love, and I don't think I've ever even seen meringue cookies before.

"I want to make a blueberry orange custard pie for Felix," she continues. "I already have the crust ready, and I figured maybe you could help me get the rest ready."

I pause. That actually sounds... really fun. I don't know why it strikes me so much in this moment, but I haven't done something just plain fun in a while. "Yeah, I'll help."

She smiles brightly, and my stomach twists into knots. She pushes a little pink journal toward me, its face open and up. "Alright! Here's the recipe. How about you start measuring the sugar, flour, and butter? I'll separate the egg whites from the yolks and grate the orange zest."

There's something comforting about the slightly unfamiliar motions - I've always worked with my hands, but I haven't had time to sour on the feeling of scooping powders and cutting sticks of butter the way I have cutting flower stems and arranging bouquets. It's even a little relaxing, a feeling that cuts in and out whenever Summer's arm brushes mine or she passes close enough for the warm scent of vanilla and something ineffable that just says 'bakery' to fly up into my nose.

Unlike me, each of her movements is poised, perfectly practiced and natural. She seems to float through every step, a frustratingly gorgeous sense of ease permeating everything she does. I almost feel flushed to be stumbling through her greatest talent alongside her, like a kitten chasing a leaf next to a hunting tiger. She takes on the hard parts with no trouble, using a handheld whisk like an industrial mixer and watching the oven like a hawk for the precise moment her confection is complete. While it cools in the fridge, she demonstrates using two forks to delicately roll blueberries in a syrupy sugar mixture and into a small dish of fine powdered sugar. The berry emerges as if from a day in the snow, coated in white and shimmering subtly.

She offers me her tools with a kind sparkle in her eye. My knees go weak. "Want to try?"

I can already smell disaster at the thought of my inexpert hands fiddling with the tiny fruits, but I accept them and clumsily go through the motions. My result somehow looks less magical than hers - more sad and wet - but she smiles like a light bulb. I feel wobbly.

"You're a natural," she says. I don't quite believe it, but she gets two more forks and we start combining our efforts.

Pulling the pie from the fridge, she looks over her shoulder at me and our little bowl of sugar-coated berries. "You're the visual artist here. Why don't you place the berries?"

I'm not sure why this causes such an uprising in my stomach, but it's as if every microorganism within me stirs at the suggestion. "That pie looks *amazing*. I think your art is plenty visual." I flush at my inadvertent compliment, but it's *true*. The soft, smooth look of the custard would certainly make my mouth water if-

"I insist," she says, setting the pie down in front of me.

I pause. "...with my fingers?"

She actually *laughs* a little bit, amused by my fish-out-of-water awkwardness, and the sound fills me with butterflies. "You can wash your hands if you don't feel clean."

After doing just that, I stare down the pie and the berries like one of them will suddenly start talking and give me the intel I need. But of course, I'm on my own. I've never been so stressed trying to arrange something in a neat, tidy array.

To make matters all the more nerve-wracking, Summer watches over my shoulder. "Very nice," she says with an approving cluck of her tongue as I gingerly place the final blueberry. "Only one thing left to do now."

"What's that?"

She holds up a triangular knife with a bent handle. "Give it a try."

Once again, I can't help but admire her as she cuts and plates a slice, an effortless attention in her eyes and a fire-red strand of hair falling across her face. She wipes off one of the sugar forks with a paper towel and takes it to the pie, which cuts like warm butter. Her face is stony as she brings the bite to her full, pink lips, and the expression changes gradually toward satisfaction.

"That's Felix, alright," she says, nodding. She looks almost confused when she looks up at me, standing back with my arms tucked to my sides. "You can have some, you know." A playful gleam flashes in her eyes. "You made it, after all."

I freeze up for a second, looking between her and the slice. My stomach feels funny, but not quite like it usually would, more like - God forbid - butterflies.

I shouldn't do this. Maybe I shouldn't have even helped her make it. But I've done worse things because someone pretty asked me to, and it *does* look really good…

I can have a bite. It'll mean giving in to these *I-might-like-you* feelings a bit, but it's not as though anything will come of that. She doesn't even like me. *And she certainly won't after she sees me eat,* something deep in the recesses of my mind reminds.

Feeling skin-crawlingly observed, I pick up another of the sugar forks and clean it the same way Summer did. It's all I can do not to shake as I scrape off a piece and put it in my mouth.

And *holy shit*. Suddenly my brain is firing on all synapses, and I feel my eyes sting with the hot beginnings of tears.

Summer's eyes go wide. "Are you okay?"

I can barely formulate a response, too focused on finding something to say that won't make me sound as crazy as nearly crying at a bite of pie is making me look. "I'm… I haven't… I didn't… I forgot…"

Her dark brown gaze is gentle and understanding, and I manage to take a deep breath which slows my thoughts and helps keep the tears at bay. Still, everything feels heavy, like something slowly crushing me from the inside. "I, uh, I haven't had any, like, desserts in a long time. I just broke up with this girl who, uh..." My exhale shudders, even my body acknowledging the immense weight of this admission which I've never made to anyone else. "She made a lot of comments about my body, and what I ate, and so I stopped having desserts or big portions in front of her, and then I sorta just, uh... stopped having desserts and big portions at all. I mean, it was easier than having to *look* at my body all the time while I tried to work it off."

She furrows her brows even further, her lips parting in the most picture-perfect, Disney Princess show of concern I've ever seen.

"So I guess I kinda forgot how good pie tasted," I say apologetically, my throat still frustratingly groggy with the threat of tears. "And, knowing your reputation..." I motion lamely toward the plate. "Probably better than most pie."

It's a second before she says something, her voice breathy and quiet. "Sadie..."

"It's really good," I say with a nod, averting my gaze. With any luck, I'll be able to steer the conversation back onto the course and pretend this little detour never happened. "The, um, oranges taste really... orangey." *Nice one, Sadie.*

"Sadie, I'm so sorry somebody would do that to you," says Summer, still hushed.

The thing is - Felix knows that Gabby dumped me "for being too fat", and when I told him, he reacted with the appropriate amount of outrage. But what he doesn't know is that I listened to her. That I tried to appeal to her for months before she finally decided to cut things off because I wasn't doing a good enough job. That I started to hate my body just like she did. The thought of it fills me with hot, raging shame all up and down my chest. She shouldn't have talked to me that way, I know, but I shouldn't have let her.

"You're *beautiful*," Summer continues, her emphatic delivery almost enough to make me believe the obvious platitude. "And even if you weren't, that's just... it isn't ever okay."

A genuine frustration seems to build behind her comforting words, and I cast a short glance at her and back to myself. We're both rather firmly midsize; not trim and lean like Felix or Georgia, but not as plump and proudly fat as Rio. I'd never gotten bullied for my size in school like I know Rio did, but I've never felt small like so many of my peers did growing up. I wonder if Summer has felt that way.

"Did people ever say that kind of stuff to you?" I venture, feeling like the first step onto a frozen lake.

"Sometimes," she says simply, her gaze still fixed onto me.

Even more carefully, I let myself ask: "Did you… ever believe it?"

"I think teenage trans people basically *invented* hating their bodies," she says lightly, and I let out the smallest chuckle. After a second, she turns more serious and continues, "It's hard not to believe things you hear all the time. I socially transitioned when I was *ten*, and I'd still have these… really bad days, up until, like, sophomore year of college."

There's something to the tone of her voice, to the things she's saying that actually does start to wind me down.

"I think we have more in common than we thought," she says, finally looking away from me to study the countertop pensively.

"Yeah?"

"When Julian and Felix first got really serious, I'd just started dating this guy Landon," she says, leaning against the island and absently pushing that loose strand behind her ear. "He was really sweet, and I didn't really hang out with other people a lot. I didn't want to, you know? I liked him so much." She looks up at me lightly. "That's probably why we never met. I barely saw Julian, let alone anybody else."

I suck in my lips, not liking the sound of this story. I nod.

"A few months in, Landon got a job in Chicago," she continues, back to the counter. "It felt totally crazy. But he asked me to go with him, and I wanted to. So I packed up everything and moved. And then I had even fewer friends, because they were all back in Roseport seven hundred miles away, so I just worked twice as hard at this coffee shop I ended up at. The hours really sucked, and I hated just making these corporate, predetermined recipes that I wasn't allowed to change. So finally I started making Sweet Summer posts, trying to sell my own desserts. And *then* I was working three times as hard as before."

My stomach churns. I almost feel like I'm watching a horror movie with Past Summer as the protagonist I'd like to yell warnings at from the theater seat.

"So, last June, Landon sat me down and told me he'd cheated on me," she says, a frown taking over her face. I feel myself gasp ever so slightly, a sharp pain in my chest. "He said I worked too much, and didn't have any friends. He wasn't happy with me anymore." She grimaces. "So I moved out, and he kept half my shit."

"Jesus Christ," I hiss. "What the fuck, man?"

"Yeah," she says with a nod. "So, I get it. You're not alone."

My heart thrums hard against my ribcage. *Why* exactly that leaves me so speechless, I can't say.

"I'm sorry," I tell her after a moment. "For how I've been. I'm weird around… new people." *Around pretty people*, I should say. *Around people I know I could like.* Knowing how it always ends up for me, I can't risk something like that. But, I realize, neither can she.

The anxious ball in my chest finally starts to loosen. She feels safe. We can be friends.

She nods. "It's okay."

I look up a little sheepishly. "Can I try a meringue cookie?"

Her sweet smile grows mischievous, a glint in her eye that says *now you're speaking my language*. "Let me set aside a few cookies and a couple slices for the boys," she says almost wickedly. "The rest is ours."

We spend the rest of the evening on her couch, laughing over some bad reality TV show about tanned straight people kissing one another on a beach. I relish in the sweet, fruity taste of the desserts, never quite getting over how nice it feels not to be worried about them, or about the way I look eating them. I'm calmer altogether - Summer's whole aura, comforting and warm, certainly doesn't hurt either.

"Baby!" Felix cries as he opens the door, jumping up and down like a little kid in an honest-to-God *pajama set* printed with little bunnies.

"I come bearing gifts," I tell him, holding out the bouquet I arranged for him and the container with his and Julian's "signature desserts" from Summer while he leans forward and kisses both my cheeks. "Happy birthday, babe."

"I'm so fucking excited," he says. Then, looking down at the food container: "What's this?"

"The signature desserts of your wedding," I reply, pointing to each treat as I identify them. "*The Felix* and *The Julian*."

"Holy shit," he says, snatching it from me. I push up my glasses. "That Summer McConnell really is a miracle worker. Jules, come see!"

Julian emerges from the hallway. "Was just gonna get out of your hair. What do you need, sweetheart?"

"Come try these with me," he says, hurriedly getting silverware.

No surprise, they're a huge hit. I make note to text Summer about it later. Julian kisses Felix goodbye and leaves us to it.

Every year since we were five, Felix and I have celebrated his birthday with a solo sleepover full of snacks, movies, and makeovers. He's already turned the living room couch into a blanket fort pointed directly at the TV, and within a few minutes I've changed into my own PJs and joined him in the cushy cave he's made.

"This is *so* fucking good," he says, eagerly digging into his second slice of The Felix pie while I put our well-loved childhood copy of *The Princess Bride* into the DVD player.

"You know, I helped make that," I say, allowing myself to preen as I settle into my spot in the fort.

"I knew you and Summer would work well together," he teases, pointing his fork at me.

"Shut up," I protest, shoving his shoulder.

"But really," he says, "do you like her?"

I don't quite know how to respond for a minute. "I meant what I said two months ago," I decide. "I'm not ready to date anybody. Not yet. Maybe not ever. Gabby..." I pause, picking at my nails nervously. "I really took a blow to my confidence." I'm downplaying it by a lot, I know. But he's *Felix*, and he's my best friend, so of course he feels the weight of my statement through my smokescreen. His mouth falls open and his eyes go wide, a soft breath whooshing out of him like a deflating tire.

"I'm so sorry, babe," he says, setting down his slice to put his hands on my shoulders. "I had no idea. That shit's so..." He huffs. "I'm just sorry, babe. Take as long as you need. And if you ever need to talk-"

"I know," I say, a smile growing on my lips.

"I still think you should fuck somebody, though," he teases, pushing my shoulder. "You're so tightly wound, you're going to snap in half if you don't have a good time every once in a while."

"Not that it's any of your business, Felix," I reply, "considering I've known you since we were *four*, but I think you'll rest assured that I'm twenty-seven years old and perfectly capable of 'having a good time' on my own." I scrunch my nose at him, resisting the childish urge to stick out my tongue, too. "Now shut up, the movie's starting."

He gasps with offense and tosses his pillow at me.

"Felix!" I cry, grabbing it and my own.

He laughs, throwing his arms up in front of his face like a shield. "Not the glasses, not the glasses!"

"You've been using that bullshit since we were kids," I protest, flinging his pillow back at him. "*I'm* wearing *my* glasses, too. I'm just not going to take it easy on y-"

Suddenly, he takes a violent swing and hits me across the chest with his pillow.

"Felix, *ow!*" He giggles smugly, pleased by my pain. "You little asshole, *some of us* still have boobs. That fucking hurts!" I launch myself at him, but even the tackle doesn't stop his laughter. "God, you're such a fucking *child.*"

I'm picking one last dog toy out of the vacuum's path when there's a knock at the door. I turn it off to answer, momentarily ceasing Ethel's shakes. Summer's there when the door swings open.

"Oh, shit, I'm sorry," I tell her, shoving the vacuum out of the way so she can get inside and out of the doorway. "I've been picking up and I totally lost track of what time it was and when you were coming."

"This place looks..." She trails off, looking off into the living room with wide eyes.

"I know," I reply. Every pair of shoes abandoned right inside the door, every piece of trash sitting right next to the trash can, every pile of random magazines and junk mail stacked on every surface, every overflowing laundry basket destined for the washing machine downstairs, plus a fair buildup of dust, dirt, and dog fur - all gone in the face of my spontaneous cleaning frenzy after work today.

"Any particular reason?" she asks, dropping to her knees behind the couch to greet Ethel, who merrily trots up to her.

I'd asked myself the same thing when I'd gotten home, ditched my shoes, and suddenly felt the urge to pick them back up, and then to break the vacuum cleaner out of its near-permanent spot in the back of my closet. I'm still coming up blank.

"Just time for a change," I tell her with a shrug, wrapping up the vacuum cord.

"Well, it smells great," she says, standing up. Her face turns to surprise, settling on the vase on the counter full up with a voluminous arrangement of bright yellow flowers. It's quickly taken over by a smile. "Those are so pretty!"

I'd thought the same thing when I decided to bring them home from work - it didn't seem strange to anyone else because I took flowers home all the time. But that was always for Felix or for wedding planning. Today I had looked at my arrangement of sunflowers, roses, goldenrod, and asters and just felt like I wanted to see it more. I hadn't felt that way at work in a while, so I bought them.

"Thank you," I say, smiling faintly. "So. You ready to get started?"

Chapter Six

Summer Slows Down

"Hey," Sadie greets me brightly, rearranging some more flowers in a vase with her back turned toward me. Over the last week, it's been as though we never had that rocky, awkward patch. I set down my bag on one of her kitchen chairs, wiping a bit of flour off my face.

"Hey," I reply. "I just came straight from work, so I'm sorry if I smell like So Sweet threw up on me."

She turns, her head cocked to one side. "I thought you worked the morning shift. Doesn't that start at, like, four AM?"

I can't help but laugh. "Sort of how it works, yeah."

"Jesus," she says, "with a shift like that, you must get your forty hours *no problem*." Her eyes bug with realization. "Summer, you're working twelve-hour shifts four days a week, plus your own business *and* wedding planning?"

Wincing, I nod. "It's... a bit much, I know."

"We've planned enough this week," she says suddenly, that same caring fervor from the day she made me take a nap coming back with a vengeance. Maybe, I realize, this is how she is when she's actually your friend - fiercely supportive and kind, as well as the teasing wit I'd already associated with her.

"Okay..." I say slowly, smiling through mild confusion. "I mean, I'm already here. Do you want me to just turn around and go home?"

"I want you to take a break," she says. "I'm starting to wonder if your arms keep mixing phantom batter while you sleep."

"When I *do* sleep," I add playfully, and her face shifts to an overblown exasperation. She honestly looks like she's turning red. I almost feel guilty for dangling the other thing I know she cares about regarding me, but she's made it perfectly clear that in the name of friendly banter, everything is fair game.

"You're going to drop dead before you turn thirty if you don't pump the brakes," she says, pointing an accusing finger at me. She holds my eyes, her demeanor shifting back toward the sympathetic view she'd started this whole thing with. "I mean it. We've got nine months to plan this wedding. I understand if you can't drop your *job* or your passion project, but this can definitely wait."

And just like before, my body seems to agree with her before my brain can even fully comprehend. My arms are sore and heavy, and my back aches. Suddenly I can't even remember *why* I work so much. "You're probably right."

She raises her eyebrows ever so slightly. "You can stay if you want. Just have a... regular friend hangout." The words come out a little awkwardly, but I have to smile at the effort and the sentiment.

"Yeah," I reply. "That sounds nice."

She insists I sit down *immediately*, and her couch is welcoming against my tired body. She disappears down the hallway and returns a minute later with a set of Uno cards.

I grew up with three brothers, and still somehow as we play round after round, I learn that I had no idea that Uno could feel this cutthroat and competitive. I'm almost afraid of Sadie, whether she wins or loses. (Though, she mostly wins.)

But, as we laugh and talk, I start to realize that maybe I do know why I've been driving myself into the ground lately.

"Thank you," I tell her, placing a card down in the pile.

"What for, kicking your ass?" she asks, setting down her own card.

"You know what for," I prod. "I think maybe the reason I've been working so much has to do with all the Landon stuff."

She perks up, the competitive fire flickering out. "Yeah?"

"I started spending all my time on work when we moved to Chicago and I didn't have any friends," I tell her, a knot starting to unravel in my stomach. "And then when he dumped me because I worked too much, I was stuck in the habit. And if I were to stop now, it'd be like..." I breathe in, knowing what I'm about to say is silly. "Like I threw away a two-year relationship for nothing."

"What? No," she says, looking so personally offended you'd think Landon had cheated on *her*. "You were doing what you needed to do to make money, pursue your passion, and keep yourself afloat in the city you moved to *for him* and that asshole managed to get *mad* at you for it." She shrugs off some of the anger, softening her tone. "Besides, I know what it's like to be creative. Working a lot is kind of a given."

"I know," I reply, smiling a little. "But, you know... now I have friends. It's starting to feel okay to relax again. Work isn't the only thing in my life." I make sure to meet her eyes directly when I add, "Thank you for reminding me."

She smiles back, that prominent canine peeking from behind her lip, and I'm beginning to count myself incredibly lucky to be Sadie's friend, if it means I get to see these room-brightening smiles directed towards me.

"You're welcome," she says, "and *you're welcome.* Blue." She sets down a wild card, and I groan at the three yellow cards in my hand.

"I take it back," I grumble playfully, drawing card after card until I find a blue one. "I'd rather work myself to death."

Her eyes shine, and it seems that I might as well have paid her a genuine compliment. "Be my guest," she says grandly as she sets down another blue card and sends me fishing in the draw pile once again.

"Great work today, Summer," says a voice behind me as I'm turning off the "open" sign in the So Sweet window. I turn to see my boss, Brandy, at the cash register.

"Thank you," I respond without much thought, and then something shifts in my chest. "Hey, could I talk with you for a minute?"

She looks up. "Sure."

I'm not even sure I'm really going to say it until I'm saying it. "I think I wanna cut down my hours." I gulp a bit. "Maybe more like twenty, twenty five a week?"

She knits her brow. "Well, sure, but may I ask why? You're about the most talented we've got on staff."

I flush at the compliment. "I've been, uh, working on my own personal baking brand for about a year now, and I want to put some more focus into growing and maintaining it."

She clicks her tongue. "I was afraid of that. I've lost a lot of damn good people that way over the years." She crosses to me from behind the counter. "But I think that's the way it should be." A breath of relief escapes my mouth. "I've been in this business a long time, and I know it takes a lot of courage to take that leap, kid."

"I appreciate it," I reply a little breathlessly, surprised by the depth of her support. "But I'll still be around."

"I know it," she says. "But it's only a matter of time before you're out of here and on to bigger and better for yourself. I'm proud of you, Summer, and I wish you all the best. I'll have everything fixed starting on next week's schedule."

"Thank you," I say, my chest puffing up a bit.

This newfound confidence and freedom drives me back to my apartment like a flash, and I take advantage of the burst of energy. Setting up my phone and going into an absolute fugue state, I make more social media content for Sweet Summer Confectionaries than I have in the last few months combined, using trusted old recipes and a couple I make up on the spot. I make instructional videos, timelapses of my process, detailed decorating videos - all of this for a cake, two batches of cookies, half a batch of cupcakes, and a few cake pops made with the extra bit of cake I cut away while leveling it. I even do a photoshoot for each treat once it's done. I stand back and look at my countertop in awe - this content will last me a month at the least.

And, it occurs to me a moment later, it is now on the later end of 2AM and I have an entire cake, two batches of cookies, half a batch of cupcakes, and a few cake pops sitting on my counter with only me to eat them. I pull out my phone and make a familiar call.

Julian is there at my door in what seems like two minutes, with his mullet sticking up in all different directions and his tattoos on full display in a bright pink Hello Kitty-patterned tank top which matches his pajama pants.

"Cute outfit," I tell him with my hand still on the door. "Goes great with your beard."

He scratches the aforementioned stubble. "I still look cool in Hello Kitty and you know it," he says, shoving past me and strolling into the kitchen to preview my smorgasbord. "I would venture to say I still look cool in *any* Sanrio character."

"You struck me as more of a Badtz-Maru kind of guy," I reply, "but I concede the point."

"I couldn't get Felix out of bed," he says, picking up a cookie. "He's gonna be *really* pissed in the morning."

"I already made a container for you to take home," I say, holding it up to show its packed nature and setting it back down.

He groans in appreciation at the first bite of the cookie, then asks, "What's the occasion?"

A huge grin can't help but form on my face. "I cut my hours to part time at work so I'll have more time for Sweet Summer stuff."

His eyes go wide. "Summer! Holy shit, that's amazing."

"I know!" I squeal. "So let's celebrate by eating all of this tonight."

He snorts. "Don't tempt me."

So we pull up chairs to the island and dig in, not caring about manners or cleanliness. We don't even cut the cake past the initial slice I'd cut for the camera and then put in Felix's to-go box - we just dig straight into it with our forks. Julian's teeth are quickly covered in colorful icing remnants and chocolate crumbs, and there's a tiny swipe of edible glitter nestled in his mustache hairs just under his septum ring that I decide not to mention.

Sitting here like this, I feel like someone else - but not *new*. I feel like Summer at twenty-five, Summer before Chicago, Summer before Landon.

"You know what this reminds me of," Julian says, his fork poised over the cake. "Freshman year, that day you came back from your little cousin's birthday party-"

"Oh my god, that Spider-Man cake!" I cry out with recognition. "I worked so hard to make it, and he and his friends ate, like, two slices."

"Best day of my life," he says. "I was *so* glad he didn't finish it. We sat on the floor of your dorm and ate practically the whole thing."

"Yeah," I recall, "that was just like this. If Georgia were here, it'd be uncanny."

He raises his eyebrows, a rare mischievous glint in his eyes. "We shouldn't."

I match the expression. "No…"

Georgia is there within ten minutes, looking self-possessed and wide awake. "Alright, motherfuckers," they say right as the door opens. "Show me the cake."

The three of us, true to my memories, finish nearly the entire cake and about half of everything else as the night progresses, talking and joking like we're still eighteen on the floor of my dorm room. My heart is almost achy with gratefulness for them, still the same wonderful friends even after all the years that have passed and all the things that have changed. They both finally bid me goodbye around 5, and as they leave I feel more like myself than I have in a long time.

Chapter Seven

Sadie Comes Out

I'm about neck-deep in a mindless binge-watch of that awful reality show I watched with Summer back in September (which I've now learned is called Tropic Like It's Hot, and is even worse than we'd thought it was) when my phone rings. Upon seeing that it's Summer, my heart beats dully and I pick up the call.

"Hey."

"Hey," she says, "are you busy in, like, an hour?"

"It's my day off," I reply. "I'm…" I glance at the scantily clad singles on the TV. "…not up to much."

"Do you want to come thrifting with me?" There's a feeling in my chest like a flint lightly sparking. "Khalil invited me to his and his partners' Halloween thing and I don't have a costume."

"Sure," I say, an odd tingly feeling running through my body. "I don't have a costume yet either."

"Cool," she replies. "How about I pick you up at your place around two?"

"That works."

"Alright, cool. See you then, Sadie."

"See you."

I feel a little gross when I peel myself up off the couch and look down at my frumpy sleep clothes, the disturbing realization coming to me that I haven't gotten dressed for anything but work or a quick run to Felix and Julian's house in a *long* while. This little bit of self-deprecating shame looms over my head as I get ready, still avoiding the mirror. A quick glance is enough for now to tell me that I look presentable - I'll get better at looking, I promise myself. Someday.

My first thought when I see Summer in the parking lot is that she really does live up to her name. It's a chilly autumn afternoon, but her red hair shines like a raging fire.

"Hey," she says as I climb into the passenger seat.

"Hey," I say, my breath catching ever so slightly.

"So, Khalil said the party has a theme?" she asks as we push open the double doors to the big box thrift store down the street.

"Childhood favorites," I tell her, starting toward a rack. "They pick a theme every year for all the costumes to revolve around. Last year was 'hot topics'. *That* was brutal. Now we've all got outdated topical references gunking up our closets."

"Childhood favorites definitely seems more approachable," she agrees. "Any idea what you'll dress as?"

"Maybe Silvermist from those Tinker Bell movies," I reply, thumbing through a clump of blue t-shirts. "I watched those *constantly* as a kid. Honestly, I blame her, Roxanne from *A Goofy Movie*, and Julia Roberts in *Pretty Woman* for turning me gay."

"Oh, man, I wanted to *be* Roxanne," she says with a laugh. There's a hiccup in my chest. "But as a kid, I basically wanted to be every girl I saw on TV. I shouldn't have been surprised when my parents reacted the way they did to my coming-out."

I flick my eyes upward toward her. "Yeah?"

"Not surprised at all," she says, grinning wistfully and looking up as if she can see her parents in the store's rafters, "mostly just proud."

This warms my heart, but also comes with that inevitable twinge of jealousy like a short pinprick at my chest.

"It was really nice," she continues. "You know, I'm not even the one who picked 'Summer'."

"No way."

"Yep. I have three brothers," she explains, "and when I came out, my mom said she'd always had the name Summer picked out for if she had a girl. And as soon as she said it, I knew it was my name."

"That's so sweet," I muse, genuinely taken over by the story and by the look on her face.

"They were always really supportive," she says. "Still are. We're all so lucky to have had them, you know? They always made us feel safe and heard, so none of us were scared to come out. They were just as cool when I told them I was bi, and when Cameron and Wyatt came out, too."

There's another one of those strange hiccuping feelings when she says she's bi. I mean, I'd *assumed* something along those lines, since she told me about her ex-boyfriend and, well, straight people certainly aren't *common* in Julian's social circles. I try to push the feeling down and away, having gotten to a batch of blue skirts that might work for my costume.

"You're definitely all lucky," I agree. "Even the one straight brother." I say this with a pitying tone.

"Ryan's the luckiest of any of us," she says with a smile, looking through the rack opposite mine. "Cam and his boyfriend don't want kids, and Wyatt is aroace. *Ryan* got married and had kids. Our parents can be as liberal as they want, but I think it's hardwired into everybody over fifty to view becoming a grandparent as their ultimate purpose."

I laugh. "Point taken."

"How about you?" she asks. "What are your parents like? If you want to talk about that." She looks over her shoulder and says this part gently, trying her absolute hardest to be sure I'm not offended. It's sweet. Pardoning the pun, sweet really is what Summer seems to do best.

"They were alright," I say slowly, not sure how I'll vocalize these thoughts and emotions that have raged wildly within me for years. "Not perfect. Kind of strict sometimes, a little old-fashioned, but supportive of whatever I wanted to do for the most part. I, uh..." My breath comes out ragged, but I push through. "I knew how my dad was, so I didn't come out until I was twenty-four. I mean, I *came out*, just not to, like, anybody over thirty because I was afraid they'd tell my parents." I force out a laugh, because my mind seems to oscillate wildly on whether this story really is funny. "When I was sixteen, I hid under my own bed with a girl for, like, an hour and a half because my dad came home early from something. She was *pissed* at me afterward, and I had to have Felix lie that I'd been at the library with him."

She cocks her head to the side, her lips drawn tight in an almost quizzical frown. I feel exposed under her dark brown eyes, and I turn my back to feign a deeper interest in the clothes in front of me.

"When I finally told them, it, uh..." I squeeze my eyes shut and bite the inside of my cheek. "Well, let's just say they're still not totally over it."

"Sadie, I'm so sorry," she coos. My stomach churns.

"It's cool," I say a little too quickly. "Things definitely could've been worse."

She doesn't seem to know what to say, seemingly picking up on my reluctance to dwell on what definitely isn't *cool*. I let the silence hang.

"You know," she says after a minute, a bit further down the rack. "I didn't pick Summer, but I did pick my middle name."

"Yeah?" I ask, turning to look at her, then letting a burst of laughter break through as I glance between the short purple dress she's holding and the insinuating look on her face. "No way."

"Daphney with a y," she says with a shrug, "but yeah. I mean, she was a girly ginger with a cool gang of friends. She was everything I wanted to be." The dress is, indeed, a dead ringer for Daphne's from Scooby Doo. It's just missing the lighter lavender bits and a green scarf.

"Jesus," I remark, "I've heard of people naming themselves after fictional characters, but that is..."

"My costume for Khalil's party?" she says, ceremoniously folding the dress over her arm. "Absolutely."

Toward the back of the store, she disappears into a section stuffed with kids' toys while I meticulously thumb through a collection of old prom dresses.

"Here you go," Summer says, appearing at my side with a pair of kids' costume wings in her hand. "Fairy, right?"

"Wow," I deadpan. "You should *definitely* know better than to call me something like that."

Her laugh almost sounds like it's surprised by itself. "My sincerest apologies."

I take the wings from her, trying to reign in my smile. "Help me look for a dress."

"That *hiding under the bed* story," she says, joining my search, "that's badass. My parents *knew* I was into girls, but I was still super scared to bring anybody around them."

"I don't know if *badass* is the word I'd use to describe the desperate acts of a scared teenager lying to her parents," I reply, a bad taste coating my tongue. "Shit like that was what always got me dumped."

"What? It's like a spy movie," she jokes. "Stealth. Intrigue."

"Words that describe the closet perfectly," I agree sarcastically. "But at least I stopped being such a pisspoor girlfriend when I got out of their house."

"I'm not sure I can imagine you as a pisspoor girlfriend," she says, and there's a strange prickly feeling at the nape of my neck. "A sore loser *and* a sore winner, sure, but-"

"You *can't?*" I reply with an emphatic disbelief. "Here, this'll help: I've played card games with every one of my exes."

"Oh, I see it now," she nods, then pulls a dress from the rack. "How's that?"

I step back to give it a good once-over. It's long, with a one-shoulder top and sequins focused at the bodice. "That'll do."

"Are we the best thrift shoppers in the world?" she asks, handing it to me. "We've been here, what, ten minutes, and we already found everything we were looking for?"

"Is that what you consider an accomplishment?" I prod, glancing down at the sizing tag on the dress.

"You don't?" she asks, following me almost like a duckling to its mother as I head toward the registers. "Would you rather spend three hours looking for a dress and a pair of fairy wings?"

"Once you've spent an hour and a half hiding under a bed in your own house with your angry girlfriend, nothing else seems to take very long," I counter.

"I can imagine," she says. "But the worst thing that's ever happened in my dating life - aside from the obvious - was when my prom date and I didn't communicate well enough and ended up in the same dress." She giggles. "I thought it was kind of cute, but they were *not* pleased."

"So, you realize how *you're* the good guy in this story," I tease. "That doesn't exactly make me feel better, Summer."

"Did I say it was supposed to?" she says, and a laugh escapes from me almost like a burp, short and quick and loud. She looks a little smug at this, and it occurs to me how *easy* being her friend feels. Despite seemingly being the literal sweetest person on earth, she has absolutely no trouble matching my snark blow for blow.

"Do you want to go for coffee or something?" she asks as we exit the store with bags in hand. "We can swap more dating horror stories."

"You mean *my* horror stories, and *your* after-school specials?" I grin. If it's horror stories she wants, I'm definitely the person to look to. Gabby was just the latest in a string of awful experiences. There's a reason I'm sworn off dating. "I'm down."

Summer drops me off back at my apartment around 4 after two hours of annoying the patrons of the local artisanal coffee house with our uproarious outbursts of laughter.

"It was really nice hanging out with you today," she says, unlocking the car door.

"You too," I reply, and I realize I'm beaming. I also realize I don't stop all the way into the building, up the elevator, and into my apartment. *Okay, noted- going out and having fun is…* fun. *Truly a shock.*

At the sound of the door, Ethel sits up from her dog bed and begins her slow beeline toward me. I take advantage of her excitement and quickly scoop up her daily dose of pills, the wag of her tail telling me I've successfully passed them off as enticing treats. They're down her throat before she realizes she's been swindled and gives me a look of droopy-eyed indignation.

"Complain all you want," I tell her, stooping to scratch behind her ears. "But I swear to god, dog, you're living forever."

She gives no indication that she understands, just rolls onto her back to expose her tummy and shoot her big brown eyes at me. Unlike her to me, I comprehend: *Shut up and scratch.*

About five minutes and an incomprehensible amount of dog hair later, my phone rings in my back pocket. I stand up and internally cringe at the caller ID.

"Hey, Mom," I say into the phone, masking it all.

"Hi, sweetie." Her voice, as always, sounds a little wavering, like somebody about to step onto a rickety rope bridge, and so sickly sweet it makes my teeth hurt. "I just wanted to call and see how you were doing."

Reeling from a breakup with a woman. Planning my best friend's gay wedding. Home from hanging out with one of my many queer, trans friends. This is all something I *could* say, but while nothing would stop the quaver, that certainly wouldn't help the matter. "I'm great. Working hard. Ethel says hi."

"Ohh, hi Ethel," she says, then sort of sighs. Like everything else, it's a sort of choppy sound, like she's not even sure about sighing. "Not up to much around here either, I'm afraid. I'll be looking forward to seeing you for Christmas this year, and I'll be sure to get all our old junk moved out of your room by then. That'll convince me to finally go through it all, get rid of some things."

"That's great, Mom," I reply, even though every bone, nerve, and muscle in my body is telling me that the absolute *last* thing I want to deal with is Christmas back home. But I promised her last year, and despite everything I can't quite bring myself to back out.

"It'll be so nice to have you," she says. "It'll be our first Christmas without… without Daddy."

And *there's* the thing about my mom. She patently avoids everything except the one thing I'd like her to ignore, and *that* she sugarcoats to high heaven like she's trying to give medication to a flailing toddler. I know without a doubt that Christmas will mostly consist of her cozying up next to me on the couch with photo album after photo album to show me all our good memories with my dad and musing about what a good man he was. Just the thought of it makes my stomach turn.

"Yeah," I reply faintly. "I've, um, I've got some laundry I need to go take care of, but I'll talk to you later, alright?"

"Of course, honey," she says. "I love you."

"I love you too." I flop into the couch as she hangs up, feeling almost physically drained. My phone buzzes after a second, and I pick it up with dread.

It's a text from Summer, an image attachment with the accompanying message: *World, meet Summer Daphne(y) Blake.*

In the photo, she holds her phone up in front of a mirror to show off her red hair, straightened and flipped outward into huge '70s Farrah Fawcett waves. It's genuinely a little impressive.

Oh, I text back, *I see how you are.*

Her response is almost lightning-quick. *What is that supposed to mean?*

I can't help the smirk that grows on my face as I type, *You definitely seem like someone who'd take Halloween that seriously.*

The typing bubble appears, then disappears, then reappears, and disappears again, until finally: *I've never heard anyone say something so evil. Halloween is gay Christmas. It's basically Pride Month 2.*

It takes me a minute to realize I'm audibly chuckling to myself. Summer Daphney McConnell, who loves smutty robot romance novels, named herself after a Hanna-Barbera character, and thinks of Halloween as *Pride Month 2*. What a friend to have.

It looks great, I reply finally.

Thank you, comes her response. *I know how hard it is for you to admit that.*

I roll my eyes. *I'm not a Halloween cynic, Summer.*

Then I'll have to call off the three ghosts.

This actually makes me *giggle*, and I feel like a kid again, sort of like when I'm with Felix. Almost all of the discomfort from talking to my mom lifts off of me and drifts away.

"Sadie!" Macy cries, springing up from her chair when I enter my coworker Crystal's house.

"This doesn't count as 'getting me out'," I tell her flatly as I set down my gift bag on a long table full of them. "Crystal's birthday party is basically a work event."

"Does this look like Inspiration Florals to you?" she asks, gesticulating with her cup and flicking her long dark hair, now sans ponytail, over her shoulders. "I consider it a win." She cranes her neck back to call into the kitchen, "Hey, Crystal! Look who it is!"

Crystal, who even at her own birthday party looks perpetually bored, leans into the living room. "Hi, Sadie."

"See?" Macy says. "The people crave you."

"They're practically foaming at the mouth," I deadpan, sitting in the chair opposite her. I'd stopped at home after work to change, and seriously debated not coming at all. I don't even *like* Crystal, and I barely speak to anyone else.

But instead I sit through Crystal opening all her presents like a preschooler sitting on a throne of wrapper paper. Her vibrant personality positively *shines* as she gives the same forced reaction to every gift, her lackluster smile never even trying to reach her eyes.

"These people are so boring," I have to whisper to Macy as Crystal and her entourage eventually shuffle off into the kitchen to cut the birthday cake. "I think if any of them even tried to do something interesting, they'd drop dead on the spot."

"Crystal's a lesbian," she offers with a shrug, apparently under the impression that I can't tell high femme from hetero.

"I'm allowed to be bored and annoyed by gay people just as much as straight people," I counter, pulling my purse strap further up my shoulder. "Besides, we live in the queerest town in Pennsylvania. You can't throw a rock around here and *not* hit somebody sapphic."

"I think that'd be a hate crime," she says, then flicks her gaze downward to my bag. "Where are you going?"

"Figured I'd go for the old Irish goodbye," I respond, already making eyes at the door. "My dog's been home alone all day and my contacts are getting itchy."

"Spoilsport," she chides.

"See you later," I reply, turning and stepping out the door.

It's a great relief to change out of my party clothes and curl up in bed with Ethel. How can it be that hanging out with Summer the other day was such a good time, while Crystal's party felt so draining? Well, I think, *other* than my opinion on Crystal…

I'm lulled to sleep by Ethel's slow breathing and faint doggy snores before I can figure out the answer.

Chapter Eight

Summer Shows Off

Just as I'm parking my car outside Khali and his partners' house, I catch Sadie getting out of her own car. Even from a distance, I can tell she's rocking her costume even more than I'd thought she would when I first pointed out that dress.

I take on a light jog to catch up with her, and her soft features light up with a crooked smile when she senses me at her side. "I think the word I'm looking for is... jeepers?"

"You learned that for me?" I coo in an overly saccharine tone that I know will make her roll her eyes. "Those Ghosts of Halloween really did change you for the better."

She scrunches her nose, and I take in her appearance from my improved vantage point. The blue sequined fabric hugs her curves, and the costume gives a whole new meaning to her cute pixie cut. "Hey, I haven't seen the movie since I was a kid, but didn't Silvermist have long hair?"

She raises one eyebrow, lengthening the block of shimmery blue shadow on her eyelid. "Well, now she's an adult bisexual who didn't wanna *also* pay for a wig."

"Please," I reply, "Silvermist was *always* bisexual."

She locks her eyes on mine, the green glittering with humor. "Just like Daphne Blake?"

"Exactly," I reply as we reach the front porch. The door flies open just as I'm about to reach for the knob, and there's Khalil, beaming in a pair of khaki pants, a blue denim shirt, a red neckerchief, and a wide-brimmed fedora.

"Hey, ladies!" he says, giving the biggest smile I've ever seen on him. A short, petite woman I quickly recognize as his partner Eleanor rushes to the door, dressed all in white with a similar hat to Khalil's and a painted-on white beard. She throws her arms open. "Welcome to Jurassic Park!"

"*Ohhh*," I say audibly, only now getting their costumes.

"They pick a different movie every year," Sadie leans toward me to whisper. "If Halloween is Pride 2, this house is the parade."

"You look great," Khalil says, ushering us in. "Daphne, Silvermist."

"Dr. Grant," I reply, then cut my eyes toward Eleanor. "Mr. Hammond." She grins.

As we walk in, I realize Sadie's observation is unabashedly correct. Every inch of the place is decked out in decor. There are costumed twenty- and thirty-somethings filling out every nook and cranny, draped over every chair and congregating in every corner. The classic Halloween decor clashes with the guests, who more resemble a Cartoon Network, Disney, and Nickelodeon reunion sharing a convention center.

Buzzing with energy, Khalil re-introduces me to the rest of his partners: Cecily (a tall, supermodel blonde dressed in her best Ellie Satler), Matthew (a bespectacled brunette whose unbuttoned Ian Malcom shirt exposes a huge moth tattoo on his collarbone), and Axel (an enby with a bright red mullet and a khaki vest with three stuffed velociraptors tacked to their back in a play at Robert Muldoon). Georgia stands at the end of the line in a false mustache and a yellow jacket, the picture of a heavily pierced, blonde buzz-cut-sporting Freddie Mercury.

"And you know Georgia, who continues to wantonly ignore our theming," Khali says, motioning at them with a mock offense.

"Who are you to say Freddie wasn't my childhood favorite?" she replies, taking a nonchalant sip from her drink. "I don't exist to cater to your little power trip, Doctor." Their dark blue eyes flick upwards to Sadie and I. "You two look sick."

A short Black woman comes jogging up to Georgia, her dark curls and white dress covered with trickles of red. "They're out of TP."

Georgia turns to the polycule, pressing their mustache back onto their lip. "You guys are out of toilet paper."

Eleanor squeaks and rushes off to the bathroom. I look to the new person at Georgia's side. "Hi, I'm Summer."

"Sadie," adds Sadie. "And you are?"

"Carrie," she says, and I suddenly recognize the femme from Spectrum, Georgia's girlfriend of three months, who I've still only seen a few pictures of. "Actually. And *somebody* didn't tell me about the 'childhood' theme."

"I'm sorry I didn't want you to have to do Halloween under totalitarian rule," Georgia replies.

"You can just tell people they based the book off of you," I offer. "*I'm Carrie. It was* my *childhood.*"

"Good idea," Carrie says, showing off straight, white teeth as she smiles. "It's really cool to finally meet all you guys."

"You, too," Sadie says.

"Summer! Sadie!" Rio comes running into the room, their short stature swallowed by a big blue turtleneck and their backward red baseball cap adorned with a pair of floppy black dog ears. Georgia and Carrie turn back toward Axel, picking up whatever conversation they'd been having.

"Nice costume," Sadie says, looking Rio up and down. "Animaniacs?"

"Wakko is a nonbinary icon," they reply with a serious tone.

"Did you need something or were you just that excited to see us?" I ask, and Rio's face lights up.

"Oh! Right," they exclaim, then cup their hands around their mouth to call into the next room. "Baby!"

A tall, muscular woman in a detailed '80s She-Ra costume jogs shyly into the living room and stops at Rio's side, her face flushed. "This is Tae," Rio says with a huge grin. "She's my new girlfriend."

"Nice to meet you," I say, shaking her hand. "I'm Summer."

Sadie takes the next turn, introducing herself and leaning in ever so slightly as she says, loud enough for Rio to catch, "Let us know if Rio showing you off like a piece of meat gets to be too much."

"*Bitch*," Rio says, and Sadie breaks into a chuckle that Tae hesitantly shares. "She's a hottie with a body. Am I supposed to be ashamed?" The flush on Tae's face only grows darker.

"I am so fucking nervous right now," Tae says, absentmindedly reaching for Rio's hand.

"You've got this, Princess of Power," I assure, offering her a fist bump which she returns with a weak smile. "We're not that scary, I promise." Her smile strengthens a bit.

"Thanks, Daphne," she says.

"Just don't tell the folks at Filmation that you fraternized with someone from Hanna-Barbera," I warn. "They'd have your head cut off with the Sword of Protection."

Tae laughs a bit breathlessly, and I hope this signals the beginning of her nerves starting to unravel. But they seem to dissipate completely when Rio gets on their tiptoes to kiss her cheek and the two bid us goodbye and walk off hand-in-hand.

"Are those two really not enough to make you believe in love?" I ask Sadie, realizing a second too late that maybe the reason she told me she "didn't really believe in all that love stuff" was because of her awful, fat-shaming ex.

"I was actually just thinking about how big a nerd you are," she says. "But come on. They *just* started dating. 'Love' is probably a pretty strong descriptor."

Or she's just a cynic. "Maybe I'll have to send some Valentine's Day ghosts your way next."

She physically cringes. "Ugh, *no*. I *hate* Valentine's Day. I think every florist in the Valentines-celebrating world carries an obligate hatred for that horrible day."

"I hear you," I agree. "The business part of it could definitely be smoother in the baking world, too."

The door swings open loudly, and I grin as we turn to look in the direction of the noise. "Speaking of love."

Felix saunters toward us in a sparkling red evening gown, long purple gloves, heavy sultry makeup, and a bright red color sprayed onto his dark hair. Julian - pun absolutely intended - hops along beside him looking extremely silly in a diminutive pair of red overalls, an oversized polka dot bow tie, yellow gloves, and a pair of bunny ears.

"Oh my god, look at us," says Felix, grabbing Sadie by the hand and pulling her tight against his flat chest. "Sparkling fabulous in our beautiful gowns. It's just like-"

"Junior prom," she finishes for him, pulling away. "I know."

I cast my gaze at Julian. "What's up, doc?"

"First Hello Kitty and now this?" he says, pressing a gloved hand to the white chest binder under his overalls like an old lady clutching her pearls. "When are you going to stop mocking me for not fitting into your strictly defined ideals of masculinity?"

"I have absolutely no qualms with Jessica *or* Roger Rabbit," I reply with my hands up like a shield. "I've just never seen Roger with a mustache, a septum piercing, and sleeve tattoos."

He shrugs. "What can I say? The world's gone woke."

"Now that we're here, the party can officially begin," Felix says, pulling upwards on the sweetheart neckline of his dress. "C'mon, ladies, let's drink." Without even waiting, he starts walking toward the kitchen.

"Hop along," I say to Julian with an exaggerated nod. He rolls his eyes and turns to follow his fiancé. Sadie and I are close behind.

"Okay, okay, okay," says Felix, waving his glass and trying to silence us. "Do you guys remember..." He gulps a little before continuing. "Do you guys remember that girl Danielle that Georgia dated, like, three years ago?"

"Oh my god," Sadie says, leaning forward with wide eyes. "Not the married one."

"Yep," Felix says grandly, "found her on Instagram."

"There's no way they're still together," Sadie says.

"Everyone, place your bets," he says, clutching his phone to the glittery fabric at his chest.

"I mean, I definitely *hope* they broke up," I add. "I'll guess not married."

"You guys didn't *meet* Danielle," says Julian. "I'm going married."

Felix takes in a huge, presentational breath. "Mr. Jefferson, just like the day you met me..." He takes a loaded pause, then turns his phone. "You have won."

We all burst into an uproar.

"Pregnant with baby number three," says Felix, "and she told Georgia she's *never* been attracted to a man."

"God, that poor woman," says Sadie. "At least when I was closeted, I wasn't *closeted* closeted."

We're all sitting on the floor in a corner of the house, where we've been for a few hours, drinking and gossiping about mutual acquaintances, and even people we don't all know (I now hold a burning hatred for an old client of Julian's and for Sadie's ex Reagan).

"Okay, who's next?" Felix asks, holding up his phone again. "Ooh, I know! Let's look at Julian's mom. God, I miss her."

"Oh, alright, I know what that means," Julian says, springing to his feet and gently holding Felix's shoulders. "He only brings up how much he misses my mom when he's had too much to drink."

"Her hands are so warm and she smells like honey and oatmeal and sunshine!" Felix half-wails, suddenly seeming a lot drunker than I'd thought a minute ago.

"In fifteen minutes, he'll be on the phone with her and sobbing," Julian tells us, then pats his fiancé's back. "Come on, love." Felix clambers to his feet and tucks himself under Julian's arm (a rather comic sight, considering their five-inch height difference is only made larger by Felix's stilettos).

"Hey, no fair!" Sadie says playfully. "What about us? You can't just steal the life of the party."

"Yeah, he's the only one whose phone hasn't died," I add. "How are we supposed to keep ourselves entertained now?"

Julian's gaze flicks to the table above Sadie's head and, with the hand not wrapped around Felix's shoulder, he grabs a huge plastic bowl full of candy and plops it onto the ground between us. "Knock yourselves out, kids. We'll see you later."

"See you later," Sadie repeats, squeezing Felix's hand, then Julian's. "Love you."

"Bye, guys," I add. "Don't forget about dinner next week."

Felix gasps. "I'm *so* fucking excited to see what you guys have been planning."

"You're gonna love it," says Sadie. "Bye, babe."

The Rabbits make themselves scarce, and when I look up at Sadie sitting across from me I suddenly start to feel the buzz of the party's signature "Monster-ita". I couldn't even taste the alcohol when I first started sipping it, but now I'm knee-deep in that warm, happy sensation. The Brown-Fuller-Kennedy-Manners-Wykowski household certainly doesn't play about its cocktails. Now I'm *really* glad we've got this candy.

"Okay, so you weren't kidding," Sadie laughs as I start rapidly unwrapping a Starburst. "You are a total Halloween devotee."

"It's costumes and candy," I say through a mouthful, my hand over my face to mask my chewing. "What's not to love?"

She lets her head hang to one side as she props herself up on her hands, adjusting her sitting position. "Scratchy sequins, loud parties, gross bulk candy, cavities-"

"Is there *anything* you love?" I say this before it can pass through any filters, and practically before I know I'm saying it. The change in her expression feels like a shot in the heart. My mouth falls open and an unbearable heat washes over my face. "I'm sorry, I just- You know, you poke fun about- And I know you- I didn't mean to-"

"I love flowers," she says softly, and I stop my babbling. She isn't looking at me, just sort of wistfully at the floor. "I don't show it as much as I used to, but I always have." She sighs. "I guess it's been a while for anything else. I mean, I love Felix, and Ethel, and my friends. But you're right, I joke about that, too." She runs a hand through her hair, finally looking up at me with a masked bit of discomfort in her eyes. "I don't know, everything I owned as a kid had butterflies on it. Does that count?"

A lightbulb turns on in my brain, and I hold up a 'one minute' finger, then focus my gaze downward at the Starburst wrapper in my other hand. A few seconds later, I hand her a tiny origami butterfly.

She takes it delicately, her eyes wide. "God," she says breathily, "you just keep showing off."

I cock my head to the side. "What do you mean?"

"*They wrote* Carrie *based off of me. Don't tell Filmation we were fraternizing*," she says, shaking her head and doing a silly voice. "I don't know, you're just... people like you. You're charming and fun in this, like, genuine way. You can make a *butterfly* out of a Starburst wrapper. You're not... prickly and snarky."

My chest feels heavy hearing how she supposedly thinks of herself. "People like *you*."

Her gaze is locked on the floor again. "Loving things out loud, unapologetically, like you do... that's the right way to do it."

I'm not quite sure what to say, but something in me itches to soothe her worries. "I think you're great the way you are."

Her expression goes stony. "I used to."

My heart sinks even further. "Sadie..."

"It's been hard to *love* things my whole life," she says. "I didn't just *not come out* to my parents. By the time I was a teenager, I barely told them about anything I liked. Because if I did, it would be like... my mom wouldn't say anything. But I knew she was judging me. And my dad..." She shakes her head. "Joking about it gave me an out. But eventually it was just easier not to feel that way to begin with."

"You can start small," I offer. "Maybe try and find something in this room that you really love, no irony."

Her whole demeanor seems to brighten a little bit, and it brings mine right along with it. She makes eye contact with me, leaning forward and giving a serious expression. "Summer."

"Sadie."

She holds her palm upward, the tiny pink butterfly sitting atop it. "I fucking love this butterfly. No irony." The huge grin on her face is infectious.

"I am so proud of you."

"Maybe one day I can unironically love *all* butterflies," she says.

"That might be a little fast," I reply, relishing in the return of her joking demeanor as she giggles. "Better take it slow."

"Baby!" Felix cries at the front door. "Come in, come in, come in!"

Arms full of flowers, Sadie comes in to join the rest of us in the kitchen. Julian's eyes light up like a child's at the sight of her stash.

"Those are incredible!" he cries. "Felix, do you see?"

"Yes, honey!" Felix says, smiling in that just-for-him way and kissing the top of his head, affectionately running his fingers through Julian's hair. "We're so excited, you guys."

"We are, too," I reply from my spot leaning against the counter, casting my eyes sideways to Sadie. "Do you want to go first?"

"Sure," she says, setting down the flowers, a colorful feast of shapes and sizes. It's like a sunset, all shades of yellow and orange and pink. Julian looks like a kid in a candy store.

"I figure I'll wait to place certain flowers until you guys pick out your outfits next week," she explains, arranging the flowers on the table as the boys lean over, watching intently and nodding. She's in her element in a way I don't even necessarily see when we're working on wedding stuff together - she looks focused and carefree, a single strand of short hair hanging ever so slightly out of its style and pointing down toward her button nose, soft chin, and full lips. "But we can put bouquets on tables, at the altar..."

"Oh!" Felix says. "What if you put some at the dessert bar, too?"

"Sure," she says. "Anywhere you want."

"Maybe I could even decorate some of the desserts to match," I pipe up. "Not to brag, but I can make a wicked flower out of frosting."

"Yes!" cries Felix. "Oh my god, that would be so cute."

Sadie looks up at me, smiling. That single strand is still falling out of her bangs, just above her eyelashes. "I love that idea." She gives a meaningful pump of her eyebrows, and there's a feeling in my stomach like champagne bubbles. "We can implement it at the next planning session."

"Alright," says Julian, "as much as I'd like to stare at these flowers all night, I think it's time to spoil our dinner."

"Perfect," I say, stepping forward with my food container. "Here's a retrospective of your dessert bar picks thus far." We all sit down at the table, and I take off the lid, motioning to each dessert as I refer to it. "Our signature desserts based on the grooms: *The Felix*, a blueberry orange custard pie, and *The Julian*, vanilla meringue cookies with raspberry and blackberry."

Felix grabs a cookie almost like he's not supposed to. I go on, "We have a chocolate, caramel, and pretzel cake. If you guys like it enough, that can be what you cut. We have chocolate-covered strawberry brownies, mango passionfruit cupcakes, honey lemon bars, and macarons in three flavors. Almond, green tea, and banana. If you want more flavors, I can do that, too." I look between the couple. "Is there anything else you guys might like?"

"Maybe some cinnamon rolls," says Felix, biting into a macaron. "Mm. And this in, like, five more flavors."

"Ditto on the macaron," Julian says. "Something with coconut would be nice."

I nod. "Coconut and cinnamon rolls. I can do that."

"What do you think, Sadie?" Felix asks.

She pauses, one of the lemon bars an inch from her lips. "It's not my wedding."

"But you're my maid of honor," he counters.

"I don't know what you want me to say," she says. "It's all good."

"That's all I needed to hear," he says with a nod. "Dinner time?"

A few minutes later, we're eating Julian's homemade chili and listening to Felix and Sadie reminisce over their shared childhood.

"I swear, your mom used to make chili just like this," Felix says, pointing his spoon at the bowl. "On our 'Girl Scout' trips."

"You guys were Girl Scouts?" I ask.

Sadie rolls her eyes. "It was 'too dangerous'. My mom didn't want me out of her sight, so she created our own Levine Girl Scouts so I never had to brave the wilderness all alone." Her tone is dripping with irony. "I'm lucky that Felix's mom let him join so I wouldn't be an even bigger loser, just sitting in my living room on a 'camping trip' with my *mom*."

"It was way better than real Girl Scouts would've been," Felix adds. "Air conditioning, TV, Mama Levine's homemade chili, and s'mores in the backyard."

"*Mmm*, those s'mores," Sadie says, closing her eyes as though imagining the campfire treat. "Now there's a fond childhood memory."

"God, I used to love s'mores!" Julian says. "But I didn't like graham crackers, so it was basically just hot marshmallows and chocolate."

"So it sounds like s'mores for dessert tonight?" I ask.

"Absolutely," says Felix quickly.

It seems that this promise makes everyone eat just a little bit faster, and before too long we're all putting our bowls and spoons into the dishwasher and Felix is rooting through the pantry.

"I can brown the marshmallows in the oven," I say aloud, pulling a baking sheet from the cabinet.

"Not so fast, Miss Professional," says Sadie, stepping between me and the island. "There's only one right way to do s'mores."

Julian grins. "I'll get the fire pit started."

We all follow him into the backyard, my skin prickling with goosebumps in the chill of the early November evening. The backyard is spacious and the fence is lined with Julian's little garden, flowers in every corner and vines snaking up trellises. The greenery hasn't all gone to sleep for the fall yet, a few flowers and evergreen trees in the distance hanging tight to their summer vibrancy.

Felix hops about the yard just like a former 'Girl Scout', fetching sticks and handing them to Julian with the kind of enthusiasm usually reserved for puppies. Julian stacks the sticks and some leaf litter in a little brick fire pit, lighting the pile and settling into a chair. We follow suit. Slowly, the fire builds with a satisfying crackling sound. The heat emanating from the flame begins to warm my body in the brisk air. Sadie passes out the ingredients, and we all get roasting.

"How am I about to marry you but I never knew you burn your marshmallows like that?" Felix asks his fiancé, sliding a lightly browned marshmallow onto his graham cracker.

"What, is this a dealbreaker?" Julian replies, drawing his pitch-black marshmallow from the fire for a moment to gesticulate with it. "Alright, it's been a good run. Let's give back the rings."

"No!" snaps Felix. "Don't you even joke about that."

Julian grins. "Didn't know you liked the ring that much."

"Shut up," Felix pouts, "you know I love *you*."

"I love you too," he replies. "Even though you're judgy about other people's s'more-making habits."

"Doing okay there?" I ask Sadie next to me. She sits with a half-demolished s'more in one hand, licking melted chocolate and marshmallow off the other hand.

"Fantastic," she says, then straightens her posture. Her face glows orange in the firelight. "I fucking love hanging out with you guys, and I fucking love s'mores. No irony."

I break into a grin. Felix "aww"s loudly.

"Me too," I say.

Chapter Nine

Sadie Takes Charge

"Alright, boys, if you're not ready in five minutes, the Groom-mobile is leaving without you!" I call from the hallway, my voice bellowing like a movie drill sergeant's.

Felix pokes his head out of the door to the bedroom, his torso bare and his expression apologetic. "I really appreciate you doing this, Sadie."

"Of course, babe."

"Have you seen my nude underwear?" *There it is.*

"No, Felix, I have not seen *your* nude underwear," I reply, crossing my arms. "Come on, dude. You've known we were going wedding outfit shopping today for, like, a month and a half."

"I'm sorry!" he whines. "I swear I had them-"

"They're right here, darling," says Julian's voice from within the room, and Felix's eyes go wide.

"Thanks, love," he says, and looks at me sheepishly.

"Tick tock, nearlyweds," I say with a stern raise of my eyebrows, and he ducks back into the room, the door slamming behind him.

By some miracle, the boys end up in my car with everything they need and we arrive at Roseport's premiere (and only) gender-neutral wedding attire shop "Find Your Forever" a few minutes before their appointment. It was converted a few years back from a traditional bridal store when its old owner retired, and as with every other place in town, Rio tells us they have "connections".

They're right inside the door waiting for us when we enter the building, their wild hair pinned back and their usually extravagant attire exchanged for a casual (still colorful) sweat suit.

"Thanks for setting this up," I say, giving them a quick hug.

"It takes a village," they reply with a shrug. "Now. How are we feeling, gentlemen?"

"I'm so fucking excited," Felix says with a childlike grin.

"I'm a little sad I won't get to see what you pick," says Julian, grabbing his hand. "You're gonna look so amazing."

"But," Felix reminds, "just think of how much better it'll be to see it for the first time on the day." Julian's face lights up, and they stare adoringly at each other.

Khalil comes in shortly after, dressed in his usual business casual best with an honest-to-god Polaroid camera hanging from his neck.

"You look like a film noir news reporter," Felix says immediately.

"It's for posterity," he replies, tapping the camera lightly. "You're going to want to document everything. It's a special day, boys."

This sentiment seems to win Felix over. "I'll allow it."

Georgia's next through the door, giving each groom a hug and a kiss on the cheek. "Good morning, everybody," she chimes cheerfully, despite the fact that it's decidedly the afternoon.

"Somebody seems happy," I remark as they move on to me.

"Ask Georgia whose house they've been at for the last four nights," Rio says with an innocent bat of their eyelashes.

"Shut up," Georgia replies immediately, her hand flying to the tight pink jersey they're wearing - about a size too small and definitely not their style. Her face goes red. Quietly, she adds: "Carrie didn't have a chance to do laundry before I left."

Summer sneaks in just as the clock hits 2, giving Julian a tap on the back of his elbow and a warm smile. He returns it.

"Hi there," says a black-clothed woman as she rounds the corner from deeper within the shop, "Nguyen-Jefferson for 2?" Her eyes flick up from her clipboard, wide. "Daphne?"

"She-Ra!" Summer cries, and indeed, the bespectacled brunette in black is Rio's girlfriend Tae.

"I didn't realize Nguyen-Jefferson was you guys!" she cries, hugging Felix and Julian. "Everything went so fast at Halloween, I guess we weren't properly introduced."

"Rio, you didn't tell us the stylist was your girlfriend!" Felix says, turning to them.

"It's more in the vein of, I didn't tell you I started dating the stylist," they reply.

"No way," Georgia says. "Jesus, Rio, you could pick someone up *anywhere*."

Tae flushes. "I'm really excited to help you guys find your outfits. Come on, let's get started. Why don't you tell me what you're looking for?"

Tae leads us down a corridor heavily stocked with dresses and suits to a bank of dressing rooms which rest on a platform ever so slightly up off the ground. She sends Felix to the nearest one and Julian to another a few doors down. The rest of us sit down in a group of chairs, both men well within our eyeshot.

"Okay," Tae says, looking back and forth between them. "So, black suits only for Julian, and Felix, you're interested in seeing both suits and dresses. Right?" The boys nod, and she opens up a partition wall between them. "This partition will keep you from seeing one another's picks, but your friends will still be able to help out. I'm going to go grab your first round of outfits."

"Thank you, Tae," Felix calls behind her as she starts back down the corridor. "Oh my god, I'm *so* fucking excited."

"I'm so glad, babe," I tell him, reclining in my chair and pulling out a notepad so I can jot down any ideas for flower pairings that come up.

"Me too," says Julian, straining toward the partition like he's hoping to be able to touch his fiancé through it.

Khalil's camera flashes. Tae appears back on the scene with both arms full, and Julian cranes his neck to peek at the white fabric in the pile.

"Turn around," Rio snaps, and he does so like a kid caught with his hand in the cookie jar.

"Alright," says Tae, dropping off a couple of white dresses and two white suits with Felix, and then the rest of her armload with Julian. "Let's try these out first, and if we haven't found the one yet, I'll keep looking." Both boys disappear into their dressing rooms, and Tae backs up to where the rest of us are sitting and perches on the armrest of Rio's chair.

Julian emerges first, a black tuxedo sitting loosely on his body with the button-up open at his collar and the bow tie untied and hanging around his neck. Rio lets out a wolf whistle, and he blushes.

"Okay, good-lookin'!" Georgia cries.

Khalil's camera flashes. I scribble some notes.

"Julian, you look like-" Summer starts, and then the sound of her ringtone fills the space. Her face goes white. "Shit, I'm sorry. I'll... I'll be right back."

She scurries away and Felix emerges from his own dressing room, the door slamming open in classic grand entrance style to reveal himself draped in a long mermaid style gown, the sweetheart neckline gapping ever so slightly at his lack of chest. Again, the group erupts with approval.

"What do we think, boys?" Tae asks, standing up and positioning herself a few feet in front of the partition wall.

"I really like it," says Julian. "The fit is great, but I think it's a bit too traditional."

"I want something with a little more *presence*," says Felix, throwing his arms open. "And some lace wouldn't kill me."

Tae nods, face screwed up in thought. "Alright, let me refine what I've already brought you and see if there's something that'll be a bit more in line with your vision." She jumps up onto the platform with Julian and starts sorting through the stack.

They eventually both go back into their dressing rooms with a more specific option, but Summer's hasty exit nags at the back of my mind. She returns before either of them step out again, but something seems off in her demeanor. I try to funnel my focus back toward the grooms-to-be as Julian steps back out.

Several suits, dresses, and camera flashes later, Felix steps out wearing his fifth option and my jaw drops.

"Oh my god, babe!" I cry, setting down my notebook.

He already looks gleeful - this attitude is enough to say this one is special. "Yeah?" he beams.

The dress is bright white, with a long A-line cut and tight lace sleeves that compliment Felix's long, graceful arms. The lace runs up the bodice into a high neck and down the skirt in floral appliques. He looks elegant and ethereal, and best of all very happy.

"Felix, that's gorgeous," says Summer, leaning forward in her seat.

"You look amazing!" cries Rio.

Khalil's camera flashes once, twice, then three times. "I love it!"

"It's so you, Felix," agrees Georgia. "I'm calling it, that's the one."

Julian comes out of his dressing room, once again straining as though he'll be able to see. His smile is huge.

"Tae," Felix says, "get the bell."

We all cheer, and Tae hands him a massive cowbell, which rings out through the store. A few other customers join in on the cheering from the far reaches of the building.

"Let me make note of any tailoring we'll need to do," she says, pulling the measuring tape from around her neck. "Are these the shoes you'll be wearing?"

"Felix," Julian calls across the partition, "is it pretty?"

"It's *really* pretty," Felix replies, beaming.

"Hell yeah!" he cries. "I'm so happy for you, love."

"Okay, Julian," Tae says, crossing in front of the partition and onto Julian's platform. "What do we think here?"

He looks down at his black suit and gray floral shirt. "I don't know. It's nice, but I just don't think it's the one."

"Okay," she says, nodding. "Is it the shape? Or the color? Pattern? Are you liking the floral direction?"

He nods. "Definitely. I just..." He trails off, and suddenly his eyes go wide. "Sadie?"

I sit up straight in my chair, a "Maid of Honor" switch flipping in my brain. "Yeah?"

"Do you think you could find something that matches-"

"Spoilers!" Felix cries, slapping his hands over his ears.

I hop up on Julian's platform, too, and he leans forward with a conspiratorial look in his eye and whispers, "Something to match the flowers."

I grin. "I think that would be awesome." I look over at Tae.

"You're the one who's seen them," she says. "Come with me and we can find something together."

She leads me down the hallway and expertly takes a couple of turns until we're in an area of colorful accent pieces. "This is probably your best bet."

I focus on the yellow, pink, and orange options - quickly bypassing the brightest ones, which I know Julian won't like -

until finally I settle on a light pink vest with a faint floral print which I can see pairing perfectly with the orange and yellow flowers I've picked out.

"Do you think he'd like this?" I ask Tae. "Maybe with that one suit, the one that you put with the black shirt."

She nods. "I think that'd be really lovely. Good eye, Sadie."

I shrug. "Pairing colors is sort of a big part of my job."

Julian's eyes sparkle excitedly when he sees us coming back with our pick. He seems a bit more eager to disappear back into the dressing room after Tae's told him what to wear with the vest than he has with the last several outfits. He looks even more so when he steps out again, to the delight of the group. Khalil's camera flashes wildly.

He's in one of the more trim black suits he's tried, with a white button-up open at the collar and the pink vest bringing out the dewy quality of his dark skin and giving an alternative edge to the otherwise mostly traditional look of the suit. He looks irrevocably *cool*, and I can already see the orange-and-yellow boutonniere in his lapel.

"I really really like it," he says, grinning.

"Oh my god," says Felix from the other side of the partition, back in his street clothes. "Is this the one?"

Julian looks out at us. "What do you guys think?"

"It's perfect," says Georgia.

"*So* cute," adds Rio.

"You look so handsome!" Khalil says.

"Julian, if you don't wear that-" says Summer, shaking her head. Julian lights up like a lantern.

Almost shyly: "Can I have the bell, Tae?"

We all cheer once more as the bell chimes joyously.

"Hurry up and change so I can kiss you!" Felix cries, bouncing up and down like a caffeinated preschooler.

Julian laughs and rushes into the dressing room. It seems like a couple of seconds later that he's racing back out in his street clothes and running to Felix in front of the partition. They throw their arms around each other and kiss as though they're reuniting after years apart. The group erupts in wolf whistles and catcalls.

"Jesus, do you two love each other or something?" Georgia calls.

"Get a room!" says Rio.

I feel sunshiney inside like I did the day they got engaged. Despite what I told Summer back in July, I do believe in love. Looking at these two, I *have* to. I just don't know if I'll ever be where they are. Even if not everyone is like Gabby or Charlie or Reagan or Ben... who could ever love me as much as Felix and Julian love each other?

I shake my head, trying to clear away the thoughts.

"Alright, boys, wrap it up," I call. "Don't forget who drove you here. I can leave without you."

"We'll just have to handle payment and fill out a contact sheet for your tailoring, Felix," says Tae, standing up again. "The rest of you can wait outside. We won't be long."

Chapter Ten

Summer is Stuck in the Middle

The front door of "Find Your Forever" slams as I step out onto the sidewalk and the cold air accosts me, my heart already racing.

"Hello?" I say into the phone, keeping my tone even.

God, I shouldn't have picked up. Before even hearing his voice, I want to scream and cry and chew him out for everything that happened, for dragging me to Chicago and letting me get almost my entire identity wrapped up in his, for punishing me for that by sleeping with someone else and then *telling* me. Not to mention barely letting me back in the apartment long enough to make off with the bare essentials of my *own* belongings. A red hot ball is raging in my chest at what he could possibly want from me now.

"Hey, Summer," Landon says, and the feeling ignites even further. That same chill, go-with-the-flow inflection he's always had grates on me now like sandpaper on an open wound. "How's it been?"

I could puke. "Great," I reply, seething. "And you?"

"Can't complain," he drawls, and I can practically see him reclined in the big blue chair we bought together for the new place in Chicago two years ago, one hand holding the phone to his ear and the other behind his head like he's lounging on the beach. In this admittedly inaccurate mental image, he's even got on sunglasses and a backwards baseball cap like some frat boy. The easygoing nature that used to draw me to him has turned unmistakably sour, and now I can't see him as much more than an apathetic asshole.

My tone grows more clipped. "What did you need?"

"Look, Sunny, I was going through the apartment," he says.

My mind races to unpack every insufferable thing he managed to pack into that one sentence. *Sunny*, the nickname he gave me when we were dating, that to this day sounds like something he'd call a guy friend. *The* apartment, like I still live there, months after he kicked me out. That sickeningly casual way he has of delivering every piece of news, like nothing is more or less important than a grocery list.

He continues, "I found a few of your things shoved into the back of the closet. I guess you forgot 'em."

I want to rip his head off. The *nerve*, the absolute balls he must have to try and act as though I 'forgot' anything. I hold my tongue.

"Couple of photo albums," he says. "Box of stuff. Kinda looked like keepsakes."

My ears perk up at this. Most of what I hadn't been able to grab had been replaceable - expensive, in the case of some, like my favorite hand mixer and a few of my hair care products, but replaceable. Those photo albums and keepsakes weren't.

"Anyway, I'll be back in state for Thanksgiving," he adds. "I figure if you want we can meet up then and get them back to you."

The absolute last thing I want is to see him again. But my heart aches thinking of the sentimental trinkets and grainy Polaroids of college days currently collecting dust in a closet in Chicago. My stomach churns.

"I'll let you know if I'm free," I say finally.

"Great," he says. "Good catching up with you, Sunny."

I don't reply, just hang up and try to catch my breath. How can he act so casual when *he's* the one who ended things, and practically tore me apart in doing so? I shudder at the memory of that day he sat me down, the nonchalant way he shrugged his shoulders and told me I wasn't enough for him anymore, that I worked too much and had no friends, that he had gone out and found someone better. And now, what, he wants to chat and be friends and *catch up?*

And why did he have to do this, of all days, when Julian is wedding suit shopping? All I want in the world today is to support my best friend, and now my mind is racing with the fact that I may actually be considering seeing my cheating ex again, if even just to get my stuff back.

I reign in my nerves and turn back toward the building. I *will* still be here for Julian, no matter the circumstance.

"We'll just have to handle payment and fill out a contact sheet for your tailoring, Felix," Tae tells the boys, climbing out of her chair. She's undoubtedly feminine, and her tall stature and impressive muscles - even under the black long-sleeved shirt she's wearing - make me wonder how I ever managed to be dysphoric. "The rest of you can wait outside. We won't be long."

As the group files out of the store, I'm squirming with the impulse to tell someone. I feel like I'll explode if I don't let it out. But I definitely can't bother Julian with it, not *today*, and Georgia would drive straight to Chicago and carry Landon's body back in her truck bed.

"Sadie," I find myself whispering, catching up and tapping her shoulder lightly as everyone else disperses to their cars. She turns around, looking ever so slightly up at me with her eyebrows raised receptively. The fresh scent of spring is ever-present on her, even today when she hasn't even been working. "Can I talk to you for a second?"

"Is something wrong?" she says, seeing right through me in a way that feels less like a callout and more like a soft hand on my shoulder. We stand under a tree a few feet away from the store. Dappled sunlight falls onto her face, cracking her eyes into a hundred shades of green.

"My ex-boyfriend Landon called me," I tell her. "He's going to be back in town for Thanksgiving and he wants to meet up and give me back some stuff I left in Chicago."

She blinks hard for a second, a crinkle trying to force its way between her eyebrows. "That's... I'm so sorry, Summer."

It feels a bit better just having gotten off my chest. Still, my stomach is like a bag of knots. "I don't know what to do."

She bites her lip. "I mean... what is it that you left?"

"A box of keepsakes and some photo albums," I reply, sighing. "I don't want to see him."

She shakes her head, the shadow of a frown creeping onto her face. "I don't blame you."

"But I want my stuff back," I add.

She nods. "I think... you should do whatever you think is best."

I have to smile a little bit at her forced calm. She's definitely not saying everything she's thinking. I bump the toe of my shoe against hers. "But...?" I reply expectantly.

She cracks the smallest smile. "Fuck him. Do whatever you want."

Laughing, I say, "There's the Sadie I know."

"He sucks," she says. "Like, he's the worst. If you want your stuff back, you should get it, regardless of whether or not it means seeing his slimy ass."

"Thanks," I tell her. "You're right. I don't want to see him, but I can't let that hold me back."

"Damn right," she says forcefully. "You are way too brave and awesome to let that loser dictate what you do and don't do." She blinks. "Or, um... y'know, whatever you think is best."

I chuckle. "Which is it?"

"I'm just..." She flushes. "I'm still new at being your friend and I'm trying to do a good job."

My heart warms. "You're doing a great job." She smiles sheepishly. "And, for the record, I'll always want you to give me your honest opinion."

"Good to know," she says. "So, would that include my honest opinion on your shoes?"

My hand flies to my chest as if she's shot me. "Why not? You've already given your honest opinion on my favorite book, my favorite holiday, and my sleep schedule. Let's see if this time you can land the killing blow."

She rolls her eyes, reaching out a hand to lightly swat my shoulder. "I'm just fucking with you. Your shoes are fine."

"This is my favorite day so far," Felix yells out as he and Julian exit the store doors, Tae waving from the lobby behind them. "Sadie, get in the car, we're getting froyo!"

She snorts, looking over her shoulder at them. "What is it, 2014?"

"In the car, woman!" Felix calls, and Julian covers his laugh behind his hand. Sadie turns back to me, rolling her eyes.

"At least it's not day drinking," she says. "I'll see you later?"

"Wedding planning at my place this Tuesday," I confirm.

And then she steps forward and gives me a hug. Instinct carries me through for a second before I realize *we've never done this before*. She squeezes softly, and the floral scent is a hundred times stronger with her head on my shoulder.

"You can handle this Landon thing," she whispers in my ear. "You are strong, confident, and badass."

"You're a good hugger," I say before I can think. My face goes red hot, and she laughs, giving me one last squeeze before pulling away.

"Bye, Summer," she says, then turns and starts walking toward the boys. "Alright, everybody in the car!"

Felix whoops, and I find myself watching them go with a smile on my face and a calm, warm feeling in my chest.

I'm about three steps into the door when my phone rings. My body is achy, and every molecule in me wants to let it ring and just collapse face first onto my bed. I take in a deep breath and pick up.

"Hello?"

"Hi, is this the number for Sweet Summer Confectionaries?"

I light up like someone's flipped a switch. "Yes, it is. I'm Summer. What can I do for you today?"

"We heard about you from a friend," says the woman's voice. "And everything on your Instagram is just so cute."

"Thank you so much."

"Well, my son's birthday is coming up," she continues. "We were wondering if you ever do shape cakes. He's just crazy about football."

"Absolutely," I reply. "When would you need it?"

"The 18th," she says, and I wince. Even though I've cut back my hours, a few of my So Sweet coworkers will be gone that week, so I volunteered to cover for them. I'll be working long hours for days leading up to the 16th. There's absolutely no way I'll have time to prepare a cake, especially to the standard of a paying customer.

"I'm so sorry, ma'am," I say, my stomach sour. "I'm entirely booked for that whole week."

"Oh, that's unfortunate," she agrees. "Well, shoot."

"I can offer you a discount on your next order if you'd like to try again another time," I say carefully. I'm making this policy up as I go - I've never had to do this before.

"That's so kind," she says. "We'll take that, for sure."

I apologize again and take down her name, then defeatedly slump onto the couch. I thought that going part-time at So Sweet would prevent things like this, and yet here I am. I never imagined I'd *turn down* Sweet Summer clientele, even when I was working full time.

Sinking further into the couch, I sigh.

Chapter Eleven
Sadie Has a Little Faith

"Good afternoon, beautiful people!" Felix sing-songs as he and Julian stride into the restaurant.

The rest of the group chimes their greetings, an unseasonably sunny morning lighting our brunch table through the window. Julian takes a seat across from Summer, and Felix remains standing, flashing a small stack of papers in his hands.

"Guess what came in today," he says brightly.

"The save-the-dates?" Khalil says, raising his eyebrows.

"Bingo, Mr. Brown!" Felix cries, and Julian grins up at him. "I thought it would be very special to distribute these to you now. And that way we'll save on postage."

"Alright, let's see them," says Rio, opening and closing their hand like a child saying 'gimme'. "I wanna judge your graphic design choices."

"Rosario Hernandez, plus-one for Tae," he says grandly, setting a card on the table in front of them. He turns. "Georgia

Terrell, plus-one for Carrie. Khalil Brown, plus-four for Eleanor, Cecily, Matthew, and Axel."

He sets the last two down in front of me and Summer on my left. "Sadie Levine and Summer McConnell."

I can't help but feel a bit embarrassed looking down at my card and Summer's, a matching pair of "check one" boxes asking whether or not we'll be bringing a plus-one. I place my hand on my card and scoot it under my purse, quickly flicking my eyes away from the other card sitting there. As far as I know, Summer isn't seeing anyone, but I don't even want to think about the possibility of being the only one going alone to my best friend's wedding.

Felix slides into his own chair across from me, all smiles and songbirds, just like he usually is anytime the wedding is brought up. "Those will give you all the info you need," he says.

"Semi-formal?" Rio reads. "Come on, I've got a *sick* formal dress I've been waiting to bust out."

"You really want to wear a gown in our backyard?" Julian prods, leaning forward to look at them across the table. "Be my guest."

"This is going to be a beautiful affair," Khalil says. "Putting the wedding colors on the card is very classy, gentlemen."

"It's going to look awesome in the pictures," Felix says. "Imagine it, all our best friends gathered around us, and we all match the flowers. We'll look like all those picture-perfect Pinterest gays."

"I don't think I own anything pink, yellow, or orange," Georgia pipes up. "Unless you want me there in my Freddie jacket."

"Ha ha," deadpans Felix, just as Julian sits up straighter.

"Actually," he says with a lopsided smile, "that sounds kind of awesome, if you style it right."

"Julie, you're a genius," Felix says, slamming his hand on the table. "Georgia, you put a button-up and some dress pants under that jacket and you've got yourself a deal."

She shrugs. "Perfect."

"I'll send you all my options," Khali says.

"Knowing your closet, that could take days," says Julian.

"I'll send mine too," adds Rio.

"Jesus, you won't be done in time for the wedding," Felix says, sticking out his tongue.

"God, forgive me and Khalil as the fashionistas of the group for trying to elevate your Pinterest power," Rio replies. "I'll just show up in a trash bag if that'll serve you better."

"Whatever you pick will be great, Rio," Julian says.

"But in all seriousness, do clear your selection with one or both of us at least three months before the wedding," Felix adds, leaning forward onto his elbows to look at everyone.

"We've got it, Groomzilla," I tease, reaching across the table to tap his hand. "Now, you haven't even looked at that brunch menu. Since when can you resist French toast and a mimosa at 2PM?"

"Point taken," he says, giving a flippant hand wave and reaching for the menu.

"I love you. Don't have too much fun at work," says Julian, giving Summer a hug.

"I'm not worried about it," she replies. "I'll see you later, man. I love you too. " She turns toward Felix and I. "Bye, guys."

"Bye!" Felix exclaims, hugging onto her.

"Bye," I add, my skin prickling ever so slightly as she wraps her arms around me. She waves one last time and turns out the door, leaving just me, Felix, and Julian.

"I'm gonna use the bathroom and then we can head out. Okay, sweetheart?" says Julian, standing up and affectionately running his hand through Felix's hair.

"Okay, love," he chirps, and Julian walks down a hallway toward the bathroom.

"You two are so sweet," I say, shaking my head and swishing around what little is left of my drink. "By the way, I appreciate the plus-one, but I don't think I'll be using it."

Felix's eyes get big. "Are you sure you want to decide right now? May's a long way away."

I push a strand of hair back into my bangs. "I mean, would I like to spontaneously meet my Julian and have somebody wonderful to take to your wedding? Obviously."

His gaze is understanding as I shift in my chair. "But I don't know if somebody like that exists for me. And even if they do, I think I'm too fucked up to be with them."

"Baby," Felix breathes, his mouth falling open. "You're never 'too fucked up' for love. If it's something you want, you deserve it."

"I don't know. I didn't mean it like that," I reply. "Just... all this stuff with my body. I don't want to be constantly wondering what they *really* think of me, you know?"

"Babe, I'm not trying to push you, so if I am *please* stop me," Felix says, leaning forward and putting his hands on top of mine. "But I know how it feels not to feel so hot about yourself and to be with someone wonderful." I avert my eyes. "It's possible. More than possible." He squeezes my hands. "I totally get not wanting to date for a bit after everything that happened. But if eventually finding love is what you want... don't give up hope."

I squeeze back. "Thanks, Felix."

"Of course, babe." He reaches up and touches his hand to the side of my face. "I just want you to know how fucking awesome you are, and how you deserve the entire earth and someone sexy who would move mountains for you and loves every inch of you."

"I know," I say, giving a performative eye roll and standing from my seat. "I'd better be going. I love you. Tell Julian."

"I love you too, babe," he says, standing up only to crouch back down and kiss my cheek. "See you later."

I'm weirdly in my head as I walk out of the restaurant and to my car. I can't quite seem to stop myself from slipping in and out of focus as I make the short drive home. A Queen song comes on the radio, the lush harmonies and wailing guitar cutting through my senses like a rock-and-roll knife. I pull into my apartment's parking lot just as the song crescendos to its end, a gospel-esque choir chanting out in a broad, joyous harmony. I don't even realize until I reach up and touch my face that there's a tear on my cheek.

"Hey!" Summer's smile is bright as I open the door. Her hair is tied back and she smells like I'm shoving my face directly into a freshly baked cake.

"Hey," I smile, stepping out of her way to let her in. "Thanks for coming over. Work today was *rough*."

She chuckles, pulling the hair tie from her hair and letting the ginger locks cascade onto her shoulders. "Tell me about it."

"Yours, too?" I ask as Ethel trots toward Summer.

"No, I meant 'tell me about it'," she says, leaning down to pet the dog. "Your rough day."

"Oh." I blink, walking over to the couch. Summer joins me. "Well, I was working with this woman who'd just gotten engaged on some flowers for her bridal shower. Not even her *wedding*, and she was just so incredibly particular. Like, everything had to be exactly this tall, and exactly this big, and exactly this color." I cut my eyes sideways towards Summer. "She literally had a handful of hex codes printed out."

"Holy shit," she laughs as Ethel climbs up onto the couch and lies down against her leg. "Yeah, I can see how that might be a little straining."

"She sounds extreme, but that's far from the worst I've seen," I add. "Like, just wait until she comes back for the actual ceremony." Summer laughs. I go on, "That's when it really amps up. They're all zen until it's down to the wire. That's when the claws come out."

"I didn't realize Bridezilla had claws."

"Some do. Those wedding day manicures." I mime a slash of imaginary claws, swinging my hand through the air. "But it's not just brides. I've had people of all genders go absolutely apeshit over weddings. It's the one thing that unites all of humanity."

"You mean to say that everyone who's ever gotten married, or will ever get married, goes full 'zilla?" she asks, stroking Ethel's fur as the latter quickly dozes off. "That can't be right. *You* wouldn't."

"Oh, I'd be the biggest 'zilla of all," I correct, and she laughs. I continue, "Plenty of people manage to keep their cool. But when that happens, the person they're marrying is always a control freak with a perpetual stress headache and a *very* detailed vision board. So guess who *I* end up talking to."

She nods, grinning as she says: "Such is the way of life."

I laugh. "This lady today, with the hex codes, she came in with her fiancée, who I swear didn't say a word to me the entire time. Really quiet, mild-mannered girl."

"Sort of an odd couple," Summer says.

"Sort of," I concede. "But when she did talk, it was always, like, whispering sweetly to Hex Code Lady and, like, petting her hair until she calmed down a bit. That's how I managed to sneak some *slightly* differently colored roses in."

"Aww," she says. "That's nice."

"It was," I say, leaning back and looking off kind of wistfully. "I guess, *maybe*, if any person on earth could calm Hex Code Lady from the brink of conniption, I would say that..."

"Go on," she says, leaning forward with an intense gaze, like she already knows what I'm getting at and just wants to hear me say it.

"I guess that could possibly, maybe, perhaps point to the existence of love," I admit, and I can't stop myself from cracking a small smile.

"Oh, could it?" she replies, laughing smugly. "Jesus, for you, that was practically getting on one knee and proposing to the concept of love."

"I've actually been working on something," I tell her, sitting up straight. "For you."

She raises her eyebrows, her smile as thousand-watt. "Oh yeah?"

I clear my throat ceremoniously and announce, "I love this couch, no irony. I love my crappy apartment, no irony."

Her laugh is like a bell.

"I love taking care of my dog, no irony," I continue. "I love spending time with my friends, no irony. I love being creative, no irony. I love those Valentine's Day candy hearts that taste like chalk, no irony. I love winning at Uno, no irony. I love bad reality TV... very little irony."

"I'm so proud I could cry," she says, still giggling a bit behind her hand as she flutters her long, black lashes to fake tears.

I stretch, putting my arms behind my head. "I know, I'm amazing."

"Well, I was about to suggest some Uno, but I think your head would blow up enough to fly away," she says, leaning forward in an attempt to poke me. Ethel wakes back up, disoriented. "So how about some bad reality TV?"

A few hours later, I'm lying in bed and I can't get to sleep. It could have something to do with the glowing cell phone five inches from my face, but I wouldn't bet on it. Felix and Georgia - basically everybody - would scold me for it, but in the middle of an hours-long doom scroll, something pulled on me, and now I'm looking at Gabby's Instagram. I've only given in and checked it maybe twice since we broke up, and just like last time it's full of aesthetic photos of her food, her travels, and most of all herself.

She's as pretty as I remember, thin and fashionable with an ineffably cool air, like everything comes easy to her. But I feel a little different looking at her than the last time I let myself sneak a peek. Instead of missing the coffee dates and late nights, I remember how small *and* large she could make me feel, like all my worth was based on her approval. Absentmindedly, I swipe away and into the app store.

I blink for a second, my finger hovering over the 'redownload' icon next to the dating app where we met. I wouldn't have to go on any dates, I tell myself. I wouldn't even have to swipe. Maybe just having it on my phone would make me feel better.

But I don't press the button. I just click my phone off, set it on my nightstand, and roll over, restless.

Chapter Twelve

Summer Gives Thanks

"Would you pass the potatoes?" Khalil asks me, his voice overlapping with Rio and Georgia's heated debate over cranberry sauce.

"Here you go," I reply, passing the dish.

"Felix, this stuffing is so fucking good," Sadie says, squeezing her eyes shut. "Best Friendsgiving ever."

"Jules made that," Felix half-yells over the noise.

"Julian, this stuffing is so fucking good," Sadie repeats, raising her voice a bit. "God, this is just like real Thanksgiving. Except nobody's said anything racist."

"So, where's everybody headed tomorrow?" Felix asks, his brow knit. "Georgia? Rio? We're all family here."

"Sorry," says Georgia. Rio nods apologetically.

"Jules and I are staying in town," Felix continues. "The joys of house ownership - we get to *host*, like real grown-ups."

"You won't feel so grateful a year from now," says Khalil knowingly. "Some parents just can't be trusted in your house without trying to move everything. I have to watch my mom like she's an errant toddler. Axel thinks we should put child locks on the cabinets."

"I guess we'll cross that bridge when we get to it," says Julian with a dry laugh. "My parents should be here tonight, and Rashida's flight gets in tomorrow morning."

"Is your mom not coming up from Virginia?" Sadie asks, flicking her eyes over to Felix.

"She said a flight would be too expensive," he replies, rolling his eyes a bit. "I'm trying to convince her to just move here, but she says she couldn't bear to be away from her book club."

"My dads didn't want me to drive all the way home for Thanksgiving when Hanukkah is so close," says Georgia. "So we're making the family recipes on Skype together."

"You three are so sweet I could puke," Rio says. "While you have your cute virtual celebration, I will be carpooling with my siblings the four hours to my dad's house, where he'll turn on football at full volume and ignore us all the whole time."

"I've only got a half-hour drive to my parents' in Serenton," I pipe up. "I'm planning on heading there after dinner."

"After dinner?" Felix repeats. "We're having Friendsgiving *lunch*. Why the wait?"

My stomach churns, and I set down my fork. "I, uh, I'm actually meeting up with Landon."

Georgia hits the table, and I watch Felix's mouth fall open with shock. Sadie looks down at the table.

"What?" Georgia shouts.

"I'm just getting some of the stuff I left in Chicago," I clarify.

"Who's Landon?" Rio asks, brows raised.

"My ex-boyfriend," I reply, and Khalil and Rio give their belated gasps of outrage.

"Who cheated on you," Georgia reminds. "You've gotta let me come with you, so I can kill him."

"No, no no no no," Julian mutters, patting Georgia on the back soothingly. "Murder is not the solution."

"I think I would appreciate some moral support, though," I say. "I'm going after lunch."

"Why don't you and I stay here for a bit and have some pumpkin pie?" Felix asks, crossing behind the table to Georgia, taking over in the job of comforting them.

"You are awesome, Summer," she says fiercely. "He's a jackass."

"I know, Georgia," I reply. "Thank you."

"Do you want me to come with?" Julian asks, leaning in ever so slightly. I nod, but there's still an uncomfortable jitter in my heart. I look over at Sadie, still staring at the table and fiddling with her fingers. I remember the way she reacted when I first told her about Landon, and when he called me.

"Sadie?" I find myself asking. She jumps a little, like she'd forgotten we could see her. "Would you come, too?"

"Of course," she says, her eyes wide. "Of course I will."

"I really hope everything goes well for you, Summer," says Khalil, nodding solemnly.

"Yeah, girl," adds Rio. "Good luck. Exes are the worst."

"Thank you guys," I say, perking up a bit. "I really appreciate having you all in my life."

"And what a perfect time to say it," says Felix. "Happy Friendsgiving, everyone."

Even though it's about halfway full with irony, everyone responds in unison: "Happy Friendsgiving."

After we all finish eating, Julian and Sadie pile into my car and I drive to a strip mall on the very border between Roseport and Serenton, realizing with a prickle that it's only a couple minutes away from a little hole-in-the-wall Mexican place where Landon and I had our first and many subsequent dates before we moved. I pull into a spot in the almost totally empty parking lot. I'd recognize Landon's little blue convertible even if he weren't currently leaning against it.

"Hey, Sunny," he says as I step out of the car, his blonde curls messy in the typical fashion. "Didn't realize we were bringing guests."

Actually *seeing* him again brings back a rush of emotions, and I tighten my fists in the pockets of my jacket. He's tall and thin in overlarge clothing, everything about him the picture of "couldn't care less".

"How is Julian?" he asks, squinting at my tinted windows and giving a casual wave. "I heard he's getting married?"

I press my lips into a thin line, holding back a million things I want to say, absolutely *none* of which pertaining to Julian or his engagement.

"Aw, c'mon, Sunny, don't be like that," he says, lightly kicking a loose bit of gravel with his shoe. "Come on, I've got your things in the trunk." He goes around and pops it open, and I feel like I'm rescuing a hostage when I finally see the beat-up old printer box I brought to Chicago two years ago.

"Thank you-" I'm starting to say when Landon steps between me and the trunk, leaning against the suspended lid with his arm straight. I take a step back without even having to think about it; I don't like the way he's leveraging his height against me, and I definitely don't like the look in his eye.

"Being back here is so crazy," he says, looking off into the distance. "It's like, everything is the same, and everything is different. When did the movie theater go out?"

I feel a painful twinge. Is he *trying* to bring up associations with our past here? We must have spent four nights a week in that theater when we first met, laughing through dollar movies and fighting over the giant popcorn bucket. I cast my gaze sideways, trying to avoid his. "Winter before last."

"Bummer," he says. "Where are all the awkward kids supposed to go watch classic films and throw M&Ms at each other now?"

Something in me burns white-hot. "What are you doing?"

He leans forward a little more, bringing his face closer to mine. Every hair on the back of my neck stands up.

"I've been thinking, Sunny," he says. "Back in June, we both said some stuff we didn't mean. We're different people than we were when we met, but that doesn't mean we shouldn't keep trying. I think you should come home."

I don't even realize I'm talking until it's out. "Oh, so your new girlfriend left you?"

A wrinkle appears between his eyebrows, and his hand falls from the lid of the trunk to his side. "Sunny-"

"My name is Summer," I say forcefully, some mix of adrenaline and righteous outrage carrying me through the telling-off I never gave him, the one that my body has apparently been saving ever since the day he kicked me out. "I never liked that nickname, and even if I had, you categorically lost the right to use it when you dumped me."

He almost looks emotional, his perpetual calm finally upended. This only fuels me. "Do you seriously not understand that I would *never* want to get back together with you? I moved away from all my friends and family *for you*, and when I worked because I had nothing else to do, you found somebody else to fulfill your needs." He opens his mouth to speak, but I don't even let him start. "And *then* instead of communicating with me about your issue, you kicked me out and, might I add, held on to a sizable portion of *my* stuff. What part of that makes you think I would be *at all* interested in coming back to you?"

"That's not exactly the way I remember it," he says, stuttering ever so slightly. "I think if we could just go and talk for a bit, like over at *Gordita's Cocina*, maybe we could-"

"No," I snap. "You don't get to bring up all these 'happy times' we had together and expect me to just fall into your lap. I'm not going anywhere with you no matter what you say. But the least you can do is admit some semblance of fault in the situation."

He steps forward again. "Summer, I think maybe you're overreacting a bit-"

My heart is beating in my ears. The sound of my car door opening behind me is faint, and Julian's voice, Julian's hands gently moving me backwards. "Summer, get in the car. I'll handle this, man to man."

Breathing heavy, I stumble back into the driver's seat. The door shutting behind me cuts straight through the haze between my ears, and I let out a shaky sigh.

"Oh my god," I find myself murmuring, and I feel Sadie's hand on my shoulder, softly rubbing back and forth.

"Yeah," she says, "that guy's an asshole." She breathes deeply, in and out, and instinctively I match her. My heartbeat starts to slow.

"Are you okay?" she says gently.

"I don't know." There's a dull stinging sensation behind my eyebrows, no doubt the start of some terrible headache. "I knew I wasn't going to like seeing him, but *Jesus*, I did not expect that."

"You handled it like a champ," she says, her hand still resting on my shoulder. "I was hoping you'd punch him."

I laugh weakly, not even caring that it makes the stinging flare. "I might've, if Julian hadn't stepped in."

"I have no doubt you could've handled it," she says, squeezing my shoulder with a raise of her eyebrows and a smile that's perfectly half-humor and half-comfort. "I just don't think he deserved a single second more of your energy or your time."

I was right, it occurs to me, about Sadie being a caring friend. Her words, her touch, even just her presence radiates support.

"Thank you," I tell her, rubbing my forehead with my palm. "God, this has *majorly* fucked up my day."

"At least you'll get to head home and see those lovely, supportive parents of yours," she says, her tone only a little mocking. "I bet they'll wrap you up in a blanket and give you some hot cocoa, and you can forget all about it."

"Something like that," I admit. "How about you? You headed to your parents' later?"

She shifts in the passenger seat, taking her hand off my shoulder to adjust her hair. "Not this year." She swallows. "Ethel needs a lot of really specific care. I don't have anyone to dogsit, and I definitely can't travel with her. I'll have to figure something out for Christmas, but..." She shrugs. "Seemed like a lot of hassle for turkey and Black Friday with all my hillbilly cousins."

"Alright, ladies," comes Julian's voice along with the sound of the door opening. I watch him slide my keepsake box into the seat behind Sadie. "Let's get going."

"What did you say?" I ask, leaning forward to see Landon's car pulling out of the parking lot.

"I told him he'd massively fucked up, and that a girl like you deserves a hell of a lot better than him," he replies, sliding into his own seat. "I also may have mentioned that my fiancé is about an inch taller and ten pounds heavier than he is, and I have no problem whatsoever physically overpowering him and pinning him to the ground."

Sadie laughs shortly, her mouth wide open. "*Julian.*"

He smirks. "What, like Felix doesn't give you all the details?"

"I cannot believe you threatened my ex-boyfriend with physical violence," I say, grinning. "You really are the best friend I've ever had."

"I swear, guys like him see a Black man with tattoos and a piercing and automatically their knobby little knees start knocking," he continues. "I barely had to get out of the car."

"I wish I would've been recording," says Sadie.

"Me too," I add. "Thank you so much, Julian." I flick my eyes sideways to Sadie. "Thank you, too."

Her lips quirk into an almost shy smile. "Don't mention it."

Chapter Thirteen
Sadie Branches Out

"Which of these looks the most like the flowers?" Summer asks, turning a plate of cupcakes toward me, each one featuring a differently shaped frosting flower.

I cross around the counter for a closer look, Ethel darting out of my way as she circles the kitchen on a quest for food scraps.

"Well, this one is the closest to the roses," I say, pointing to it. "And this one reminds me of the lantana. But you know better than anyone that none of the flowers are going to be white."

"I figured I would show you the options and let you color the frosting," she says, brown eyes fixed on mine as she gives an exaggerated shrug. "You're the expert there."

"I'm not the Hex Code Lady," I reply with a laugh, leaning against the counter and crossing my arms. "You know what pink looks like. Besides, I don't know anything about coloring frosting."

"It's not rocket science," she says, pulling a small box from her purse. "You put some food coloring in, you mix it, you add more if you want it darker."

"Then why do you need me to do it?" I prod, poking her shoulder.

I've noticed the shift in our relationship more and more lately - not just with the increase in teasing, but ever since she told me about Landon calling her at the fitting, and especially when we went with her to meet him. We've been friends for a while, but now I feel like maybe we're even close. It occurs to me as she raises her eyebrows and grins that I feel distinctly lucky to be close with her.

"I don't *need* you to," she says with a mocking shake of her head. "You said yourself you love being creative, and I was trying to give you an opportunity to be creative. I thought you might have fun, so sue me."

I roll my eyes. I *did* love helping her make the signature desserts all those months ago, and I'm not up to much else at the moment. "Scoot over and hand me the dye."

"See? You don't have to be so difficult," she says, making room for me at her end of the counter and setting the box in front of me.

"Sure I do," I reply, jabbing my elbow at her as I grab the big metal bowl of frosting. "Would you get me two more bowls from the cabinet? I want to make a few colors."

She obliges, not doing a very good job of hiding the smug smile on her face. "Here."

And of course she's right about it being fun, the creative process lighting up the elusive inner child usually locked inside my chest. Some itch in my brain is scratched watching the colors manifest from a few little drops to a couple swirls to the entire bowl.

"Look at you," she comments dryly, looking over my shoulder. "You figured it out!"

I scrunch my nose at her. "It was touch-and-go there for a second, but I pulled through."

"I'm so proud," she says, scooping a glob of orange frosting into the empty piping bag in her other hand with a spatula.

She leans down to an unfrosted cupcake, her face shifting into a focused expression. Her eyes go stony and her tongue peeks out from between her teeth as she expertly extrudes the frosting into another rose shape, and I watch intently. It's satisfying in the same way coloring the frosting was, with the added finesse of her hands making it look incredibly simple. It takes me a second to realize I'm staring and look away - I *hate* it when people stand over me and watch me work.

After one last flourish, she lifts the piping bag and turns to me. "You wanna try?"

I snort. "Absolutely not."

She cocks her head to the side, her red hair shining in the little streak of sunlight coming through the window. "Why not?"

"Because-" I sputter ever so slightly. "Because I can't do that."

"It doesn't have to be perfect," she replies. "It's just fun. You don't have to if you don't want to."

I run my tongue across the back of my teeth. With her big brown eyes and the way she's holding her head, she looks just like a freckled ginger puppy. "Show me again."

She smiles, that close-lipped one she does that narrows her eyes and has just the slightest hint of smugness. She turns back to the frosting bowls, refilling the piping bag. I let myself focus in on her movements, carefully piping each shape onto the top of the cupcake from the outside in, curling inward just like rose petals. The little brown freckles on her wrist momentarily pull my attention, trailing all the way up her bare arms.

"Think you've got it?" she asks, and I flick my eyes back up to her face. I nod, and she hands me the piping bag like she's passing down a sacred heirloom.

My hand shakes as I start to gently squeeze the bag, leaving a wobbly line of frosting on the edge of the cupcake. The rose takes shape, and I can almost hear that silly "womp womp" trombone sound effect as I take in the underwhelming result.

"So, it seems my skill in flowers ends at buttercream," I quip, crossing my arms and critically gazing at my creation.

"It takes practice," she says gently. "But did you have fun?"

I shift my weight, turning to look at her. "Do you get off on being right or something?"

Her face cracks into a huge, toothy grin. "So I'm right."

"That isn't what I said," I reply, falsely rigid.

But of course she is. The part of me that wasn't laser-focused on the poor quality of my output was distinctly tickled by the action, the novelty of turning something into something else. It's a feeling I don't quite have when I'm arranging - that's component elements coming together into a greater product. I don't have experience shaping a raw material into something new, not since crayons and colored pencils on printer paper. Summer's baking is reminiscent of childhood in that way.

"Well, I'm sorry to have put you through so much duress," she says, taking back the piping bag.

"Thank you," I say, and she almost jumps. "For letting me try."

"Of course," she says, pleasantly surprised. "Do you want to do another? It gets easier the more you do it."

"Sure. Get another piping bag, I wanna try the yellow."

She smiles. "Yes ma'am."

"Hey, babe," I chime, picking up the phone and holding it in the crook of my neck between my shoulder and my ear. "What's up?"

"You'll never guess who you're talking to right now," comes Felix's voice, enthusiastic like a sugarhigh preschooler.

"If it's not Felix Nguyen I've gotta change the contact," I reply, shuffling around the flowers in the vase in front of me.

"You're talking to the associate vice director of efficiency for the Roseport branch of Synergistic Strategies."

Knowing Felix personally (and knowing his personality), it's easy to forget about his boring corporate job, especially because of how little of it I actually understand. "What does that mean?"

"Not a damn thing," he replies. "Just a sizable bump to my pay, and a fancier desk."

"Are you Khalil's boss now?" I wonder, sliding a piece of greenery into the vase between two similarly sized-and-colored daffodils.

"No," he replies, a little disappointedly. "They made Khalil associate vice director of *competence* a few months ago."

"Damn," I say. "The rich get richer."

"It's basically nothing, but I'm still pretty proud of myself," he continues. "I do damn good work there, and I'm glad to be getting a bit more money for it."

"I'm proud of you, too, babe," I agree. "Tell you what, Mr. Associate Vice President. I'm working on an arrangement right now. It was going to be for me, but now it's got your name on it. Wanna come pick it up?"

"Absolutely," he says. "I can be there in, like, fifteen. Just don't be shocked when you see the Secret Service scouting the area."

"Thanks for the heads-up, Your Excellency," I laugh. "I'll unlock the door. Love you. See you soon."

"Love you!" he replies, following it up with a barrage of kissing noises and then hanging up.

He's there about as soon as promised, grandly pushing open my apartment door, his round glasses replaced with a cosmopolitan pair of movie star sunglasses. "Hey, that's beautiful. What are those, daffodils?"

"Yep." I turn, opening my arms up for a hug. "How was your day, outside of the inauguration?"

"Good," he says, ruffling my hair before I can shove him off. "Brian won't stop stealing my lunch, though."

"Put food coloring in your sandwich," I suggest. "Or cake frosting instead of mayo."

"Speaking of cake frosting," he says, looking intently at the bouquet, "do you wanna hang out with me, Julian, and Summer next week? We were gonna do a late lunch at that new cafe, then maybe walk around Main Street and do some shopping."

"Sure," I reply, and I can't help but feel a little sunny. I've really loved spending time with the three of them lately. "That sounds great. I just have to make sure I'm home by six so I can give Ethel her pills."

He raises his brows. "She needs her pills at a specific time?"

"The vet said she should have medicine with or slightly before food," I reply, pointing my chin to where she stands, still nosing around her mostly empty bowl. "And if she eats too late, she gets grouchy and tears up her toys."

"And when she tears up her toys, she swallows fabric and has to go to the emergency vet," he finishes for me with a nod. "I remember, that happened sophomore year."

I nod. "So it's just easier to always be home somewhere in that four-to-six window."

"Why don't you get a dog sitter?" he asks. "I know you're planning on finding someone for Christmas, but why not see if you can get somebody to come around a bit more often?"

"It would be nice to have that extra free time," I concede. "But do you really think there are people who'd be willing to come to my apartment and dote on my dog?"

"Sure I do," says Felix. "People will do anything if you pay them."

"Spoken like a true associate vice president of efficiency."

"This is even one of the better things you can be paid to do," he continues. "Taking care of a sweet, old-ass dog is a way more plush position than probably two-thirds of the present-day job market."

"She *is* pretty adorable," I say, scrunching my nose in her direction. "Come here, you little stinker."

She trots over loyally, her tail wagging. She seems more or less ambivalent to Felix's sudden appearance, just allowing us both to pet her with her head held high like an elegant queen accepting praise from her adoring subjects.

"So, I'll call you later about lunch," Felix says, standing up and grabbing the vase off the counter.

"Sure," I reply, still scrubbing behind Ethel's ears. "And don't forget to give me my vase back."

"Babe," he says, his hand on the doorknob, "with my new associate vice president money, I can buy you *ten* vases."

I roll my eyes. "Thanks for that shameless little brag." As the door opens, then slams: "I mean it, I want my vase back!"

"This has been really fun," says Summer brightly, pulling a shopping bag up onto her elbow. "Are you having fun, Ethel?"

Ethel continues panting, and I re-wrap the leash around my wrist. "She's never had this much fun in her life."

"Mostly because Felix kept feeding her," Julian teases. His fiancé nudges his shoulder, almost tossing him off the sidewalk and into the street.

"She has the eyes of a Dickensian orphan," Felix defends. "If she'd been staring up at *you*, she would've gotten your whole burger."

"We've both had a lot of fun," I cut in. "Thank you guys."

"What are you all up to after this?" Summer asks. "I'm off all day."

"I have a client," Julian says. "Session number three of this *giant* griffin tattoo. It's already looking great, so I can't wait to see it at the end of this session."

"Ethel and I are going to Witch's Brew in a bit to interview a potential dog sitter," I say.

"Aw, that sounds so fun!" Felix cries. "I don't work today, either. Can I come with?"

"Sure," I reply. "I don't really know what to look for in a dog sitter, so the more the merrier. You wanna come, too, Summer?"

"You mean spend more time with the world's best dog?" she grins, tossing her curls over her shoulder. "Absolutely."

Ethel wags her tail like she knows she's being complimented. "Alright, then it's settled. Have fun at work, Julian."

Felix slings his arms around him, tilting his fiancé's head upward to kiss him. "I'll see you at home, my love."

"See you later, man," Summer adds.

"Thanks, everyone," says Julian, then bends to look at Ethel. "Bye, Ethel." She looks up at him and graciously accepts the quick stroke to the top of her head.

"Can you drive me home after, Sadie?" asks Felix, giving Julian one last kiss before he heads off to their car.

"Of course."

Felix, Summer, Ethel, and I set up shop at Witch's Brew, the less pretentious option of Roseport's two coffee shops. Ethel stretches to the very end of her leash to sit outside of the patio's shade as we settle into our chairs. Summer looks down at the menu.

"Hey, they've changed this since I left," she chirps. "Half of these drinks are new."

"Yeah, they did a bit of an overhaul last year," says Felix. "It's all pretty good."

"I've always just stuck with my regular," I say.

"I can take everybody's orders inside," Summer offers. "Once I decide what I want."

"Aren't you the sweetest," Felix says, scrunching his nose at her.

Before too long, we're joined by a put-together young girl who looks fresh out of college, who first introduces herself as Olivia and then immediately drops into a sitting position on the pavement with Ethel.

"She's gorgeous," she says. "How old?"

"She's fourteen," I tell her, smiling at the way Ethel enthusiastically sniffs her face. "I've had her since middle school."

"Oh, you two must have been through a lot together," she coos to Ethel. "You're just a puppy, aren't you?"

"How long have you been dog sitting?" Felix asks, stirring his coffee. "You certainly seem to have a passion for it."

"Oh, I *do*, sir," Olivia replies, and Felix clutches his chest like he's been shot. She goes on, "I started when I was about eleven. My next-door neighbor was a very old woman who had a lot of mobility issues, and I volunteered to take her dog on walks for her. It felt really good, to help a person *and* a dog."

Summer smiles. "That's really lovely."

"What kind of schedule would you be able to keep?" I ask. "She needs her food and medication in a certain time window, and I'll be leaving the state in a couple weeks for Christmas."

"I'm a full-time dog sitter," she says, "so I can work whatever timing you need into my schedule with my other clients. And I'll be staying in Roseport for Christmas, so I can definitely check in on her while you're gone."

Ethel rolls onto her back, and Olivia gasps, obliging her request for belly rubs immediately.

"Is she good being alone?" Olivia asks. "Or should I plan on hanging around with her?"

"She's pretty low-maintenance," I say. "Most days you'll probably just need to feed and medicate her, but while I'm out of town she'll want a bit more attention."

"Gotcha," she nods.

"I think you would be a great dog sitter for Ethel," I say.

"Oh, yay!" Olivia says. "Let me give you my information. You can let me know at least three days ahead of time when you'll need me, and provide more detailed instructions then."

"Great." I say, and I feel a small weight lifted from my shoulders. "Thank you so much, Olivia."

"Thank *you*, Ms. Levine," she says brightly, and I wince.

"You've gotta stop that, kid," I laugh, looking over at Felix. "You're making us all feel old."

"I don't feel old," Summer jokes.

"Sorry," says Olivia. "It was Sadie?"

I nod. She thanks us all again (including Ethel) before frolicking away. "She's a nice young lady," I say aloud, then cringe at the sound of my mother's voice coming out of my mouth. "Oh, God. Am I really that old that a twenty-two-year-old looks like a pigtailed schoolgirl to me?"

Felix laughs. "She called me *sir*. I think we *are* old."

"Speak for yourselves," Summer says, exaggeratedly curling her hair around her finger. "I don't turn twenty-eight until April."

"Oh, shit, you *are* the baby," Felix exclaims. "You're younger than Julian!"

"By a month," she says with a nod.

"I've still got another month," I announce. "Why don't we just say Felix is the old fart for now?"

"Shut up," Felix says. "Twenty-eight is the new twenty-five."

I laugh. "Sure, Felix."

"I'm glad you found a dog sitter, babe," he says, leaning forward. "How do you feel?"

"It'll be nice to have a bit more time for myself," I say. "And to know somebody's taking care of Ethel while I'm out. I haven't... you know, *been* out a lot lately. But it'll be nice to have that freedom."

Summer nods. "Yeah."

"I don't know that I *will* go out more," I admit. "I want to, but it's just so *easy* not to."

"It's okay, babe," Felix says. "At least you've got the option now."

"Yeah," I agree, then lean down to look at Ethel. "Did you make a new friend, pup?"

She rolls over to give me her belly.

"We can do our part, too," Summer says. "To get you out."

I can't help but grin. "That would be great."

Chapter Fourteen
Summer Takes a Leap

"Morning, Summer," says Brandy, emerging from the back door.

"Morning, boss," I reply, flicking on the "open" sign.

She rolls up her sleeves and straightens the tip jar and business card holder on the counter. "Were you the one who frosted those chocolate donuts? They look great."

"Thank you," I reply, turning over my shoulder to flash her a smile before taking the broom from where it leans against the wall to sweep the entryway. "Trish was the one who made the glaze, though."

"I'll be sure to give her the brownie points, too, then," she says. "I hear you had a big catering job last weekend?"

"Yes ma'am," I tell her. "A very literal Sweet Sixteen."

"Very cool," she says, nodding. "I'm proud of you, kid. It seems like you've really been growing."

"I have," I agree, and a twinge of anxiety shivers up my spine. "Actually, I wanted to talk with you."

She nods. "Let me guess- it's time."

"I wanted to put in my two weeks," I say. "Not leave you totally blindsided."

"I'm far from blindsided, Summer," she says, smiling warmly. "In fact, set down the broom for a second and come with me."

My eyes go wide. "O-okay."

She leads me back past the kitchen and the restrooms into her little office, a tiny room with pink-painted walls, a cluttered desk, and an array of dessert-themed wall decor. I stand in the doorway as she crouches behind the desk. She re-emerges a moment later with a bottle of champagne in her hand.

"I bought this the day you went part-time," she says.

"Wow," I breathe. "Brandy, that's... that's so kind."

"You can take this home," she says, holding the bottle out and beckoning me into the room. I take it. "I don't delude myself into thinking you'd want to drink with this old lady." I have to laugh a bit - she's probably only in her mid- to late-forties.

"But if you'll sit and have a little chat with me," she continues, "I'll be satisfied."

I gladly pull up the chair on the other side of her desk and she sits in hers. "Sure."

"I just have to tell you again how proud I am," she says. "It takes a lot of guts, dedication, and talent to do what you're doing."

"Thank you," I reply, flushing a bit.

"I certainly hope you're proud of yourself, too," she adds.

A shy smile works its way onto my face. "I am."

"If you ever need anything, you have my number." She shifts in her chair, leaning forward onto the desk. "I know I don't seem like I know much, but I've been in this business a long time."

"Brandy," I cut in. "I absolutely trust your knowledge. If I need something, you'll be the first person I call."

"You know," she says, her expression shifting ever so slightly toward the solemn. "You're a sweet kid. You remind me of mine."

I raise my eyebrows. I'd never heard of her having a kid. "Yeah?"

"My baby, Sky." The tremble in her voice is unmistakable now. My heart aches at this unprecedented melancholy. "Kindest kid you ever met. They told me and my husband they wanted to be a painter. So we bought them everything they needed, and it was so wonderful to see that passion in their eyes. It's the same as you've got."

Everything she's said has been kind, but I can't misread the air. There's another part to this story. I brace myself for it.

"They got in a car accident a couple years back," she says, pushing her hair behind her ears. "So I hope you'll forgive me if I hold a little tight to you sometimes. I'd just like to see you succeed, since I never got to see that for Sky."

"I'm so sorry," I say.

"It's alright," she assures. "I don't say that for your pity. It's just good to see sweet kids like mine achieving their dreams."

"I'm really glad, Brandy," I add. "Thank you again."

"Of course." She stands. "Let's get to work then, shall we?"

"Yes ma'am," I say, and she gives me one last smile before following me out of the office.

"Alright," says Julian over the group's chatter, standing from his chair and holding up his glass. "Everyone, we are gathered here today to celebrate Summer Daphney McConnell and the emergence of Sweet Summer Confectionaries as a full-time business."

The group cheers, clinking silverware against cups and wolf-whistling.

"Throw your hats in the ring now for the privilege of paying for her meal," Julian continues, and everyone thrusts their hands into the air like they're at an auction.

I laugh, my cheeks burning. "Guys, please."

"Khalil already paid you for Axel's birthday," says Rio. "It's somebody else's turn."

"That doesn't seem relevant," protests Khalil. "I deserve as much of a chance as anyone."

I clear my throat. "Guys."

"I just got a promotion," Felix says. "I've got the extra cash."

"Summer gave me a million free cupcakes throughout college," Georgia jumps in. "I should get to pay her back at least a *bit*."

"*Guys*," I say louder. "You don't have to do that."

"Everyone quit it," Sadie says, then cuts her eyes sideways toward me like a cheeky grin. "We'll ask the waiter to split her bill six ways."

"Sadie," I scold.

"We won't if you really don't want us to," she says, "but we're proud of you and we want a way to show you."

"Just speaking from experience," Julian adds with a nudge to my shoulder, "but when your own independent business is all the income you're getting, I say take the handouts."

I roll my eyes. "*Alright*, you guys, fine."

"I propose a toast," says Felix, taking his turn to stand up. I have to cover my face. "Summer: our beloved friend, our talented baked goods dealer. A full-time entrepreneur! To Summer."

"To Summer," everyone echoes, and the restaurant seems to fill with the sound of clinking glasses.

"We could have just cracked open that champagne in my living room," I whine. "I feel like everybody's looking at us."

"Let's hope they are!" exclaims Rio, whipping their head around. "Did you bring any business cards?"

"Let's please talk about something other than me for a minute," I say. "What else can we talk about?"

"I know," Sadie chimes. "Everyone, with the recent development of my acquisition of a dog sitter: I can stay out as long as I want."

This brings about a similar cheer, and Sadie beams. My insides feel warmer, and I let out an enthusiastic whistle. Her smile grows even bigger, her eyes squinting so I can only see a sliver of the sparkling green.

"Let's also hear a little commotion for my fiancé, the new associate vice president of efficiency of Synergistic Strategies for the Roseport location," Julian says, and Felix tucks his hair behind his ears with a fake shyness. "Cementing him forever as the primary breadwinner of the Nguyen-Jefferson household."

"Hear, hear!" Khalil bellows, and we all follow suit.

"But don't fret, my friends," Felix says, waving his hand humbly like a young royal. "My staggering success and incredible wealth will have no negative effect on our friendship."

"I was really worried, Felix," I joke. "That's good to hear."

"Carrie and I are going to move in together," Georgia says shyly, fiddling with one of their many ear piercings. "She was already looking for a new place, and we decided I'd go ahead and look with her."

"Aw!" Felix squeals. "God, I love love."

"I can't say I'm surprised," Sadie says. "It seems like you haven't slept at your own place for more than a couple nights in months."

Georgia's face goes red. "Someone else talk," she says, uncharacteristically meek.

"Tae and I said 'I love you' last week," says Rio, primping their bright blue-and-green hair with a smug grin.

"Rio, we know," says Sadie dryly. "You texted the group chat, like, the minute it happened."

"Oh, I'm sorry, do I not get to play?" Rio says, pouting exaggeratedly. "I think I'm entitled to brag."

"I'm still happy for you, Rio," I cut in, catching Sadie's gaze out of the corner of my eye. "Tae is *so* cool. How many buff, gorgeous wedding stylists are there in the world, let alone in Roseport?"

"*Thank you*, Summer," they say, shooting Sadie a jokingly loaded glance. She pokes her tongue ever-so-slightly out of the side of her mouth, her brows raised, and switches her eyes from Rio to me. There's a private, playful edge to the look as she seems to ask me *really? You're going against me on this?*

"Forgive my cynicism," Sadie says, putting her hands up in concession. "Congratulations on love."

"Aw, Sadie, you softie!" Rio cries, and scattered laughter sounds around the table.

"Alright, alright," she says, rolling her eyes as a slight pink colors her cheeks. "Let's not forget why we're actually here, huh?" She cuts her eyes toward me again, cocking her head to the side and lifting her glass.

"Speech," calls Julian through cupped hands, the same winking irony in his expression.

I tuck my hair behind my ear, holding back a smile as I pick up my glass. "I want to thank you all for being here tonight to celebrate me and my business." I'd thought I was kidding about making a speech, but suddenly my throat starts to feel stuffy with tears, and I have to go on. "I started Sweet Summer Confectionaries when I was having a really tough time in Chicago. I felt like I had lost myself and the things that I was passionate about. Sweet Summer was my way of trying to get all that back. It was my baby, and my brainchild, and in a way it was my identity. It's so amazing that my work and my recipes have been able to get this far, and I can't wait to see where it goes from here."

"I'll drink to that," chimes Khalil, and everyone else's agreements roll in like a waterfall. I wait a second before taking my sip, looking out at all my friends. My heart warms - right now, I think I have everything I wanted two years ago, directionless and lonesome in a new city. I can't believe how far I've come.

"We're gonna head out, babe," says Felix, returning from the bathroom. "Woah, you're still not done eating?"

"Get off my back," Sadie cries, slowly pushing the fork across her plate. "I don't have to be home anytime soon, so I can take my sweet time finishing this delicious food."

He chuckles, and Julian hugs me. "Congrats again, Summer."

"Thank you," I reply. "Bye, guys."

"Bye," Sadie adds, her mouth full. Felix ruffles her hair affectionately, and she swats at him with one hand, the other still gripping her fork.

"Love you guys," Julian says, touching Sadie's shoulder as he passes her.

"Love you," we both chorus, and they head out the door.

I look over at Sadie, similarly nursing the remnants of my dinner. It's just the two of us left. She seems almost triumphant in her lingering stay: it's proof that she *can*, of that little bit of freedom she's gained. I'm hoping to sit in the high of today for just a little bit longer, to soak in the feeling of my friends' support so I can never forget it.

"So, are you planning on spending the night here or what?" I ask her, stirring my food before scooping a bite onto my spoon.

She laughs shortly, rolling her eyes. "Yep, already booked my room. You?"

"Same," I reply with a false nonchalance. "I hope you weren't planning on using that booth over there. I already called dibs."

"Damn," she says, swinging her arm and snapping her fingers. She looks down into her plate. "I know you've heard plenty of it tonight, but I really am proud of you."

I smile. "Thanks."

"Just promise me you won't forget to relax every once in a while," she prods, glancing up from her food with a knowing look in her green eyes. "I want you to make some time for yourself so you don't die and leave Sweet Summer without Summer."

Something feels like it's blossoming inside my chest, and looking at her my smile gets a little bit bigger. "Only if you promise me you'll get out once in a while."

She raises her brows, and there's no judgment on her face, but my cheeks still burn. "Not, like, dating, if you don't want to. Just not staying confined to your apartment when you could be out having fun."

"It's a deal," she says, sticking out her hand. I can't help but feel stupid for accidentally implying I thought she should date, especially knowing about everything that happened with her ex. Part of me thinks she should be at least a little pissed at me, but her gaze isn't anything but friendly and warm. When I shake her hand, it feels the same.

"What are you eating?" she asks, her attention returning to her plate. "If it's half as good as this pad thai, you must be in heaven."

"Crab fried rice," I respond.

"Holy shit, that sounds good," she groans. "I fucking *love* Thai food." My lips quirk at the phrase.

"Wanna try some?"

"*Yes*," she says, picking up her plate. "Here, we'll trade."

A bubbly feeling builds at the pit of my stomach seeing the sparkle in her eyes as she passes her plate across the table and I replace it with mine. She's practically bouncing in her seat.

"Oh my god," she says after her first taste. "Can we actually trade? This is delicious."

"Absolutely," I nod, mouth half full of noodles. "So good."

We stay there until the food is gone, which judging only by my internal clock, could be anywhere from a few minutes to an hour. Conversation is easy with her, and time flies without making much of a fuss as it goes. When we've finally cleared our plates, we both stand up and gather our things.

"Again," she says, pulling on her coat, "congrats on Sweet Summer. I'm really happy for you."

"I'm happy for me, too," I say, putting on my own. "And it was really nice hanging out with you."

She smiles, her crooked tooth flashing. "You too, Summer."

I hug her, and for a second I think to say *love you* like we both do to the rest of the group. But even thinking of it feels wrong on my tongue, weird and inappropriate, even though I've known her just as long as I have Rio or Khalil. I suppress the thoughts, saying just "Bye." as I pull away.

"Bye," she says, and turns toward the door. I stand there for a second as she goes, a faint buzzing in my ears, then follow her out.

Chapter Fifteen

Sadie Has a Cup of Cheer

"Hey," says Summer excitedly from her kitchen island as I open the door to her apartment. "How was work?"

"The usual," I reply, dropping my purse onto a chair and joining her in the kitchen, where she's spread out ingredients, cookie cutters, and mixing bowls. "A nearlywed screamed in my face about filler flowers and I was ankle-deep in poinsettia all day. How about you?"

She grins almost smugly. "Pretty great. I've got a birthday cake in the fridge that I'm delivering tomorrow morning."

"Are you sure you don't just want to watch TV or something?" I ask, surveying the stuff on the counter before us. "You *do* bake all day, every day. I'd understand if you wanted a break."

"This is baking for pleasure," she says definitively. "Besides, I couldn't sit idly by after hearing you haven't made Christmas cookies in..." She pauses. "How long?"

"Since elementary school, I think," I reply, then shrug. "I don't know, I didn't figure it was that important of a tradition."

Her brown eyes are shockingly complex, a million different shades, as she looks at me with a playful smile. "Then why did you agree to do it?"

Because you're my friend, and I want to spend time with you. But that's too vulnerable for me to say aloud, even though I'm pretty sure she knows it. I put my palms flat on the countertop. "Where do we start?"

"I've got everything measured out already," she says, turning her attention to the spread on the counter. "First, we put the butter and sugar in this big bowl. We'll add everything else in a second."

I nod, reaching for the little bowl full of sugar. "Glad to see you've Sadie-proofed the process."

She raises her eyebrows, her hand stopping midair. "What does that mean?"

"You made it so I couldn't fuck anything up," I reply casually. "I think even *I* can handle pouring things into a bowl."

"I didn't mean it that way," she says, her tone so earnest it almost hurts. "I'm sorry if I-"

"No," I say quickly, my cheeks getting warm. "I just know my baking skills are far from a professional's."

"We're having fun," she says, her voice soothing. "It isn't a big deal if you're 'skilled' or not." Her smile grows a bit more playful. "Besides, cookies are easy. I don't think anyone could fuck them up."

I look down at the measuring spoon full of vanilla extract so I don't have to look at her. It isn't just her assuring words that make my stomach squirm - it's the realization that I don't talk about myself like she or Felix or any of our friends would. We're all constantly joking with one another, but nobody would ever imply I was too dumb to make *cookies*. I feel almost ashamed for sweet, genuine Summer to have caught me talking bad about myself like it was a reflex.

"Sorry," I say carefully. "You're right."

"You don't have anything to be sorry for," she says, her smile warming me from head to foot. As she turns to dump the butter in, I can't help but notice the bright red hair tied at the back of her head and the skin it exposes. Her pale neck is dotted with freckles, more sparsely than on her face. She looks back at me, and in my mind I snap to attention like I've been *caught* somehow. "Alright. Would you give me that?"

I pick up the hand mixer at the edge of the counter, noting that it's heavier than I'd expected when I hand it to her. Her fingers brush mine on the handle for the slightest of seconds, and an electric tingle runs up from the source of her touch and through my entire body. Horrified, I try to ignore the growing blush on my cheeks and focus on *anything* else.

She brandishes the mixer like a Charlie's Angel with a revolver, an easy confidence to her stance. "Have you ever used a hand mixer before?"

"My mom didn't trust me not to fling batter everywhere," I say. "I can't say I blame her."

"Okay, I'll get things started so you can see how it's done, and then you can take over when you feel confident," she says, lowering the mixer so that its metal arms rest in the bowl.

I waver. "I don't-" But her voice from just a second ago rings in my head, and I swallow the sentence. "Okay."

She pushes a small lever on its side and the appliance roars to life, shaking furiously inside the bowl but not even seeming to wiggle in her grip. I force myself to focus on the mixer and not the way her eyes look, dark and half-lidded and focused.

"I think I can-" I approach her after a second like she's a wild animal, and she presses her hand to my shoulder blade, gently pushing so I'll step closer. My brain suddenly feels jumbled.

I take the handle, her hand lifting off it as mine makes contact. I'm too loose at first, and the machine starts to wobble, but Summer looks at me proudly when I stabilize the motion.

"Very good," she says, nodding appreciatively. "Now keep like that until the mixture looks creamy."

"Yes, chef," I bark, and her eyes go narrow when she laughs.

We go about this way for a few more minutes, her adding vanilla and salt and baking powder and letting me mix them, until finally all her pre-portioned ingredients are gone and the bowl before me contains a clumpy bunch of dough.

"This is the fun part," she tells me, grabbing a bag of flour from next to the stove. "Well, one of them."

"Oh, yeah-" I sputter as she dusts a generous helping of flour onto the island in front of me, the powder flying up into my face.

"Sorry," she giggles, not sounding particularly truthful in the matter. I frown, rubbing the back of my wrist under my nose.

"God, I'd have rather you used mustard gas," I choke.

She shrugs, her cutesy appearance and the nonchalant gesture not quite managing to mask her wicked grin. "Mustard gas doesn't stop the dough from sticking."

"You're sick."

"And proud of it. Hand me the rolling pin?"

I do, and she quickly gives me instructions before getting to work herself. Instead of helping, though, I fall back into watching her as she uses her hands to pull the dough from the bowl and pat it together onto the counter, her movements so practiced she looks like an assembly line robot.

"What?" she says, turning over her shoulder with raised eyebrows. "If I'm going to be the one making these cookies all on my own, you're gonna have to start paying me."

I step forward, looking down at the mostly flat mass of dough on the countertop as she picks the rolling pin back up. "Doesn't look like you needed my help."

She starts to say something, but snorts with laughter when her eyes lock on my face. She covers her mouth with her hand for a moment before raising it to hover in front of my cheek. "Sorry, you just have a little…" She trails off, wiping away the speck of flour under my left eye. Another giggle bubbles up from her throat, and my heartbeat quickens as her fingertips brush my skin again. "Okay… maybe a lot."

"That's what you get for engaging in chemical warfare with the flour," I remark, averting my eyes from the sunny smile on her face.

"Poor baby," she says through an exaggerated pout, then holds up the rolling pin at eye level between us. "Can I venture a guess you'll need a demonstration on this, too?"

"There's more to do?" I ask, purposely acting a little more clueless than I really am, if only to see her eyes crinkle at the corners when she laughs at me.

"Watch and learn, my protégé." She rolls up nonexistent sleeves with a grand flourish, then pushes the rolling pin across the dough, flattening it more each time. It's as smooth as a fresh piece of printer paper when she straightens again, visibly proud. "That's how it's done. Like a hotel bedsheet."

I nod, clicking my tongue. "Unwashed and paper thin."

She rolls her eyes. "Very funny."

"Not pretty under a blacklight."

"Take a look at those cookie cutters and tell me what you want to use, Comedy Hour," she says, her eyes glittering and her lips squeezed together to hide her smile.

Suppressing the urge to give her a sarcastic salute, I start thumbing through the bag full of cookie cutters. She seems to have every shape imaginable, not stopping at the classic Christmas shapes: hearts, stars, butterflies, leaves, flowers, shamrocks, animals of every kind. But my hand definitively stops at one specific shape.

"This is the one."

Summer looks up and snorts. "Not very festive of you, but I'll allow it."

"Why exactly do you have a penis-shaped cookie cutter?" I ask, waving the phallic metal outline.

"You'd be surprised how often people want it," she tells me, rooting through the bag for her own, more Christmas-y selections. "Bachelor and bachelorette parties, gag gifts. 'Eat a dick'. You know, that kind of stuff."

"*Gag gift* is right," I murmur suggestively, and she giggles and focuses back on the flat sheet of dough before us.

We cut out the cookies and transfer them to a baking sheet and into the oven, and the feeling of her hand on my fingers, my back, and my cheek finally begins to fade from my memory. I relax back into the familiar rhythm of our friendship, but there's still the tiniest pinprick at the corner of my mind, like a pea under a stack of mattresses. This miniscule upset stays with me as we take the cookies out of the oven and decorate them. I feel disturbingly aware of where her hands are, to the point that I'm mostly watching them rather than what I'm actually doing.

"So," she asks, adding the last little touch to her snowflake cookie, "did I manage to give you the Christmas cookie experience Little Sadie always dreamed of?"

"Absolutely," I reply, then hold up a dick cookie on which I've shakily drawn a smiling face and a bow tie. "Meet Ricky." I pause, giving the cookie another once-over. "Willy."

"Peen-elope?" she offers, a crooked grin on her face.

"You're a genius."

This makes her look, if possible, even prouder than when she'd been showing off her rolling pin skills. She beams down at the counter as she starts frosting a tree-shaped cookie. "Let me know when you're ready for the taste test."

"I don't know if I can do that to Peen-elope," I tell her, sticking out my lower lip and making my eyes go wide. "We've grown so close."

She rolls her eyes, once again suppressing an affectionate grin, then looks at me seriously like she's about to give me some real straight talk. "Sadie?"

"Yeah?"

Her chin points defiantly upward. "Eat a dick."

This genuinely catches me off guard, and my laugh comes straight from my stomach, loud and full. Having officially been convinced, I take a bite of the cookie.

"Well?" she says expectantly.

"Christmas morning," I reply, practically seeing stars. "That's fucking amazing. This cookie tastes like *Christmas morning*."

She covers her face with her hand, her cheeks pink. "Stop."

"You've definitely given me the full Christmas cookie experience," I tell her. "Thank you."

"Of course, Sadie," she says, cocking her head to the side. "You can keep whatever we don't eat today."

"*Yes*," I hiss, pumping my fist. "Wanna watch some more Tropic Like It's Hot? The holiday special came out a few days back."

"I think that certainly counts as 'not working too hard'," she teases, and we go over to the couch.

"Morning," Macy chirps, only a couple steps ahead of me as I enter the back door of Inspiration Florals.

"Morning," I reply, plopping the container of leftover Christmas cookies onto the break room table as she ties her apron.

"What are those?" she asks, eagle-eyed.

"I made some Christmas cookies," I say as nonchalantly as possible, grabbing my own apron.

"No shit," she says, incredulous, flicking her ponytail out from under the neck strap of her apron. "Just when I thought I had you figured out." She immediately cracks the top off the bowl, picking up one of Summer's meticulously iced angels. "*You* made these?"

"In a manner of speaking," I concede, knowing all of Peen-elope's siblings are long gone.

"You are just full of surprises, Sadie," she remarks, nodding her head suspiciously. Her eyes go wide when she has a bite. "Oh, I *really* don't know you at all. What the fuck is this? Is it made of real angels?"

I start to tell her that I can't take the credit for Summer's recipe and a good deal of her work, but I've barely ever spoken to Macy about my personal life in all the years I've worked here. And somehow I get the feeling that if I start talking about Summer, I don't know if I'll stop. I don't like the idea of crossing that boundary with Macy - or with Summer. I don't go around gushing about my other friends.

"Just don't eat all of them," I reply instead.

"No promises," she says, pointing the beheaded angel at me and biting off another chunk. I shrug, heading into the front of the store.

"Sadie!" cries Rio, throwing their arms around me right as the door swings open. "Hey, hot stuff."

"Hey," I echo, squeezing them back. "Happy holidays."

"Happy holidays! Come on in," they say, patting my back. "Summer says she'll be late, but everybody else is already here."

Rio's place isn't quite as big as Khalil's, but it makes for a pretty decent party venue, too: a winter wonderland of decor spread out over every surface. Even their army of handmade stuffies, who sit year-round on every surface, are decked out in little Christmas sweaters and Santa suits. Gathered around the couch, everyone and their partners come into view, chatting and laughing in different festive outfits.

"Baby!" Felix exclaims, jumping up from the couch in a sweater wrapped with multicolored tinsel.

"Hey, babe." I slide into his spot before he can protest, and he perches on the arm. His hand slips naturally into my hair, and I can't quite summon the energy to stop him from messing up the style.

"We were just talking about holiday plans," Julian says, gently tapping the back of his hand against my arm. "Felix and I are spending Hanukkah with my family."

It sticks in my mind that they don't mention Felix's mom, but I don't dwell on it.

"I'm headed back home then, too," says Georgia, Carrie tucked into her side. "My dads go all out." They scrunch their nose at their girlfriend. "You're gonna love it."

"I can't wait," Carrie responds, her nose pressed to Georgia's.

"All our families are coming down here for the holidays," says Khalil. "We just have to hope at least some of them behave."

"It's pretty much just my parents we need to worry about," Matthew pipes up. "Your mom can be nosy, but my folks..." He shakes his head. "I'll consider it a win if we can get through the season without a screaming match."

"The season *is* a screaming match at the Hernandez house," says Rio from Tae's lap. "Is it too late for me to plan on hitching a ride to somebody else's festivities?"

"I'm staying here," Tae says in a tone I think she means to be casual, but which certainly belies some nerves. "I mean, you don't have to go to your parents' if you don't want to."

Rio's eyes go wide and a devilish grin spreads across their face. "Tae, are you suggesting what I think you are?"

She looks like a deer in the headlights. "I- I... Yeah."

Rio squeals, flinging their arms around her neck and peppering her face with kisses. "You're the *best*." They turn to the rest of the group, bouncing. "Did I mention who sewed all my plushies' new clothes?"

"Okay, you two, get a room," Axel bellows.

"Let them be," coos Cecily, nudging their knee with hers.

"Yeah, don't you remember how you and Matthew used to be?" Eleanor adds, and Axel sticks out their tongue.

"Are you headed back to Virginia, Sadie?" Felix asks.

I grit my teeth. "I leave for the airport early tomorrow morning."

"I know that look," says Georgia, sitting forward in their seat. "What's back in Virginia?"

There's a tightness in my chest. "I haven't done Christmas there for a couple of years. And, uh, things with my mom have been…"

"I don't need to hear any more," says Felix suddenly, and I let out a tiny breath of relief at not having to find the perfect way to articulate the jumble of feelings. "I know *exactly* what you need."

As it turns out, Matthew orchestrates the party's cocktails whether it's at his home or not, and in a matter of minutes he's taken Felix and I to the kitchen, mixed up a bright green drink, and presented it to me.

"What is this?" I ask, leaning against the kitchen cabinets and inspecting the neon color.

"I call it Grinch Punch," Matthew says proudly.

"No," I ask, taking a sip and confirming I can't taste any alcohol whatsoever, "what *is* this?"

"Christmas cheer," Felix says, lifting his own glass of the stuff. He's right about that much - it's delicious, sour and fruity with a hint of sugar. I have another sip.

"Just vodka and a bunch of juice," Matthew says. "You like it?"

"Truly a masterstroke," I confirm, and he grins, bumping his fist against mine before heading back to the living room.

"I don't think I realized stuff was that bad back home," Felix says solemnly, looking down at the floor.

I shrug. "I don't know, it's..."

"I feel like I've kinda dropped the ball as a best friend," he says, and it's like a stab to my heart. "First about how much the Gabby stuff hurt you, and now..."

"Felix, no," I say quickly. "It's just... I don't say things, because I don't want to talk about them or think about them. It's not your fault."

"What's wrong with your mom?" he asks, brown eyes full of concern. "I thought she was doing better than..."

"She was." I feel a shiver run up my arms. "But after last year, it's like... I don't know. It's not like she was in a great place before, but she's lost anything she had. We can't talk about anything, and what she *does* want to talk about..." I trail off, instinctively taking another sip of my drink. "Whatever. I don't want to worry about it tonight."

"Absolutely, babe," he says, his voice automatically comforting me. He crosses the kitchen to hug me, my face going into the place just above his collarbone but just below his shoulder like it has since we were in middle school and he had that pesky growth spurt. I tighten my grip around him, and some of the pent-up feeling seems to seep out of me, at least for now. I breathe out and let go.

"So how about we just have fun tonight?" I ask, lifting my drink.

He grins, clinking his glass to mine. "I'll drink to that."

I snort. "You'll drink to anything."

"But especially my best friend in the world," he defends, then takes a sip of his drink. I follow suit, the tiniest twinge of a buzz starting to come to me. With it, I feel just a bit more of my worry slip away.

As the party rages - for lack of a better term - I nurse my drink, though its influence never quite seems to go away, nor does an irksome itch at the back of my mind, only growing slightly smaller with each sip. Still, I can focus a little better as Tae regales us with horror stories about nightmare nearlyweds in the shop (I reciprocate - the tale of Hex Code Lady sends Eleanor in particular into hysterics) and Georgia somehow convinces Khalil and Julian to join in on an impromptu and mostly tonedeaf performance of "Little Saint Nick".

"Hey, there she is!" cries Rio, breaking from their thunderous applause and turning over their shoulder toward the door. My eyes follow theirs and there's Summer, rosy-cheeked from the cold outside in a way that greatly accentuates the quietly dramatic angle of her cheekbones. I haven't thought in a while about just how striking of a sight she is, with fiery red hair and freckles and long, dark eyelashes.

The group choruses their own greetings as she grins and makes her way around the circle hugging everyone individually.

"Sorry I'm late," she says hurriedly. "I thought I'd be done with this rush order *way* sooner, but what can you do?"

"No worries, *Boss Babe*," says Rio, putting on a valley girl affectation and ruffling Summer's hair as she leans down to hug them.

"What'd I miss?" she asks, getting to me last of all. She hugs me quickly, then easily slides into the seat next to me.

My skin pricks- she's so *close*. She's definitely been close to me before, probably even this close, but now something about it puts an odd feeling in my stomach. I notice, maybe for the first time, that her top lip with its heavily defined cupid's bow is markedly thicker than the bottom lip. *Had she asked me something?*

"For once I'm not the drunkest," Felix says, and I feel myself relax. Even without knowing it, Felix has saved my ass once again. "If you ask nicely, I bet the Three Musketeers over here will be willing to give an encore performance."

Summer looks over at Julian, Khalil, and Georgia with a bemused smile. "Oh yeah?"

The weird bubble of anxiety in my stomach starts to deflate, and I can't quite figure out where it came from in the first place. I run my hand through my hair, tasting the sour punch on my tongue a bit more than I had before.

"We are phenomenal singers," Georgia says, their words ever-so-slightly slurred. Carrie giggles into her hand.

"I remember," says Summer. "Like junior year, at that karaoke bar. You two really pulled off Diana Ross."

"Believe me," adds Georgia, out to the room, "I'm a *musician.*"

Tae leans towards Rio's ear. "Is she?"

"They're a bassist," Carrie says. "*Not* a singer."

"I remember," Tae parrots, with an exaggerated shudder.

"It's settled," Georgia announces, grabbing Julian and Khalil by the hands and yanking all three of them out of their seats. "The golden trio sings once more!"

A cheer breaks out, quite clearly led by Carrie. Khalil shoots a desperate look toward his partners, who seem to offer little sympathy. When Georgia starts snapping a rhythm, he rolls his eyes good-naturedly and cuts in with his low harmony.

Summer laughs as Julian and Georgia join in, dissonant and out-of-time. Her arm brushes against mine as she rocks forward, and the touch feels almost electric. I stiffen my posture and take a sizable sip of my drink.

The woman in the bathroom mirror looks about as disoriented as I feel, something beyond the Grinch Punch buzz floating around my head and fucking me up. I stare at the Sadie above the sink, her chubby face and stubby nose, hoping she'll have a better idea than I do as to what's happening to me. Instead, my eyes leave their own reflection and travel down my body.

I'm *fine* with my body, I really am - I've gotten better at eating around people, at eating dessert without feeling guilty. Sober, I can look at my body in any angle and lighting and not fall apart. But now, my stomach churns at the sight of my squishy upper arms, the outline of my stomach in my t-shirt, and the overlarge swell of my chest.

There's an image in my mind as I stare down my soft physique like a single puzzle piece discarded from the box. I don't know *why* I'm feeling this way. It occurs to me that I probably should, but everything is too muddy. I hadn't thought I was that drunk. I'm *not*, if the very slight fog in my brain is any indication. Just a bit tipsy.

I steel myself now, gripping the edges of the sink. "Be normal," I mutter through gritted teeth, the silliness of it not lost on me. The Sadie in the mirror seems to tell me it's a much-needed reminder, so I push on. "Don't be weird."

Seemingly unrelated thoughts start to drift around in the forefront of my mind. My mom. My dad. Felix. Summer. I tighten my hands around the sink.

"Stop it," I say, staring into my own eyes, daring myself to try me. I take in a deep breath, and this tiny solace seems to be as good as I'm going to get. I shake the tension out of my shoulders and turn to the door.

Just when I rest my hand on the knob, it swings suddenly open and knocks me off balance. I stumble forward and catch myself, stopping just before Summer.

"Shit, sorry," she says, her hands out like a safety net in case I start to lose my balance. "Are you alright?"

I suddenly can't tear my eyes off her face. Her cheeks are slightly pink under her freckles- and oh, her *freckles*. They're most concentrated on her long, thin nose, but they occupy every area of her skin in all different sizes and frequencies, blindingly complex. Her entire face seems to have this same intrigue to it, her features coming together unexpectedly. I think anyone else with her same sharp jaw and bright hair would seem imposing, but everything about her somehow points toward the warmth of her character, like you could tell how kind she is just by looking at her.

Her voice cuts through my focus. "Sadie?"

"You're really gorgeous," my mouth says before me, and the sound of my own voice is immediately sobering. My heart pounds, and my breath hitches in the millisecond before she responds.

"Thank you," she says, completely and utterly casual aside from the tiniest quirk at the corner of her mouth. "Do you need help getting back to the living room?"

She thinks I'm drunker than I am. Which explains why she's so nonchalant about what I've just said. This should calm me down - I'm getting out of my verbal misstep scot-free - but my heart rate doesn't slow. "I'm alright. Thank you."

She nods, a faint smile curving on her mouth as she closes the bathroom door behind her. I half-consider repeating my earlier pep talk, but the potential embarrassment of her overhearing this outweighs the current embarrassment, and I make my way back to where the party rages on. Felix is on the coffee table doing a Mariah Carey impression with an impressive amount of accuracy and Khalil is dead asleep with his head on Cecily's lap. I settle onto the couch next to Julian, who is rapturously watching his fiancé's attempt at whistle notes.

Sensing my presence, he turns. "Sadie, it's getting kind of late. Didn't you say you've got a flight early in the morning?"

I blink for a moment. "Oh, yeah, I guess you're right. I'll wait here to sober up a bit and then get home."

"We'll miss you, babe," Felix says, jumping off the table and onto the couch, sitting sloppily on mine and Julian's laps.

"Hey, Superstar," I say as he kisses his fiancé's cheek and then mine. "I think I can hear Mariah crying from here."

"Everything's gonna be okay," he adds, looping his arm around my shoulders. "And call me if you need *anything*, alright?"

"Thanks, babe," I say. "I will."

The sound of the alarm is an unwelcome knife through my sleep, and I feel like flattened roadkill as I peel myself up from the pillow and out from under the covers. I didn't even drink that much - I let Felix finish off my Grinch Punch - but it's 5AM and I know where I'm going. I've never felt this exhausted.

Olivia is at the door, perky and bright, at 5:30 on the dot. She smiles, her blonde hair neat and shiny. "Good morning, Sadie."

I feel like a gnarled old witch, so I lean into it and point a shaking finger at her. "Don't *ever* drink."

She laughs. "Noted. Is there anything specific I should know that I don't already?"

"No, I think you've got everything you need," I say, then sigh. "Thank you, Olivia."

"It's my job," she says, dropping to the floor to pet Ethel, whose tail is wagging as quickly as it can manage. "So, you said you're going to see family for the holidays?"

"Yes," I confirm, patting down my pockets as I try to think of anything I've forgotten. "I'll head for the airport here in just a minute."

"Well, have a great time," she says, and I can't quite control my dubious expression. Her brows knit, seemingly having clocked the change. "Or should I say, *good luck?*"

"Something like that," I grumble, straightening my purse strap on my shoulder. "Have a happy holiday, Olivia."

"You too," she says.

The lack of human interaction as soon as the apartment door closes behind me turns me back into a sleep-deprived zombie, and I swear I'm settling into my seat on the plane a second later. Olivia's words ring in my ears as a text from Mom appears on my phone.

Good luck.

Chapter Sixteen

Summer Makes the Yuletide Gay

"Summer!" The second the door to my parents' cute suburban home opens, my mother springs forward and wraps her arms around me. She's still a few inches taller than me even in her sensible ballet flats, though not quite as tall as when I was a teenager. She lets go and holds me at arm's length, her brown eyes searching every inch of my face. "Oh, I've missed you, baby."

"I've missed you, too, Mama," I reply as she reaches up and runs a hand through my curls. "How have things been?"

"Oh, same as always," she says, turning to straighten the wreath on the door. "The gophers are back in the garden. Your dad's almost gone crazy trying to get rid of them." She turns over her shoulder, locking eyes with me while her lips draw into a thin line. "And Janet from next door is having an affair. I'm sure of it."

I hold in a laugh. "Really?"

She nods her head. "Positive. I keep seeing another car in the driveway when Terry's not home, and this young man-"

"With brown hair and a college t-shirt?" I cut in, smiling at her. "I'm pretty sure that's their son. We chatted at Thanksgiving, he comes over every couple of weeks to do his laundry."

"Oh." Mom shrugs her shoulders. "Well, I've got to entertain myself around here somehow."

"I'm sorry I didn't get here sooner," I tell her, putting my hand on my suitcase. "I was delivering my last few holiday orders."

She tuts. "You work too much."

I can't help but grin, the image of a certain short-haired florist edging its way into my mind. "I get that a lot."

"Well, come on in," she says, her hand on my back. "Everyone's going to be so happy to see you!" The smell of Christmas fills my senses as she pushes me through the door, and so does the sight and sound of Christmas. The house is as warm and colorful as it's been every December since I can remember -

the fireplace roaring, carols playing, and every available surface covered in holiday paraphernalia.

Dad turns from the coat closet, his face lighting up when he sees me. "Well, hey there, Sunshine!"

He's an inch or two shorter than I am, and when he hugs me his dark red beard scratches my earlobe. "Hi, Dad."

He's the round and jolly ginger Santa Claus to Mom's tall, dark, and freckled. People always thought they seemed like an odd couple, but I never did. Dad grabs her waist and gets on his tiptoes to kiss her cheek, and she giggles like a flustered schoolgirl.

"How's life in the big city?" he asks, and I chuckle. Neither Serenton nor Roseport is exactly a metropolis, but Roseport makes this sleepy little suburb look like Las Vegas.

"Great," I reply. "I've been getting a good bit of business lately."

"Good," he says, rubbing his hand over his shiny, bald scalp. "And how is the planning going for Julian's wedding?"

"Oh, they must be so excited," Mom coos, starry-eyed. "I still remember our wedding."

"Best day of my life," says Dad, once again going to his tiptoes to nuzzle his nose against hers.

"It's going really well," I nod. "I'm working with Felix's best friend to get everything arranged. She's a florist."

"You know what flowers I always liked," says Mom. "Daisies. Has she thought about daisies?"

I grin. "I'll ask."

"How is Julian?" Mom asks. "Oh, and Georgia! And all your new friends. I could just chat with you for hours."

"Well, let's not hold you hostage anymore," says Dad, ushering me toward the living room as if I don't know where it is. "Everyone else will want to get their hug in, too."

"Look who's here!" Mom choruses as we enter the living room, and seven heads turn. A couple of voices cry out my name.

"Form an orderly line," says Dad, and they actually do. One thing that time apart from my family as an adult has provided is a good sense of perspective - as a teenager I wouldn't have found this type of signature McConnell sentimentality as insanely amusing as it is.

Cameron is first in line (having pushed to the front), my perpetual 'baby brother' now a towering bear of a man. His dark hair is messy, and his thick Freddie Mercury 'stache has grown in since Thanksgiving - Georgia would be jealous. His embrace engulfs me.

"I'm suffocating," I croak jokingly, and he squeezes harder.

"This is for building a better sandcastle than me when we went to Florida," he whispers into my ear.

"That was only because you stole my favorite teddy bear," I protest, pushing the heels of my hands into his shoulder to wrench him off of me. "Now let go, Squirt."

He grins at the nickname - a product of his long years before the growth spurt which was *definitely* worth waiting for. "Good to see you again, Summer."

Then there's Wyatt, thin and freckled like Mom but with mine and Dad's same red hair, who pushes up his glasses before offering me a fist bump which naturally turns elaborate. I don't know if I'll ever lose the muscle memory of our secret handshake. When he'd first taught it to me, I'd idolized him and

Ryan as my cool older brothers (twins, three years my senior) and had practiced it for hours on end. Wyatt's cooler than me to this day, wearing a hoodie with his own incredible art printed on it.

"How's the business?" he asks.

"Good. Busy. How about yours?"

He laughs faintly, raising his eyebrows. "Turnabout's fair play, I guess. It's good. Busy, too." The handshake finally reaches its conclusion, a quick hug. "Don't worry- I won't ask you to bake."

"I appreciate it, Wy."

"As long as you don't ask me to draw," he says, holding his hand up at eye level and pointing at me.

"Wouldn't dream of it." He nods, satisfied, and steps out of the way for Ryan.

His hug comes about as quickly as Cam's, and with a kiss on my cheek. His face is just like Wyatt's, with Mom's strong jaw and Dad's more round snub nose, but his build is much thicker and his hair is brown and neatly styled. "Hey, Sunshine! We've all missed you."

He steps aside so his wife, Emily, can give me a hug too. Her body doesn't quite meet mine so she can avoid squishing baby Joey between us. Their other two kids, Jamie and Jessica, each hug one of my legs.

"It's so nice to see you again," Emily beams, dimples appearing on her smooth skin to accompany her bright, perfect smile. Her long jet black hair is tied in a neat braid, and the girls - Jamie at five and Jessica barely at two - are already spitting images of her, borrowing only Ryan's freckles and slightly more hazel eyes.

"Hi, Auntie Summer!" squeaks Jamie, the only one of the Zhao-McConnell kids currently speaking in full sentences.

"Hi there, cutie," I reply, leaning down to her level. She grins, her little front tooth missing. "Merry Christmas."

"Auntie Summer," she giggles. "It's not Christmas yet."

"Oh, silly me!" I cry, hitting my forehead with my palm. Ryan laughs. "I forgot. Santa comes tomorrow, though, right?"

She nods precociously. "We gotta leave him his cookies."

"Exactly," I agree. "We'll make them tomorrow. Do you want to help? I can show you how."

Her little eyes light up. "Yeah!"

I hear Wyatt laugh. "So much for getting away from work."

"You shut up, Uncle Wyatt," I tell him. "I'd do anything for my niece. Isn't that right, Jamie?" The little girl beams.

"We were just about to look at some of Wy's old family scrapbooks," says Mom from the couch.

"Sounds fun," I say, standing back up. I look down at Jamie. "You wanna see some awkward pictures of your dad?"

"Yeah!" she cries, and Ryan chuckles.

"Real nice, Summer."

"I know no allegiance but to the children," I counter, and we all make our way to sit down on the big sectional couch. Jamie nuzzles immediately into my side, and Jessica toddles up to me. Emily lifts her onto the couch with her free arm, and I'm sandwiched between my nieces.

"Oh, there's Uncle Cam with his favorite toy," I tell Jamie as Mom passes me a heavily decorated photo album. In a picture right on the first page, Cameron, about six or seven, sits proudly in the seat of an electric kiddie car.

"He loved to go hot rodding," says Dad, winking at Cam.

"Oh, there you go," I say, looking to the opposite page. The four of us are lined up in front of the bush that still sits outside this very house, posed awkwardly for a clearly forced family portrait. Wyatt and Ryan are probably about eleven, gangly as all hell and muddy as though they've been dragged directly from a wrestling match in the dirt. I tap my finger on Ryan, dressed in a too-large t-shirt, a pair of ripped jeans, and flip flops. "See, there's your dad."

Jamie giggles. "Daddy looks so silly!"

Ryan's laughing, too. "Definitely not my finest wardrobe choice."

Wyatt shifts, leaning forward to look closer. "We used to call that 'Ryan Chic'."

Shooting a dirty glare at his twin, Ryan says, "Oh, like you were so fashionable." Wy grins.

"And there's Uncle Wyatt," I go on, pointing at each kid. "And Uncle Cameron. And there's Aunt Summer."

She looks from the scrapbook to me. "You look different."

"I was probably only about eight," I tell her.

"Why do you look like a boy?" she asks, her little hand resting on the picture of my young face and tracing my short hair.

My stomach turns nervously and I look up and lock eyes with Emily, who nods lightly.

"Well, when I was born, the doctors said that I *was* a boy," I try gently, realizing I've never really considered having to talk to a kid about this - not as an adult. "Just like they did for your dad, and Uncle Wyatt and Uncle Cameron."

Her little hazel eyes look up at me, fathomless.

"And they all felt like that was right," I continue, "but I didn't. I felt like a girl. So, a couple years after this picture, I talked to Grandma and Grandpa and they helped me start doing things in a way that made me more comfortable. I started dressing how I wanted, and we started using different words to talk about me, like *she* and *her*." I nudge her gently. "And *Aunt*. Even though when I was born Grandma and Grandpa thought I was a boy, I'm a girl. Just like you and Jessica and your mom."

"That's called being transgender," Ryan adds, taking the term slowly so he's sure she'll catch it.

"There's actually a trans kid in her class," Emily says to me, rocking baby Joey in her arms. "I just don't think she's ever noticed."

"If you ever have any questions about it, you can ask me or your parents, okay?" I tell Jamie, and she nods thoughtfully. "Is there anything else you want to know?"

"I think I understand," she says.

"Good, I'm glad. Do you want to keep looking at pictures?"

She nods, reaching forward to turn the page herself. Then, her face lights up at a colorful spread full of drawings of flowers and pictures of the four of us in a flower field. "Pretty!"

Wyatt smiles faintly, leaning over to look at his handiwork. "Eh, I've made better flowers."

"You were, like, ten," Cameron prods.

"And now I'm, like, thirty," Wyatt replies, mimicking Cam's voice in a less-than-flattering way.

"This is you, Aunt Summer?" Jamie asks, pointing to a picture of a chubby redhead surrounded with wildflowers.

"Yes," I say, and she giggles. "What?"

"You were always the prettiest," she says, and my brothers all make gasps of offense.

"Jamie," Emily scolds, but even she doesn't sound too angry.

"On that note," Mom laughs, "who's hungry?"

My back is tired and my stomach is full by the time I finally head to my childhood room, set down my bags, and settle into bed. It's been a long day of catching up, watching Christmas movies, and reminiscing over thirteen editions of Wyatt's family photo scrapbooks.

"I'm gonna go see a couple friends," Cam says, pulling a jacket from his suitcase on the bed opposite mine. "I'll be back around ten."

"See you later," I reply. "Have fun! And if it's anybody I know, tell them hi."

He smiles from the doorway. "Sure thing."

For a second after he's gone, I swear I can hear crickets. My fingers start to itch, the kind of restless feeling that I'd usually remedy by heading to the kitchen to make a quick batch of brownies. But I don't quite see that as a viable option here, especially after I promised Mom *and* Wy that I'd cut back on the baking. Still, the tenseness in my chest just won't quite dissolve. I take in a breath, and with the slightest bit of relief even at the idea, I pick up my phone and dial.

She picks up after only a couple rings. "Hey," says Sadie, and the sound of her voice loosens the knot a bit more.

"Hey," I reply, and I can almost picture her smile - the left side of her lip pulled way up and that one crooked tooth peeking out from the right side - and feel the soft hug she'd give me. "How are you doing?"

"Can't complain," she says, her voice a little strained, like she's tired. I wonder for a second where she is - if she's lying in her childhood bedroom like I am. "What about you? How's the Brady Bunch?"

"They're good," I tell her with a short laugh. "Actually, my mom told me to ask you if you'd thought about daisies."

She snorts. "Like, am I aware that they exist?"

"Apparently they're her favorite," I respond. "But this is the woman who mistook our neighbor's son for her affair partner, so..." I giggle. "I'd recommend taking her words with a grain of salt."

"Noted," she says, humor edging into her voice, too. "How are your brothers? And you said Ryan had kids."

I feel almost flattered that she remembers. "They're great. I swear Cam is *still* growing. He's like a grizzly bear in a Drag Race t-shirt. That's my little brother." She hums in confirmation, and I keep going. "Wyatt's an artist, and he says his business is going well. And Ryan and his wife had another baby, Joey, a few months ago. He's adorable. But my niece Jamie, that's where my heart is."

"Yeah?"

"She's five," I explain, "and *so* sweet. We're baking cookies for Santa tomorrow."

"Aww," she says, her voice low. I feel suddenly warm, lying on top of my comforter in the dead of winter.

"I actually ended up explaining being trans to her today." I gulp a little bit. "I haven't had to talk about it with a kid before. And, I don't know, I was kind of worried she'd look at me differently. I know her parents are raising them right, but... you know."

Sadie's quiet for a second. It doesn't feel uncomfortable or judgmental - somehow it just feels like she's listening.

"I've been really lucky," I go on. "Even though I transitioned really young, I've never really had any trouble with people not getting it or acting, like, outright transphobic. And I'm better now, but... I've just always felt a little different."

I can practically see her brow knitting and her lips parting as I stare up at the ceiling, my own words echoing between my ears. Gingerly, she says: "Different from cis women, or different from everyone?"

Not quite sure what my answer is until I say it, I reply: "Both."

It hangs between us for a second, dead in the air. I feel my heart pounding dully against my ribcage. Finally, she says, "I mean, you *are* different from everyone. I've never known someone as kind as you are."

My cheeks are hot. "Really?"

"Yeah," she says, then sighs. "Can I tell you something?"

"Yeah," I reply. "Of course."

"My dad died almost a year ago."

"I'm so sorr-" I say quickly, but she cuts me off.

"Please don't be." I can better place the tiredness in her voice now - more weary than sleepy. "We weren't... things were never quite okay between us, but especially not after I came out. Anyway, it's our first Christmas without him, and my mom... She's never been good at addressing anything uncomfortable, or complicated, or... you know, anything. So it's been really shitty around here, her talking so much about how hard it is to be without him and just... totally glossing over why it's so hard for *me*."

"Sadie," I breathe, "that's so-"

"Hearing from you makes me feel better," she says, almost bluntly. "Reminds me there are people who don't see me as some weird, foreign thing. Who don't see me as 'different' for being who I am."

A small smile tugs at the corner of my mouth. "I'm glad, Sadie."

"You're not different because you're trans," she says.

"I know." I press my lips together, and I can almost feel her hand on my shoulder like that day in the parking lot. "Thank you."

"Thank *you*." she says. "You're a good friend. And you've made my shitty holiday a little bit more bearable."

"Do you want to talk again tomorrow?" I ask, and my stomach is fluttery. "I could tell you more about the Osmond Family Christmas Special going on in this house."

"*Osmond Family Christmas Special?*" she asks, laughing, and her return to a more typical attitude sends a rush of relief through me. "How old are you?"

"Could my Christmas gift be an end to the abuse?" I huff, feigning offense. "Or a copy of *Drone Cold*."

"Do *not* tell me they made a sequel to *Romancing the Drone*."

"Close, it's a Christmas-themed spinoff bonus chapter."

"*Yes*, Summer," she says, her voice strained through laughter like she's trying really hard to pretend she's tired of me. "I'd like to talk again tomorrow."

A shiver runs through my body. "Alright. Around this time?"

"Yeah," she says. "Mom usually makes dinner around six."

"Okay," I nod, sitting up on the bed. Suddenly I feel even more restless than before, a faint adrenaline lightly shocking me at the joints.

"Merry Christmas, Summer," she says. "Thanks again."

"Merry Christmas, Sadie."

Chapter Seventeen
Sadie Rings In The New Year

The lights are low in Felix and Julian's house, save for a bunch of flickering candles and a couple miniature disco balls resting on various countertops. Rio and Tae are camped out under the kitchen table with a plateful of grapes, Georgia and Carrie are sitting on the kitchen island, Khalil, Eleanor, Cecily, Matthew, and Axel share the couch, and Julian and Felix themselves are nestled in one another's arms directly under the TV. There's a melancholy feeling in my stomach, and I feel a little sick as I pull my legs up under me and try not to let my eyes linger. I take another sip of my champagne. I've had just enough that it doesn't ease or erase my sadness, just covers it with little champagne bubbles.

"Hey, stranger," says Summer, joining me in the little sitting nook by the window and setting a bowl of pretzels down between us. "I swear I almost got lost in that kitchen, and *I* used to live here."

"Thanks, I was starving," I say faintly as she settles into her chair.

"Totally."

Part of me is sadistically relieved that she still isn't seeing anyone - this way, I'm not the only sad sack in a group full of happy, in-love people without that built-in someone (or someones) in their life. This way, I'm not the only one starting the year the way I'll probably end it: not utterly, but certainly alone.

Of course, she's far from the worst person to spend the time with.

"Anyway," she says, pushing her curls over her shoulder and putting a pretzel in her mouth, "like I was saying, I didn't think *Drone Cold* quite reached the same level as the original. XJ didn't make as good a protagonist as V3."

"These are the robots," I say, eyebrows raised.

"Yes," she says quickly, a pit stop on what I can tell is about to be a verbal road trip. "So, at the end of *Drone Cold*, XJ and Katie still aren't together. They've had sex, but they aren't in a relationship. And the author put out an announcement on her

Instagram last week that they're going to be the stars of her next book-"

"*Stepping Drone?*" I suggest. "*Rolling Drone?*"

"*No Drone Unturned*," she replies, a bit of humor in her voice. "Anway. XJ is, like, kind of a douchebag. I'm sure it's supposed to appeal to that, like, 'I can fix him' demographic, but it's just not my thing. I'm going to read it, obviously, I just don't know if it'll dethrone the first one."

"*Romancing the Drone*," I say thoughtfully. "With a title like that, is… *V3* not also kind of a douchebag?"

She cocks her head to the side and purses her lips. I haven't seen her in person since the Christmas party, and I suddenly remember the observation I had about her mouth that night. I can't stop my eyes from going there, tracing the soft pink lines.

"He's not the friendliest," she says finally. "Not at first. But he isn't *mean*. He's just awkward and sort of shy, and when Isla actually gets to know him, he's totally sweet. And *already* perfect for her, no 'fixing' or changing necessary."

My face is suddenly a little warm, and my legs feel jittery. I look out at our friends, all engulfed in their own little conversations. "You know, I'm not sure I ever got the New Years hype."

"Yeah?" she asks, shifting in her chair.

"I mean, what? It's just a random day, and then we start writing the date differently on paperwork." I can feel her eyes on me, and I refuse to meet them. "I don't see what the big deal is."

She shrugs. "I guess I always just saw it as a good opportunity to look back on the year you've had, and how things have changed. I mean, a year ago, I lived in Chicago with Landon and had no friends. And look at me now."

"Sure," I concede, "I get that, even if I haven't exactly had the best year to look back on. I guess I just mean the big party, and the glitter, and all the cheering."

"Oh, so now you have something against glitter?" she says, and this forces a laugh out of me.

"You must think I'm the biggest grouch in the entire world," I say.

"I mean, you *have* professed to hate my favorite book, the entire concept of Halloween, standard Christmas cookie shapes, *and* sunshine," she says, and I reach out to lightly hit her arm before I really even think about it.

"I don't think I said *all* of that."

"I get what you mean, though," she continues. "It's kind of a lot for just a change in calendars." She makes a sweeping gesture to the rest of the house. "Even the old people, just sitting around watching a televised ball drop and waiting for that midnight kiss."

I snort, though my face feels even warmer. "The *midnight kiss*. Why do people even care so much about that?"

"Our friends definitely seem excited at the prospect."

"They can kiss whenever they want," I say flippantly. "But, like, why is it a tradition in the first place?"

"I think I've heard that going without one is, like, an omen for a year of loneliness," she says, lifting another pretzel to her mouth. Involuntarily, my eyes follow its trajectory toward her lips.

"I'm not sure I believe that," I reply. "I kissed Charlie last New Years, and you and I both know how my dating life has been this year."

"I don't know." She brushes a lock of hair behind her ear. "I kissed Landon, and that obviously didn't work out, but coming back to Roseport... I'm less lonely than I've been in a long time."

A thought, at the back of my mind, comes quietly first. I could ask her to kiss me. We could kiss each other.

"Sorry you don't have anyone to kiss this year," I comment casually, my cheeks burning. "You know, to lock it in."

I could ask her. She might not want to, but I could ask.

"I'm not quite that superstitious," she says. "I don't imagine you guys are going away anytime soon just because there's no one for me to kiss tonight."

A low chant comes up from all around the living room and kitchen. "*Ten.*"

"No," I tell her, my fingers itching. "We're not going anywhere."

"*Nine.*"

"I must just have enough good karma left over from the last two years of New Years kisses," she says.

"*Eight.*"

"Yeah." I can barely feel my face. "You must."

"*Seven.*"

"How about you?" she says, her brown eyes flicking downward ever-so-slightly. "Have you really felt so lonely this year?"

"*Six.*"

"No," I reply. "I don't guess I have, not with all these friends."

"*Five.*"

I could ask her. I *should* ask her.

"*Four.*"

"So maybe that kiss last year *did* work," she says.

"*Three.*"

"Yeah," I say, my heartbeat pounding in my ears. "Maybe."

"*Two.*"

She takes a breath, her mouth open before she even speaks. "Do you-"

"*One!* Happy New Year!" the voices erupt through the house, and I quickly join in on the exclamations. I gulp, cutting my gaze sideways at Summer for the smallest of seconds as she cheers along with everyone. I shake my head, trying to shake away the thoughts, too. I must be more intoxicated than I thought.

"Did you want some more champagne?" Summer asks, holding up her own empty glass.

"I'd better not," I tell her, trying to will the red flush out of my cheeks. "I have work in the morning."

I'm seeped in the smell of shame when I get back home around two in the morning, and Ethel's right in front of the door as I wrench it open, tail wagging rapidly.

"Hi," I coo. "Did you miss me?" She proceeds to give me one emphatic lick across the face, her whole body shaking with the force of her happiness.

"I know," I tell her, stroking the top of her head. "I wish I could play with you for a bit, but it's bedtime. How about tomorrow?"

She dutifully follows me to the bedroom and into bed, her tail standing straight upward like a salute and making her look overall like a droopy-eyed little soldier at attention.

She snuggles into my side eagerly and lets out a sigh as she gets cozy. I pull my arm out from under the duvet and scratch lightly behind her ears.

"Good dog," I tell her with a yawn, already getting a little drowsy as her breaths grow deeper and heat emanates from her body.

"Look at you," says Macy as I walk in, "bravely pretending not to be hungover."

"I'm not hungover," I reply, pulling on my apron and joining her at the counter.

"Since you still refuse to come out and party with me, I've just been forced to believe that you're into even crazier shit than I am," she says, flicking her ponytail from one shoulder to the other. "Admit it, you spent the night doing ketamine in some back alley outside an exclusive nightclub with a bunch of models and musicians."

"In Roseport," I deadpan.

"Maybe you caught a five-hour red-eye flight from LA to get to work on time," she suggests. "I don't know your life."

"What are we doing today?" I ask, stepping away from the clock-in computer. "I'm thrilled to be off of poinsettias."

"Rob wants us to make a display," she says. "There are a bunch of new flowers in the back. Let me go get them."

I nod, and a second later she's back with an armful of white and light blue blooms. I grab a vase and some ribbon from under the counter as she sets them down.

"So," she says, "any New Years resolutions?"

"I don't really do that stuff," I reply, absentmindedly moving the flowers around on the table to see them in different positions. "I'm a little too old to actually believe I'm going to fix anything about myself."

"I'm going to be more bold," she declares.

This gets a laugh out of me. "*You?* What's left to do? Streak across the freeway?"

She laughs, cutting a long piece of ribbon to go around the neck of the vase. "See, I always forget how fucking mean you are. I love it."

"You would," I retort, and she giggles like a little kid.

"I guess if I were going to delude myself into thinking I'll change something this year," I offer after a minute, "I'd say it was to actually get out of my apartment every once in a while. I've been doing alright lately, but *god* is the call of the TV enticing."

"That just seems like something you'd say to get me off the trail of your wild partying," she says. "I won't be fooled, Sadie."

I press my lips together. "Then I suppose that's your prerogative. Pass me the scissors, please."

"I'm so glad our schedules finally aligned," Felix says, settling onto his couch opposite me. "It's been too long since we had a girls day."

"Yeah, like thirteen years," I reply.

"Don't be so rigid," he scolds, emphatically punching the buttons on the remote. "I swear, you cis people. Do you wanna watch *Clueless* or *13 Going On 30?*"

"*Clueless*," I reply without hesitation.

"How has work been?" he asks as the opening credits start to play.

"Work," I say simply.

"You love florist-ing," he says, and I choose to gloss over the gross misuse of my job title as a verb.

"It's not as fun when it's not for your wedding," I respond, reaching to steal a handful of popcorn from the bowl in his lap.

"How is that going, by the way?" He tries to smack my hand, but misses by a hair as I pull it away. "Anything new?"

"Summer and I haven't had a chance to do any more planning yet." My stomach churns ever so slightly at the mention of her name - even though she never caught wind of it, I can't help but be mortified by what I was thinking at the New Years party the other day. It's not even like I *actually* want to kiss her -

but if I did, why on earth would I ever be so deluded as to think she'd want to kiss me?

"That's okay," he says. "It doesn't sound like you have much left to do, do you?"

"No, not much," I confirm. "So how is *your* job treating you? I assume the diamond-encrusted Mercedes is in the garage."

"How tacky do you think I am?" He flattens his palm to his chest in a display of righteous outrage. "It's a *Bugatti*."

What would usually only earn an amused eye roll instead brings me out into giggles, probably just for the pure absurdity of his performance. After a second he falls into them, too, and it's like we're nine again and about two minutes away from my mom ripping the top blanket off our fort and telling us *time to go to sleep*.

"I think I might've found something to wear to the wedding," I tell him as the laughter dies down. His eyes go wide and he scrambles to pause the movie.

"I'm so fucking excited," he says. "Tell me everything."

"I saw this top at that one boutique on Main," I tell him, turning my phone to show it to him. It's a dark orange satin material with thin straps, a low-cut cowl neck, and a dainty brown flower pattern. "What do you think?"

"Sadie," he coos, taking the phone out of my hand. "It's so cute!"

"Yeah?" I frown a little bit. "It's not too…" I gesture vaguely.

"Sadie," he says, narrowing his eyes at me, "your tits are fantastic and you would be doing the world a *disservice* not to show them off."

"*Felix.*" I laugh. "Okay, point taken."

"I think it'd be perfect," he says. "With a pair of, like, white cigarette pants? You'd look stunning."

"Really?" I nudge his leg with my foot. "You'd let me wear white to your wedding?"

"You've seen my dress," he replies with a cheeky grin. "I guarantee, there will be *no* confusion about who to pay attention to."

"I should have known," I concede. "I don't think I could pull focus from you if I tried."

"Not on my wedding day," he says, shaking his head so that his fluffy black hair bounces with the movement. "Oh, but speaking of pulling focus! Are you excited for the 16th?"

I suddenly feel a little sick. "Sure."

"I know you've never been *crazy* about your birthday, but you deserve a day to celebrate the amazing, talented, gorgeous person you are," he prods, leaning forward to poke my calf. "You can spend the day holed up in your apartment if you want, but you can also do literally anything else."

I still feel uneasy, but I nod. "You're right."

"How about Jules and I throw you a little party here?" he offers, his hand now making soothing circles on my knee. "None of the big to-do, just our friends and a night of *How Great Is Sadie*."

"World's worst game show," I comment lamely.

"More like *world's best*," he cries. "I would absolutely win that game. Loving you is, like, my favorite hobby. So what do you say?"

With a performative eye roll, I nod my head. No matter how anxious the idea of my birthday still makes me feel, I can't deny him this. Not when it makes him look so happy.

"Yes!" he yells, and springs forward to hug me, effectively crushing me into the couch. "Sadie, this is going to be so great. I'll take care of everything. You won't even have to lift a finger. I'm so *excited*."

I can't help the smile that grows on my face, even as I shove him back to his side of the couch. "Just play the movie, dork."

Chapter Eighteen

Summer Celebrates

"Hey!" Julian and Felix chorus, hugging me as soon as I walk through the door.

"Hey!" I reply, squeezing Julian a little tighter before letting go. "Where's the birthday girl?"

"I think Rio's holding her hostage in the kitchen," says Julian, straightening the collar of his leather jacket.

"We're just about to eat," Felix says. "Come on in."

I follow them into the kitchen, where indeed Sadie leans against the countertop opposite an animatedly talking Rio. I drop the card in my hand onto a spot on the counter where a few other ones sit, and Sadie's eyes drift upward toward mine.

"Hey, Summer," she says, a small smile on her lips. She's a bit more dressed up than usual, with her pixie cut slightly more gel-slicked and her typical t-shirt replaced with a turquoise blouse which stands out in contrast with her dark hair and light skin.

"Hey!" I cut between her and Rio to give her a hug. She smells like perfume instead of the usual floral scent. "Happy birthday!"

She pulls back, her smile not quite reaching her eyes. "Thanks."

"Okay, kids, soup's on," says Julian from the stove, and Georgia lets out a whistle from the table.

"Since there's no cake, can we sing happy birthday over the pasta?" she asks.

"I'll kill you, Georgia," Sadie replies, moving past me and toward them. "Don't think I won't."

"We'll all just sing it in our heads," Khalil offers as I sit down.

"I'll hear you," Sadie warns. My stomach turns - she seems a bit more upset than she is joking, a balance she's usually far on the other end of. There's something unusually jagged in her tone, and I can't find the comical light in her eyes.

"Has she always been like this?" Rio asks Felix as they both slide into their chairs.

"Yep," he says. "As far as Sadie's concerned, today is just another day. Everyone act accordingly."

So maybe this is just normal. Sadie just hates her birthday, and there's nothing else wrong. I try to soothe the nerves scrambling across my body, but they won't quite go away.

"Alright," Georgia says with a shrug. "Does anyone have a recommendation for a good toaster?"

Khalil snorts as Julian begins to set everyone's food down in front of them. "Pardon?"

"Carrie and I had been using this, like, hundred-year-old toaster her mom gave her, but it totally crapped out, like, a month ago," they continue. "We've been looking for a new one, but nothing so far is living up to our standards."

"Your *standards*?" Rio repeats. "How much toast are you people eating that it has *this* big of an effect on your daily life?"

"The toaster at your place is shitty," Georgia says dismissively, waving her hand at them.

Their jaw falls open. "When have you made toast at my place?"

"Khalil," Georgia says, turning to him like a vulture. "What kind of toaster do you guys use?"

He puts his hands up defensively. "I didn't buy it. You'd have to ask Cecily."

"My toaster is-" I begin.

"I unpacked that toaster," they interrupt me. "I've got to say, I think it's too fancy even for Carrie and I."

"It's fancy?" I ask.

"You can go look at our toaster," offers Felix, turning over his shoulder to point to it.

"After I finish my pasta," she says. "Are we doing anything after dinner, Sadie?"

"Don't look at me," Sadie deadpans, and the concern in the pit of my stomach bubbles up again.

"We're all gonna sit in the living room and watch *The Princess Bride*," Felix says, casting what I can tell is a playfully loaded glance her way. "It's what we've done since we were kids."

"Cute!" Rio cries. "Are we changing into our PJs, too?"

"Felix certainly will," says Julian with a slight nudge to his fiancé's shoulder.

Sadie seems restless as we all settle in in the living room and Felix starts up the movie. The ancient DVD player is loudly whirring with effort and the previews have barely started when she stands up out of her chair.

"I'm going to go check on the pansies I planted," she announces, heading toward the back door.

"Are you sure?" Felix asks, twisting around in his seat. "You'll miss the beginning."

"I could recite it from memory," she retorts, but the fire I've come to expect from this kind of response feels dim. "It'll be alright. I'll be back in a second."

"You don't want me to pause it?"

"I'll be back in a second," she presses, and still I can't help but feel the slightest edge to her voice. Without any further discussion, the door closes behind her.

I look around the room for a second, unable to shake the feeling that something's wrong. A quick glance at Felix's face tells me he's fighting similar doubts, and I lean forward.

"I'm gonna go..." I trail off, cutting my eyes toward the door. Felix sucks in his lips and nods.

Sadie doesn't turn when the door opens and closes behind me, just stays squatted in front of a patch of magenta flowers.

"Hey," I try quietly.

"Hey," she replies faintly. Her voice is uncharacteristically soft.

There's a heavy weight of anxiety in my stomach. Now that I'm out here, I don't know exactly what my plan is. "Are those the pansies?"

She nods. "They could be doing better, but they're alright."

"I think they look really nice." She still doesn't turn, and I awkwardly slide into one of the patio chairs.

A silence hangs in the air for a moment, and she stands up to look out at the whole garden. In the dark, I can almost see where Felix and Julian will put a makeshift altar and where they'll walk down the aisle.

"I wish I had something like this," Sadie says, almost under her breath.

I perk up. "What, a house?"

"I mean, yeah," she laughs, turning. Her gelled hair has the slightest sheen in the moonlight, but there's a steely sardonic light in her eyes as she sits in the chair next to mine. "But..."

Her voice trails off, and I ache to comfort her and to cover her hand on the chair's hand rest with my own. I suppress the urge, trying not to let my stare bore into her as she seems to process her thoughts.

"Twenty-eight isn't old," she says finally. "*Thirty* isn't old."

I nod.

"But I just feel like I don't have anything permanent to, like, show my successes," she continues. "I don't have a house, or a big impressive job title. It's like... I don't know. I've done so much, but I don't have anything to show for it. You and Felix and

Julian and all our friends... it's like you're all actually adults and I'm just pretending."

My lips part, but I can't quite find the words. "Sadie... I'm so sorry you feel that way."

She rests her head on her fist, looking out at the yard absently. "Yeah."

I reach out and lay my palm against her arm. "I think *most* people our age feel like they have 'nothing to show for it'. I mean, yeah, Khalil and Felix and Julian have houses, and I own my own business. But you're not *behind*."

She takes in a big breath and nods slowly.

"And not to sound cheesy," I add, stroking my thumb across the skin of her forearm. She leans ever so slightly into the touch, and the knot in my chest loosens. "But even with my business this year, there's one thing I'm prouder of."

She rolls her eyes, but the smile on her lips is undeniable. "God, don't say it, I'll puke."

"I wouldn't have been happy in Chicago even if I'd been able to take Sweet Summer full time," I tell her.

"I know," she says with a mocking edge. "You're happy because you have *friends*."

"*You* have friends," I correct. "There are a bunch of people in there who love you, and who don't care how 'successful' you are. And for the record, *I'm* proud of everything you've accomplished, whether you have a house or a cool job title or not." I don't add what I maybe could add - that I'm not just happy because I *have* friends. I'm happy because of who those friends are, and she just may be the one I'm happiest about.

She presses her other hand to mine, squeezing gently. "Thank you, Summer."

My lips quirk upward. "Of course."

"Let's head back inside before we miss it," she says, pulling herself up out of the chair. Her smile still isn't quite as radiant as usual, but it's much better than before. I return the smile and follow her in.

"Guys," Felix hisses an hour and a half later, "Sadie's crying."

"Shut the fuck up, I am not," Sadie replies froggily, frantically wiping her face with the back of her hand as Westley, Buttercup, Inigo, and Fezzik ride off on their white horses.

"Sadie!" coos Rio. "Don't feel bad, babe! I've cried on every single birthday since I was ten."

"It's a good movie," Sadie croaks.

"Yes it is, baby," says Felix, rubbing her back.

"Do you want to look at your cards now?" Julian asks her as the credits start to roll.

"Are you guys *trying* to make it worse?" she replies with her usual humor, wiping under her eyes again.

"I'll go get them from the kitchen," says Georgia dutifully, hopping up from their seat like a dog anticipating a game of fetch.

A minute later, Sadie is holding a pile of envelopes and the rest of us are sitting in a semicircle around her. She grandly shuffles the stack like a deck of cards, finally drawing a bright orange envelope. Felix pops up.

"Oh, that's not all there is to that one." He darts into the hallway that leads to his bedroom.

"You asshole, I specifically said no gifts!" Sadie calls after him. I can't help but notice that the tension in her shoulders is all but gone, and she's carrying herself in a much more carefree fashion than she did earlier this evening. I feel warmer as Felix races back into the room, a small gift bag in his hands.

"Don't be a baby," he replies, handing it to her. She gives a performative huff and opens the envelope. Her gaze softens as her eyes scan the card, and finally they flick back up to Felix's face.

"You're a son of a bitch, you know that?" she says, and he's already leaning forward to hug her. They hold each other for a moment, and when Sadie pulls away she says, "I don't even need to ask what this is, do I?"

He shakes his head as she pulls the gift bag into her lap. "Nope."

She pulls out a little clay pot glazed with a sweeping rainbow arch. We all "ooh" as she shows it off.

"I'll put it with my twenty-three *other* hand painted clay pots," she says, sticking her tongue out at Felix.

"Twenty-*two*," he corrects, pointing a finger at her. "You broke the one I gave you for your seventh birthday when you were moving into your freshman dorm."

"And you'll never let me live it down," she replies, setting the pot on the coffee table and picking up another envelope. "I'm moving on."

As she slides her finger under the flap of the envelope, I recognize it as the card I brought. My body tenses. Her lips quirk up at the corners as she reads the little note I wrote, and I try to imagine which words align with which expressions - is that flash in her eyes about *happy* or *grateful?* Is that cute scrunch of her nose in response to *can't wait to spend more time with you* or *hope this year is the best one yet?*

Her smile is positively luminous when, after what feels like hours, she finally looks at me.

"Thank you so much, Summer," she says, briefly biting her bottom lip between sentences. "That's really sweet."

She gets up to hug me, and as I feel her soft embrace I find myself not wanting her to let go. Everything in my body seems to relax at her touch. There's just something about the way she fits into my arms like a puzzle piece, her head on my shoulder and mine on hers. She squeezes me once and lets go, and without consulting me in the matter my eyes flick straight to her lips and glue themselves there. Luckily, she turns back around before she notices and I lightly shake my head, trying to rid myself of the thought. She starts opening the next card.

Suddenly, though, I can't stop thinking about what would have happened if I'd actually asked her to kiss me on New Years. I can't stop imagining her arms around me and her mouth covering mine. I blink rapidly as Sadie reads Georgia's card, trying to make sense of myself.

I'm laser-focused on every minute detail of her: the way she pushes her hair behind her ear, the way her blouse drapes over her collarbones, the way her green eyes carefully move over the card and the way her lips curve upward when she looks up at Georgia. *Why am I feeling like this?*

My stomach drops. *Oh, shit.*

Chapter Nineteen

Sadie Takes Care of Business

"I can't believe they would vote Tisha off," Summer says, the newest episode of Tropic Like It's Hot blaring on the TV in front of us. "She was the glue holding the entire group together! Now the whole show is just gonna be Chloe and Kaley getting into fights over Aaron."

I nod, not tearing my eyes away from the screen even as I pick up and eat a cookie. "That is, if the producers don't decide to bring Jasper back just for the drama." My words ring in my ears, and I have to marvel for a second that I've managed to get this unironically obsessed with a trashy heterosexual 'dating' show.

"No way," she replies. "He's already come back to the island *twice* this season. They can't keep going back to that well."

Just then, the camera moves to follow a mysterious figure as he walks onto the beach where the rest of the cast is hanging out. The dark curls on the back of his head are pretty unmistakable - especially for the two of us, who've been watching the show all year - but Summer leans forward incredulously, only sitting back when Jasper turns to show his face to the camera.

"Son of a bitch," she breathes, half defeated and half impressed.

The commercial break starts, and she turns to me. She looks soft and cozy in a light pink sweat set with her red hair in a bun, messier than the kind she'd wear while baking. "What are we even going to do for the next few weeks when we're too busy at work to watch the episodes as they come out?"

My face feels oddly warm. "I won't watch them without you if you won't watch them without me," I offer, raising my eyebrows.

She nods immediately, her face serious. "Deal."

Ethel, nestled between us, lets out a hearty snore. Summer giggles, leaning forward to pet her, and there's a tickly feeling in my chest.

"So." I reach for another cookie. "I assume that means you're all booked up for Valentine's Day, too."

"Yep," she says. "If I don't eat or sleep for the next two and a half weeks, I can get it all done no problem." She cracks a smile immediately, as though she already knows how I'll react.

I take the bait. "Don't even joke about that." This just makes her giggle even more, and my stomach flutters.

"I'm sure it's nothing compared to what goes on at the flower shop," she says. "I'm kind of just picturing the aftermath of a tornado through a giant rosebush."

"Yeah, that's pretty close." I shrug. "Just add a bunch of people running and screaming like they're in a zombie apocalypse, and you've pretty much got it."

"Well, I'm glad you get your last moments of sanity before then," she says with a motion toward the TV, and I almost don't register the irony of Tropic Like It's Hot being included in "moments of sanity".

"I'm glad I get to spend some time with you before we both get busy," I say before I can think better of it. She gives me a smile that makes her brown eyes look especially warm. I almost feel a chill through me when the show comes back on and her gaze goes straight back to the TV. It's a split second before mine joins her.

On February 14, Inspiration Florals is a war zone. Endless shades of pink and red are burned into my retinas, and for once I'm thankful for my ability to do the job on autopilot as my mind circles the drain. I'm manning the register and doing my best to keep everything moving as quickly as possible, but the line still trails out the door.

Macy, who started her shift with a hundred little meticulously drawn hearts around her eyelids in place of her usual thick winged eyeliner, is sweaty and messy as she races around the store with Crystal, Vivian, and Ollie.

"Hi there," I say brightly as a man leaves the line and another takes his place. "Welcome to Inspiration Florals. How can I help you today?"

"I'm here to pick up an arrangement I ordered online," he says, straightening the collar of his dress shirt. "Last name Collins."

"Gotcha," I reply. "You'll actually want to go see Rob over there." I point at my boss in the far corner of the countertop by the store phone, supervising the case of already-prepared online orders with an iron fist. The man nods and heads that way.

"Hi there," I say again as a woman shifts to the front of the line. "Welcome to Inspiration Florals. How can I help you today?"

"I'd like to get a custom arrangement," she says, and I cringe internally. Someone always has to be *that* guy right when we're already incredibly busy. Still, I nod and start to open my mouth to respond. She just keeps on trucking.

"I'll need it to be ready pretty quickly," she says, raising her voice slightly over the sound of the phone ringing, "so you can use whatever flowers you already have, I just have some specific-"

"I'm gonna go ahead and send you over to my coworker," I say forcefully, craning my neck to see who's the least busy. "Macy, would y-"

"Sadie," Rob's voice echoes across the store and I turn my head quickly. He raises the phone in his hand. "There's a call for you. She says her name is Olivia."

My heartbeat all but stops, then promptly begins racing, and I turn back around, eyes wide. Macy meets my gaze, her face quickly turning to concern. I motion vaguely at the spot where I'm standing, and she quickly replaces me. Rob, looking grave, hands me the phone.

"What's wrong?" my voice quivers into the receiver.

I can barely hear Olivia over the blood pounding in my ears, but everything I need for now is evident in her voice alone. I look at Rob with what must be a great deal of desperation in my eyes, and he nods silently.

The Pennsylvania cold seems especially biting as I rush out the back door toward my car, still haphazardly pulling on my coat with one hand while I use the other to shoot off a text to the group chat explaining that I'm headed to my apartment and then to the emergency vet.

Just as the car door closes behind me, my phone rings. I put it on speaker and start the car. "Hello?"

"Sadie," says Summer's voice, and I feel a rush of chills through me as a blast of cold air erupts from the vents. "I'm headed to my car right now. I'll meet you outside your building."

My whole head suddenly burns, and I have to steel myself to focus on pulling out of the parking lot and onto the road. My lips feel numb as I reply, "You don't have to do that."

"I want to," she says, the sweet cadence of her voice comforting me a bit even now. I let out a deep breath.

Olivia is waiting for me in the apartment, a thick worry line between her eyebrows. She starts talking the second she sees me, following as I race to a lethargic Ethel lying in her dog bed.

"I noticed she was having trouble when I took her on her walk," she says, her words rushed and almost unintelligible. "And then she was vomiting and gagging, and there was more drool than usual, which are all signs you have to look out for with-"

"Olivia, do you have other clients to take care of today?" I kneel next to Ethel and graze my hand on the top of her head. Her droopy brown eyes look up at me and her tail wags lamely.

Olivia blinks. "Yes, but-"

"Thank you for helping," I say, gingerly lifting Ethel into my arms. She feels stiff, tensing up from the pain. "I can take her from here. I'll keep you updated on how she's doing."

It seems for a second like Olivia might protest, but instead she just grabs Ethel's carrier and helps me slide her into it, then follows me out of the building.

Summer is in the parking lot, her hair tied back and her clothes still dusted with flour. I feel a twinge of guilt deep in the pit of my stomach, but her eyes light up at the sight of me and the dog carrier and she follows me to my car without much greeting.

The entire process at the vet goes by in a blur. Summer sits beside me in the almost endlessly white void that is the waiting room, but she doesn't reach out or try to touch me. I'm grateful for this; I almost feel like I'm vibrating as I sit there with Ethel and her carrier in my lap, staring daggers at the bay of doors across the way.

"Levine?" comes a voice finally, *finally* as a woman in scrubs peeks out from one of the doorways. I spring upward and give a look back to Summer, who looks back and forth between me and the chairs, silently asking me where I need her. I grit my teeth and shake my head before following the woman back to an exam room, unaccompanied.

Time here moves just as slowly. The veterinarian gently pulls Ethel out of the crate and asks me some questions, which I robotically answer as she inspects the dog's body. She then tells me she'll need to perform some X-rays and takes Ethel off into another room, leaving me once again in the constricting embrace of waiting.

I don't know how long it is before the vet comes back, and immediately my stomach drops when I see that Ethel isn't with her. Her face is understanding, and she sits across from me over the exam table.

"Is she going to be okay?" I'm taken aback by how childlike my voice sounds, how small and fragile.

"She has an intestinal blockage," says the vet. "It doesn't look like a foreign object on our X-rays, so there's a very real possibility it could be an intestinal tumor."

My hand flies to my mouth almost involuntarily, and tears sting at the corners of my eyes.

"Not all tumors are cancerous," she continues. "We'll have to perform a biopsy to know that, but we'll want to remove it either way."

I nod numbly, biting down on my lower lip.

"At her age, surgery is a more significant risk," she says, "but as a rule I don't turn dogs down for that. I know how important a pet can be, and I never want to take away their chance for several more good years." She leans forward, putting a hand on my knee. "The best case scenario for this surgery, Ms. Levine, is a full recovery and several more good years, even at fourteen. But the worst case scenario-"

I hold up a hand and squeeze my eyes shut. I can't bear to let her finish that sentence. Instead, I take a deep breath and nod. "I know."

"It's up to you," she says gently. "Whatever you want to do."

The ache in my chest is so strong I feel like crumpling to the ground. I have to take several deep breaths which still come out jagged before I can even begin to formulate a response.

Chapter Twenty

Summer Drops Everything

I can't stop checking the time on my phone and staring at the door Sadie left through; ten minutes, then fifteen, twenty, thirty. I worry I'll wear a hole in the carpet with my compulsively tapping toe, only stopping when a dim figure emerges from the door with a familiar carrier in hand.

She looks like a zombie as she makes her way back, dropping the empty carrier at my feet and then flopping into the chair next to me, her head in her hands. Cautiously, I rest my hand between her shoulder blades.

"I *hate* hospitals," she says finally, her voice gravelly as she barely lifts her face out of her palms. I nod, gently massaging the spot where my hand lies. A few moments later, she finally offers: "They're going to keep her for about three days, more if she has trouble recovering after the surgery. She has something blocking her intestine, probably a tumor."

"Oh, Sadie," I breathe, bringing my other hand to her forearm.

I notice now that her eyes look puffy from tears. "Then it'll be a few days after *that* for them to figure out if it's cancer."

This knocks the wind right out of my lungs. Not sure what else to do, I hook my arm through hers and gently pull us both to our feet. "Come on, babe, let's get you home."

She nods faintly, unfocused almost as if she's sick herself. Still holding her arm, I point out my hand, palm toward the ceiling.

"Maybe I should drive."

"Bed or couch?" I ask as the apartment door closes behind us.

"I can do it," she says, but stumbles immediately out of my grasp. I pull her back toward me.

"I don't want you to hurt yourself, Sadie," I reply gently, curling my hand around her waist. "Bed or couch?"

"Bed," she says finally, and I walk her down the hallway and into her bedroom. The foot of the bed is only a few feet from the doorway, and as we pass it she reaches out to the mattress for support. I gingerly pull back the covers at the head of the bed for her to crawl in, and she seems to turn to putty as she climbs into bed.

"There," I say, pulling the blankets back up over her. "Do you think you want to sleep? Or just sit?"

"Just sit," she says, though her tone belies a certain level of exhaustion. Still, I push gently upward on her shoulder so I can fluff up her pillows, then hand her the remote from her bedside table. She turns the TV on, seeming to stare straight through it as she flicks through an endless menu of streaming services. I settle into the chair at the vanity by her bed.

She shifts, looking over at me with wide eyes. "What are you doing?"

"I'm staying with you," I say.

"You need to go back to work," she says.

My response bubbles up almost like a burp. "No." I clear my throat as if to clear away the overly emotional reaction. "I don't want to leave you alone."

"It's Valentine's Day," she says, her fingers curled around the covers like a little kid having a sick day in a cartoon. "You must still have a ton of orders you need to do."

"But-" It dies in my throat, and I'm lucky she cuts me off.

"But nothing." Her tone is as stern as she can muster, still the tiniest bit weak.

But what? I have to ask myself. *But they're not important? But you're* more *important?* What had I meant to say?

"Go," she says. "There's no way you can handle that kind of dip in your profits or your reputation, not this early in the game."

I can't help but chuckle. "Leave it to you to criticize me, no matter the circumstance."

Her face doesn't turn to its usual brightened state in response to a joke, instead falling into a light frown. "I'm sorry."

My eyes widen. "You don't-"

"You're a really good friend," she says, her voice soft. "I love you, no irony."

I tense, immediately feeling bad for my mind making the comment something it's not. Even though it's something we've never said to one another before, she's my *friend*. The way the words make my heart beat faster feels almost disrespectful to her. I swallow the feeling down.

"I love you too," I say, the admission feeling jagged and inappropriate on my tongue.

"Now *go*," she says, that beautiful laugh finally returning. "Don't deprive the lovers of Roseport of their delicious desserts."

"I'll have you know, I don't just serve Roseport," I reply. "I also have customers in Serenton, Graceburgh, *and* Petersford."

She laughs, exasperated. "Summer."

I hesitate, biting my lip and studying her face, uncharacteristically pale. "Are you sure you'll be okay?"

"*Yes*." She raises her eyebrows.

"Text me if you need anything," I say finally. "Please. I won't be able to leave otherwise."

"I will." She leans back on the pillows, her eyes falling as she disappears into her thoughts. "Can I have a hug?"

"Of *course*." I'm at her side in an instant, and she practically falls into my arms, her head resting on my chest. Just like before, her touch alone calms me down, too. I squeeze gently at first, but when her grip tightens, so does mine. I don't let go until she does.

"Thank you," she murmurs, sinking further into the blankets.

"Anything you need, alright?" I repeat, backing out of the bedroom door. "I don't care if you're just really cozy and don't want to go all the way to the kitchen for a snack. Call me."

"If I need someone to suffocate me with a pillow, I know exactly who to go to," she retorts, her usual biting tone bringing a welcome levity to my mood.

"Alright, alright, I'm going." I pause at the doorway, looking at her and her glowing smile for just a second longer. I can't believe I'm only just now realizing how incredibly happy that smile makes me. It's even staggering for a moment - I *really* like her, maybe more than I've ever liked anyone.

I shake the thought away. The *nerve* of me, to be thinking about that while she's feeling the way she is, and when there's absolutely no way she'd be interested in dating me, or anyone. "Bye."

"Bye." I force myself to turn around.

Back at my apartment, I turn the ringer on my phone all the way up before resuming my work. I only have a few more things to actually make, and most everything once I'm done with that will just be deliveries. A few notifications make me jump, but they all turn out to be different messages in the group chat of Sadie explaining the situation to everyone else and them giving their best wishes. When anyone asks if she needs anything, she always says that she'd prefer to be alone. Each time, it brings a pang to my chest.

Once all the Valentine's stuff is finally done, I get back home and exhaustedly fall onto the couch. For as tired as I am, my mind is still racing, and there's that restless feeling in my fingers. Just as I begin to stand up and go do a bit more baking to ease the feeling, my phone rings.

"Hello?" I ask immediately.

"Hey," says Sadie, and somehow I both feel calmer and more on edge, my heartbeat thrumming against my chest. "The vet called. Ethel's out of surgery."

"That's good," I say, my voice light. "How's she doing?"

"They said she seems okay," she says. "But it's too early to really tell. If everything goes right, she'll be ready to come home on Thursday."

"Good." I don't say anything else for a second, leaving the air open for her if there's anything else she wants to add.

"Did you get everything done?"

"Yes, I did," I reply, letting out a bit of a laugh. "Like fifteen minutes ago."

"Good," she says. "I'm very proud. You survived Valentine's Day."

"It was touch-and-go for a minute there," I admit dryly. "Is everything gonna be okay at work?"

"Yeah, my boss was the one who took Olivia's call," she says, and her voice sounds the smallest bit more distant. "He's not going to schedule me until I'm sure Ethel's alright and I feel okay going back."

"That's good," I say, very aware that I'm sounding like a broken record and holding back the urge to ask her a hundred cloying questions about what she needs, how she's feeling.

"What are you up to now that you're over the Valentine's hump?"

"I was actually just about to head to the kitchen and make something," I admit, and I can almost picture her brows furrowing and her mouth twisting into that angry-bunny-rabbit frown.

"Don't you dare," she snaps. "You just got through what will almost certainly be the busiest day of the year for your business. *Relax*."

"You know, you keep telling me to do that," I say, fighting back a playful smile. "I'm just not sure I know how."

"You're a smart kid," she says. "I'm sure you can figure it out."

"What if I came over and we got caught up on Tropic Like It's Hot?" It feels almost risky to ask, like some kind of boundary-crossing proposition instead of the rather normal suggestion it is.

Her line is silent for a moment. "No, I don't think so."

"Okay," I reply. "Whatever you need."

"I, uh, I think I have to go."

I feel my heart fall to my stomach at the brittle nature of her voice. I try to mask it when I respond: "Okay. Bye."

"Bye," she says. "Thank you again. For today."

"Don't worry about it," I say quickly. "Call me if-"

"If I need anything," she says, and it satiates my nerves a bit that I can almost hear a faint smile in her voice. "I will."

Friday morning, she texts to tell us all that Ethel is home. Friday evening, my phone rings again.

"Hey!" I cry. "How's Ethel?"

"I need your help," she says, and it's like a punch to the gut when I realize her voice sounds like she might've been crying. "I've been trying everything, she just won't-"

"I'm on my way."

Chapter Twenty-One

Sadie is Struggling

From the minute Summer hangs up to the minute she appears at the door, I pace in the doorway. As my foot catches on a discarded piece of clothing on the floor, I internally scold myself for letting the place get messy again.

There's a knock, and I open the door to reveal Summer. Even though I'd known she was coming, there's a small jump in my chest at the sight of her. A part of my mind hopes she doesn't look at me for too long - dirty hair, unwashed clothes, and the red remnants of tears probably still visible in the whites of my eyes.

"What do you need?" Her big brown eyes look serious, and her hair spills over her shoulders in ringlets. It takes me a second, in my frazzled state, to notice there's a plastic-wrapped bouquet in her arms.

My lips part. "O-oh. Thank you."

She looks at the flowers like she'd forgotten she has them, suddenly flustered. "I thought you might like them."

I nod, gingerly taking them from her. "They're, um, they're really nice." The thought is louder now, and I feel all the more embarrassed at the state I'm in. Every part of me is praying that her eyes don't linger anywhere on or around me.

"Ethel won't eat," I tell her, turning to show her where the dog sits, looking especially droopy in front of her full food bowl. "I tried treats, and lunch meat, and just *pretending* to put stuff in it... all the stuff that usually works like a charm."

She nods, going onto her knees while I fill a vase with water and put the flowers in. "Hey, Ethel!"

With a bit of effort, she lumbers to her feet, tail wagging, and gives Summer a big kiss across the face. I wince before remembering that she, inexplicably, finds dog breath charming - a feat of pure delusion that I'd previously assumed only dog owners were capable of.

"Hi, puppy," she says, stroking all across Ethel's fur. "Don't you look beautiful."

Ethel rolls onto her back, revealing the shaved bit of her stomach and the scar there. Summer cringes at it.

"You must have been so brave for your surgery, girl," she says, petting around the incision gently before turning to me. "Do you have any honey?"

I cock my head to the side. "Do you think that'll work?"

"Just a little bit, with some warm water," she replies. "Our childhood dog was always going on hunger strikes, and that snapped him out of it every time."

I let out a breath, and it's more sigh-like than I intended. "Worth a try. Let me go get it."

Summer prepares the honey-and-warm-water concoction on top of Ethel's kibble with the same care and focus she would a human confection, and as Ethel watches wide-eyed I wonder if this alone gives her a vote of confidence. The second we set the bowl back on the floor, she sticks an interested snout in, and a second later she's crunching away.

"Good girl!" Summer cries.

"Thanks," I say, but for some reason there's a weight in my chest pulling firmly downward. "I'm glad that finally did it."

She looks sideways at me, her gaze growing studious in all the ways I'd hoped it wouldn't. Still, there's something soft about her face that stops me from feeling judged or caught. Her voice is gentle as she asks, "Have *you* eaten?"

My knees suddenly feel weak beneath me, and I'm realizing it for the first time when I say, "No."

"Honey, you seem really tired," she says, and her voice feels like a hand stroking my face. At the observation, I feel even more tired than I already had. "How about I stay and cook you something?"

"You can cook?"

She grins. "My degree is in culinary arts. Even with a focus on baking, you don't get out of there without figuring out how to make a decent meal."

The tightness in my shoulders loosens. "That would be nice. We could..." My body feels weaker by the second. "We could watch the rest of our show."

"Sure," she says. "Why don't you go ahead and sit down while I get everything started?"

Ethel snuffs, stepping away from an empty bowl and waddling off to her dog bed.

"I can help," I offer lamely.

"You deserve the rest," she insists. "As long as you're fine with me rooting through your pantry, I think you should get cozy on the couch and start the show."

Everything feels slow. Part of me still feels like protesting her taking care of me at all. Finally, I just say: "You don't want me to wait for you?"

"I can watch from the kitchen."

My stomach is heavy. "You... you don't have to."

She locks her eyes onto mine, and I feel weaker still. "I want to." I keep waiting for some kind of slip in her demeanor, something to show that I really *am* burdening her, but there's nothing. Only that genuine kindness coming off of her in waves, just like it always does.

So I sit down on the couch and pull up our next episode of Tropic Like It's Hot. She provides commentary from the kitchen and Ethel climbs up onto the couch, and I start to calm. I'll admit I don't fully tune in to the drama of the show like I usually do - more so, I fall into a half-sleep trance, the worry about Ethel's food off my shoulders. I wake back up when I feel the couch shift beside me. Summer hands me a plate.

"How's that?" she asks as I scoop up a bite of stir-fried vegetables and meat, her expression anticipatory.

The food fills me with warmth and a shot of energy. I nod appreciatively with my mouth still full and Summer's face lights up.

"Good!" she says. I keep chewing, the fullness in my stomach also bringing back a guilty sort of wait. I don't know how she clocks this tiny change, but exactly as I'm feeling it her face turns once again toward concern. "How do you, uh... how do you feel?"

I swallow both the food and a lump in my throat. Only one goes down. "I'm, um. I'm good."

It's an obvious lie, and she knows it. Her brow is knit and her eyes are kind, and I find myself hoping she'll call me on it.

"It's tough," I offer, surprising myself. "It's *been* tough. Ethel being sick."

She nods, her hand going to the dog, who's already happily snoozing. "Yeah."

"You know, I've had her since she was a puppy," I tell her, setting down my plate and scratching behind Ethel's ears. "I was thirteen."

"You guys have been through a lot," she says. "I bet she's been a really good friend."

There's a hot rush of tears behind my eyes threatening to come falling out. I grit against them. "Yeah. She has."

She doesn't say anything, but the silence doesn't feel awkward. It's as though we can both just tell that I'm not done. Something within me feels like a thread slowly unspooling.

"I still won't get her biopsy results for a few more days," I say, my breath coming out just the tiniest bit ragged. "So even though she *seems* fine now, it's just..."

Summer's hand moves up from Ethel's fur and up onto my arm, as if she knows how much her touch always soothes me. I take a few breaths, smoother now, and lick my lips. "I know I don't have much time left with her. I've been preparing for years for, like, whenever she'd get too sick. But now, knowing she might have *cancer*..."

A tear falls down my face against all my will. Summer leans even closer, her lips parted and her eyes huge.

"And these past couple of months, I've actually been trying to spend *less* time with her," I say, my throat bubbly with sobs.

"Sadie," she says, her soft fingers running up and down my arm. "Honey, it's okay."

"I should have... I should have..." *I don't know*. But I feel so desperately that I could have prevented this somehow, if only I'd done something differently. The sobs grow stronger.

Summer makes a small sound, her soft touch suggesting me toward her embrace. I let myself fall against her chest, Ethel still asleep between us. Her hands tentatively tighten around my back.

"Sadie, you didn't do anything wrong," she murmurs, her voice barely audible over my own cries. "It's all going to be okay."

"How could I be so selfish?" I blubber.

Ethel wiggles, awakened by the sound, and crawls up onto my lap. Her wet nose forces its way between Summer's chest and my face, and her tongue finds my wettened cheeks.

"Hi, baby," I say tearfully, pulling out of Summer's grip to look at the dog's droopy face. With a breath in, I realize it feels good to have let the tears out.

"See?" Summer says, her voice still hushed. "She's happy, and she loves you. You're not selfish. Everything's going to be alright."

I look up at her, her eyes nearly as big and brown as Ethel's. She looks unbelievably sweet sitting there across from me, red curls framing her pale freckled face and a hesitant smile on her full, pink lips. It occurs to me, all at once, that I want to kiss her.

I blink in the realization and immediately begin to deconstruct it. It's just because of how I'm feeling, and that she's beautiful, and comforting me. I pass my hand over Ethel's head, trying to wipe the thought away.

"Thanks," I say, sniffing hard against my still-stuffy nose. My gaze goes to the mostly untouched plate on the coffee table. "For everything."

She nods. "Do you... want me to stay for a while?"

"Yeah," I reply, pressing my lips together. "We can catch up on the show, and maybe put on a movie?"

"Of course," she says.

"I need to clean up." The thought leaves my mouth essentially as it appears in my mind, my gaze lingering on the messy floors.

"You don't need to worry about it right now," she says, her fingertips brushing across my wrist in a way that sends electricity through me. "Just relax."

As if trying to help Summer make her point, Ethel stretches in my lap and curls into a ball, only seconds away from another nap.

"Well," I sigh, already smiling in anticipation of the way Summer's face is going to light up, "I can't really argue with both of you."

The grin that appears on her face is even better than I'd imagined.

The first thing I do when Summer leaves is finally take a shower. The world seems just a little bit brighter now that I'm clean, and without much thought I pull out my phone and dial.

"Baby!" Felix cries. "How are you, love?"

"Not my best," I admit. "But I'm going to be alright."

"Good! And how's Ethel?"

"She's good," I reply, looking over at the couch where she's still lounging. "Just waiting on the biopsy results to see if that tumor was cancer."

He tuts. "Poor baby."

"I'm kind of driving myself crazy over it," I tell him, falling onto the couch next to Ethel. "Like, I hadn't showered. And shit's a mess."

"Aw, baby. I'm so sorry I haven't been able to drop by," he says. "We had this whole disaster at work where an entire server went down, and we almost lost a *shitload* of data-"

"Enough corporate talk," I poke. "You're already losing me."

"I'll come over soon, okay, babe?" His voice goes distant at the end, like he's pulling away from the receiver. "Hold on, babe. I'll have to call you back."

"I always knew this would happen," I tell him with a smirk. "I always knew you'd make it big and leave me behind."

"Yes, that's exactly what I'm doing," he chirps. "Goodbye, Riffraff. It's Fame and Fortune calling."

"Love you, Felix," I say. "Just call me and let me know when you're coming over."

"Love you too, Sadie."

A couple days later, Felix hugs me before I can even fully get the door open. My vision is flung into darkness as his body covers my face.

I squeeze him, one hand still on the doorknob. "Hi, baby."

"Hi!" he exclaims, drawing out the syllable and squeezing me tighter. "Oh, I've missed you."

"I've missed you, too," I say into his chest. "Are you gonna let me go now so I can let you into the apartment?"

"Ten more seconds," he says, and I snort.

After what I'm very suspicious is actually ten seconds, he finally lets go and I can see a little gift bag in one hand and a bouquet in the other.

"You bastard," I hiss with narrowed eyes.

"Wait," he says, holding out one arm as I start to swing the door shut. "Don't close it yet."

"What are you-" I step back, and on perfect cue the hall is suddenly filled with a stream of people - Julian, Georgia, Rio, Khalil, and Summer - all with gifts in their hands.

"Surprise!" Felix declares, then whips around to look at everyone else. "Really? Nobody? C'mon, Jules, we practiced in the car!"

"Sorry, love," says Julian. "I really dropped the ball there."

"You guys..." I trail off, petrified in my spot with one hand still on the door.

"We all brought you and Ethel some gifts," says Khalil.

"We figured we could throw a mini-party to celebrate her recovery," Georgia adds.

I scan over the crowd of smiling friends. "Wow, I..."

"Well, let us in!" Felix cries. "I know Mama Levine taught you better than to leave your guests out in the cold."

A bit dazedly, I step out of the way and let the Friend Procession into my apartment.

I finally start to gain my footing as everyone's setting their things down in the kitchen and Ethel comes trotting in from the living room as if she knows it's a party for her. "Thank you guys so much. This is-"

The sound of champagne uncorking is briefly deafening, and we all turn to look at Rio, the foaming bottle a proverbial smoking gun.

"What?" they ask with a nonchalant shrug. "I thought somebody was getting the glasses."

I laugh, pushing past Felix and Julian to get down everything I have even remotely resembling a champagne flute.

"Here, baby, open my gift first," says Felix as Julian gets out a vase for all the different bouquets everyone's brought.

I do, quickly cutting the tags off a squeaky toy and tossing it to Ethel. The bag also produces two kinds of dog treats, another toy, and a box of my favorite chamomile tea.

"Thanks, babe," I coo as Rio slides a wine glass full of champagne into my hand. "We both love them."

"I know," Felix preens. "Who's next?"

As I go through Julian, Rio, Khalil, and Georgia's gifts, I get a package of scented bubble bath, a pair of fuzzy socks, a bottle of wine, a hot pink vibrator (Rio seems to have absolutely no shame about including this for its more literal "self care" meaning), a handmade stuffy, a plush blanket, a bag of chocolates, and a handwritten note from each of them.

Ethel, too, makes out like a bandit. There's at least six types of treats, a huge rawhide bone, a bunch of toys, a spiffy new collar, a fluffy dog bed, and even a little t-shirt that says *free kisses*. The counter is practically flooded with gifts by the time Summer, last in line, hands me her gift bag.

My jaw drops at the first thing I pull. "No fucking way."

Her smile is thousand-watt.

"I can't believe you found this!" I cry, waving the Tropic Like It's Hot card game ecstatically. "I thought it wasn't supposed to come out until next month!"

"I found it just sitting out on some random shelf," she says, the upturn of her lips not going away even as she talks. "They told me it had been put there by mistake and that they weren't allowed to sell it until March, but I, uh..." She flashes a proud grin. "I may have used my feminine wiles and convinced them to take my money."

"Oh my god," I laugh. "What did you do?"

"Flash them your tits?" Rio pipes up.

She gives a coy shrug, tossing a strand of bright red hair over her shoulder. "I may have cried a little."

"Classic Summer," Georgia chimes, and Julian nods along.

"I love it," I tell her. "Thank you so much."

"Of course," she says. "Just don't play it without me."

"As if I would," I scoff, and open my arms for a hug. She steps forward and seems to click into my embrace like a LEGO brick. "Although, I have to say I'm surprised you'd willingly play a card game with me again."

"I'll make a special exception this time," she says, her chin on my shoulder, and a laugh bubbles up and out of my mouth.

"It's kind of a theme gift," she tells me when she pulls away. "I got Ethel a couple toys that look like beach toys. I even found a squeaky bikini top." I grin as I pull the aforementioned toys from the bag, squeaking a stuffed seashell so enthusiastically that Ethel points her snout in the air toward the sound.

"It's perfect," I say, passing Ethel the seashell as she attempts standing on her hind legs to see what's going on. Tail wagging like a jet turbine, she races to her dog bed with her treasure.

"This is really, *really* nice," I tell Felix, the two of us the only ones still lingering in the kitchen as the rest of the group gets cozy in the living room, some dog-themed romance movie that Georgia picked out already blaring on the TV. "Thanks for getting everybody in on it."

He cocks his head to the side as he shuffles everyone's empty glasses into the sink. "I didn't. I mean, I was already going to drop by and bring you and Ethel some goodies, but it was Summer's idea for everyone to show up and make a party of it."

I blink. "Oh."

"You two have definitely gotten pretty close," he says with the slightest smirk on his face. My face warms. He pulls up his sweater sleeves as he leans against the sink and crosses his arms. "I know that everything with Gabby put you off dating for a while, but you're sure there's nothing... there?"

All at once, this question catches me completely off guard and feels perfectly expected. I turn it over in my mind, the concept feeling totally foreign. Quickly, though, the conclusion is obvious - I can't feel that way about Summer. It isn't possible. Sure, I might occasionally have the urge to kiss her during couple-centric holidays or moments of personal weakness, but the thought of *dating* her, of letting her see and touch those flabby deposits of fat that Gabby used to abhor? Fat chance.

I shake my head. "She's my friend, Felix."

"Absolutely," he says, seeming to drop the subject completely like he's been trained with a release word. "She's a *wonderful* friend. That's why she and Jules have stayed so close."

I nod, and I feel almost naked admitting: "I'm really grateful to have her."

"I'm glad, baby," says Felix with a grin. "But I may have to be mad at you for getting another best friend."

I shove him lightly, and he's already giggling. "Fuck off."

"Alright," he says, hands up like a shield. "I'll fuck straight off to the living room with all the cool people."

My phone rings in my pocket, and my heart leaps into my throat. "I'll be there in a second." I pick up the call as he turns his back to me and jumps into Julian's lap. "Hello?"

"Is this Sadie Levine?" asks a chipper female voice.

"This is she," I reply, and my brain starts to sound like TV static. My whole face feels numb. A minute later, with a goodbye to the receptionist, I look into the living room. "Guys."

Summer lowers the volume on the TV as they all turn to me, eyes wide and brows raised. Everyone seems to unite in one single anticipatory inhale, and for a second time is frozen.

"Ethel's tumor," I say, hot tears once again pricking at the corners of my eyes. I can't even begin to care. "It wasn't cancer."

The room erupts into cheers, and soon everyone's off the couch and running at me. All six of them make impact one after the other, trapping me in a euphoric, bone-crushing hug.

"It wasn't cancer," I say again, and the hug mass grows tighter. I whisper it to myself over and over, joyful tears streaming down my face as all my friends' hearts beat around me.

Oblivious, Ethel gleefully bites into one of her new toys, creating a loud squeaking sound. She gives a cheerful yip, just like a puppy.

Chapter Twenty-Two

Summer Explains It All

"Happy birthday!" I exclaim, rushing toward Julian the second my car door closes. He laughs, stumbling backward on the pavement as he absorbs the shock of my half-tackle hug. "How does twenty-eight feel?"

"Good," he says with an introspective nod and a light smile, looking confident in a white tank top that displays all his tattoos. "Just waiting on my old-age-mandated back pain."

"My baby's aged like a fine wine," says Felix, wrapping his arms around him. As always, Julian goes fluttery like a grade schooler holding a handmade Valentine from his crush.

"This is such a cute idea for a birthday celebration," I say, looking up at the unassuming facade of our neighboring city Petersford's premiere art gallery. A standing sign by the door reads *THIS MONTH ONLY: YOUNG QUEER ART FROM AROUND THE COUNTRY*. "How did you hear about this event again?"

"Wren from work told me about it," he says. "Her wife has a couple pieces on display."

A familiar little silver car pulls up right next to us, and my heart pounds when Sadie climbs out, her smile bright.

"Happy birthday!" she says, wrapping her arms around Julian. "You look great."

"Thanks," he replies. "My youthful beauty hasn't faded yet."

"And by the way, a blue minivan cut me off about a block back, so the others shouldn't be far behind," she adds, coyly raising an eyebrow. Right on cue, Khalil's car pulls up, Rio and Georgia hopping out the second it's stationary.

"Hey, birthday boy!" says Rio. Khalil and Georgia line up to hug him, too, and we all file into the gallery.

As we stand in the lobby while Julian checks us in at the ticket table, I can't funnel my attention away from Sadie: the soft roundness of her cheeks, the delicate upturn of her eyelashes, the short hairs at the nape of her neck. And the final wrench in my already shoddy composure: the dark red lip shade she's sporting. I'm thoroughly disgusted with myself: who knew that a red lip was all that stood between me and dizzying thoughts about one of my best friends?

As if the universe senses my inner turmoil and wants to exploit it, Sadie leans toward me, her shoulder rubbing with mine. She smells like fresh flowers, and I wonder if she came straight from work. Her breath is warm against my cheek, sending chills down my spine, as she whispers from the side of her mouth, "How much do you want to bet that about half of this art will go straight over my head?"

"Give yourself some credit," I whisper back. "There'll probably be written explanations next to them."

She snorts, a gleeful spark in her eyes that makes me feel wobbly. It seems that now, when Sadie isn't at her lowest point, my brain sees no issue in being devastatingly attracted to her.

Julian turns from the ticket table, flashing us all a smile. "We're good to go."

"Excellent," Khalil pipes up, striding forward on his long legs and looking immediately like the ideal art gallery patron. We all follow suit, the group moving like an amoeba into the exhibition.

The artwork around us is incredibly diverse - paintings, sculptures, sketches of all kinds and subject matters line the walls. It's candy to the eye for everyone, but Julian especially looks like a kid in a theme park, his already huge brown eyes wide and starry.

The first piece we all settle at is a painting of a lavender night sky with delicately and painstakingly painted constellations, a rhinestone representing each star. A stray rhinestone, though, is placed more toward the bottom of the canvas like a fallen star lost in the grass.

"That's beautiful," says Georgia. "I love those wavy lines." They lift their hand, tracing the wobbly patterns in the air in front of them.

I nod along with everyone else, but almost the entirety of my brain power is zeroed in on Sadie's hand hanging at her side just centimeters away from mine. I swear I can feel electricity zapping in the space between us.

"The way it combines intense stylization and more realistic elements is incredible," says Julian. "I think those are real constellations."

"Cool," says Felix, nodding.

"But what about this little sparkle on the bottom?" Sadie asks, bringing her hand up to point toward it. I almost hold my breath when her skin brushes past mine.

I look at the piece of paper hanging next to the piece, but it does not, in fact, explain the significance of the symbols. All it provides is the title (a date, about a year and a half ago), the artist's name, her pronouns, and her state of origin.

"That couldn't be the day a meteor hit Portland, could it?" I try, and my heart skips a beat when Sadie giggles. I force my gaze to leave her red-painted lips as my hands go clammy.

"Maybe it's supposed to be a firefly," says Rio.

"It kind of reminds me of an engagement ring," adds Georgia.

"I bet it's symbolic," says Khalil, pushing up his glasses. "The beauty and majesty of the cosmos falling to earth in the form of glorious queer culture."

"And to think *I* was expecting to be the most pretentious asshole tonight," Julian tells him with a smile, which Khalil returns.

"I'm gonna look it up," says Georgia, plopping onto a bench a few feet away and pulling out her phone. "I'm really interested."

Julian nods and leads the rest of us further into the gallery. The next piece we stop in front of is tiny, an impressively detailed portrait only about as big as a business card.

"Wow," breathes Felix. "That's gorgeous."

"I can't see it," says Sadie from the back of the pack, resting both hands on my shoulders and springing up onto her tiptoes. I freeze, swallowing hard to try and quell the imminent freakout at her proximity. Julian catches my eye, and just like always I think he can see straight through me.

"Oh my god, it *is*," Sadie says, leaning her body even more against my back. I think if she were to touch my face, she'd burn her hand.

"*Babylove*," Rio reads off the information page, cocking their head at the butch, bearish subject of the picture. "Cute."

"Happy birthday again, Old Man," I say softly, leaning my head against Julian's shoulder as we stand in front of a luminous digital painting of a smiling trans man. The rest of the gang mills about in the far corners of the gallery, each having chosen a favorite piece to stare at. "You had fun tonight?"

"Making my friends analyze a bunch of kickass queer art," he replies, linking his arm with mine. "What could be more fun than that?"

"I'm glad." My tone falls flat a bit, and he shifts, holding onto my arm but turning his body so he can look at me.

"Are you alright?" He frowns. "You've been kind of... reserved."

I bite my lower lip. I've been expecting some version of this talk, but I hadn't given any thought to what I'd say. "I, uh... I think I have feelings for Sadie."

He nods, raising his eyebrows.

"But I know she doesn't want to date," I add quickly. "And I just feel really guilty for, like, making our relationship something it's not."

"Yeah," he says thoughtfully. "That sounds really tough."

"She's so..." I huff, the words dying somewhere in the back of my mind. "She doesn't deserve that from me, you know?"

"What do you mean?" he says, his tone neutral like a therapist's.

"I'm supposed to be her friend," I say with a sigh. "She doesn't want to date anybody, but here I am, just, like, lusting after her."

"First of all," he says, "I doubt you're *lusting* after her. You like her, because she's kind and funny and beautiful. Right?"

I flush. "Right."

"So it's not like you're just fantasizing about having sex with her," he clarifies. "There's nothing disrespectful about liking your friend. You can't help the way you feel. *And* it's not like you're trying to get past her boundaries and make her date you."

Everything he's saying is right, but something inside me still feels squirmy. "I just..."

"You care about her," he presses, jutting his stubbled chin out with an almost defiant look on his face. "Because you *are* her friend. You don't even want to think about making her uncomfortable. But you haven't done anything wrong, Summer."

I take in a deep breath, steadying myself. "Thank you. You're right." I give him a weak smile. "Sorry to do this on your birthday."

He rolls his eyes good-naturedly. "I guess I owe it to you. You've helped me enough over the years."

My smile grows a little. "Have I told you lately how *incredibly* proud of you I am, by the way?"

He covers his face with his hand. "No, you haven't."

"Just think about how happy Baby Julian would be to see you now," I say, poking him lightly in the ribs. "You're a thriving tattoo artist and a homeowner, you have officially grown into the coolest man alive, *and* you're about to get married."

He beams. "You think I'm cool?"

"Are you kidding? You're basically my icon."

"Really?"

"I want to be you when I grow up," I confirm, and his grin only grows.

"Don't underestimate yourself, Summer," he says.

"I've only got a month," I reply cheekily. "I don't think I'll be able to catch up."

"Stop kidding." He nudges my shoulder.

"I'm proud of myself," I concede. "I've come really far, even from a year ago."

"You know," he says, cocking his head to the side. "I don't think you need to treat Chicago like your life's big mistake. I know it sucked, but… you're here now."

"I started Sweet Summer there," I add, smiling wistfully. "I don't know what I'd have done if I never moved."

"I hope you're happy now," he says. "You deserve to be."

I nod. "I am."

I'm hunched over my kitchen counter with a bowl of dough, the only light coming from the overhead fixture as the windows are nothing but black. My phone chimes, and I reach forward to pick up and turn on speaker phone before returning my full attention to the bowl. "Hello?"

"Hey," says Sadie. "What are you doing?"

"Working late," I reply. "I've got an early delivery to Graceburgh in the morning. How about you?"

"Also putting in a little overtime," she says. "The boss is really nagging me."

"Yeah?" I ask, sensing some irony in her voice as I scoop the dough onto the baking sheet in front of me.

"I'm playing with Ethel," she says, and I hear a characteristic squeak in the background. "She suddenly thinks she's two again."

I laugh, sliding the baking sheet into the oven. "I'm glad she's feeling better."

"So, it's almost your turn," she says. "Any plans for the big two-eight?"

I lean against my kitchen island. "I figure I'll invite everybody to my apartment and have some cake. Nothing fancy."

"What do you think you want?"

You, says an intrusive voice in my mind. I recoil at it. I have really got to get myself in line. "I don't know. Nothing specific."

"You're impossible," she says, and I can picture her rolling her eyes and smiling at me.

"Proudly," I reply. "But, to be fair, you didn't even *let me* get you a birthday present."

I relish in imagining her cutely frustrated expression. "I don't see how that's relevant."

"Just get me anything," I tell her. "I'll love whatever you choose."

"How can you be so sure?" she says. "You wouldn't know this, but I'm a famously bad gift-giver."

"I can't imagine that in the slightest, Sadie."

"You know, I think you have too much faith in me."

"I think you don't have enough." It comes out before I can think about it, how frank and even slightly flirty it sounds. The line is silent for a second.

Finally, she says: "I guess you've got me there."

Chapter Twenty-Three
Sadie Comes to Terms

"Hi there. Welcome to Inspiration Florals. How can I help you today?" I say robotically as the bell over the door chimes. A teenager in a hoodie walks up to the counter like they're afraid I might bite them. Even at first sight, I'm already a little fed-up with the kid; my shift is almost over, my feet are killing me, and teenagers in the flower shop are almost always an interesting experience.

I cast a quick glance at Macy on my left and Crystal on my right - *dammit*, both busy. I'll have to suck it up for twenty more minutes and, if need be, foist my responsibilities onto somebody else as soon as the clock hits five.

"Hi, uh..." The kid brushes a strand of dark hair behind their ear, fingers barely emerging from their sleeve. "I wanted to get a bouquet."

The uncertainty is always one of my biggest pet peeves in customers - it's like calling to order a pizza and making the delivery driver read you the whole menu.

"That's great," I say, putting on my best customer service face. "Do any of these here on display work for you, or would you need something a bit more specific?"

Their eyes dart toward the tile floor. The gesture, for some reason, sticks in my brain. "A, um... a custom arrangement would probably be better."

Of course it would. But naturally they couldn't have a shred of clue what they'd want for that custom arrangement. That'd make my job too easy. "What's the occasion?"

"It's, uh..." They pull their other hand from their pocket, fidgeting with a crumpled wad of bills. "I wanted to get a bouquet for my, um... my best friend."

It strikes me incredibly suddenly- this kid is *me*, sixteen and closeted. The secret money, the shifty gaze, the 'best friend'... Sympathy floods away all the animosity.

"How about something with marigolds?" I try slowly. "That's what I always used to give my ex-girlfriend."

The kid blinks as if processing what I've said. "I couldn't do marigolds. She's really into the Victorian flower language."

I raise my eyebrows. "Oh?"

They nod, measured. "Marigolds mean grief and jealousy, and I'm... I want to give them the bouquet to say that I..."

I wish I could project an image of myself at this age to them. I remember this feeling - any adult is unsafe. I want them to know that isn't true. That they can say what they mean.

"What about camellias?" I offer, mentally crossing my fingers and banking on my limited knowledge of the Victorian flower language to be correct.

Their eyes pop wide open, making them look like a deer in the headlights. "Yes," they say, a bit shakily. "Some camellias would be a good start."

"My name is Sadie," I offer gently. "I can help you with your arrangement."

"Micah," they reciprocate a bit clumsily, a pink flush gradually falling from their cheeks as they seem to come to terms with the fact that they're not about to be ratted out to their parents.

"Tell me a bit about your friend," I say. "But I'll just let you know up front, I don't know much about the Victorian flower language."

Their soft, young face lights up, and from the same pocket as the wrinkled cash, they pull a pristine scroll of paper covered in writing. I have to chortle. "I see I'm dealing with an expert."

"Not really," they reply sheepishly, fiddling with the list. "I just... it really matters to Inez."

Micah ends up telling me all about Inez and even a bit about their parents (who are, as far as I can tell, the only homophobes in Roseport) as they share their extensive Victorian flower language notes with me and together we construct a beautiful arrangement with pink, red, and white camellias, red and white chrysanthemums, and red tulips.

"How much do I owe you?" Micah asks, pulling out their money and carefully straightening out the folds. I quickly count the values.

"What you have will do," I reply, a little too quickly. They look up at me almost suspiciously, but the expression becomes appreciative nearly immediately. They pass me the bills, and once their attention is enveloped in the bouquet, I pull a few more from my own pocket.

"Thanks a lot, Sadie," they say, eyes still fixed on the arrangement. "I think she'll really love it."

"I think so, too," I add. "It's been a really big pleasure meeting you and helping you, Micah."

Their smile seems to take up their whole face. "Thank you. Really, thank you."

I'm so full of emotions that I feel like a cup running over. The look on their face reminds me of Julian's when I show him flowers for the wedding, full of joy and wonder. It clicks for me, for the first time in possibly years, just how special my job is, and how much I really love it. "Thank *you*."

When I check my watch as they're leaving the store, it reads 5:15. I head toward the back door, already taking off my apron, and Macy looks incredulously at me from where she leans against the wall.

"Just when I thought I might have you figured out," she says.

"What do you mean?" I ask, hanging up my apron.

She grins. "I had no idea you could be *nice*."

"Maybe you could try being a child," I offer. "Don't you still have work to do?"

"I got off at five, just like you," she says.

I turn, raising an eyebrow. "So, what, you just stood there and watched me talk to a customer for fifteen minutes?"

"Uh, *yeah*," she says, moving her ponytail over her shoulder. "That was the most inspiring shit I've ever seen. It's, like, what the job's about." Her gaze cuts toward the ground for a split second as she shifts her feet. "And, I, um. I was going to wait for you anyway."

I cock my head to the side. "Do you need something?"

"I've been meaning to ask you for a while," she says, suddenly shy in a way I've never seen her. "I feel like we have a lot of fun at work, you know, and I always joke about, like, wanting to get to know you better... Do you wanna go out with me?"

I stand there for a second, just gawking. My mind races. I know immediately what my answer is, but what I can't quite place is *why*.

"I'm sorry," I tell her. "I'm not interested in you that way."

She nods. "That's okay. Honestly, I'm kind of just glad I finally got myself to ask. I've been, like, agonizing over it for months."

"Good on you," I reply. "I hope you find somebody really nice to be mean to you someday."

Her smile is wide, effectively washing away a lot of the nervousness that had still been sitting in her expression. "That's the dream." Her eyes soften. "Thank you."

"Sorry I'm late," I say, my brain still scrambled as I set my bag down in the empty chair next to Felix at one of the cute outdoor tables at Witch's Brew. Julian scoots his coffee out of my way as I sit down. "Work went a little long."

"No worries, babe," Felix says. "How was your day?"

"Really good, actually," I say, putting my car keys into my bag. "I helped this kid arrange a bouquet for their crush. It was really sweet."

"Aww," Julian coos. "That's so cute!"

The incident with Macy still nags at me, but for some reason I don't want to bring it up to Felix. Normally this would be exactly the kind of thing I'd tell him, but the event is still rolling itself over and over in my mind, and I can't begin to share it until I figure it out for myself.

"I had a really nice client the other day," Julian says, already smiling at the thought.

I know I don't want to date Macy. That's sort of a given. But the thing that makes me think that isn't that I'd be terrified of her seeing my body and being like Gabby - which is sort of the blanket reason I've avoided even the idea of dating for months now.

"He was getting this tattoo to honor his childhood mentor," Julian continues. "I think he said it was an old teacher who he used to visit at her house and they would, like, read and crochet together."

I just don't *like* her that way. I like talking to her. She's funny and easy to talk to. But I don't get excited to see her enter a room. She doesn't make me feel flustered or energized. I don't miss her when she's not there or hope to see her more than I do.

It's been so long since I've had the luxury of making this kind of discernment, but the issue isn't just that I don't want to date. Ever since my breakup with Gabby, that's been the end-all be-all. But somewhere along the way, I've regained my ability to say I don't want to date *that person*.

"He was super kind, and he came in with this gorgeous hand-drawn design based on a letter she'd written him once," says Julian, and I nod dazedly. The pieces are coming together, however slowly.

Does this mean I'm finally healing? Does it mean I've *healed?* That I can look at someone and not stop at *I don't want to date*? It's almost empowering to think that now I can look past the initial fears of being hurt again and tell that I don't like someone enough to date them, that I don't like them like-

"Hey, Sadie!"

I whip my head around as Summer emerges from within the coffee shop and sits down next to me. My heart, out of nowhere, starts pounding like a bass drum.

Like I like Summer. I blink, everything clicking. *Like I've liked Summer for a long time.* I feel like the dumbest person in the world.

"Hey," I say, trying to sound casual while I'm pretty sure my entire person is vibrating.

"Sorry to interrupt," she says, turning to Julian and pushing her hair behind her ear. "Go on."

He does, but now I can't help but fully tune him out. My brain sounds like a thunderstorm. *I like Summer.* It's the most obvious thing in the world, but I've just been repressing it for who knows how long.

I let my gaze wander to where she sits, intently listening to Julian's story, and the way she looks just confirms everything. I'm almost impressed with myself - so I *am* still capable of feeling these things.

"So," Felix says, bringing his hands down on the table with a sound that wakes me up. "About our bachelor party."

My skin is still humming. I try to swallow the electric feeling all over me, purposely moving Summer out of my periphery. "Yeah?"

"We don't want anything too crazy," Julian says. "But we thought it was kind of a bummer that nobody would get to be, like, *really* dressed up at the wedding."

"Where are you going with this?" says Summer, and her voice sends shivers through me in a way that I realize maybe it always has.

"We're gonna have everybody over to just drink wine and reminisce on the single life," Felix says. "But we wanna do, like, formal dress. It'll feel super fancy."

Something in me deflates. "You're going to do a *formal dress* bachelor party?" I imbue the question with a playful tone, but alarm bells are going off in my head.

What the hell am I going to *wear*? I don't own a single formal outfit I'd feel comfortable in. And this is what brings my whole mood dwindling down to reality. I *can't* be with Summer. I'm just a bundle of body issues that's nowhere near good enough for her. There's no way she feels like I do, even in the slightest.

"That sounds fun," Summer says, and I swallow hard.

"Yeah, for sure."

Standing in the hallway outside of Summer's apartment, part of me wants to run away. I've hardly seen her since that day at Witch's Brew, and knowing how I feel about her just makes me feel naked - like, any minute, someone will catch me looking at her and see straight through me, and everyone will laugh that I can even imagine a world in which she'd be interested in me.

It's more than a little dramatic, but the fear is there. I take a deep breath, trying to remind myself that I'm an *adult* and most likely will not die of embarrassment under any circumstances, and knock on the door.

It swings open and the whole hallway lights up under the glow of Summer's smile. Her curls fall lusciously over her shoulders and her skin is dewy and flushed, her foundation light enough that I can still see her freckles through it. Her long, dark lashes are even more dramatic than usual under a layer of mascara. I try not to let my eyes linger on her body in the flowy purple dress she wears, which nips in at her waist and plunges at her neckline.

"Hey!" Her eyes flick to the giant bouquet in my arms, and she gasps. "Oh my god. Sadie, that's beautiful!"

My face burns. I basically arranged this in a fugue state, just thinking about her hair and her smile and the way she makes me feel. It's bright and fragrant and, well, summery. I have to preen a bit at the way she regards it, gently taking it from me. "Let me get a vase."

I follow her into the apartment, floating awkwardly by the island as she sets the flowers up. I quickly assess that I'm the first one here, and I can't tell if that makes me more or less nervous - no one to notice my moony-eyed stare, but also no one to act as a buffer between us. I turn my attention to the beautifully frosted cake sitting on the counter and the carefully piped roses adorning its light pink frosting.

"I can't decide if it's impressive or sad that you made your own birthday cake," I prod, trying desperately to act normal.

"You won't wonder anymore once you try it," she says with what would've been an arrogant smirk on anyone else, but on her is only adorably proud like a kid who's won a spelling bee.

"Like I don't already know how talented you are," I say, my tone sneering despite the compliment in my statement.

She turns over her shoulder to look at me, a flattered smile on her lips. "Wouldn't kill you to say it a little more often."

She'd be surprised just how much I could say about her. I bite my lip, trying to shrug it away. "You own a successful business based off your talent. I'd figured it was common knowledge."

I retreat into myself as everyone else starts showing up and we cut into the cake. No surprise, she's right about the cake, delicious vanilla and strawberry flavors melting on my tongue. If I were half as fucked up and even a third as good a person as her, I'd marry her for this cake alone.

Once we're all done eating, we gather around the kitchen island, in the great tradition of birthday parties, to stare at Summer while she opens her gifts. It's the kind of thing that's always made me unspeakably uncomfortable, but she looks natural and effortless even under everyone's gaze. My breath hitches when she picks up my gift, a compact rectangle wrapped in pink paper.

"Gosh, I wonder what this is," she says in response to its clearly bookish shape, locking eyes with me. She's already smiling before she even unwraps it, and my heart races. "Oh, Sadie!"

She proudly turns a shiny new copy of *No Drone Unturned* toward the captive audience. Julian laughs.

"I almost bought that, too," he says.

"I'm easy to please," she replies with a shy smile, running her fingers gently across the cover and studying the artwork. Her hand travels to open the cover, and once again my heart skips as a slip of pretty stationery paper slips out. "What's this?"

This had seemed like a good idea two weeks ago when I prepped her present, before it occurred to me that I was head over heels for her. Now, with that informed perspective, I'm laid bare.

She smiles wider as she reads, and I force myself to stop reciting it in my head along with her after *I also bought a copy of.* When she's done, her eyes lock onto me. "You didn't."

Regaining my composure is a feat which warrants an Olympic medal. I manage a humble nod.

"You're really willing to do that for me?" she asks almost cautiously, and I shiver.

"I can't promise I'll *love* it like you do, but it's probably in my own best interest that I get some real exposure. No irony involved."

Summer's eyes sparkle as she smiles at me almost conspiratorially. She looks so unfathomably beautiful I think I could pass out.

"What is it?" Georgia asks.

"She bought herself a copy of my favorite book," Summer says, turning the note around so the group can read the largest lettering: *IOU no less than three hour-long book club discussions.*

"Aww," Rio exclaims.

"Thank you so much, Sadie," she says, touching my wrist lightly with only her fingertips. Even this feels all-encompassing. "I love them both. *And* the flowers you brought me."

"You're going to make the rest of us look bad, Sadie," Felix jokes. "I basically just spun around blindfolded in the baking aisle and grabbed whatever I landed on."

"I'm sure I'll like that, too," Summer says, reaching for her next gift. It takes what feels like a few minutes for my body to finally calm down, her gaze and attention no longer focused on me like a concentrated ray of sunshine.

I am in *trouble*.

Chapter Twenty-Four
Summer Reigns It In

There's an only-slightly embarrassing spring in my step as I move around the kitchen preparing for my last wedding planning session with Sadie. The morning sun is a soft shade of yellow as it floods my apartment, making everything feel bright and cheerful.

The bouquet from my birthday a couple days ago catches my eye, still lively and vibrant on the kitchen island. Just looking at it brings a shy smile to my face, and I allow myself the self-indulgent urge to lean forward and take a big whiff. It smells like hugging Sadie, and that is just one more point in its favor.

There's a knock at the door, and I feel equal parts excitement and like I've been caught with my hand in the cookie jar. I don't exactly want Sadie to know I've been dreamily smelling that bouquet she gave me every chance I've gotten. I take a deep breath, trying to exude *chill* as I walk to the door.

My eyes almost pop out of my head when it swings open. I take a second to collect my thoughts. "H-hi."

"Hello!" cries my mom, throwing her arms open and closing them around me.

"Hi, Sunshine," adds my dad, joining in on the hug.

"This is a surprise," I laugh, patting both their backs.

"Oh, I know you weren't expecting us," Mom says, pulling back to gesticulate. "But we just felt so bad for not coming down on your birthday, so we figured we'd drop by for an hour or two." She looks to the side. "Also, your neighbor sure has a lot of newspapers piled up outside their door. Do you think they're alright?"

"I wouldn't know," I manage, more than a bit bewildered.

"I'd check if I were you," she says with a short nod. "Janice was just telling me about the time her old neighbor's mailbox overflowed and they finally went to investigate. Poor thing had fallen and hadn't been able to move for days."

"Look, it's really nice of you to come, but..." I feel myself flush. "I'm kind of expecting company."

Mom's brows shoot up. "Like a date?"

"No no no no no," I say quickly. Am I really *that* obvious? "Just the friend I'm planning the wedding with."

"Oh, how nice," chimes Dad.

"Well, we'd love to meet her!" says Mom. "If you don't mind."

"Uh... sure," I say, ushering them inside. "We'll just be working on-"

"Why's the door open?" comes Sadie's voice, right on cue, and her eyes go wide when she steps into the doorway. There's quite a bit of surprise to her tone, so much that it drains the phrase of its usual politeness. "Oh, hello."

"Hello!" my parents chime, and suddenly I'm fifteen again and *majorly* embarrassed.

"You must be the McConnells," she says, blinking rapidly as her smile grows more friendly. The tooth makes its adorable appearance.

"Paul," says Dad, sticking out his hand. She firmly shakes it.

"And I'm Heather," chirps Mom, offering her hand as well. Sadie lets out a muffled "oh" as Mom pulls her into a hug. I want to scream.

"I'm Sadie," she says when Mom lets go. "I'm Felix's best friend. The florist."

"Yes, yes, we know who you are," says Mom coyly, and even though I've told her almost nothing about Sadie, suddenly my greatest fear is that she'll spill how crazy I am about her like it's casual conversation. "You are *gorgeous*."

Her lips quirk at one corner and she cocks her head to the side. "Thank you, ma'am, but you don't need to lie to me."

"No!" Mom crows. "We're not blowing smoke up your skirt. Paul, isn't she pretty?"

Dad nods, tucking himself at Mom's side, and I resist the urge to shoot him a death glare. "Very pretty."

"And so modest," Mom tuts, shaking her head. "I never saw the sense in being humble." Her eyes go to the bouquet. "Oh my goodness. Is this your work?"

Sadie smiles, cutting her eyes to me with a bemused look. "Yes, ma'am."

"Well, you are just fantastic," she cries. "Tell me, Sadie, are you seeing anyone?" She purses her lips suggestively and looks between us.

This does it. "*Mom.*"

"What?" she squawks. "I'm making conversation."

"You can make conversation about anything," I counter. I would rather die than let my mom make Sadie uncomfortable. "She has a job, and friends, and a dog."

"A dog!" Mom cries. "Oh, tell us about the dog."

Sadie laughs. "Are you sure I wouldn't be boring you?"

"Boring us!" Mom repeats. "I would pay for this kind of entertainment back at home. It's not every day I get the chance to talk to a sweet young florist."

"Even about dogs?" Sadie asks, and I get the distinct impression that - luckily - she is more amused by my parents than mortified.

"Especially about dogs," Dad assures. "We haven't had one in years, and neither have our neighbors."

And so Sadie tells the enraptured seniors every detail about her dog, and then her job, and then her friendship with Felix. She keeps shooting me these little meaningful glances, like we're the only two people in on a really funny joke, and each time it makes my knees feel less and less secure beneath me.

Finally, Mom and Dad declare they don't want to overstay their welcome and start heading out.

"Bye, Sunshine," says Dad, kissing my cheek.

"We love you!" Mom sing-songs.

"It was nice to meet you both," adds Sadie.

"I like her," Mom tells me like it's a secret, even though she's speaking at full volume.

"Bye, guys," I say. "I love you."

They give a few more goodbyes and even manage to each hug Sadie, then finally make their exit.

"Sorry" slips out of my mouth almost the second the door's shut.

"Don't be," Sadie says, crossing her arms and leaning against the island. "It was fascinating to see them in person. They're even more perfect than I imagined."

"They're... *something*, alright," I concur.

She raises her eyebrows. "Now I see where you get it from."

My whole body tingles. She's making fun of me - I *know* that - but still, Sadie calling me perfect does something to me.

"You should meet Ryan and Wyatt," I reply, trying to push the feeling away. "I just got what was left over after they were born."

"I'm sure they're great," she says. "And your younger brother, who I guess I have to assume is *im*perfect."

"They're all really wonderful," I tell her. "When I came home for Christmas, they all stood in a line to hug me."

Sadie snorts, and even this fills my stomach with butterflies. "Okay, so maybe you were right about it being an Osmond Family Christmas Special." She pushes back her hair, looking wistfully toward the door. "I like them. It would've been nice to have parents like that."

I raise my eyebrows, not quite sure how she wants me to respond. "Yeah, they're pretty cool," I reply. "They did manage to set us back quite a bit on our planning, though. Do you want to get started now?"

She nods, seeming to brighten. "Absolutely."

"It is *so* fucking hard to drive in heels," Rio says, sitting at Felix and Julian's dinner table and sticking their foot in the air, their bedazzled pump sticking out from the slit in their bright green floor length gown.

"You know, you could've just driven barefoot," Georgia points out, straightening her bow tie.

"Don't encourage them," Felix says, uncorking a bottle of red wine. "They're dangerous enough behind the wheel when they've got shoes on. I don't want anyone getting in an accident tonight."

"Then put away the wine," Khalil remarks, and the doorbell rings.

"I've got it," says Julian, adjusting his cufflinks and disappearing around the corner to the front door. My stomach tightens - Sadie's the only one missing, and I'm definitely not ready for her in formal wear.

Right on time, she and Julian round the corner and I swear my heart stops. She's wearing a long blue sleeveless dress that hugs her torso and hips then flares at her thighs. The sweetheart neckline shows the soft skin of her shoulders, collarbones, and a cruel bit of cleavage. Her hair is slick to her scalp and her eyeshadow perfectly matches the dress's shade of blue, bringing out the green of her eyes. Holy *shit*.

"Hey, babe," Sadie says, hugging Felix and kissing his cheek. "Happy bachelor party, you two!"

"Thanks, baby," Felix chirps. "We were just about to start the slideshow. Here, have some wine and we'll head into the living room."

"Don't mind if I do," she says, taking a glass just as he finishes pouring it. "Long day," she adds, and I feel myself shiver when her lips rest on the rim of the glass. I look away.

We all move onto the couch - a bit of a funny sight with all of us in our tuxedos and formal dresses - and Felix cues up a slideshow, complete with sentimental music. Everyone "aw"s when a baby-faced picture of Felix and Julian pops onto the screen, probably of their first meeting. Jules's curls are shorter and he has fewer tattoos, and Felix's face looks rounder and his makeup more amateurish than the elaborate looks he'll occasionally sport these days. They're sitting side-by-side with awkward smiles.

The picture melts away to reveal a more recent one; Julian on his tiptoes with his arms wrapped around Felix, his pink rose tattoos matching the flower behind Felix's ear. I recognize the background after a moment - So Sweet, the day they got engaged. I venture a glance at Sadie, who's sitting next to me on the couch and is about an inch and a half from giving me a heart attack. I don't have the strength to imagine how I would react if her bare shoulder were to brush mine.

"Nice picture," I comment, leaning slightly toward her to whisper. That's why - totally not because I want to smell that fresh floral scent that's ever-present on her.

She grins coyly, whispering back, "I know."

The slideshow is full of precious pictures from the boys' six years in each other's lives, from when they met at 22 and started dating the next year and all through their relationship. It's touching and hilarious and sweet, and the wine certainly isn't lessening the emotional effect. The slideshow comes to an end with the beautiful closing flourish of the song.

"Aw, you *guys*!" Rio wails, hugging onto Julian.

"Shh," Felix hisses, and there's an outbreak of disbelieving laughs and groans as a *second* slideshow begins.

"*Felix*," Sadie scolds. "Baby, read the room."

"Hey," he snaps back. "It's *my* bachelor party, and if I want you all to sit here and watch five slideshows, you *will* sit here and watch five slideshows. Right, baby?"

"Absolutely," Julian says with a serious nod.

"*Five* slideshows?" Georgia laughs. "Guys, seriously."

"Alright, maybe it's more along the lines of seven," Felix says sheepishly, fiddling with his glasses.

"I'll get more wine," says Khalil, standing up and heading back into the kitchen.

As the photo montages have continued into the night, we've all spread out a bit. Georgia, Rio, and Khalil are in a semicircle around the TV, chatting and playing some sort of drinking game around the contents of the slideshow. Felix and Julian, seemingly a little wine drunk, are slow dancing in the kitchen, the kind of slow dancing that's more a giggling hug on your feet. Sadie and I are in the same corner where we sat on

New Years, and I start to wonder if I liked her then, too - when I almost asked her to kiss me, just so she'd have someone to kiss. At the time it hadn't been a selfish thought - even though I'd *wanted* to kiss her - it was more that I didn't want *Sadie* of all people to go unkissed. I try to push the thought away as Sadie lowers her wine glass from her mouth.

"I can't believe they're getting *married*," she breathes. "This *month*. It's fucking wild."

"I know," I say. "I've known Julian for *ten years*. I can't imagine how you must feel with Felix-"

"Twenty-four years," she says, nodding. This even shocks me, hearing it laid out like that. I knew they'd known each other since they were kids, but *damn*. "You're right. It's weird. I've known this man since we were in preschool, and now he's an adult with a house and a fancy job, and soon he's going to have a *husband*." She smiles faintly. "I've met everyone he's ever dated. It's not that many guys, but... I'm definitely glad it's Julian."

"Yeah?"

"Yeah," she says. "He's everything I ever imagined for Felix, you know? They're perfect for each other."

"They really are," I say, grinning. "That's, like, exactly what I thought when I met Felix. Outside of my parents, I don't think I've ever met two people who were just so perfect for each other." Absently, I bring my wine glass up to my mouth. "That's what I want. To fall in love with somebody who feels more like a friend."

The second it leaves my mouth, it feels like a mistake. It's not exactly a love confession, but it's still too close to my chest, too close to the truth. There's no way she can read into it what that really means, but I watch her squirm ever so slightly and my stomach drops.

Even if she doesn't pick up on the fact that I'm maybe, *possibly* wishing that I could fall in love with someone an awful lot like her, I've just brought up love and life partners. *Again*. To Sadie, who has told me time and time again that that kind of stuff hurt her, and she isn't interested in pursuing it anymore. How insensitive could I be?

Before I can apologize, she cocks her head to the side and says quietly, "I really hope you find somebody perfect for you."

My lips quirk up at the sides. "Thank you."

She crosses her legs, the slit in her skirt exposing her knee. I feel like a colonial puritan for a second, endlessly enticed by the flash of skin. Shame comes a second later - what the *hell* is wrong with me, pining over my friend right as I'm reminding myself that she doesn't want to date?

"Look," she says, her green eyes flashing upward to the TV. I follow her gaze, and in the slideshow there are two smiling little kids with missing front teeth holding up a pair of paper hand turkeys. My jaw falls open - they both look so different, but it's unmistakable. Sadie's hair is long and a little wavy, but her button nose and the curve of her smile - with that same little crooked tooth - is the same as I've always known it.

"That man is about to have a wedding," Sadie says with a smirk, and it's only now that I really look at Felix, black hair in pigtails and little wrists covered with bracelets.

"Definitely hard to believe those two are grown-ups," I say with a nod. The picture slides to the left to reveal another, and Sadie laughs. Julian, Georgia, and I are nineteen years old and arm-in-arm like the cast of The Wizard of Oz. Julian is clean-shaven and free of tattoos, Georgia has only a few of their now-copious piercings, and my curls are frizzy and wild, tied up at the top of my head.

"Hard to believe those *three* are grown-ups," Sadie says, giggling. "How hungover were you?"

"We weren't," I reply, leaning forward. "I remember that night. Somebody on Georgia's floor of the dorm invited us to play a game of hide and seek, and it ended up lasting until, like, four in the morning."

"Holy shit," Sadie laughs. "And now here you are in a formal gown sipping wine, and I'm sure you'll be asleep in bed by ten tonight."

"Eleven," I say, and she laughs. The sound still fills me with feelings, but I try to push them away. "Funny how time changes things."

She nods. "It really is."

I think about how different my life looked even ten months ago, in July, when I moved back to Roseport with a broken heart and hadn't had much contact with my two best friends for two years. My life looks so different now; my business, my social life. When I left Landon and Chicago, there was no image in my head of my next great love.

Now, no matter how hard I try to change it, that image is of Sadie.

Chapter Twenty-Five

Sadie Makes A Move

"I'm so fucking excited," says Felix, as he usually does on matters related to the wedding. His bouncing knees shake the table, and I make a quick grab for my coffee so it doesn't topple. "It'll be really nice to talk wedding stuff with you two as the maids of honor and not the masterminds who planned the whole thing."

"Mastermind may be a little generous," I counter, coffee still in hand. "I put flowers in vases."

"Better than anyone I know," says Julian, and it would sound like a diss from anyone but him. The sincerity in his dark eyes is so thick that they look like gooey, half-melted chocolate truffles. I shrink a bit.

"The new cold brew is fantastic," says Felix, his cup pressed against his lips. "As if Witch's Brew wasn't already getting enough of my monthly income, they have to go and drop this delicious concoction."

"Hey," says Summer, pulling up the chair next to mine. Her red curls are pinned up at the top of her head, but the bun is messy and her hair's a bit frizzy. "Sorry, I was dropping off an order."

"No worries," Julian says, patting the back of her hand. "How are you doing?"

"Great," she chirps, but her tone feels shallow. My stomach churns. There's something bothering her, and my mind kicks into overdrive trying to tell what it could be. She doesn't look like she did when she was overworked and tired... could she be feeling sick? She certainly doesn't look like that either.

"Do you wanna get your coffee before we get started, Summer?" asks Felix, taking another large slurp of his cold brew.

Summer shakes her head. "I had some earlier. I'll get jittery if I have any more."

"Alright. So! Wedding stuff," Felix continues, clapping his hands together. "Have I mentioned how excited I am?"

"We figure you guys can set everything up on the day while we're getting dressed," says Julian, sipping his own coffee. "And once that's done, you'll join us in the house."

"Jules will be in the guest room, so you can join him there," Felix tells Summer. "And Sadie, you'll be with me in the bedroom."

"Once we're both ready, you guys will meet in the living room," Julian goes on. "That's where my parents will be, too. You guys will go down the aisle first and go to either side, then Felix will go, and then my parents will walk me down the aisle."

"Your mom isn't walking you?" I ask, raising my eyebrows. It occurs to me now that I haven't heard anything about Alison for a while.

"I just never dreamed of being walked down the aisle like Julie did," he says. "She's coming, though. She said she's really excited."

"Great," I reply. "It'll be nice to see her again. It's been so long."

Felix nods. "She's really been thriving in that new neighborhood. She made a lot of new friends. I've barely seen her either."

I nod, my eyes still skating back toward Summer. Her brown eyes are uncharacteristically dim as she rests her cheek on her hand.

"Hey, Summer, are we still on to watch the new episode of Tropic Like It's Hot tomorrow?" I ask, and my heart flips when she smiles, even though it's weaker than usual.

"Of course," she says. "Wouldn't miss it for the world."

"You two are the cutest," says Felix, and my face feels red-hot. He links his arm with Julian's. "I'm so happy our best friends became best friends. Now we're just one big happy group!"

Summer's mood doesn't seem to improve much as we stay and chat - she participates just like she normally would, but there's something missing from her smile, her laugh. It stays with me even when I go home, and into the morning of the next day as I'm preparing for her to come over. I ache at the thought of some unknown shadow covering the brightest light I've ever known. Slowly, an idea forms in my mind.

I'm not sure what I already have in the pantry, but maybe I could bake something for her. It wouldn't be as good as if she'd made it, but it could be something to show that I care about her. I open the pantry, Ethel watching lazily from her dog bed in a post-dinner slump. As I notice chocolate chips, flour, and sugar, the notion strengthens. I read the recipe from the back of the bag of chocolate chips and gather the ingredients, which I miraculously have just enough of.

I feel like a little kid finger-painting as I mix everything together and use my hands to transfer balls of dough onto a baking sheet, but I think I'm better at it all than I would've been last year, before I met Summer. I'm actually excited as I put the baking sheet into the oven. I can picture the look on her face when I present her with my homemade cookies, and it makes me shiver.

Suddenly I feel underdressed in my sweatpants, even though that's what I wear every time we watch TV together. I try to tell myself it's alright, but my feet still carry me to my room and into my closet. The next several minutes see me absorbed into every article of clothing I own, until I emerge back into the kitchen in a simple buttoned blouse and a pair of jeans. A quick glance at the kitchen timer tells me there are only a couple minutes left on the cookies.

Ethel lets out a noisy snore from her bed, and a second later there's a knock at the door. I'm a flustered little kid when I open the door, and for some reason Summer takes me aback even more than usual. She's just in a t-shirt and jeans with her hair in a low ponytail, like she is for most of our hangouts, and by all means I've found her stunning every time. But there must be something specific in the light today.

Her brown eyes gaze warmly at me from behind long lashes, and her cheeks and lips are a beautifully enticing shade of pink. A few curls fall from her ponytail, framing her sharp cheekbones, and her clothes are just tight enough to accentuate her hips, her chest, and the subtle inward dip of her waist. Everything about her is just so overwhelmingly perfect that I feel weak.

She raises her eyebrows, her freckled nose crinkling. "Sadie...?"

I come to my senses, my eyes popping open as I smell a hint of smoke. Shame floods through me. "Oh, *shit*. I was..."

As if taunting me, the kitchen timer chimes angrily. I whip around and pull the cookies out of the oven, a soft plume of smoke rushing out of the door as I open it. The cookies are almost black, and my shame doubles, heavy on my shoulders like a pack of bricks.

The baking sheet clatters to the floor, and I drop to my knees along with it. I sense her sinking down to meet me.

"God, Summer, I-" My breath heaves. "Fuck, I'm so sorry."

Her brown eyes search for mine, and I tilt my chin toward my chest to avoid them. My entire body feels like it's burning. Her voice is gentle and earnest. "What are you sorry for?"

"It seems like you've been feeling bad lately," I explain lamely, sliding my oven-mitted hand under the metal sheet. "I just wanted to do something special for you to make you feel better. You're so... wonderful, and kind, and you light up a room when you're happy, and it just makes me feel sick when you aren't." *I just wanted to try and make you happy, and* of course *I managed to fuck it up.*

I venture a look up at her, and I don't feel confident taking in the inward angle of her brows. Slowly, she tells me, "A few days ago would've been three years since moving in with Landon."

My heart drops and I lose grip of the baking sheet, oven mitt and all. "Summer, I'm so sorry."

"Don't be," she says, brushing her hair behind her ear. "It's okay. I've barely even thought about him since Julian put the scare on him after Friendsgiving." This forces a weak chuckle out of me.

"Just... difficult sometimes, thinking about how rough things were when I first left Roseport, and how things ended in Chicago." She shrugs, then catches my eye and flashes that sunny smile. "It makes me really happy that you thought to do something for me."

"Of course," I say instantly, a hard tug in my chest. She doesn't know the half of it. "You're amazing, Summer. You've done so much for me, and I-"

"Are you kidding?" She says, beaming. "What about everything you've done for me? You're amazing. You're so caring - more than you give yourself credit for - and you're smart, and creative…"

Her eyes are glittering like a disco ball and the smile on her face makes me feel weak. If I weren't already kneeling on the ground, I think I'd faint.

Something dawns on me slowly as her freckled nose scrunches up, her lips stretched into the cutest smile. She's talking about me. *Summer* looks like this while talking about *me*.

My head is spinning. It comes out before I can think: "Can I… can I kiss you?"

Her jaw drops, and I can't quite assign an emotion to the slight pull at the corner of her mouth. "Sadie…"

My heart pounds. "I'm sorry. I-"

"Sadie," she says, her mouth hanging ajar in an incredulous smile, "you *want* to kiss me?"

I can't help but let loose a breathy laugh, my lungs constricting and my heart pounding. "Are you fucking kidding? Summer, how could I-"

In one swift movement, she's shoved the baking sheet out of the way and grabbed me by my hips, pulling me flush against her and into a kiss. Her lips are hot and needy against mine, and that pull toward her that's been there from the beginning ignites in my chest. I hold her like she's the only thing keeping me from plummeting off a cliff, trying in vain to bring her even closer as our mouths move together. Her fingers are tight around my hips, and as she eagerly reciprocates every touch of my lips against hers, the intoxicating possibility comes to mind that she's been wanting this as much as I have.

"Please," I say, my voice raspy from lack of breath, "*please* can we go to my bedroom?"

She laughs with a similar breathlessness, her palms soft against my cheeks. "God, yes."

"Let me pick up the baking sheet," I murmur, the tiny sliver of my brain which remains reasonable fighting to the forefront. She nods seriously, her eyes locked onto mine.

We stumble down the hallway, giggling like teenagers while she unbuttons my blouse, throwing it aside, and I pull her shirt off over her head and unclasp her bra. I nearly trip on the trail of scattered clothing right as she nudges me through the door to my bedroom and reaches for the button of her jeans.

I fall back on the bed, eyes wide as her pants hit the floor, the buckle of her belt making a faint clinking sound against the tile. She stands there, miles and miles of smooth, white skin dotted with freckles. I want to take in every inch of her; want to trace every curve and line with my lips. There's the devastating angle of her collarbone, as sharp as her jaw, paired with the gorgeous softness of her stomach, her thighs, her boobs.

"What?" she says, both eyebrows raised and a coy smile playing at her plush pink lips.

"I… you…" The words go slack on my tongue, all descriptors for the insane effects her body is having on me gone from my mind. Her panties hang loose around her pelvis, but there's no mistaking the bulge there, and my heart rate quickens. I look back up to her face, swooning all the more at those big, kind eyes and the almost playful expression on her striking features. I can't believe I can look at her like this – not even that I'm allowed to, but that I physically *can*.

"That's how I feel," she says, "looking at you."

It doesn't compute. She's an angel goddess woman with all that smooth skin and silky hair, and I'm just…

Just then, she leans forward and pushes a strand of hair behind my ear. She slowly climbs onto the bed, straddling my hips and cupping my cheeks as she kisses me. She cradles me like something precious, and I feel all wobbly. One hand leaves my face and travels down my body, leaving a red-hot trail of anticipation on every inch of skin it touches. She's discarded my bra before I even really realize, my head high and drunk on the feeling of her lips, her touch.

My stomach churns for a second when she settles at the closure of my jeans, just above my navel. I know this shouldn't throw me - her body doesn't look that dissimilar to mine, and hers is *gorgeous* - but I can't shake the image of the last person to take my pants off. All the little comments, the digs that cut into me a little deeper each time…

Summer pulls back, her brow furrowed with concern. "We don't have to."

I take in a deep breath and look up at her, stunning and caring and perfect. She's *Summer*. My heart pounds. "I want to."

She smiles almost shyly and holds my eyes as she takes off my pants, my underwear sliding away with them. I shove them off my ankles and onto the floor, suddenly eager.

Her gaze locks onto my body, the wide-eyed expression on her face something she couldn't fake.

"Sadie," she half-whispers, her eyes reverent, "you're so beautiful."

I spring forward, wrapping my arms around her neck and pulling her back on top of me, and kiss her like I'll never need to breathe again.

She breaks it after a few minutes, practically panting. There's a crazy, urgent glint in her eye that ignites a fire in my stomach. She sits up, still straddling my legs. "Where can I touch? What can I do?"

Her hand is already sliding down my waist, and my brain is deliciously scrambled. "Everywhere," I breathe. "Everything."

She takes this to heart, wasting no time in bringing her hands down to my pelvis, gently and ever-so slowly forcing my legs open. I yelp like a dog at the teasing touch, and she looks up, worried.

"Please," I whimper. She adjusts herself, putting her legs between mine, and the expression turns almost cocky, a crooked grin on her face I've never seen before. I like it. I *really* like it.

She starts slow, her fingers giving an agonizingly careful rub against my clit. All manner of moans and cries escape from my lips as she gradually gains speed and pressure, and I lose sight of that sexy, confident smile as I'm forced to throw my head back and squeeze my eyes shut.

I feel her weight shift, and I weakly lift my head to see her sliding to the floor and onto her knees, warm palms resting on the tender insides of my thighs. She pauses, raising her eyebrows at me. Shivers run all the way up my body.

"God, Summer, yes," I manage to say, and her face disappears between my legs.

It occurs to me to be almost angry at her and the pace she takes, covering the sensitive skin of my upper and innermost thighs with the most delicate and chaste of kisses. A moan erupts from me like a formal complaint, and right on time her tongue presses into me, tracing a line up the length of my vulva. I melt into the bed with a satisfied groan, and she settles her attention again on my clit, unraveling me further with every motion. It could be anywhere between ten minutes and two hours that she spends there, but it still feels like seconds later that the accumulated tension all suddenly releases and I come against her lips, my hand clamped over my mouth to muffle the sound.

Overtaken, intoxicated by the dizzying feeling throughout my body, I reach out and pull her back on top of me. I let every urge take over: my palms explore the warmth of her boobs, tracing and teasing my thumbs over her nipples; I bury my face in the crook of her neck and kiss, bite, suck, and lick the soft skin there with a ferocity I've never felt before. The sounds she makes in response affect me like a drug, my heart rate soaring as she whines and murmurs *god* and *Sadie* and *fuck*.

Then, with a weakening burst of forcefulness, she pushes us both further onto the bed, a pillow cushioning my head. She eagerly reciprocates my touch, her hand ghosting across my nipple, there one moment and gone the next. I whimper, feeling her growing hotter and harder through her panties as she presses against me.

I clumsily claw at her waistband, my lovesick mind suddenly recognizing only the immediate and urgent goal to liberate her from her underwear. She takes the hint, rolling them down her gorgeous legs and tossing them carelessly aside. I dig into my bedside table and triumphantly produce a condom, practically shaking as I hand it to her. I lie back, admiring once again the beautiful roundness of her torso, the smattering of freckles, and now the sweat glistening on her pale skin. She puts her legs together, and I spread my own on either side of her, the skin of her hips brushing enticingly against the inside of my thighs.

Her eyes lock onto mine as she leans in and guides her dick downward, silently asking my permission once again. I nod desperately, breathlessly. She slides into me and I let out a guttural gasp, pleasure coursing through my body, as much for the sensation as for the overwhelming sense of *finally, finally we're doing this*. Only now does my head really begin to clear, and as she begins to stroke inside of me, the feeling momentarily takes a backseat to the wonderful realization sinking in that Summer and I are really doing what we're doing.

My breath shudders in tandem with each thrust, and our voices join together in a chorus of swears, sighs, and moans. I look up at her through half-lidded eyes, disheveled and glowing and utterly unbelievable. Her eyes roll back and her lips remain permanently parted, her chest heaving with each little sound which bubbles up from her throat. I hook my legs around her, pulling her forward so her lips can meet mine as she continues rocking inside of me.

This - *she* - is too good to be true, I can't help but think. This can't be real. But I feel each movement echoing through my body, a sensation larger than life as I lose myself in the rhythm of her hips. This, too, goes on without cognizance toward time. I kiss her and she moves in and out of me, and it's as though neither of us has ever done anything else. It's as though I've always been here, breathing and acting as one with her.

Her pace ever so gradually builds and builds, and her voice grows higher and messier, the groans more insistent, until one last cry dies halfway out of her mouth. Her face freezes for a moment in an extraordinary ecstasy, and then she slumps against my shoulder with a drained, satisfied sigh.

Like second nature, my hand goes to the back of her head, my fingers burrowing into her hair and lightly scratching against her scalp. "Jesus Christ, Summer."

"Jesus Christ, Sadie," she agrees, her voice muffled and her lips still hot against my skin. "Do you want to get cleaned up?"

"Just a second," I reply, taking my first real breath in what seems like days. "That was..." I can't find a sufficient description to finish my thought, but she seems to understand.

In the shower, she washes my body with the same care she used to pleasure it, and I have to treat her with that reverence, too. I haven't stopped reeling at the way her body looks, the way it feels. We end up back in bed, freshly cleaned and clothed in my spare pajamas, with her arms around my waist and her head on my chest. I almost miss the scent of baked goods on her hair.

"You know," I find myself saying with a wistful smile at my lips, "Felix wanted to set us up back in July."

She lets out a short, shocked laugh. "God. I'll give him this, it could've saved us a few steps."

"I didn't want to like you," I say, absentmindedly curling a still-wet ginger strand around my index finger. "Or anybody, after the Gabby stuff. I knew that feelings like that could hurt me. They had. A lot." I laugh incredulously. "And you were so *pretty*, I couldn't do anything but be an asshole."

She shoves me lightly. "You were not an asshole."

"I was, too," I reply, shoving back. "I couldn't let myself like you, because I knew I'd *like* you."

She adjusts herself, sitting up so she can look at me. Her brown eyes make my knees feel weak. "I'm just glad we got here." She grins. "Very glad."

I have to kiss her, and it feels like the easiest thing in the world. Falling asleep by her side feels easy too.

In fact, everything feels easy, right up until she leaves for work the next morning.

"I'll come over tonight after work," she says as I pull her in for what must be my millionth kiss, leaning against my open apartment door.

"I'm off today," I reply, frowning deeply and tightening my grip on her hand.

"Poor thing," she says, her other hand cradling the nape of my neck. "Guess you'll just have to sit around and wait for me."

She's kidding, but I just nod.

"We can finally watch that episode," she adds, quirking her eyebrows. I laugh, pressing a kiss to her knuckles.

"Do you really have to go?" I ask, and she laughs.

"You *are* always telling me I need to work less," she says with a smirk, then pulls me in by the back of my neck and kisses me. She still holds me when she pulls back, her eyes huge as she looks at me. "I'll see you tonight, okay, darling?"

My knees get so weak, I half expect to collapse to the ground. "Jesus, Summer, are you trying to kill me?"

She chuckles softly. "You like 'darling'?"

"I'd like anything you called me," I tell her, my tone the slightest bit too earnest. But, no- I don't want to hide my feelings from her. I don't have to, because as amazing and incomprehensible as it is, she feels the same way.

Her smile lights up the whole hallway. "See you soon, Sadie."

I shiver. That may just still be my favorite.

"See you soon," I say, "sweetheart."

And I steal one more kiss.

"Hey baby!" comes Felix's voice on the other end of the phone. "To what do I owe the pleasure?"

"Can I come over in a bit?" I'm so excited I'm practically dancing in my chair. I wasn't like this when we were kids - pseudo-closeted and too insecure to act happy - but this is how I imagine gushing to a preteen Felix about my newest crush would feel.

"Sure!" he says. "How about here in, like, thirty minutes? I'm just going through all the RSVPs again to make sure everything's good."

"Alright," I beam. "I was gonna stop by So Sweet for a snack on the way. What can I grab for you?"

"Sadie, you're scaring me," he replies, and I can hear the smile in his voice. "Did somebody put vodka in your coffee this morning?"

"Unless I *really* slipped up in the kitchen, I don't think so."

"Seriously, babe," he says. "Don't take this the wrong way, but you sound really happy. What's going on?"

"Don't worry about it," I respond. I could tell him now, but this feels too monumental for a phone call. Especially knowing that Felix of all people is going to *freak* at the news. "We'll talk when I get there."

"Alright," he says. "I'll take your word for it, Sadie. Grab me a cupcake. Whatever flavor looks good."

"You got it, Boss," I say. "See you soon."

"Just let yourself in when you get here," he says. "Love you."

"Love you, too." I'm bouncing with excitement when I kiss Ethel goodbye, lock the apartment door behind me, and make my way to the car.

"Felix!" I call, heading down the hall toward his bedroom. "They had a few flavors that I thought you'd like, so I just got you-" I stop in my tracks as the door swings open and my gaze focuses on Felix in bed. "Oh my god, babe, what happened?"

He gives a loud sniff, using the back of his hand to push his glasses up onto his forehead and wipe away a stream of tears.

"I just..." A sob bubbles up from his throat, and I hurriedly sit down at his side, setting the cupcakes at the foot of the bed.

"It's okay, baby," I murmur, rubbing his back. "It's all going to be okay." He takes a deep breath in the way he always used to when we were kids, clenching and unclenching his fists along with it.

"My mom called," he says slowly, and my heart pounds. "I thought she was... We'd said..."

"It's okay, babe," I coax. "Take your time."

"She's not coming to the wedding," he says shakily. "I knew she was having a little bit of trouble, but we'd always agreed she would be at the wedding. But she just called and said she can't come."

"She can't make it?" I ask, sickeningly hopeful. "Or she won't?"

Felix whimpers, leaning onto my shoulder.

"Hey, hey, baby, it's okay," I say, rubbing his back.

"I know I shouldn't care," he wails, fist closing around the hem of my shirt. "But I just want my mama, Sadie."

"I know, honey," I tell him, and I *really* do. Every part of me aches. I'd always thought Alison was better than my parents - the way she nurtured both Felix and me as a single mother, it had seemed when I was a kid like she would kindly accept anything I told her. Somehow, I can't quite corroborate this behavior with the Ms. Nguyen I knew.

"I thought we were getting better," he says. "She's been using my name and pronouns for years, and she was so nice when she met Julian the last several times. I thought she *loved* him. I don't know what happened." He sniffs. "I just want her to accept me. How dumb is that? I'm almost thirty and here I am crying about my mommy."

"Honey, no," I say quickly, stroking my hand over his shoulder blades. "No, it's not dumb. I understand. Cry as much as you need, love."

He sniffs again, loud and long. Then, weakly: "What kind of cupcakes did you bring?"

I squeeze him like I did when we were little. "Okay. This one is dulce de leche, this is cookies and cream, key lime..."

Chapter Twenty-Six

Summer At Your Service

Work goes by quicker than it ever has. I'm only half-conscious through preparing orders and making deliveries, and I see Sadie's face, glowingly grinning as she tilts her chin to kiss me again and again, every time my mind even slightly wanders. It almost doesn't feel real when, at the end of the day, she opens her apartment door to let me in.

"Hi," I breathe, pulling her toward me and brushing my lips against her forehead. She brings her face upward to give me her lips, which I gratefully cover with mine. She seems to melt in my arms.

This feels too good to be true. Leaving this morning, I'd almost had the impression that Sadie and her apartment would disappear behind me like some magical other world I was only allowed to visit once. But here she is, beautiful and kissable and real. She wraps her arms around my neck, and my whole body feels dizzy.

"How was your day?" I ask when we pull away, tucking a lock of hair behind her ear.

"I missed you," she says, then bites her lip and looks away almost shyly. It feels like butterflies in my stomach.

"I missed you too." My hand slides up and down her back.

"We can watch our episode," she says, clearing her throat. "But I'm, uh, I'm gonna be packing."

I nudge the door shut behind us. "Packing?"

She turns around and paces a bit, all the tension returning to her body language. Discomfort creeps into my senses at seeing her like this. "Felix's mom told him she isn't coming to the wedding."

My jaw falls open. "Oh my god."

"I'm going to Virginia to talk to her," she says, her voice wavering. "I *know* she's better than this. She's better than..."

I rest my hands on her shoulders, stopping her frenzied walk. She breathes deeply, sliding onto the couch. Ethel waddles toward us and I boost her up, where she immediately curls up on Sadie's lap. I join them both, Sadie still trying to collect herself.

"My dad didn't react well when I came out," she says finally, leaning onto my shoulder. "I was *twenty-four*, and he acted like I was some disobedient kid who was just doing it to piss him off. He didn't say a word to me the whole week I stayed with them for Christmas. So, the next year, I didn't go." Her face screws with some mix of emotions I can't quite read. "Or the next year."

I rub her back gently, and she plays absentmindedly with Ethel's ears as she goes on. "It was a few days after that Christmas that he was admitted to the hospital. I showed up because, you know, he was still my *dad*." She presses her lips together, sliding a hand to her tear duct under the lens of her glasses. "He wouldn't even look at me. *Still*, two years after I'd told him I was bi. But, I mean, what was I going to do? I stayed in the hospital for hours while the doctors looked at him and argued about what to do with him, until he just kind of *died*. It was over so fast, and… it was like I hadn't been there at all."

"Oh, Sadie." I squeeze her, and she leans into the touch.

"I don't regret standing my ground with him," she says slowly. "I don't, like, wish I'd spent more time with the man who was throwing a hissy fit about my identity. But the fact that he dropped dead before he could even consider trying to accept me..." She shakes her head. "Felix doesn't deserve that. And Alison is *not* my dad."

She's still tense in my arms, and her breaths are jagged. An idea turns over in my mind, half-baked. "Honey, this seems like it's really working you up. Would it help you if I, like, came with you?"

She looks up, her green eyes huge. "I couldn't ask you to do that. Don't you have work to do?"

"I only have one order this week," I tell her. "I was already cutting back my available slots since the wedding's so close. I can deliver that order first thing in the morning and be on the plane with you right after."

"You would do that?" she says slowly, rubbing the back of Ethel's neck. The dog's tail makes a thumping sound against the couch cushions as it lazily wags.

"Absolutely."

She squirms. "You don't have to."

"I want to."

Her gaze bores into me, eyebrows slightly lifted and expression anticipatory, as if she's waiting for me to falter. It melts away after a second, something liquid in her eyes.

"Thank you," she says after a second, her voice hushed, and she caresses my cheek before pressing her lips to mine.

"I can't believe V3 and Isla took so long to get together," Sadie says, her brow knit as she lowers her copy of *Romancing the Drone*. "He's liked her from the beginning, and she told Katie and XJ that she wanted to take him to the Human-Droid Relations Gala, like, five chapters ago."

I laugh, adjusting in my cramped airplane seat, my elbow rubbing against hers. "How good of a story would it be if they got together halfway through?"

"And that grand gesture," she goes on, waving the book around emphatically. "He reprogrammed her whole security system in a single night just because he wanted her to be safe. How did she not catch on that he wanted to be with her?"

Shrugging, I pull up the blanket across my legs. "I mean, what did you think when I came to the vet with you on Valentine's Day?"

Her lips part and she blinks at me. "That was *months* ago. You mean... you liked me on Valentine's Day?"

"Yeah," I reply meekly, suddenly a little bashful. "I hope you didn't think the other night was just, like, some spur-of-the-moment thing."

"I didn't," she says quickly. Then, casting her eyes toward the aisle, "It wasn't for me, either."

A grin cracks my face. "No way." It's not like I'd thought she decided in that very moment to fuck me out of nowhere, and she told me about why she was cold when we first met, but it kind of boggles my mind to think she'd been actively crushing on me, too. "When did you..."

"When you rushed off work to help me with Ethel?" she suggests flippantly, moving a strand of hair out from behind her glasses. "When we made penis cookies together? When you fell asleep on my couch? When I first saw you with your hair down?"

She tugs gently at one of my curls, and I feel like squealing like a schoolgirl. "I don't know. Maybe kind of since the beginning."

I'm taken aback for a second, a flower blooming in my chest. "You know what? I think, me too."

She smiles, almost privately. "Wow."

"What?"

"Still surprising," she murmurs, resting her hand on my wrist and gently tracing her fingers across the sensitive skin.

"You're surprised that I like you?" I ask, sliding my arm so her hand fits into mine. "You're, like, magnetic. And so *funny*. Seeing you smile, and interact with our friends... it was there from the start."

She bites her lip, a familiar glint in her eye. "Do you want to be my girlfriend?"

My heart skips. "Yeah, I do. Of course I do." She smiles, squeezing my hand.

"Okay." A blush runs up her round cheeks. "Cool."

"Yeah," I reply, grinning at her. "Very cool." I can only describe the feeling across my senses as some kind of dancing, like maybe if we weren't buckled into airplane seats, I'd pull her up and start moving to some inaudible tune from my mind. It's a delightfully childish feeling, the kind I thought was long behind me at fifteen, let alone twenty-eight.

"Anyway, you're right," she says, lifting her book and taking away her hand after another quick squeeze. "XJ is a douchebag. He's really gonna have to shape up in the sequel if I'm supposed to believe he's good enough for Katie."

Maybe it shouldn't, but this takes me aback. "You're going to read the sequel?"

"If I can borrow my girlfriend's copy," she says casually, with a twinkle in her eye that tells me she knows about the electricity that runs up and down my spine when she says that. I grin, patting her thigh.

"It's all yours."

"Oh," she says, brows raised and her nose buried in the gutter between the pages. "Now they're having sex. Is this gonna be weird?"

"Only a little," I reply, shrugging. "You know V3's designed to be *mostly* human."

"I hope that isn't you hinting about wanting a reenactment," she says. "I hope you noticed, I don't have a robot dick."

"I don't either," I add. "Exactly what we've done is what I want."

"*Woah*," she chimes, face somehow even deeper in the book. "That was fast. Not wasting *any* time climbing onto that man-shaped vibrator."

I chuckle. "She knows what she wants."

Sadie nods, turning the page. "Good for her."

When we finally arrive at Sadie's mom's house after a long ride in an Uber following the trip on the plane, the sun is just starting to set. The door swings open almost the second Sadie's foot hits the curb. A gray-haired woman comes sprinting onto the sidewalk with us. Sadie doesn't turn to her immediately, just goes around to the trunk to get her suitcase. I cautiously step out after her.

"Welcome home, sweetheart!" the woman coos, her dark eyes fixed hard on Sadie's face as she smooths a palm across her daughter's hair. "How was your flight?"

"Good," Sadie says, her jaw set. She turns her chin toward me, flicking her gaze back. "This is my mom."

"Cassie," she offers almost reflexively, her demeanor growing awkward when her eyes settle on my face. She clears her throat, pushing a bit of long gray hair over her shoulder. "Sadie didn't tell me she'd be bringing a friend."

Sadie looks at the ground, her teeth gritting behind her lips. I give my best 'you're an unaccepting sexagenarian, but I still want you to like me' smile. "I'm Summer. It's nice to meet you."

"You too, dear," she says, the slightest trembling under her voice. She turns back to Sadie. "How long are you going to stay, sweetie?"

"I'm leaving tomorrow after I talk to Ms. Nguyen," Sadie says bluntly, pulling shortly up on the handle of her suitcase and grunting frustratedly when it doesn't budge. My hand goes to her back like it always does, making small circles. She looks at me, smiling weakly.

"That'll be nice," Cassie nods. "You can tell Alison hi from me."

The handle finally goes up smoothly now, and Sadie starts toward the door. I follow, my hand still on her back.

Sadie travels familiarly through the house, neat and tidy, until we reach a white door painted with flowers. I cock my head to the side, grinning at her. "*Please* tell me Baby Sadie did that."

"Felix helped," she says with a small smile finally cracking through, opening the door and pushing it out of her way so she can pull her luggage into the room. I take it in- cluttered yet empty in that characteristic way of a room where nobody lives anymore. Picture books and little trophies mingle on shelves and dresser tops, and the sheets on the queen-sized bed don't match the comforter.

"How soon is too soon to start snooping?" I ask, setting my bag on the bed next to her suitcase and craning my neck toward the knickknacks on top of the bookcase.

She rolls her eyes, her lips curved in a smile. "You could just ask Felix if you wanted dirt on me."

"How dare you imply it'd be *dirt*," I reply. "I'm looking for all the butterflies."

Sadie's mouth hangs open for a second, an incredulous smirk pulling at the corner of her lips. "You remember the butterflies."

"Of course I do." I reach out and touch a little clay butterfly. "This is so cute."

"Oh, you should've seen the one David made," comes Cassie's voice as she strolls in through the open door. Sadie tenses. "Do you remember? I couldn't go to that little pottery class with you, and Daddy didn't want to waste the money." She chuckles, then looks at me with a melancholy expression. "He tried his best, but art never was David's strong suit."

Knowing how much Sadie's dad hurt her, this cute talk about him bravely taking a butterfly-themed pottery class with his daughter turns my stomach. "That's sweet."

"What are your parents like, Summer?" She cocks her head to the side and keeps intense eye contact, but I get the feeling that there's something between her question and a genuine interest. Sadie turns to her suitcase, busying herself with pulling her toiletries out.

"Really great," I reply. "My brothers and I are still really close with them."

"*Ohh*, the only girl," coos Cassie. "They must have been so excited when you were born."

"They actually didn't find out they'd had a girl until a few years later," I quip, and she blinks.

"Oh," she says, a tremor in her bottom jaw carrying through to her voice. "I- I couldn't even tell."

Sadie slams the lid of her suitcase shut. "I'm going to the kitchen."

She shoves past her mom and is out the door in a second. Cassie looks between me and the door for a second before shifting awkwardly on her feet and looking at me. It's an odd kind of look, hesitant and studying.

"You're the first one I've met," she says slowly, and at first I think she means *trans person*. But that can't be it- she knew Felix when he was growing up, even though he didn't transition until later. It dawns on me that what she really means by that is *Sadie's girlfriend.* "I don't..."

Her face seems to screw up with effort. Where exactly is she going with this? Sadie didn't mention her being outright unaccepting like her dad was, but there's a definite uncomfortable twinge to her expression.

"She seems to really like you," she says finally, her voice thick. "You'll... you'll take care of her." She raises her eyebrows- it's a question.

"Yeah," I reply quickly. "We'll take care of each other."

I can't measure his discomfort in linear terms; there's a change in her expression, but whether she's soothed or even more anxious is entirely unclear. She gives a wavering smile. "I can show you the guest room."

My gaze flicks to the open door Sadie left through. "I don't..."

"Of course," she says, clipped. Her eyes shift, and she's already halfway out the door when she says, "I'll... let you get settled, then."

Chapter Twenty-Seven

Sadie Moves On

I hear footsteps coming into the kitchen just as I'm pulling a water cup down from the same cabinet they've been in since I was a kid.

"That Summer seems like a very sweet girl," says Mom, a cautious lilt to her voice as she passes behind me and heads toward the cabinet where she keeps her tea. I tense. There's a surreal feeling about Summer being here, my *girlfriend*, a concrete being, where my mom's house has always been the land of vagueness, of discomfort and implications. I almost don't want my mom to be able to see her - she's too sacred.

"She is," I reply shortly, filling my cup.

"Did you have any trouble on the plane?" she asks, crossing the kitchen to get her mug. "I know how you used to get scared of the turbulence."

I grit my teeth. I can't stand this- I just stormed out of my room in a huff like a toddler, and she's here talking to me about turbulence? I can't take it anymore.

"Why do you have to talk about Dad like that?" I say, the words leaving my mouth like a gust of wind. Mom turns, blinking like she's stepping into the sun after a long movie.

"Like what, sweetheart?" she says, the words brittle. Something glints behind her eyes.

"Like he was the most fantastic man in the world," I reply. "Mama, he didn't say a word to me the day he died."

She bites her lip, looking down at her shoes.

"I know you miss him," I go on. "But he wasn't a good dad, and any chance I had of having any sort of good relationship with him died when he did."

"You know how he was," she says, not meeting my eye.

Stubborn. Ignorant. Tyrannical.

"He... he wasn't ever going to change."

Something in me feels a little braver than I ever have. This is the closest she's ever come to acknowledging things with Dad, and she's still so far away. "But you can," I say a little weakly.

I've fractured something, that barely-breathing polite composure, but I haven't broken it. She looks at me curiously, telltale fingers frozen on the string of her teabag. "What do you mean?"

"You must notice I'm not comfortable here, Mama," I say, years of resentment seeping into my voice. "It's because *you're* not comfortable with *me*. We haven't talked about Felix, my best friend in the world, in ten years because he's a man. I finally got up the nerve to tell you and Dad that I like women, and we never talked about it again. And now, when I finally bring a woman home, a woman who really matters to me, you can't act even a little like it's happening." I let out a whooshing breath, full of pressure. "I want to be able to talk about things. *Real* things."

Her mouth seems to form the beginning of a hundred different sentences, her eyes slowly moving across the countertop. "I don't know what to say, Sadie."

"I never felt like I could tell you things," I say softly. "As a kid. I think you've always shied away from tough topics, and I understand it. But it hurts me when you do that. It always has. It's part of why I hid being gay for so long."

"Honey, I want you to be happy," she says. "I just... I don't understand it."

"You don't have to," I press. "But I want to be able to have hard conversations with you, Mom. Like about Dad."

She casts her eyes downward, something darkening on her face. "I know that wasn't easy for you, honey."

"It was more than not easy, Mom," I say, leaning forward onto the counter. "It was like he wasn't even my dad anymore. And you didn't help. You just let him ice me out."

"I didn't want to..." Her interjection dies out halfway through. Lamely, she finishes: "...cause a scene."

"I don't need you to change how you feel about him," I say quietly, pushing myself back up off the counter. "But I need you to acknowledge that I'm not mourning him the same way you are. You lost a husband. I don't know if I can even say I lost a dad."

"I'm sorry you feel that way, honey," she says, wringing her teabag string around her forefinger. "I'm... I'm sorry."

"Summer is my girlfriend," I say carefully, and it feels strange and new and exciting - equally due to my present company and to the fact that those words are still so new that I've never said them out loud before. "I want to be able to talk to you about that."

"She's..." Mom clears her throat. "She's lovely. And she makes you happy?"

"Yes, Mama," I reply, an ache growing in my chest. "She does."

She nods. "Good. That's what I want." She swallows, pointing her chin up like a brave soldier. I find myself almost a little proud.

"That's all I want," she goes on, reaching across the counter for me. I let her cover my hand with hers. She clears her throat. "I'll try to be better, baby."

"Thank you," I say plainly.

"I'll need my time," she says. "But I'll try."

"I know." I take a breath, and it feels easier than a minute ago.

"Hey." My bedroom door closes behind me, and Summer looks up from where she sits, perched on the end of the bed.

"Hey," she says, her smile brighter than the overhead light. I set my water cup on my nightstand, then sit down at her side. She flicks her eyes toward the door to the kitchen. "Everything okay in there?"

"Actually, yeah," I reply, leaning against her shoulder. "We kind of ended up talking stuff out."

"That's great!" she says, squeezing my arm.

"It'll be good prep at least," I add, standing up and getting my pajamas from my suitcase. "If I can convince *Cassie Levine* to put a brave face on her internalized homophobia, what's one more mother?"

"I think it goes without saying that I believe in you," she says, leaning back on her hands.

"But you *could* say it," I say, turning around and lifting my shirt over my head. In what seems like an instant, I feel warm skin against my back. I roll my eyes. "Why, yes, Summer, you *can* help me change into my pajamas."

"You looked like you were having trouble," she says shamelessly, her breath hot and ticklish against my neck as her fingers slide up to the clasp of my bra. "Just trying to do you a favor, Sadie."

With only a little token resistance, I let her slide my bra off. She presses a kiss to my back and goes to slide down my sweatpants as I reach for my sleep shirt.

I turn after pulling it on. "Definitely a two-person job."

"That's what I'm saying," she says, then gives an exaggeratedly glum look down at her clothes. "But how will *I* get changed?"

"It's a real predicament," I agree, already sliding my hands under the hem of her shirt.

It's surreal on multiple levels, sliding into the sheets of my childhood bed with her, but the one at the front of my mind is that we haven't slept in the same bed since that first night. Last night, she went back to her apartment so she could leave early to make her delivery. For a second the least logical parts of my brain are terrified that everything was a fluke, and that my last 72 hours with her will be the end of everything. But she snuggles into my side like it's the most normal thing in the world- and I guess it really is. She's my *girlfriend*. I grapple wondrously with the fact that someday this will feel totally commonplace.

"So..." she draws out the syllable, her cheek against my chest. "We fuck now, right?"

That shocks a giggle out of me. "I can forgive you for thinking that, considering it *is* what happened the only other time you took my clothes off." I move my nails slowly against her scalp. "But we'd probably better let Mom take this whole thing slow. I'm not sure she's even accepted that I know what sex *is*."

"Aw," she says, "I was really looking forward to doing it in full view of that framed glamor shot." My eyes follow hers to a shelf on the opposite wall, and I slap a hand across my mouth.

"Oh my god," I groan, the sight of my own adolescent face caught in an awkward half-smile against a cheesy photo backdrop proving to be physically painful. "I cannot believe my mom left that out. *Audible farts* make her uncomfortable, but she can stand to look at that abomination."

"It's cute," she says, scooting up to look at me. "I forgot your hair was wavy."

"So were my teeth," I quip, then give a performative shudder. "Braces can only fix so much."

"Hey, I love your little snaggletooth," she protests, pinching the sensitive spot on my torso where my waist dips in.

"You flatter me," I deadpan, slapping her hand away.

"I *love* you," she presses. "I mean it, it's cute."

"You... you love me?" Under the sheets, twenty-eight and grown, I feel like a kid, fluttery and hopeful.

"Technically you said it first," she says with a shrug, though her face is less nonchalant. There's a distinct pink running under her freckles, and I'm almost sickly delighted at the thought that Ms. Cool is blushing about *me* (as if we aren't literally girlfriends).

"Sure, coward, go there," I say, raising my eyebrows like a challenge. This'll be where she backs down, but if I can at least use this moment to get another piece of proof that she *actually* likes me, I'll consider it a win.

Her brown eyes look bigger than I even thought they could. There's an almost calculating edge to her expression as her smile grows, still the tiniest bit meek. "I love you."

My whole body feels weak. It must show on my face, because her joy only seems to strengthen.

"I already have as a friend," she says, smoothing my hair over my ear. Chills run through me. "And I know it hasn't been that long, but… I do."

"Me too," I say slowly, my heart pounding in my chest.

"Can I hear you say the words?" she says, pushing her hair behind her ear and then grabbing my hand. "Darling?"

She might as well hit me over the head. "I love you," I say, and the words spill from my mouth like water. She beams, her hand sliding from mine and up to my cheek.

"I'm going to kiss you now," she says through the smile. I don't put up a fight.

Bright and early the next morning, Felix's childhood home looks just like I remember it. I used to admire Alison's perfectly manicured flower beds, begging her to let me help her with them. They're just like they always were, lined up perfectly on either side of the front door. I breathe in shakily, my knees shaking beneath me as I suddenly revert to a preteen here on the driveway.

Summer's hand slides into mine, and she presses a short kiss to the back of my neck. "This can be a phone call if you need, love."

Love is a shot of adrenaline. I squeeze her hand. "No. I have to do this in person."

"I believe in you," she says again.

"Now or never," I murmur, striding toward the door and knocking before I can stop myself. After a second, the door swings open and there's Alison. She's shrunk even since I last saw her, though she was never exactly tall, but her short dark hair is still as starkly jet black as it was when I first met her.

Her dark eyes crinkle at the corners, though her smile doesn't mask her surprise. "Sadie, hello! To what do I owe the pleasure?"

"Hi, Alison," I say. "I was in the neighborhood. This is Summer. She's Julian's friend from college. Can we come inside?"

Chapter Twenty-Eight
Summer Has Your Back

The living room is just as neat as the facade of the house, little knickknacks carefully placed alongside countless framed photos of Felix across twenty years and two little floral couches facing one another with an ornate coffee table in between. Felix's mom fluffs a pillow on one couch while Sadie and I settle into the other. There's a faint scent of honey and oatmeal hanging in the air.

"Can I get you girls anything?" she says, adjusting her glasses. "I just made a batch of pink lemonade. It was supposed to be for book club tomorrow, but I can make another."

"No thank you," says Sadie. Her demeanor seems bright and friendly, but I can tell it's stiff. I rest my palm for a second on her knee, squeezing it. She flashes me a quick smile.

"How have you been?" Alison asks, now fussing with a little cat figurine on the shelf behind the couch. The restlessness to her posture and shiftiness in her eyes remind me, suddenly, of Mrs. Levine. "It feels like it's been so long."

"I've been good," Sadie says, her gaze flicking to me for half a moment. "Busy. Lots of work."

Alison nods. "You must be very popular. I remember those bouquets you used to give me and your mom. So beautiful."

Sadie gulps almost imperceptibly, her neck craned to look up at Felix's mom. "I'm actually doing the flowers for the wedding."

There's the smallest shift in Alison's face as she turns around, brushing her fingertips against the back of the couch. "How sweet. I'm sure it's going to be lovely."

Sadie's voice is gentle. "Why don't you come and see for yourself?"

Alison squirms, a false smile on her lips as her hands grow more vigorous, smoothing the blanket over the back of the couch. "Oh, I'd just make the whole thing a lot less fun. You won't even notice I'm gone."

"Felix really wants you there," says Sadie. "He'd hate that I'm telling you this, but he misses you *so* badly. He just wants to see you."

She crosses in front of the couch, lightly pacing. "I just can't, honey. I'm sorry."

"Why can't you?" Her tone is still soft, without a hint of accusation. Alison freezes for a second, then finally sinks onto the couch.

"It's just all so strange," she says quietly, her eyes fixed on the coffee table behind the thin frames of her glasses. "I've learned to accept my son. I know Julian is a good, kind man. But this wedding... this, this backyard wedding where two men who used to be women wear whatever they want and then marry each other..." She runs a hand over her opposite palm. "It's all so strange to me. I'm too old. I know Felix is happy, and I don't want to take that away from him."

"You being there would make Felix happy," says Sadie. "You've been a great mom, Alison. Our whole life, I saw how hard you tried for him. He doesn't need you to be perfect. He never did."

"I would just ruin everything for him," Alison murmurs, her eyes still lowered.

"You don't have to understand everything," Sadie says, leaning forward. "But I know you can try. You always took care of us when we were kids, even when you didn't get it. Remember that summer right after we met, we were both obsessed with making mud pies in the backyard?"

Alison lets out a little laugh, apprehensive but true. "God, I'll never forget. Especially that day you tracked mud all up and down my house. I spent an hour mopping up all those little footprints."

"But that was when you took us to that pottery place," Sadie adds with a grin. Her tooth flashes, and somehow all of a sudden it makes her look like a kid. "My mom wanted to stop letting us in the backyard, but you wanted to try something different."

"Is that when that was?" Alison asks, her smile quirking up a bit more. "Huh."

"That really stuck with me. You were the parent I wished I had."

She squeezes her eyes shut. "I never did like the way David and Cassie talked to you."

"You never judged us," Sadie tells her. "That's all that mattered. You're why my best friend is who he is. You're a good mom. And Felix knows you've been trying. You've always tried, our whole lives. That's what matters."

I'm in absolute awe. Sadie was so nervous, but here she is delivering this whole heartfelt speech like it's nothing.

"You can come back to Roseport with Summer and I tomorrow morning," she goes on. "It's up to you, but I really think you should. You'd have a few days with Felix to talk some stuff out."

Alison swallows hard, then looks up. "Thank you, Sadie. I think I will." She nods. "I will. I'll start packing." She stands up, and Sadie follows suit. I do, too. "Thank you."

She looks at me with a short, breathless laugh. "And it was nice to meet you, Summer." Her dark eyes dart to Sadie, a cheeky grin on her face that reminds me of my own mom. "She's really cute."

Sadie laughs, the back of her hand momentarily going to her eye. "Thanks, Ms. Nguyen."

Alison clicks her tongue. "Don't you 'Ms. Nguyen' me, girl." Then she pulls Sadie, almost abruptly, into a hug. When she lets go, Sadie's hand falls incredibly naturally into mine.

"I'll see you tomorrow morning," Alison says.

"See you then," Sadie says, and Alison leads us back out the front door. The moment it closes behind us, Sadie collapses into me with a sigh that sounds like all the air coming out of a balloon.

"That was the scariest thing I've ever fucking done," she says with a shuddering laugh, her cheek pressed against my shoulder. I squeeze her hand.

"But you *did* it." I turn my head, pressing a kiss against the top of her head. "Felix is gonna be so happy."

"Speaking of Felix," she says, righting her posture and leading me on the short walk back to her mom's house. "Who do you think should tell him?" She raises our interlocked hands.

"Oh my god," I chuckle. "You're right. He'll be so excited."

"There's a word for *smug* I've never heard," she says with a wicked smile.

"I mean, he *is* your best friend," I offer.

"And he did tell me back in July that I should make sweet, gay love to you," she adds, and I sputter.

"He said that?"

"Something to that effect," she says with a shrug.

"Then I think it's settled," I reply. "You should tell him you finally listened to his advice."

She shoves me with her shoulder. "Thank you for being here, by the way."

"Of course, darling."

"Not just *here*," she says. "Virginia. With me. All of it."

I stop, pulling her around to face me. "I need you to understand that there is literally nowhere else I would rather be."

She rolls her eyes, but her smile stretches across her whole face. "God, you're so corny."

"I love you," I add, raising my eyebrows.

Her lips pull into a straight line, but even that can't conceal her expression. "I love you, too."

"Sadie!" Felix's voice cuts through the airport as we pass the front desk, bags in hand. Sadie speeds up, flying like a projectile into Felix's arms. I arrive a second behind, catching Julian's eye and smiling.

"I will literally never forgive you for going off and doing this," Felix says, his back curved so his chin can perch on Sadie's shoulder. "Thank you *so* much, babe."

"Where's Alison?" Julian asks.

"She's in the bathroom," I reply. "She spent the back half of the flight squirming, but she refused to go in the airplane bathroom."

"That's Mom," says Felix, holding Sadie at arms-length. "I can't believe you actually got her to come."

"I just reminded her how important *you* are," Sadie replies, reaching up to ruffle his hair.

"She also managed to talk to her *own* mom," I add, a shameless bit of pride building in my chest.

"No way," Felix says, his jaw dropping. "You had a *conversation* with Mama Levine? And she was in the room?"

"Yes, yes, it was all very impressive," Sadie says, waving her hand dismissively. "But, look, there's something I think you'll be interested to know."

He raises his brows so high that they're actually visible over the big round frames of his glasses. "Was somebody having a loud, dramatic phone conversation on the plane?" He shoots his gaze to Julian and me. "Eavesdropping on strangers' phone calls has been a foundation of our friendship since middle school."

"Not this time," she says. "So, uh, I asked Summer to be my girlfriend a couple days ago."

His jaw drops, and his wide eyes immediately laser onto me. "And you said...?"

"Yes," I say, suddenly a bit flustered. He turns back to Sadie, grabbing both her hands and jumping up and down.

"Oh my god, tell me absolutely everything. Better yet, tell me when it's just us so you can tell me things she wouldn't want you telling me." Sadie laughs, and his bouncing starts to look more like a jaunty little dance. "I'm *so* fucking excited."

"I was waiting on an *I told you so,*" she says, her hands still in his.

"Baby, this far transcends *I told you so*," he says. "I manifested this shit into existence, like, ten months ago. I'm motherfucking *God*."

Sadie snorts. "Glad to hear this development isn't going to your head, Felix."

Julian looks at me with a smirk, his big brown eyes full of implication. "Nice 'unrequited' feelings you've got there, Sport."

I smile, cocking my head to the side. "Yeah, sorry I ruined your birthday party bitching about it."

He holds his arms up, palm-out like a shield. "Hey, you can bitch at my birthday party anytime, as long as it's about your future wife." He raises his eyebrows, the gesture loaded. "Is she?"

"Are you kidding?" I cut my eyes sideways to where she's still whispering about something with Felix before looking back at Julian. "It's *Sadie*. Of course she is. If she'll have me."

"What's Sadie?" she asks, turning.

"Nothing," I reply quickly. "Don't worry about it."

She rolls her eyes good-naturedly, tucking herself under my arm. "I guess if Felix is gonna get every detail of our sex life, you and Julian can have one secret."

I lock eyes with Felix. "Every detail?"

He narrows his eyes almost defiantly with a wicked grin. "You have no idea."

"Guess I should get better at it," I joke.

"Ope," says Sadie, craning her neck. "Incoming."

Alison bolts up to us like a shot from a gun, her bags falling from her hands halfway as she springs into Felix's arms. She's dwarfed by him, muttering something into his chest as he kisses the top of her head.

I can't catch everything she's saying, but I do hear Alison quite clearly when she tells him, "I'm so sorry."

"Don't worry about it, Mom," Felix says, crouching once again so his chin rests on top of his mom's head.

"You don't tell me what to worry about," she scolds, holding him tighter. Julian trots back up to the group, having retrieved her luggage. She swivels, snatching him up in his own hug.

"I'm sorry to you, too, Junebug," she says, looking only slightly less tiny next to him. "Don't tell your mom what a shit I was. I don't want her to stop sending me those sweet cards on the holidays."

"She'd never," he says.

"I'm so excited for the wedding," she says, clawing blindly to her side until she catches Felix's wrist and can pull him into their hug. She squeezes both men.

"Holy shit, I forgot there was a wedding," says Felix, his eyes popping open wide.

"That's how you know it's been a very big day," I remark with a smile, touching the side of my head to Sadie's. "I was under the impression that was all you thought about."

"Let's all head home," Sadie pipes up. "I can show Ms. Nguyen to the B&B."

"A bed and breakfast?" Alison squeals with delight. "Oh, how cute. I should come here more often."

Chapter Twenty-Nine
Sadie Is The Best

"Sadie!"

Felix's wail of need like a dying cat's cuts through the house and straight out the open door to the backyard. Summer looks up from the other side of the doorframe, where she's huddled over the dessert table. The air around me is still slightly wet, the lingering remnants of this morning's rain hanging in the atmosphere.

"Sounds like Baby needs you," she says, smirking. It still looks incredibly sweet on her, and the usual butterflies are only made stronger by knowing that she's *mine*. I return the smile, tying one last bundle of flowers to the chair at the end of the aisle.

"Maid of honor, reporting for duty," I chirp, opening the door to the bedroom. "What do you need, babe?"

Felix turns to look at me, half-dressed and bedraggled, his hair sticking up in a hundred different directions and his makeup smudged and heavy around his eyes like a raccoon mask. "Ohh. You look... *so* cute."

"Help," he whimpers.

I scoot onto the vanity bench next to him. "Okay, baby, just breathe."

"I'm a mess," he says, flapping his hands.

"It's gonna be okay, babe," I coo. "I can do your hair while you fix your makeup, then I'll help you get your dress on."

He sniffs. "I don't want to keep you from the flowers."

"I'm all done," I fib. "Besides, you're not going to be able to fix this disaster without a *lot* of help."

I stand up and pull the gel out of his drawer, knowing exactly where it is, while he takes a wipe and cleans his face. My hands move naturally through his hair, smoothing it out like second nature. It is. Something hard builds in my throat.

"Don't start crying on me, babe," he warns, powdering on his foundation.

I yank on a strand of his hair, my voice still a bit froggy. "I'm not."

"I'm already near hysterics," he says. "I need you to be my rock."

"Can do," I reply rigidly like a soldier.

"Thank you, baby," he says with a soft sigh, carefully dusting a soft, peachy pink into the crease of his eyelid.

"How did this even happen?" I ask, gently working a knot out of his short hair. "Honey, are you getting cold feet?"

"God, no." An iridescent glitter goes over the pink. "I'd marry Jules in a dirty barn surrounded by newborn pigs. Or in a city courthouse in our work clothes." He makes a face. "I'm just *nervous*."

I tuck a strand of hair behind his ear, smoothing it down with gel-covered fingers. "Why are you nervous, babe?"

"I know how much we love each other," he says. "But I'm so scared something is going to go wrong, you know? And I know it doesn't matter. But what if the flowers attract bees? Or it's really windy and nobody can hear the vows? The rain delay already had me freaking out a bit. I've been so excited about this wedding, I think I'd *die*."

"You're right," I tell him. "It *doesn't* matter. You and Julian are in love, and that's what you should focus on. And *if* anything goes wrong, you have a fantastic maid of honor who will personally fix it for you. I'll punch a bumblebee in the face if I have to."

"And if it starts raining again?" he asks, his eyebrow raised almost like a challenge.

"I'll punch the sky," I say matter-of-factly.

"How did I get this lucky, Sadie?" he asks, turning his head to look at me and causing my fingers to slip out of his hair.

I give a performative shrug. "Thank kindergarten for introducing us, I guess."

"I'm serious," he says, swatting my arm.

"I'd do anything for you, babe, you know that," I say. "God knows you've done any and everything for me."

"I mean, I *did* give you the tip about your girlfriend," he says with a wicked grin.

"Thank you," I say, with not a small amount of genuine gratitude.

He scrunches his nose at his face in the mirror. "Tell me again that everything's gonna be okay."

"Everything's gonna be okay." I lightly knock his head to the side before pulling it back into my grip. "You're gonna look hot, you're gonna eat delicious desserts, you're gonna hang out with your friends, and you're gonna marry the love of your life."

His staring contest with himself goes on for a few seconds more, something shifting in his brown eyes, an expression toward determination. "I *am* gonna look hot."

I curl a strand toward the front of his face onto his forehead. "That's the spirit, Felix."

Once his hair and makeup are done, I help him into his dress. Seeing it again, now all styled, I'm hit with another sudden wave of emotion.

"How's it look?" He's young again, looking at me with a shy upward tilt to his eyes. I gulp against the lump in my throat.

The lace bodice and sleeves, now tailored, cling tight to his thin frame, and the skirt billows ever so slightly around his legs. With his eyeshadow light and shimmery behind his glasses and his hair perfectly tousled, he looks like some kind of ethereal femboy angel.

"Really, really perfect." I cock my head to the side. "Well, almost."

The look is completed with a bunch of lantana slid behind his ear. He adjusts his glasses in the mirror, admiring my addition.

"Perfect," he agrees with a nod.

Summer looks up at the sound of the bedroom door closing as I emerge back into the living room. Her brown eyes sparkle, her curls flowing down freckled shoulders and her body complimented by a pale yellow dress with a plunging neckline and a gently flowing skirt.

"Felix all ready?"

"Yep." I slide in next to her at the dessert table, rearranging some of the flowers she's laid in the empty spots between dishes. "Julian, too?"

"He's almost done." She smells *amazing*, like cinnamon and chocolate and fruit and everything warm and tasty. It's almost worth the night we spent apart - her staying up late baking and me making sure all the flowers would be ready for today.

"You gave him his boutonnière?" I pick up an extra pair of white peonies from the edge of the table.

"Yep."

"Then there's only one thing left." I hold up the flowers to show her before gently threading the stem of one behind her ear. It stands out perfectly against her pale, freckled skin and bright red hair. "So everyone knows we're in the wedding party. Groom's orders."

She giggles, taking the other and putting it behind my ear. "So pretty!"

With the realization still exciting as ever that I *can*, I kiss her.

"Did Mr. and Mrs. Jefferson already open the wine?" Summer asks after I let her go, craning her neck toward the kitchen. I follow her gaze to where Julian's parents stand, giggling. Mrs. Jefferson is a tall, curvy woman dressed in peachy pink with a truly impressive curly hairstyle, and Mr. Jefferson, her equal in height, looks dapper in a black suit and hat with a bright yellow shirt.

"Yep," I chirp, my eyes locking on the red-filled glasses in their hands. "Brace yourself."

"I think it'll be alright," she says. "They're pretty level-headed."

"That's right, you've never done weddings," I say, smiling. "The thing about weddings is that they're the second thing on the list of what makes people crazy." She raises her eyebrows, a bemused whisper of a smile on her lips. "And the first is wine. *Hey,* guys!"

"Hey, sugar," says Mrs. Jefferson, the two of them on a brisk jaunt toward us. "Is my baby almost ready?"

"He'll come out once Felix has gone," I say, and Mr. Jefferson leans forward ever so slightly, a sizable drop from his glass going directly to my white pants like they're magnetized.

"Oh, I'm so sorry!" Mrs. Jefferson coos. "John Michael, you had better watch your step."

"My apologies," Mr. Jefferson says, tilting his trilby at me.

"Oh, no," Summer says.

"No worries at all," I say, grabbing my bouquet from a chair next to the dessert table and holding it in front of the stain. "See? Like nothing happened."

"Are you sure?" Mrs. Jefferson says, rather intently studying my crotch. "I've got a surefire method for washing that out. We just need some baking soda, milk, and hydrogen peroxide."

"We're already behind schedule because of the rain delay," I counter. "And I'd rather not do my maid-of-honor duties in a pair of Julian's cargo pants."

"At least let me blot it dry," says Summer, grabbing a napkin off the table.

"Thanks, love." I turn toward Julian's parents. "So, do you remember the order?"

With quite a bit of corralling - including a hand-off of their wine glasses to Julian's sister Rashida - we finally get the Jeffersons, well-meaning but tipsy, up to speed with their responsibilities.

"Do you think they've really got it?" I whisper to Summer as we walk up to the back door.

"They'll be fine," she whispers back, giving my hair one last adjustment. "You ready?"

I position my bouquet carefully and we walk down the aisle, splitting to either side of the altar. The ground, thank god, is dry.

When I see Felix on the horizon, I make a small gesture beckoning everyone to stand. It isn't a difficult audience to reach - Georgia, Khalil, Rio, Alison, Rashida, Carrie, Eleanor, Cecily, Matthew, Axel, Tae, and Julian's elderly grandmother (a sea of pink, orange, and yellow) all catch my drift immediately and turn to look down the aisle, oohing and awwing as Felix floats toward us in that gorgeous lace dress. I'm even more choked up than I was, watching the joyous look on his face barely contained under a serene composure. He squeezes my hand when he gets to the altar, finally letting out the toothy grin he'd been holding back.

And all the air seems to leave the backyard when Julian appears, sandwiched between his parents, bright and beaming. Felix grabs my hand again, his other hand covering his mouth as his eyes well up. Julian, similarly, seems to register Felix's appearance and quickly grow emotional. He speeds up, his mom laughing and kissing his cheek. His dad adjusts his yarmulke, but Julian's eyes don't move from Felix.

"Oh my god, baby," Felix breathes when Julian reaches the altar, grabbing his hands as Mr. and Mrs. Jefferson sit down next to Alison. Alison squeezes Mrs. Jefferson's arm and blows a kiss to the altar.

"Are you kidding?" Julian replies. "Oh *my* god."

"You're so fucking hot," says Felix. "You look like-"

The officiant clears his throat, and Felix smiles sheepishly. "Sorry. Marry us, please."

"Thank you," he says, then shifts into 'officiant' mode. Even he wears a light orange tie to blend in with the wedding colors. "Good afternoon, everyone. We are gathered here today to join Felix Nguyen and Julian Jefferson in marriage."

Rio gives a sharp wolf-whistle, which quickly brings the entire procession into a wave of applause and cheers. Felix waves like a film star and Julian looks at him that way he does, his eyes filled with love.

"I understand you have your own vows," says the officiant, looking between them. "Felix?"

Felix hands me his bouquet and unfolds a piece of paper. "I'm reading this back now, and I think I'll have to improvise a bit," he says, his voice stuffy. "There's a lot about your butt."

Julian laughs, along with most of the procession.

"It's really good," he says, laughing. "It's a really great ass. But it isn't anything compared to your heart. You are the most kind, caring, wonderful man I've ever known."

Summer catches my eye across the altar, her smile huge.

"I've gotta keep this brief or I'll actually start crying," he says, delicately sliding his finger under his glasses to dab at his tear ducts. "You're so supportive, and talented, and passionate, and just all-around perfect. You make every day a great day and you make me want to be a better man. I can't imagine my life without you, and I can't wait to spend forever with you."

Another short cheer, this time led by me, before attention shifts toward Julian.

"As it turns out, my fear of public speaking still stands even in the company of family," he says, "so I'll keep my statements short and sweet, too." He squeezes Felix's hands. "There's not much I can say up here that I don't try to remind you of every single day. I love how outgoing and funny and totally yourself you are. There's nothing better in this world than seeing someone shine as bright as you do. And if you're going to have one impression from this, I want it to be that I am the luckiest man alive for getting to know you, let alone love you."

Felix gives another cry-like attempt at words, just like the day Julian proposed.

"At this time, Felix and Julian will exchange rings as a symbol of their bond. Not of possession, but partnership," says the officiant. Dutifully, I pull the rings from my pocket. The guys put them on so fluidly I wonder if they've practiced.

"Now, Felix Nguyen, do you take Julian Jefferson as your lawfully wedded husband, to love and cherish in sickness and in health, 'til death do you part?"

"I do," gurgles Felix.

"And, Julian Jefferson, do you take Felix Nguyen as your lawfully wedded husband, to love and cherish in sickness and in health, 'til death do you part?"

"I do."

The officiant cracks a smile. "Then, as you have exchanged rings and proclaimed your commitment to one another, by the power vested in me by the state of Pennsylvania, I now pronounce you husbands. You may-"

Felix springs forward, looping his arms around the back of Julian's neck and pulling him into a passionate kiss. The officiant doesn't even finish, just smiles and steps to the side as the photographer's camera shutter flickers rapidly. The loudest cheer yet arises from the congregation, our voices chorusing in celebration.

The reception starts immediately as the boys run down the aisle hand-in-hand, giggling like a couple of kids. Everyone follows suit, briefly congregating around the dessert table, until we all end up stuffed into the kitchen. Felix pulls me into the chair on his other side, and I lean forward to look at Summer, seated on Julian's right and wiping a stray tear.

"You guys wanna go ahead and do your toasts?" Felix half-whispers.

"I thought you wanted to cut the cake first."

"Give us a minute," he says, slinging his arms around Julian's neck again and peppering his cheek with kisses. "Go!"

I stand, keeping my bouquet inconspicuously in front of my crotch. "Hello, everyone!"

Georgia whistles, then cups their hands around their mouth: "Speech!" Carrie covers her face, laughing.

"There is booze on the counter," I announce, motioning that way. "Please feel free to take a cue from the Jeffersons and help yourself."

Julian's parents, having retrieved their wine from Rashida, pump their glasses into the air. Led quite eagerly by Julian's grandma, there's a short stampede to the drinks. When the cloud settles back down, I go on.

"For those of you who may not know me-" This, alone, earns a laugh. "I'm Sadie Levine, one of the maids of honor. I have known Felix since we were four years old. He has been the greatest friend anyone could ever ask for, because I firmly believe he is just one of the greatest people on this earth."

Felix makes a soft mewling noise, grabbing my elbow with an exaggerated pout. For the thousandth time today, moisture pricks my eyes.

"In the apparent spirit of the day, I'll be to-the-point." I try to swallow the growing lump in my throat. "Felix, thank you for everything. And Julian, I love you. Take care of my boy. I know you will enjoy growing old with him as much as I enjoyed growing up with him." I raise my bouquet like a glass. Everyone gets the picture, raising their glasses and cheering. I slide back into my seat.

"Your pants," Felix says quietly. "When did that happen?"

"A bit before the ceremony," I say. "Don't worry about it."

His eyes are huge behind his glasses. "You didn't want to stop and clean your pants? We could've waited."

"We'd pushed the day back enough already. Besides, Julian's mom has a great way to get wine stains out."

He looks at me for a second like he can't quite figure me out. "Sadie," he says finally, "I think you were born to be a maid of honor."

"Is that just Groom Brain for 'you're a good friend'?" I reply.

"The *best* friend," he says, wrapping his arm around my shoulders as Summer stands up.

"I don't have the privilege Sadie and Felix did of knowing someone my whole life," she starts, "but I *have* known Julian for a full decade, so I still have a lot to say about him. Felix was not kidding when he said that Julian is incredibly kind. When we met, Julian was newly out and needed a friend. That was maybe the last time *I* helped *him* instead of the other way around."

Julian laughs, squeezing Felix's arm which is looped through his.

"Through all the ups and downs in my life, I have learned one thing: when Julian loves someone, he loves them forever," she says, "and I'm sure Felix knows this, and that it makes him the luckiest of all of us. I think we all hope for someone to support us unconditionally, and grow with us, and love us no matter what."

Her eyes soften. "Julian has been that person his whole life, and I know he used to think we would never find someone like that for himself." Her voice grows watery just as Julian covers his mouth. "I always told you you would, man."

Felix starts the applause, loud and enthusiastic, as Julian stands up to hug Summer. My heart feels swollen, almost painfully so.

"Alright," says Summer after a minute, letting go of Julian and turning to address the rest of the kitchen. "It's time to cut the cake!"

There are people now spread out all over the house and the backyard, music and laughter spilling from every orifice of the property. The parents have gone home to turn in as the party rages on. I can see almost everyone from that little corner of the living room, and there's a wistful feeling in me as I lift an almond macaron to my lips. I've already got so many good memories in this house, and this one blows them all out of the water by far.

"Hey, cutie," says Summer, sitting down next to me and letting her hand stroke my hair. "Nice spot you've got there. Mind if I join you?"

"Be my guest," I say through my bite, then notice the small bundle of flowers in her hand. "Hey, Sticky Fingers, that's *wedding* decor."

"I already asked the grooms if I could take it," she defends. "Can you blame me? You're good at what you do."

"So are you," I add, holding up my little paper plate, full of at least a little piece of everything on the dessert table.

"We make a pretty good team," she says, looking out at the house. "I might be biased, but I think this is a damn fine party."

"Definitely biased," I say, covering her hand with mine. "Definitely correct."

"Maybe we should make this wedding-planning thing a habit," she says, bumping my shoulder humorously. "Take this show on the road."

I roll my eyes through a grin. "Ever the entrepreneur."

"I think we'd make a killing," she says, brows raised playfully. "Not to mention, you know, use our talents to help couples across the Roseport-Petersford-Graceburgh area celebrate their love."

"Sounds like you've got it all planned out."

"Babe!" Felix calls from the kitchen. "Come in here, we're taking Instagram pictures!"

Summer catches my eye immediately, twin expressions on our faces as we rise from our seats unquestioningly - maids of honor through and through.

"Didn't we *just* have our photos taken with the photographer?" I ask jokingly as we reach the lip of the kitchen, where the rest of the group - partners and all - already sits.

"Those were professional pictures," Felix says. "We need to take cute party pictures for our social medias."

"Obviously," pipes Rio, looking especially cute in a jumpsuit swirled with all the wedding colors.

"Whatever the grooms say, goes," Khalil says with a shrug, catching my eye and adjusting the collar of his pink blazer.

Julian doesn't confirm his desire, but the heart-eyes he's giving his new husband tell me he's in no place to protest.

"Of course," I say with a nod, stepping forward. "Nobody get the stain on my pants in the frame."

Just like Felix wanted, we all photograph together like a dream: the boys in their fabulous wedding outfits, me in my orange blouse, Summer in her yellow dress, Georgia in her yellow Freddie Mercury jacket, Tae in an orange skirt with a black blouse, Carrie in a simple pink dress, Eleanor in yellow, Cecily and Matthew in orange, and Axel in pink and yellow.

"We all look hot as fuck," Felix says, holding his phone close to his face. "Today has been *perfect*, you guys."

"Can't agree more," says Georgia. "I can't believe you two crazy kids are finally married."

"It was about damn time," says Julian, lacing his hand with Felix's. "You're my *husband*."

"You're *my* husband!" Felix squeals, kissing his cheeks loudly and repeatedly. "Oh my god, I'm so happy."

Khalil raises a teasing eyebrow. "How happy?"

"Jules," Felix declares, spreading his arms out, "take me to bed."

"Ew," Summer says, scrunching her nose and smiling luminously.

"I'll get everyone out of the house," Georgia says dutifully, standing up. Carrie stands with her. "Congratulations again, you two."

"Congratulations," Carrie adds.

"I'm so happy for you two," says Tac. "You look so great."

"Have fun, you horny bastards," adds Rio with a jaunty salute.

"Sadie, Summer," Felix says as we all start to dissipate out the door, reaching his hand like a toddler asking for something. "Hang back a second."

We do, stepping up to where the couple sits. "Do you need something?" I ask. "Help cleaning up?"

"The wedding is officially over," says Felix. "You've been a great maid of honor, babe, but you can stop worrying now."

"You, too, Summer," says Julian, his sweet teddy bear face looking as stern as possible - which still isn't much.

"We just wanted to thank you guys for everything you've done for us," Felix says, adjusting his glasses. "I really meant it when I said today was perfect. And that's, like, *all* thanks to you."

Summer flushes. "We're happy to do it."

"You're the best friends we could ever ask for," says Julian, his smile so warm and comforting it's like he's hugging me without even touching me. "So we wanted to give you something."

Felix holds up his bouquet, grand and colorful and gorgeous. It's the one I worked hardest on by far, and it looks even lovelier now.

"God knows a bouquet toss would've been hellish with this crowd," Felix says. "It's just easier this way."

"Great," I joke, my voice thick with tears, "you're giving back the gift I gave you. Real nice, guys."

Felix doesn't even deign to roll his eyes, just gets up and pulls us both into a hug. Julian jumps in immediately, and everything in me suddenly feels complete, understood, and safe.

We give our well-wishes again before leaving the grooms alone to begin their honeymoon. Hand-in-hand with Summer in the driveway, I head toward my car.

"Stay over tonight?"

She grins, squeezing my hand. "I thought you'd never ask."

When we get back to my apartment, the first thing I do is take off my stained pants and lay them on the kitchen counter - I'll take care of them tomorrow. Ethel runs for Summer like a puppy, her tail wagging so hard her whole body seems to wiggle.

"Aw, you missed me," Summer says.

"We both did," I offer, and she looks up at me with her big brown eyes sparkling. I cock my head to the side and, like second nature, we go down the hallway and into the bedroom.

She lays back on the bed, stretching her arms out like Jesus in Rio de Janeiro, a serene smile on her face. I follow her, lowering my body on top of hers and pressing my lips to the tender spot where her jaw becomes her neck.

Her fingers play at the zip of my top, and she takes the signal when I trace my tongue against her skin. The shirt comes off over my head, and she rests both her hands on the dip of my waist.

"You know," she says in between kisses to my collarbone, "my lease is up at the end of July."

I let out a grin, not even distracted by her hand sliding up my back toward the clasp of my bra. "Really? You- you'd want to? After everything with-"

She looks up at me, her freckled face overwhelmingly sweet. It's enough to melt me. "You're not Landon," she says, gently running her fingertips along my back in a way that makes me shiver. "You're *you,* and I trust you."

This really does melt me, and I have to kiss her. It feels like seconds later that she's taken off my bra and I've thrown aside her dress. She wiggles out of her strapless bra before I can even make a move to take it off for her. I settle my hand on the waistband of her panties, and then she's laid bare before me. I almost can't handle how beautiful she looks there on my sheets, ginger curls splayed out behind her head like a halo.

"You're so gorgeous," she says rapturously, and my heart skips.

"That's what I was thinking," I say with a conspiratorial smile, touching my nose to hers.

And it occurs to me, singularly and spectacularly, that I may just have the unique privilege of spending my entire life with her.

Chapter Thirty

Summer and Sadie Plan the Wedding of the Century

Three Years Later

As we stand at the back of the packed venue, Sadie crosses her arms and looks down the aisle. A soft instrumental music floats through the air, punctuated with quiet chatter from the procession, and the June day is surprisingly temperate. White and pink flowers line the whole place, even crawling a wavy line up the tiered white cake.

"I knew I should've gone with the peonies. The entire altar arrangement looks like garbage," Sadie hisses, peeking around the corner. She looks so cute with her brow knit like that, like a toddler trying to pout.

I touch her elbow gently, looking out at the gorgeous venue and failing to keep a bit of humor out of my voice. "I think the brides will forgive you."

She shrugs the touch away, starting to pace. Her brows knit together even tighter. "That's easy for you to say. The cake looks great, but that one girl is a *bitch*."

This is a mood I've gotten used to. Luckily, I know exactly how to handle it.

"Darling?"

She comes to a screeching halt, eyes wide. "Yeah?"

A bubble of pride builds in my chest that, even after all this time, it works like a charm. I grab her hand, locking eyes with her and raising my brows. "Don't talk about my wife like that."

She scrunches her nose cheekily. "Not your wife yet."

"Then stop worrying. It all looks perfect. Let's do this thing." I squeeze her hand, looking down at her dress. It's beautiful, its shade of white a perfect compliment to mine, and the sweetheart neckline and trumpet shape accentuate her every curve.

"'Do this thing'. How romantic," she says, smoothing her hair behind her ear with her free hand.

"Would you please just shut up and marry me?" I ask with a laugh, pulling her closer. "I mean it, sweetheart. Everything is perfect. And it would still be perfect if the altar caught fire and my mom started a fist fight with the caterer.

Because as long as it's you and me and everyone we love and I leave here with a wedding band, I see nothing but success."

Her eyes soften and those bow-shaped lips curl up at the corners. "How the hell did you get so perfect?"

I cup her cheek in my hand, fighting the urge to kiss her. The reminder that I won't have to wait much longer helps. "I was going to ask you the same thing. Are you ready?"

She closes her lips tight around what I know is a huge smile. "Yes, Summer. I'm ready."

I take a long deep breath, anticipation flowing to my every extremity. Somehow, even planning the whole damn thing hadn't been able to fully convince me that it's *real*. Savoring the feeling, I turn and knock on the door behind us.

"Calling the bridal party."

The door bursts open, our friends spilling out like a stampede of well-dressed bulls.

"You guys look so beautiful," says Georgia, hugging Sadie and kissing both her cheeks.

"*So* beautiful," Rio adds, nodding emphatically.

"You ready, ladies?" asks Khalil.

Sadie grins, raising her eyebrows. "Are you kidding?"

"That's what I like to hear," he says, patting her back. "Anything we need before we go?"

"To know that we love you," I say, just as Sadie says, "Hold your bouquets at your belly button, walk down the middle of the aisle, don't look at the photographer, split the aisle left then right."

Felix cracks a smile, but Khalil, Georgia, and Rio reply in unison, "Yes ma'am." There isn't even a hint of the irony this crowd would normally imbue.

"Then I think, mercifully, the ceremony won't go up in flames," Sadie says with an exaggerated exhale. "We do, you know. Love you guys."

"Yeah," says Georgia, as Rio pipes, "We know."

"I love you," says Sadie, going down the line and giving them each a hug. "I love you, I love you. Left then right. Got it?"

"Got it," they all chirp, then Khalil holds out his elbows. Rio and Georgia loop their arms through his, and the three of them take off down the aisle, their bouquets held perfectly level.

"Left then right," Sadie whispers, staring after them. I can't help but follow her gaze, my breath hitching.

"Hey, ladies," says Julian with a grunt, and I turn to see him lifting Ethel into his arms. She's even cuter than she was this morning, all droopy-eyed and dressed up in the little pink bridesmaid dress Tae sewed for her. "How about a little pick-me-up before we head out?"

It's exactly what we need. Sadie and I both pet her fur and give her kisses, and what little nerves I had building are gone immediately. Ethel lazily licks my face, awkwardly positioned in Julian's grip.

"My favorite maid of honor," Sadie coos, squishing the loose skin on Ethel's face like she's a stress ball. "You make everything better."

Felix clears his throat, raising an eyebrow.

"And the two best best men," she says, squeezing Felix's hand. "Thank you, babe."

"Obviously," he says, looping his arm with his husband's as Julian sets Ethel back down on the ground. "We love you two crazy kids."

"And we're so proud of you," Julian adds.

We all exchange hugs and 'I love you's, and the boys start off down the aisle with Ethel. Felix turns over his shoulder, catching Sadie's eye again. "See you on the other side." Then he scrunches his nose, lowering his voice. "I told you so."

"There it is," she says, grinning, and they keep walking. I slowly slip my hand into hers, and she melts into it.

"Hey, you," she says, turning to look at me. For a second I swear my heart is going to explode under that sweet emerald gaze.

"Hey, you," I reply. "You look really beautiful."

"You do, too." She squeezes my hand, closing her eyes for a second. "The wedding is not going to be a disaster."

"The wedding is not going to be a disaster," I parrot back to her. Her next breath seems to come easier.

Her eyes sparkle. "I can't wait to marry you."

The sentiment returns like a knee jerk reaction, the truest thing I could say. Sadie smiles like the sun and picks our bouquets up off a chair. It's already a wedding band in my head as I take mine and hook our arms together.

Everyone stands up and a gentle piano melody floats up around us, but I can't force myself to focus on anything but Sadie next to me and that altar arrangement at the end of the aisle, where all our friends stand around a Sadie-and-Summer-sized gap. My heart rate climbs and climbs. I'm practically shaking by the time we finally reach the altar.

"Welcome, everyone," says Felix, shifting to the spot between us and straightening his tie. "As you know, we are *finally* gathered here today to unite Sadie Levine and Summer McConnell in matrimony."

There are a few scattered laughs from the procession, and Sadie covers a glowing smile with her hand.

"Now almost four years ago, I told Sadie I thought she and Summer would really get along," he goes on. "And it wasn't until almost a year after that when she finally listened to me."

This brings up another wave of laughter. Sadie squeezes her eyes shut and holds in a giggle.

"All of you here, as Sadie and Summer's closest friends and family, know how well these two complement one another and how anticipated it has been for them to finally be married."

His eyes sweep the venue. "But I'll grant them, they used their one-year-and-seven-month engagement to plan the *shit* out of this wedding."

The procession claps, including our friends around us. "If everything else wasn't enough to convince you of their compatibility, then just take a look around this venue. Can I hear it for this wedding?" A cheer rises, nowhere stronger than at the altar.

"Well, I think we've all waited long enough," he says, looking back and forth between Sadie and me. "Ladies, how about those vows?"

Sadie thrusts her bouquet onto Rio, and I hand mine to Julian so we can hold hands.

"You look really beautiful," I whisper. I'm sure I've told her a million times today - when we woke up, on the drive to the venue, while we were getting ready. It doesn't matter. It's the truth.

"Thank you," she whispers back, squeezing my hands. "I feel beautiful." My heart physically hurts. She really, really deserves that. "And obviously it goes without saying that you look phenomenal."

"Are those your vows?" I raise my eyebrows playfully.

"Please," she scoffs. "You'll know when I start my vows. They'll knock your socks off."

"Anytime now, ladies," Felix says.

"We've waited this long," I reply, scrunching my nose at him. "Give us a second."

Sadie breathes in, the slightest nerves audible at the edges of it. "I've had a lot of time to think about what I'd say," she says. "Nothing ever felt quite right to describe everything I feel about you. But I'll try my best." I tighten my grip on her hands. "You came into my life at a time when I didn't feel like I deserved love. And you swiftly proved me wrong by being the greatest person I'd ever met, becoming my best friend, making me fall madly in love with you, and having the absolute audacity to love me back."

A short laugh ripples through the procession and the altar.

"You make me feel like I want to be better than I am," she says, "and like I'm already really great. You make me feel hopeful, and like a kid again. I promise to try and be the person you think I am. I promise to support you in your professional life, while still making sure you always get a good night's sleep." She raises her brows playfully, and I bite my lip, my vision going misty. "I'm so grateful to have you in my life, taking care of me and loving my old ass dog like your own child and always helping me see the beautiful things in the world."

She presses her lips together, her own eyes looking rather watery. "I just really can't wait to be married to you."

I sniff. "Dammit." We both laugh through a light layer of snot and tears. Her smile is radiant.

"I'm, um, I'm glad I'm not the only one who's written and rewritten these," I say, my eyes scanning every inch of her face and cataloging all those familiar little perfections. "How am I even supposed to talk about you? You're so smart, and sharply funny, but you're also the epitome of comfort. You have strong opinions, but you're always willing to try something new for me. You're the most loyal and caring and beautiful person I've ever known. I want to spend every night of the rest of my life on the couch with you, watching trash TV or reading side-by-side or just talking about our days." Images fill my mind of our nights together these last three years, her feet in my lap or her head resting on my shoulder. My heart feels overlarge and tender in my chest. Sadie smiles, her lips tight as she rapidly blinks against tears, and I know (like always) she feels what I feel. I take a steadying breath.

"I promise to stay up with you through every problem and look at it until we can solve it," I say, running my thumbs over her knuckles. "I promise to never stop reminding you how much you mean to me, and how beautiful you are, and how you light up the world around you. I hope you never forget that. Being your wife is going to be the greatest honor of my life."

Sadie pulls one of her hands from mine, covering her mouth. "Get this moving so I can kiss her already, Felix."

He smirks, nodding. "Sure thing." He clears his throat. "Do you, Sadie Levine, take Summer to be your wife, your best friend, and your love for as long as you both live?"

She bites her lip, her smile huge. "I do."

"And do you, Summer McConnell, take Sadie to be your wife, your best friend, and your love for as long as you both live?"

I catch her eyes, my heart pounding in my chest. "I do."

Felix grins. "Jules?"

Julian stoops to retrieve a pair of wedding bands from a ribbon around Ethel's neck. Sadie gives the dog a quick pet, and her tail wags. Julian drops the rings into my waiting palm.

"I can't believe this is actually happening," Sadie whispers.

"Your hands are shaking," I whisper back, cradling her left hand in my right.

"Yours too," she says, and I realize she's right. I slip her wedding band onto her finger, where it sits flush against her engagement ring. She bites her lip again, her joy shining through on her face. She slides on my own ring.

Felix raises his eyebrows, looking back and forth between us. "You ready, ladies?"

Sadie tightens her grip on my hands, nodding. He smiles widely.

"Then, by the power vested in me by the state of Pennsylvania and by the power of your choice and commitment, I hereby pronounce you married." He folds up his piece of paper, tucking it into his jacket. "Sadie, Summer, you may now kiss your wife."

"Fucking *finally*," I chirp, and Sadie's laughing that bright, infectious laugh as her hands go to my waist and my hands cup her face and I finally get to kiss *my wife*.

"Alright, people," Georgia barks, taking on their best bodyguard stance and standing in front of our table. "Form an orderly line. Don't crowd the brides."

"This was the best idea ever," says Sadie, twisting a helping of noodles onto her fork and into her mouth. "Imagine how much worse I'd be tonight if I didn't get any food."

"You're perfect regardless," I say, scooping up my own portion. "But I'm definitely glad we're not scavenging for our own wedding dinner."

"Hello!" choruses my mom, stepping past Georgia with Dad on one arm and Sadie's mom on the other. "Oh, you girls look so beautiful! Congratulations!" She leans over the table and kisses both our cheeks.

"Thank you, Mom," I reply.

"So happy for you two, Sunshine," says Dad with a wink. "Rainbow." Sadie can't help but smile at her very own McConnell family nickname.

Cassie steps forward, smoothing Sadie's hair and kissing her forehead. "Hi, baby!" She turns, hugging me. "Hi, sweetheart! Everything is so lovely, you two."

"Hi, Mama," Sadie says. "You having a good time?"

"Absolutely," Cassie replies with a huge grin, looping her arm back through my mom's. "Heather's been telling me all about her married coworkers. I think they're going to get a divorce."

"Mom, quit corrupting her," I scold lightheartedly.

"You leave me be," Mom says, turning her chin up defiantly. "I'm making friends."

"I love you, Mom," I say. "Dad."

"Love you too, Sunshine," Dad says. "Love you, Rainbow."

"We love you," adds Mom. Cassie nods.

"I love you guys, too," says Sadie, and there's a giddy tickle in my chest.

"Congratulations again, girls," says Cassie, and my parents chime similar sentiments before all three of them head back to their own tables. A small body bolts past Georgia just as the parents are leaving.

"Auntie Summer! Auntie Sadie!"

"Jamie!" Sadie and I cry in unison. Ryan and Emily stride up behind her.

"Don't forget to tell your aunties how happy you are that you got to come and Jessica and Joey didn't," says Emily gently.

"Thank you!" Jamie choruses.

"We've been talking a lot about the responsibilities of being the big sister," Ryan says.

"What did you think of the ceremony, Jamie?" I ask.

"It was nice," she says. "You and Auntie Sadie look pretty. I like the flowers."

I raise my eyebrows, cutting my gaze to Sadie. "Hmm. Interesting."

She rolls her eyes at me. "Thank you, Jamie."

Over the next few minutes, we hear from Cam and his boyfriend, Wyatt, my old boss Brandy, a few of Sadie's coworkers from the flower shop, and at least a half dozen relatives I couldn't name without a family tree in front of me. Finally, the line dwindles to nothing and Georgia, satisfied with her performance as the bridal bouncer, sits back down between Julian and Khalil.

Ethel sniffs inquisitively at my ankle, and without missing a beat I slip her a bit of beef.

"Hey," hisses Sadie, her nose scrunched playfully. "Now she's gonna start begging at home."

"It's a special day," I protest. "She deserves to celebrate, too."

She doesn't respond, just smiles that sort of private smile she does sometimes (the one she does when she knows I'm right but doesn't want to admit it) and scratches Ethel behind the ears.

"When should I tell the DJ to get the first dance going?" asks Rio from the other end of the table, standing up and pushing in their chair.

I cock my head to the side. "What do you think, sweetheart?"

Sadie dabs a napkin at the corners of her mouth and pushes her chair away from the table. "I'm ready if you are, darling."

And then we're out on the dance floor, nestled in each other's arms and swaying to the music. I can't stop thinking as I hold her waist and press a gentle kiss to her lips: this is my wife's waist. These are my wife's lips.

"I think the dahlias are growing on me," she says, looking over my shoulder with a smirk.

"See? I told you," I reply, running my hand up her back. "Everything is perfect."

"Yeah, yeah," she says, eyes sparkling. "I believe you."

I give her a lingering kiss, and our bodies take over, perfectly executing the choreography that Khalil and Cecily painstakingly taught us in their living room while Axel, Matthew, Eleanor, and Felix yelled advice from the couch. When I dip her at the end of the song, it garners the same cheer it did when we were learning it.

Then, an upbeat tune starts playing and Felix appears at our side like he teleported there.

"Baby," he says, locking eyes with Sadie and dropping his jaw. "You *must* have done this on purpose."

Julian walks up, too, Ethel once again nestled in his arms.

"Yes, babe, I know," Sadie says, smirking at him with her eyebrows raised. "Junior prom."

"May I have this dance?" says Julian in a deep, pathetic voice, lifting Ethel to Sadie's eye level.

"Of course, my love," Sadie says, smoothly scooping Ethel up and cradling her to her chest. Felix wraps his arms around Sadie, sandwiching the dog between them.

"You put on one hell of a wedding, McConnell," Julian says as our partners dance away, dog in tow.

"Thank you very much," I reply, pretending to brush off my shoulder.

"I'm proud of you, you know," he says. "You've got it pretty good."

I look to the side, Sadie and Felix dancing and laughing with Ethel's head resting on Sadie's chest.

"We both do."

The rest of the group rushes onto the floor, all of us morphing slowly into a pulsating mass of dancing bodies.

Sadie scrunches her nose, lowering the fork from her mouth and setting it on the plate with her slice of cake. "This must be from the layer I made."

"Come on, you're being dramatic," I counter, stealing a bite with my own fork. Still chewing, I add, "It tastes great, baby!"

"Uh uh," she says, shaking her head. "I can tell the difference between your baking and mine."

"Bullshit, you cannot," I say. "*I* can't tell."

"That's because you love me and you're blinded by it," she says, waving her hand. "Carrie, come try this."

Carrie, previously focused on walking back to her table, turns to us with her eyebrows raised. Sadie waves again and she comes over, hand on her stomach.

"What do you need?"

"You had a slice from the bottom tier earlier, right?" says Sadie. Carrie nods. "Taste this."

She does, and before she's even done chewing, Sadie says, "Tastes like shit, right?"

Carrie puts her hands up, exaggeratedly swallowing. "Don't ask the pregnant lady. I was hearing the angel choir."

Sadie's brows knit, and again she looks like a kid a few seconds from a stomping fit. "Thank you, Carrie," she says grouchily.

"Thank you," I repeat, and she smiles before joining Georgia and the rest of the group at the bridal party table. Georgia kisses her cheek when she sits down.

"Face it, Sadie," I say, stealing another bite, "I have taught you well."

She snorts. "*I* have taught *you* well. Do you think, three years ago, you would've let someone else bake an entire *third* of your wedding cake, even using your own recipe?"

I shrink a bit. She's got me there. "Only because you force me to relax, you authoritarian bastard."

"Now imagine how much authority I have as your wife," she says defiantly. "You're gonna be *so* fucking relaxed."

"You're evil," I hiss with narrowed eyes, and my heart flutters when she giggles.

"You know it, baby." She bats her lashes at me, and I can't help but tilt her chin up so her lips will meet mine.

"I love you," I tell her.

"I love you, too," she says, an adoring look in her eyes, and slides her plate toward me.

The rest of the night is full of dancing and laughter and good food, but eventually people start leaving and the festivities start to dwindle. With Ethel's leash clutched close, Sadie and I face all our friends.

"Goodnight, babes," says Felix, kissing both our cheeks.

"Goodnight," we chime.

"Great party," says Rio. Tae nods, her fingers laced with her partner's.

Khalil and his partners, in impressive unison, shoot off a quick "Congratulations."

"We love you," Georgia adds, untying their tie. "But I'm glad to be headed home."

Carrie steps out of her shoes, holding them in one hand. "Absolutely. This baby is going to be a party animal, and I am not prepared to keep up."

"You can just leave them with Auncle Rio," pipes Rio. "I'll teach them the ropes."

"Enjoy your honeymoon, ladies," Julian says, winking a bit as he scoops his blazer up from the back of his chair.

"You heard the man," declares Sadie. "Nobody call until Thursday."

"Wouldn't dream of it," Khalil says.

"I love you," Felix says, hugging Sadie tightly. "I can't believe it. You're all grown up."

She sticks her tongue out at him. "You take that back."

"I *love you*," he repeats, and she rolls her eyes.

"I love you too, Felix."

"Love you," Julian says, hugging me. "Goodnight, ladies."

We all exchange goodnights and head to our cars. Sadie slips her hand into mine.

"Ready to head home, ladies?" I ask, glancing down at Ethel, happily panting at the end of her leash.

"Only if my wife drives," Sadie says, casually, as though she has no idea that hearing those words out of her mouth will basically kill me.

Our apartment feels somehow different when we cross the threshold arm-in-arm. Ethel, now freed from her collar and bridesmaid dress, makes a beeline for her bed and immediately curls up there for a well-earned sleep. Sadie drops both our purses, bouquets, makeup bags, and a ton of wedding gifts on the counter. I plop onto the couch, and she joins me a second later. I fold my arms around her, and she tucks herself against my side and relaxes into me.

"We really do throw one hell of a party," I murmur, my cheek pressed to the top of her head.

"I'd fucking hope so," she says with a breathless laugh. "We spent long enough planning it." Her soft hands reach up to my wrist, gently stroking my skin. "I'm really happy, you know. To finally be married to you."

"*God*, me too." I kiss the top of her head, and she twists around to face me.

"You're my wife," she says, giddy, a small smile forming on her face.

"That's the hottest thing you've ever said," I reply, and she leans forward to kiss me, an even cocktail of hunger and comfort and joy and adoration. She climbs into my lap, warm and soft and sweet.

It still hasn't sunken in over all the years that this is my life. Part of me hopes I never fully get used to it, this little place and these quiet evenings and *Sadie*, everything that she is. Maybe that way I'll never forget how lucky I am to have had the chance to have it all in the first place. Maybe that way I'll never stop cherishing this beautiful, amazing woman.

"You know, this wedding dress is getting really uncomfortable," she says, gently tracing her fingers across my jaw.

"Mine too," I reply, shifting so I can reach the buttons at the back of her dress. I pop them open, ceremoniously, in quick succession. "We made damn good brides, but I think there's something we'll be even better at."

Her hand finds the zip at the back of my dress, and she pulls it down without breaking eye contact. "Oh yeah?"

I slide her dress off her shoulders, and she stands up with me as her own hands busy themselves with getting my dress off. In near-perfect unison, there comes the sound of two masses of fabric hitting the floor. I hook my arms around her hips, pressing her bare skin to mine.

My lips an inch away from hers, I tell her, "I already know we're going to be *great* wives."

She runs her hand up my back, her touch sending electricity through my entire body. She holds tight to my waist, her lips brushing anticipatory against mine. "I have a feeling you're right."

Acknowledgements

Red, my muse, my inspiration: thank you for everything. I have thanked you before and I'll continue to, but I never want you to forget the part you have played.

Nora (Long), here's another gay little book. Just like the two of us, it's grown up quite a bit since last time. But I hope, also like us, they can still be great friends. I will always appreciate the stellar effect that your support has had on my writing.

It should be no surprise by now that a large part of this book is friendship, and for that reason I'd like to thank Emma, for teaching me about having and being a best friend. I don't even recognize the person I was when you met and loved me, but I am so glad that you did, because that moment has brought on a chain of events that ends with me having the greatest friend in the world. I'm so thankful for our sleepovers, trips to the mall or for froyo, and talks about anything and everything. I hope you see yourself in every friendship in these pages - because you are there.

In a similar vein, I want to thank a few of the other friends who have given me significant pieces of themselves to hide (and prominently display) within these pages:

King, for your unwavering loyalty and devotion, and for being, without a doubt, the first person I would call if I needed to hide a body.

Tess, for your support and impact on my life, even for a short time, and for never biting me, even when I probably deserved it.

Victoria, for redefining kindness and care, for gossip on shared acquaintances, and for loving me so much you once tackled me to the floor and gave me rugburn on my arm.

Nora (Garrison), for bringing fun and joy to serious times, for Thai food and questionable memes and letting me hand you the controller when there's anything to do but press A.

Kylee, for companionship that spans distance and time, for your presence as both a long-lasting tether to my past self and a mirror which grows with me.

And many more amazing friends that I have been incredibly lucky to have in my life. My sincerest gratitude is always with you.

If you've read anything else I've published, then you know that acknowledging Ms. Bristow is not optional. I have created all my life, but before her class I maintain that I had not really written.

This book wouldn't exist without the countless romance authors whose work I've loved, devoured, and idolized. I said in the beginning of the book that it's written for romance fans, and these authors are the ones who made me into my own target audience. A few specific names come to mind (maybe more than a few), but I won't include them here. What's important is how their work has made me feel - hopeful and touched and transformed. I want to thank them all for that. I hope to be able to touch that feeling with my own writing someday.

It only seems appropriate due to the nature of this story that I grant special significance to dogs past (Roxy and George, for teaching me how to love a dog, and how strongly a dog can love) and present: Henrietta and Vanya, the unlikely duo, for endless face-licking and patience-testing antics; Bella for unyielding companionship and warm, faithful snuggles no matter how late I sleep; and especially Popcorn, for growing old with me. I still forget how black your powdered-sugar snout used to look, and I'm so grateful to have been able to see that change. (And a quick side note for all you readers - with all these pups as my witness, I will never write a book where the dog dies. You may take this written statement as my sincere promise.)

Mom, my eternal cheerleader, thank you for movies, books, makeup, chai, Chinese food, and friendship. I'm so grateful for your continued support, not only of me but of my writing, and I can't wait to see your blue sticky-note annotations for this book.

Sunny: not only are you a fantastic artist, but I happen to know that you are a fantastic person. Still, let's focus on the art: this cover is so phenomenal. I still haven't been able to stop staring at it, and I cannot thank you enough.

On A Scale From 1 to 10, my first novel, *Sadie and Summer's* time-defying, younger big sister: I don't think I will ever stop being proud of myself or of you. My first finished novel, my first publication, so many different parts of me forever memorialized in print. And you're even purple... what more could I ask for?

And, as always, my final acknowledgment goes to you, whether you are a first-time reader of mine or a dedicated follower. No matter the capacity or regularity with which you're reading my work, you are supporting my dream. I cannot thank you enough.

About The Author

Elissa Marks is an author whose fiction addiction began around age four. She is a college student hoping to continue pursuing literature and musical theatre well into her adult life. Her hobbies (aside from writing semi-witty prose and poetry) include taking part in theatrical productions; watching sitcoms; reading and watching fluffy rom-coms; spending time with friends, family, and dogs; wearing giant earrings; looking at and purchasing purple things; dressing up for no reason; and jewelry-making.

Instagram: miss.elissa.marks

ALSO BY ELISSA MARKS:

  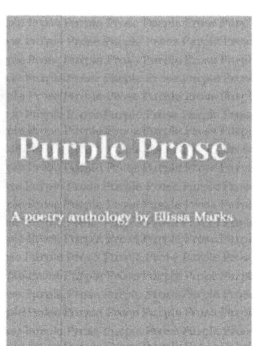

On A Scale From 1 to 10 follows Libby Saperstein and Ebony White, two overachieving high school seniors who have been locked for years in a tense academic battle for a top ten spot in their school's prestigious ranking. But when they decide to team up on an important project, affection grows. How can someone be your favorite person and the one you hate the most? Through literary debates, study sessions, cat-chasing adventures, and late night heart-to-hearts, the girls begin to realize that maybe they never hated each other at all.

The Re-Education of Quentin Whatever is a short story about high schooler Quentin as he struggles with bullying, identity, and illness.

Purple Prose is a verbose, complex collection of prose-like poetry which offers unique perspectives on theatre, sexism, and reproductive rights; and shares personal stories of high emotion from the ages of sixteen to eighteen.

One last author's note:

Please don't forget to leave a rating or review on Amazon. Your honest feedback will be instrumental in providing exposure to my work and helping me improve my craft for future pieces. You have the power to make a big difference for small creators!

Thank you again for reading!

Made in the USA
Coppell, TX
26 June 2025

51151355R00298